DISAPP'EARRING TWICE

V KNOX

Library and Archives Canada Cataloging in Publication
Knox, Veronica, 1949-
'Disapp'earring Twice' / V Knox
ISBN 978-1-7750471-4-8

Silent K Publishing
Victoria, British Columbia, Canada

www.veronicaknox.com

for *sarah* and *david*

for *sarah* and *david*

CONTENTS

TINTAGEL CASTLE RUINS — CORNWALL

It is not death
That man should fear,
But he should fear
Never beginning to live.
— Marcus Aurelius

prologue

When I was a child I learned that fairy tales contained truths too powerful to believe out loud and that storybook princesses who lived in castles were sitting targets for dark deeds.

Timing, particularly midnight, was a mixed bag of tricks. The stroke of midnight heralded the arrival of ghosts and turned coaches into pumpkins. In general, clocks, red shoes, and magic were unstable and not to be trusted. One couldn't make a move without tripping over dire consequences.

I found 'Sleeping Beauty' disturbing, beginning as it did, with a joyous celebration that moved swiftly into an evil curse delivered by a jealous fairy, only to be softened later by the counter-spell of a timely *good* fairy who turned death into dreamless sleep for 100 years.

Fairy tales were hardly the stuff to inspire sweet dreams at bedtime. While some little girls became imprinted with happy-ever-afters, I worried about strangers knocking at the door, ill-timed coincidences, deaths and other departures, and being orphaned. It was clear to me that when every dropped gauntlet stopped ticking and each slippery slope was scaled, I would die poverty-stricken and alone.

By age five, I was instilled with a deep fear of the time known as the middle-of-the-night.

At six I was encouraged to indulge in make-believe which led to the alarming notion that reality was based on lies of my own invention, and since the alternative of random events painted the world decidedly unsafe, I hid out on the dark side of the moon, otherwise known as the non-fiction stacks of the local public library.

Who was writing this stuff and why were my parents feeding it to me with smiles and cookies. I had my doubts, turned to grownup philosophy books, and knew for sure by my seventh year that making a wish was asking for unbelievable trouble.

The classics pulled no punches. I became a full-grown cynic at eight, yet strangely, the belated gift of a teddy bear proved enlightening. I was definitely no ordinary child.

But then, Virgil was no ordinary bear.

In a life beset with sharp spindles and a distinct lack of white magic, it dawned on me that growing up was a perilous journey of life-threatening surprises. My mother tried to teach me that it was best to welcome each one with the wisdom of my namesake, Marcus Aurelius.

The Emperor, Marcus Aurelius, c.78 B.C. was a philosopher warrior who declared that success can only be reached by accepting, wholeheartedly, every obstacle that comes your way. Sadly, his truth registered too late to save me. I forgot that one must have the courage and patience to recall one's childlike innocence, and remember, as the best fairy tales impart, to bring one's whole heart into play when fateful stars drop questions on your plate.

And so, I disappeared long before I ran away from home.

- Aurelia Marcus

chapter 1
MRS. M

I tried to distance myself from my mother many times before I turned thirteen and failed, but the day she threw my teddy bear from a third storey window, she died to me. Not that she wasn't already a living ghost.

I flew down the stairs and searched the asylum's grounds but my bear, Virgil, the mystic keeper of my secrets was gone. Stinging loss filled my heart, simmered into hatred, and hardened into indifference. There was nothing left to do but embrace the role of orphan. Emily Marcus became a missing person. I no longer called her Mom.

When I turned nine, my mother began to drift in ever-declining states of past and present – a precocious forty-something child dreaming the dreams of a six-year-old.

Four years later, Mrs. M retired into a permanent fog of befuddled memories and I'd become a sullen teenager who couldn't be bothered to visit the ghost of a woman who'd surrendered without fighting for me or her sanity. The bear incident, had been the last straw. I hated her.

I was an only child – the classic 'seen and not heard child' by virtue of retreating into books far beyond my years or comprehension, and somewhere in the domestic ruins of childhood I'd heard my parents discussing me, and learned that wistfulness was my defining characteristic. It was only later, as a teenager, that I became a committed worrywart.

It was true. I was a dreamy starstruck kid. A loner by nature and choice, thrilled to retreat into science, art history, classical poetry, and the unsweetened versions of the Brothers Grimm and Greek mythology. By the time my mother disappeared I was reading Dante's 'Divine Comedy' and the complete works of Virgil. Winnie the Pooh and Keats were my favorite poets.

I named my bear Virgil after Dante's blind guide in hell where he wandered searching for his beloved Beatrice, a real life girl who died tragically young – a girl I identified with because she was nine when Dante Alighieri first met her and fell in love, the same age I was when I met Zee, my best friend in all the world. It was the year my mother, whom I adored, started to disappear with a vengeance.

I removed Virgil's button eyes in a loving ceremony to honor his namesake, but I was still enough of a starry-eyed romantic in those days to scoop the two sacred buttons into a twist of wax paper and save them just in case.

Grand namesakes were big in my family. I had a succession of beloved pets named Aristotle, Socrates, and Euclid. Cat / dog / cat, respectively. I was named Aurelia after the emperor Marcus Aurelius.

Virgil, my blind teddy bear with a poetic heart, imparted to me in dreams that childhood was clearly no place for children. I kept our dream sharing a secret because invisible friends and talking bears require protection from adult ridicule and I'd made him a promise to keep him safe. My runaway imagination had already singled me out as an odd duck, so it was easy to fly under the radar of eccentricity. Besides, my instincts told me special things are best served by silence and savored alone.

And I *did* see special things. I dreamed of places I couldn't know, recalling the accent of a language I couldn't speak. I knew the flavors and scent of art, and I walked in a white landscape holding someone's hand, both unfamiliar and intimate.

Virgil and I pledged to be loyal forever, so, in true pinky-swear tradition, I swore to be faithful on my mother's life. We shared an unsettling moment. Virgil shivered and I went cold inside. *'You are an artist and artists create in their sleep,'* Virgil said. *'Be especially mindful of vows made in haste. Control what you bring into being. Lucid dreams are alive with powerful energy. Deal breaking has significant consequences.'*

Virgil had lifted my spirits after my mother abandoned me for her own magical dreams. He promised me that the inescapable growing

pains ahead would lead to wonderful things if I had the patience to wait them out.

He meant wade. Wading through family crisis after crisis became the mainstay of my life as a nine-year-old adult. But while he was with me, Virgil taught me to reach beyond the fears painted so darkly on my family's horizon and embrace the pain of inescapable setbacks.

He led me through a netherworld where his restored button eyes sought mine whenever he wanted me to remember an important lesson. *'Even if you sometimes forget this truth,'* he used to warn, *'remember that setbacks contain miraculous beginnings, and history is only a fairy tale passed forward to show you the way when the path is lost. Appearances can be deceiving,'* he said with tears in his eyes. His gentle paw stroked my cheek. *'And disappearances can be revealing. Look around you. There will always be unlocked doors.'*

Once upon a time, Virgil and I formed a pact. And then, when I needed him the most, thanks to Emily, he disappeared.

Not long after, when I was seventeen, fate conspired to send me a new guide, who, with all the irony of the unrestrained universe, blindsided me into crippling insecurity. Young and green, I made a semi-conscious choice to live in exile from my best dreams, but then 'live' is a misnomer that belies death, and lives before life, and lives after death, and especially, immortality beyond time and space.

Strange events happen now and then. But when 'now and then' occur at the same time, a mind blowing breakdown of physics occurs that encompasses always and forever, everywhere and nowhere, and before and after.

With Virgil lost, loneliness replaced the quiet joy of being alone. Guilt haunted me. I'd let Virgil down and perhaps Emily had paid the price for my tactless impulse to swear on her sad life. For a long time I wasn't fit to polish 'Great Uncle' Aurelius's sandals let alone cite him as an invisible ancestor.

And then, my friend Zee and a toy cat named Felix tried to save me.

THE MEETING

chapter 2
TRANSPARENCIES

Monmouth Senior High
– November 1 –
1965

My clearest memory is the metallic clatter that imprinted on my brain when a slide carousel shifted in the dark airless lecture hall of Art History 101. It was the sound that changed my death. I was seventeen, in love with a boy named Zee, and duly captivated by a promising future. A week of cluster headaches had a lot to answer for.

It was nearly lunch time and hunger pangs momentarily overshadowed the art until I experienced a warning vision in my right eye. I huddled in my seat, a hand pressed over my eye to quell the pulsating aura of whirling lights, a sitting target for the migraine barreling its way towards me.

Had he been there, Zee, would have serenaded me with a line from a Beatle's song about a girl with kaleidoscope eyes. It was our song. He joked that song lyrics were secret messages from outer space – a daft notion coming from a dedicated enthusiast of astrophysics.

For a brief pause, the room darkened. I sat in the front row, staring at a blank screen with my good eye, and rummaged for the bottle of Aspirin I always carried in my purse.

But the whirr of the projector reached inside me and I realized too late it was a mistake to stare into the beam it emitted. I held my breath as a sweep of dust particles and pixels caught in a stream of light cut through the dark and deposited a splash of colors onto a white canvas wall.

I was immediately transfixed by the haunting eyes of a famous portrait.

While the instructor, Mr. Hughes, spoke, his laser pointer played restlessly over the painting in a red spotlight the size of a pearl, drawing random circles around the girl's earring and mouth, and settled on her left eye. I winced as if the light had been shone in my own eyes but it was the girl who blinked.

Mr. Hughes' voice droned out dry facts from his podium as if they were vital to understanding a work of art. "Vermeer's 'Girl with a Pearl Earring'," he said. "1665. Oil on canvas. Hailed as the 'Mona Lisa' of the north. Subject unknown. Considered to be a 'tronie' – a generic portrait of no living individual. Next slide."

The image remained. "Sorry sir, the slide is stuck," a voice called out.

The chemical smell of melting celluloid made me gag, and as the hum of the projector grew painfully louder the plaintive expression of the girl in the painting changed to a frown. She floated out of her portrait, drifted slowly to the floor, and made a beeline for me.

"When you're ready," Mr. Hughes shouted to the back of the room. "We haven't got all day. SLIDE." He scowled and checked his watch.

A slide clunked into place, Mr. Hughes suppressed a yawn. Vermeer's panoramic cityscape of Delft materialized through the girl. She seemed to sense it and turned to briefly scan her former home before turning her attention back to me. For a moment her tender expression was restored. I thought she might cry but she composed herself and spoke. "The headache is on its way, isn't it," she said in a thick Dutch accent.

She stood five feet away, alone and beautiful. The painted tapestry of her home, hung behind her like a backdrop in a theatre, freeze framing seventeenth-century Delft as it once was, and still was, her world.

I was alarmed but not completely surprised. The hallucinatory effects that heralded my migraines had never taken human form before but essentially they were normal. I assumed they were becoming more artful. I played it cool and closed my eyes. All I had to do was remain patient, so I rested my head on my arms and waited for the queasiness to pass.

"Next slide," Mr. Hughes droned. And in the split second of darkness between masterpieces, as I willed the apparition of the girl to disappear, I heard the rustle of silk. In the half-light reflected from the next image, the girl had moved closer, intent on pinning me with a smile. "Hello Aurelia," she said standing over me.

Like a dolt I shouted 'go away' much too loudly and disrupted the class.

Mr. Hughes voice pounced on me from his podium. His laser pointer scanned the front row and came to rest on my chin. "Consider this hall as a library, Miss Marcus," he snapped. "Silence is all I ask. Art deserves respect. Would you care to share your observations with the class?"

I shielded my eyes. I wanted to remark that *he* had never shown the slightest respect or understanding for the inner beauty of Fine Art but thought better of it and told the truth in a weak voice. "I was only saying hello to this girl wandering…"

The projector seized as if a plug had been pulled from the wall and the room went deathly quiet. Mr. Hughes swore under his breath. "What now. Someone get the damn lights!"

A voice called out from the back row. "I don't know what happened, sir. It just stopped."

The room flooded with light. Sleepy students sat upright, pretending to look alert.

By now the girl was close enough for me to observe the fabric of her dress at eye level. I studied a fold of drapery to avoid eye contact. "Please look at me," she said in a sweet voice. "I won't hurt you."

Mr. Hughes turned his attention back to me and surveyed the room. His mood turned nasty. "A girl you say. What girl? Does anyone else see Miss Marcus's ghostly girl?" He gestured wildly on the ceiling with the washed out light from his laser pointer as he spoke.

I looked up and focused on the girl's earrings as best I could but her eyes drew me in. I hadn't intended on raising my voice. "She ISN'T A GHOST," I blurted in some distress. "There's no such thing. She was a figment of my imagination. I see things when… when I get these headaches. It was a visionary lapse that's passed. Nothing more."

I had less than five minutes to down a useless pain killer with no water.

Voices snickered. I was known for saying odd things. Flickering lights often triggered one of my 'events' so it was no stretch to blame the projector's beam. Movies often did the same.

I rubbed my temples. "I just need some water, Sir. I'm feeling faint."

"Seeing a ghost would faze most of us," Mr. Hughes sniffed. The useless red light from his pointer extinguished with a soft click.

"Maybe there's a ghost in the machine," a student volunteered cheekily.

Perspiration dampened my forehead. "It was an optical illusion, Sir. A trick of the light. She's gone now," I lied.

The girl smoothed her blue turban and brushed the dust motes from her bronze silk dress. As she spun towards Mr. Hughes, her pearls flashed a bright dagger of pain into my left eye like a shard of glass. "Tell them the truth, Aurelia," she said in a stage whisper. "You know who I am." She tossed her head slightly, sending more pearly splinters. "My earrings are quite famous."

The time for medication expired. I winced from the pearls with sickness rising in my throat, breathed in the stifling air from fifty densely-packed students, and choked on a dry Aspirin.

The projector whined into life of its own accord. "Spooky," a student commented with accompanying woo woo sound effects. The class tittered.

Mr. Hughes was not amused. "Settle down. Let's just get through this, shall we." He looked back at the screen. "You're excused, Miss

Marcus," he said in a rush over his shoulder. "Get today's assignment from a classmate. Lights off please. Next slide."

The girl with the pearl earrings strode purposefully to Mr. Hughes', leaned close into his ear, and shrieked what sounded like a stream of obscenities in Dutch before adding words that almost made me laugh. "And... I am NOT – A – TRONIE!"

She returned to my side, calmly offered me her arm, and I stumbled out of the darkened theatre hanging onto the girl's sleeve. Her right earring swung close to my face briefly reflecting my fear, distorted in its silvery sphere.

The deserted hallway seemed like a bright tunnel of Christmas lights that reached for endless miles in both directions. My knees gave way in what can only be described as a swoon, but the girl caught me. After a few deep breaths I managed to lead her to the girls washroom where sparkly white sinks and silver faucets continued to assault me. I dug through my purse for my sunglasses, stuck them on top of my head, and turned the cold tap on, full blast.

The girl stood behind me in the bathroom mirror while I splashed water on my face. She looked back at me with pity, her luscious red lips slightly pouty. Next to hers, mine pursed pale and chapped in a face flushed with fever, and much to the disgust of a few girls fixing their makeup, I retched into the sink. They jostled into each other, moving aside as I cupped running water into my hands and rinsed my mouth. My reputation as a loser was intact.

The washroom emptied fast, and the Pearl Girl handed me a wad of paper towel. I wiped my mouth, already hungering for salt to cut the dizziness, and clamped the sunglasses over my eyes. "You need food," she said.

The bell rang as we headed for the cafeteria and the hall flooded with a swarm of students rushing in several directions at once. We battled against the flow and arrived slightly battered in a line for fast food that wasn't fast enough. Upbeat Christmas music hovered over the student body delivering holly-jolly lyrics that even Zee couldn't interpret as profound.

Zee waved to me. He'd found us a table. The girl waved back frantically. After that, my own wave seemed feeble. I sent her a dirty look and ordered mac and cheese and fries with gravy. The girl pointed to my tray, her eyes wide. "Is some of that for me?" she said.

I glanced down at her feet shod in fine leather and mumbled something about real ghosts not being able to eat. "Shouldn't you be wearing wooden shoes," I said to be snotty.

Lunch with Zee was surreal. I pretended to listen to Zee's tirade about his morning classes while the girl mercifully stayed close to the door and watched us across an expanse of tables, displaying amusement, not dissimilar to a visitor observing monkeys in a zoo.

Even after my headache subsided and my vision returned to normal, the transparent girl traipsed after me the rest of the day, hovering in peripheral vision, in unnerving silence.

I ignored her as she followed me to my locker, decorated, against school rules, with stick-on snowflakes, and when she skulked through my afternoon classes.

After school she walked me home and up the stairs to my bedroom where she stretched out on my bed following my every move with obvious fascination. For a moment I thought she was real as her weight made an indent on the comforter. "What's this," she sneered waving a plush cartoon doll at me.

"That's Felix," I replied. "Please don't touch him. I don't want ghost germs all over him."

Her eyes teared up as she replaced him on my pillow with unusual tenderness. "Toys are for children," she said. "And you're *not* a child." She glanced disparagingly at the colored twinkle lights I'd draped around my headboard and the sprig of mistletoe taped to the dressing table mirror. "And that plant?"

"It's for kissing," I said. "You hold it over the head of someone you want to kiss. It's a Christmas tradition."

"So, it is magic?"

"It is. But touching it is dangerous," I lied. "The white berries are quite poisonous." I stared her down. "Although I doubt it can injure a dead person."

Felix was my saving grace, gifted to me by Zee, to commemorate the first time I laughed after my mother's heartless act with Virgil. We were at a movie featuring a cartoon short of 'Felix the Cat' who strolled unscathed through a day of killer obstacles.

Four years on, Felix had almost replaced Virgil. He'd definitely grown on me, and of course, he remained a constant reminder that I had the kindest best friend in the world.

Zee often chided me that Felix was my lost twin because his crazy eyes were as kaleidoscopic as mine. I smoothed the pillow and arranged Felix in the center. Normally, I would have kissed his nose first, but the girl was throwing me looks of deepening despair and I didn't want to feed her obvious disapproval.

She seemed bent on taunting me with insults. Failing to take the bait and humoring her rude behavior was my best chance to bore her. Sadly, it fanned the flames of her displeasure.

Felix stared straight ahead but for a moment I thought his eyes moved to assess the girl as she appraised my bookcase with approving mumbles, expressing a glimmer of hope for me.

She bored holes through me as I did my homework and surveyed the kitchen when Dad and I shared a microwave pizza, peering into open cupboards that exposed walls of tin cans. Our larder inspired an outcry of *'Acht. My Gott.'* I was embarrassed. Our shelves resembled a supermarket display of lifeless wall-to-wall products. She sniffed the inside of our fridge with its shelves stacked with leaning towers of leftover junk food. Each sniff declared her mounting disgust.

After the dishes were done I fixed my hair and dabbed some color on my lips that paled in stark contrast to the girl's crimson mouth. Something was missing in my room but Dad blasted the car horn to hurry up and I didn't have time to figure out what.

The girl sat in the back seat when Dad drove me to the library for the Stargazy Astronomy Club. As usual, he turned up the volume on the radio so we didn't have to talk. Early seasonal carols meant to serenade, bombarded us with false good cheer.

"Stars never lie," the sullen girl declared, "They told me your life was a mess." And with that, she crossed her arms and brooded for the rest of the trip. I still didn't know her name.

chapter 3
ASTRONOMICAL ODDS

The girl attended the 'Stargazy' meeting where she made herself a spectacle, if only to me, by draping herself over our boyish supervisor, hip science teacher in blue jeans, Mr. Thatcher, with her eyes glued to my face. She held the mistletoe she'd pinched from my mirror over Thatcher's head and planted a kiss on his cheek. Point taken. She could do things. Subversive things, and get away with them. I took it as a warning shot. She was light-fingered as well as annoying. If she stayed, I would have to be more vigilant with my things.

Zee was already there in his usual seat in the front row, holding two cans of ginger ale, keeping a chair for me. He patted it when he saw me, but the girl brushed past me and sat down. Silently, I threw my purse on the girl's lap while smiling at Zee, accepted a ginger ale, and took the chair on Zee's other side.

"Feast your eyes on a world you can only dream of," Thatcher said, looking directly at me. He was definitely cute. All the girls had a crush on him, including me, so when he winked, I felt a warm tingle of pleasure in spite of my anxiety for betraying Zee. The girl smiled back as if the wink had been for her which annoyed me. I was sure it had been for me.

I braved another projector in a darkened room, closing my eyes throughout a short film on Jupiter and gripped the seat of my chair but the room spun circles around me and I sipped ginger ale in order to settle my stomach. I leaned my head on Zee's shoulder. "Tired?" he asked. "Exhausted," I answered. "Falling apart," the girl said in a private stage whisper.

"Why me, why now, who is she, what does she want?" I asked

myself, but naturally, as a figment of my imagination, the girl heard my thoughts and answered me. "All in good time," she said.

"Now is as good a time as any," I replied. *"I need answers."*

Our conversation continued in my head. "You and I are kindred spirits," she said gesturing to the wall charts of constellations surrounding us. "It's the written-in-the-stars kind of right. My name is Jakobina. I want to help you."

I answered curtly. *"You and I are NOT related."*

She cleared her throat. "Aurelia, we're family. Practically sisters."

"Terrific," I said hoping to sound glib. But the word 'family' stunned me. If she was a presentment of my family's curse of dementia, she was a symptom I hoped I'd never see. I hadn't expected to succumb so soon, nor to be confronted by a such a formidable intruder.

I endured the film without a recurrence of dizziness but I was worried. My headaches had become more frequent but they were easily managed with medication and my memory was intact. I was sure of it. I was also sure there was no such thing as ghosts.

Jakobina's voice softened with compassion. She reached across Zee for my hand but I pulled it away. "Of course you'd think that," she said. "No one ever notices entire years slipping away. It's not like misplacing a key. Dementia deletes most of what was but retains a few peak moments of pleasure and pain. Human lives are written in chalk on a blackboard. Time is a blackboard eraser." She pinched my arm, hard. "And ghosts *are* real. Did that hurt?"

"And this is you helping, is it?" I snickered. *"Who's luckier than me."*

She twirled tail of her scarf around her fingers while I examined a few home truths of my own. I visited my mother every other Sunday in the institution where she lingered inside her worst nightmares, indistinguishable from her harmless childhood memories. I had seen her rapidly deteriorate into a whimpering shadow over the last eight years. Zee told me that wouldn't happen to me, and I wanted to believe him.

The girl sighed. "Aurelia, we're connected by a past life. You just don't remember."

I was relieved enough to laugh out loud. *"Wow, really?"* She was a smartassed hallucination spouting inane New-Age rubbish. *"Okay, I'm done now,"* I said. *"But you get an A+ for creativity."* I returned to real speech by mistake. "Now get the hell away from me!"

Of course, Zee heard and I had to do some fancy dancing. "Not you," I said swatting the air. "I was talking to this fly that's been bothering me." It wasn't far from the truth.

Jakobina stared into my face and adjusted her blue turban as if looking at her reflection in a mirror. "In a few days you may change your mind," she said.

Up close I noticed a thin white scar tracing her jawline, no thicker than a fine hair. For a heartbeat, it flickered red and was gone.

I remembered to think my words. *"And stay away. Forever!"*

Much to my horror, she patted my cheek the way a mother might. "It's wise not to play games with forever, little one," she said in a superior tone. "So, what does seeing me tell you? What does being confronted by a smartassed hallucination tell you?"

"That I'm overtired, my brain is overtaxed, and I need to sleep."

She shook her head. "I am only the beginning – another warning sign. Auras alert migraines. I pave the way to dementia." She dipped into a vague curtsey. "Allow me to introduce myself formally. Hello, Aurelia. I am your personal dementia guide. A precursor to instability. Your future."

"Then you're the ending too," I said making a show of popping two pills into my mouth and washing them down with warm ginger ale. *"You're a bad dream. One of my lucid nightmares. A gate-crasher. You're a toxic witch selling poison apples. I may even be asleep right now."*

"Not another headache," Zee said eying my pills. "You need to tell a doctor."

"Your synapses are thick with mental fuzz," Jakobina stage-whispered. "You're already forgetting things. Just like your mother, except with you it's more advanced but I also give *you* an A+ for creativity." She dropped the mistletoe in my lap and evaporated to the other side of the room with a snide smile. "By the way, that magic is harmless."

A cold draught shivered around me as if a door had opened. *"Suit yourself,"* I replied. *"Stay here and talk crazy to yourself. I have nothing further to say."* My brave words belied the terror forming in my brain. I suppressed the tears that threatened to spill, and wiped my dry cheek with the back of my hand. I sniffed to clear my head but teared up, anyway.

Zee rubbed my shoulders and put his jacket around me. "I think I should get you home," he said. He kissed the tip of my nose. "Hey, nothing's worth crying about, Annie," he said and sang 'the sun'll come out… tomorrow'. He tweaked my nose. "Come along, my little orphan Annie."

Tomorrow was Saturday. I feigned illness and slept all day, aware Jakobina watched me sleep.

The next day Jakobina followed me to the dementia ward that housed my mother.

chapter 4
VISITATION RITES

Sunday was visiting day at my mother's institution, although I had privileges to visit anytime. School kept me busy and I made excuses to stay home. I wanted more time with Zee.

Inside a pair of grandiose doors, Jakobina and I were greeted with a maze of corridors painted in cheerless gloss paint that offset the odors of antiseptic and bleach mingled with chicken soup. Somehow, the place looked even more bleak than usual with its tinsel garlands and gaudy Christmas ornaments. As always, I gagged. I pulled a flowered scarf sprayed with perfume from my pocket, bunched it into a ball, and breathed deeply into it like the patients I'd seen in TV hospital dramas being wheeled off to surgery with a doctor holding a hissing cup of anesthetic over their nose. Count backwards from a hundred, I told myself. You'll wake up and it will all be over. "one hundred… ninety-nine… ninety-eight," I mumbled through the silk.

"Such a fuss," Jakobina said unimpressed. "But imagination is a good thing. You're going to need it."

I made a point of imprinting the vivid blue of Jakobina's turban. "I guess we both need our scarves," I said and wrapped mine loosely around my neck.

The head nurse met me on the third floor with the words "It's a grieving day, I'm afraid." Code for low expectations. Not a great start.

I gave the woman a weak smile. "Well, maybe I can make her feel better."

"Your mother's in her room," she said. "She refused to eat lunch.

Oh, and she thinks she's found her lost bear, so that's something. Merry Christmas."

The corridors were bleak with lost souls shuffling in slippers, and abandoned carts of odd-looking appliances and metal kidney dishes draped in thin towels. We passed a food cart stacked with covered dishes of lacklustre nursery food, soft and digestible, served in an endless round of heavy plastic bowls. I snuggled into my scarf and inhaled the freedom of Chanel no.5 in long gulps as we approached the door I dreaded. A cheerless wreath of plastic pine boughs and gold baubles hung in its center and I chided myself for not bringing flowers or an artificial poinsettia.

Jakobina tried to overtake me but I stayed her arm, fixed a smile on my face, and entered first. It was the first time I touched a ghost. Surprisingly, she was warm and solid. But then my arm still showed a purple bruise where she'd pinched me.

Mrs. Marcus was hugging a small throw pillow, whispering to it as if it was a teddy bear. "You would have hated lunch," she said to it. "But I stole some cookies for a picnic." She startled at our approach.

"Hi Emily," I said. "I see you found your old bear."

She turned a blind eye towards me and hid the pillow behind her back. "Who are you? You can't take him again. I won't let you."

"It's me, Aurelia, an old friend. I've come for a visit. We can go down to the cafeteria for a sandwich if you're hungry. The bear can come with us. I promise he'll be quite safe."

Emily looked past me with a frown, shielding her imaginary bear from harm with her body. She peered around me. "Who is that with you? Only one visitor is allowed." Her face brightened as she saw Jakobina. "Oh, it's you, Aurelia."

Jakobina moved past me and perched on the bed.

Emily pulled a picture from her pillowcase – a postcard of 'The Girl With A Pearl Earring'. "This picture of you arrived after your last visit," she said. "No one will find it in here. It's our secret."

I gave Jakobina an odd stare. "And when was that?" I asked her.

She shrugged and spoke to the floor. "I guess I've been visiting your mother for several weeks, now," she replied. "Maybe a year.. or two." She coughed. "Perhaps four."

The nurse entered with a rattle of medication in a paper cup and a glass of water. "Time for your pill," she announced with brisk enthusiasm, and then, as an aside to me, "It will make her sleepy. Your mother has been agitated, anxiously awaiting you, constantly asking when you were coming. You can stay until she falls asleep." She beamed a waxen smile at me. "There's chicken soup in the cafeteria, today."

Emily swallowed the pill like a docile child. "I told you Aurelia would come," she said to her pillow bear, and obediently settled under the covers that Jakobina tucked around her.

Jakobina and I watched Emily cuddling her 'bear' with a contented smile. At least she was no longer grieving. I wondered if she'd been grieving for herself or my father or for me.

"Grief is an umbrella," Jakobina said, invading my thoughts. "It permeates everyone and everything. It's never personal. I should know."

"I'm pretty sure they didn't have umbrellas in your time. And you can stop reading my mind."

She sent me a sideways look of contempt. "I've grown, you know. I haven't been asleep for hundreds of years. I've paid attention. I want to be prepared for when I …" She paused with a frown.

"When you what?"

She took a deep breath. "Live in this century. Does that shock you?"

"At this point, I'm beyond shock. Whatever you say. It's of no matter to me."

"But it is, and ironically so, because *matter* is the word for physical. And I intend to live again. Fully. In your time. In every physical sense of the word."

I sent her a 'who gives a crap' look. "Go for it, Casper. Just go for it somewhere else. Anywhere away from me."

Jakobina raised her eyebrows and gave me a lopsided smile.

"Believe me, it will be as far away from you as I can get," she said to herself, yet somehow it didn't sound cruel or rude.

We watched Emily. I'd learned how to assess her sleep patterns by her breathing. Her alpha waves were shallow until she grew still and seemed to float slightly. When her breathing evened out into stage three, the postcard dropped from her hand, landing face up on Jakobina's foot.

Jakobina stroked Emily's cheek. "You'll be dreaming soon," she whispered. "Sweet dreams."

I looked away, embarrassed. "I lent her my teddy bear once," I mused out loud. "But she threw it out the window. By the time I got downstairs another inmate had claimed it. I've all but given up talking to a ghost." I realized my faux pas. "What am I saying. Emily is a shadow but she's at least half alive. Whereas…" I stopped. "You're 100% dead. Am I correct?"

"Almost. It's a long story."

"Do I have the time to listen before I drift away to Byzantium? Or is it Bedlam?"

"It doesn't have to be either."

"Great. Living in neither here nor there or the 'never never' is equally cheery. And what, precisely, is *almost* dead?"

"I did die, eventually, but I was immortalized in a painting as a teenager, so part of me is still hanging around. This is an important anniversary year for me. My portrait was painted three-hundred-years ago. I'm not going anywhere. I *can't* go anywhere. The truth is, I've come to see you because families help each other. Let's just say, I'm an immortal with dreams of mortality. We need to talk about the different kinds of reincarnation and how one of them can save both of us. I need to explain the déjà vu of parallel lives. A good friend of mine always says reality is the stuff of dreams." She stopped with a faraway gleam in her eye. "You'd like him." She corrected herself. "You *will* like him." Wistfulness vanished and she was all business. "And by the way, about taking your mother flowers? Some days she likes flowers. Some days she regards them as funereal offerings and bursts into tears. I've found it's best not to put her through the ordeal. She likes M&M's."

Loss is nothing else but change,
and change is Nature's delight.
— Marcus Aurelius

chapter 5
DEAR ZEE

– December 1–
1965

Tis the season of mistletoe and metaphors. Christmas break put an appalling spin on the reality of breaking up with Zee. The thought was as ghastly as it was ghostly. A full month of being tagged by Jakobina had been exhausting.

The public library was a cozy refuge from the rain that hit hard on Monday. It was homey. Warm and quiet. Christmas exams loomed around the corner. Cramming had officially begun. Students huddled together in study groups murmuring softly and rattled pages, giving the room a heightened sense of purpose. It would have been silent if Zee and I had been allowed our privacy but Jakobina hovered over our conversation like the ghost of Christmas Past – an apparition of tinnitus giving a running commentary only I could hear.

We chose our favorite table. A row of bankers lamps with green glass shades gave off a peaceful academic glow. I would be safe if I never left here.

Jakobina, a relentless maven, was an artist in her own right. She painted my future with Zee in clashing bold stripes of anguish and regret that put Ebenezer Scrooge to shame.

"Look at him, Aurelia," she said. "That boy will do anything for you. He believes love can cure a rainy day."

The gentle rhythm of winter rain drumming the roof, quickened.

"You will be his ruination," Jakobina said. "How cruel is that."

A thunderclap rattled the stained glass windows and briefly dimmed the lights. Jakobina cowered into a shadowy form and disappeared like a snuffed candle.

Zee reached for my hand and gave it a squeeze. "I love storms," he said. "This is nice. Being snug, together in a storm. I love Christmas."

Jakobina returned looking even more pale than any respectful ghost should and would not be banished. She upped her game, one barb at a time. "His happiness is in your hands. If you wait, placing you in an institution will be in his."

She'd been cruelly persuasive when we visited my mother: *Is this where you want to end your days? A nonsensical halfwit blubbering into a pillow?"* and brutal in the presence of my depressed father: *behold, desolation and wretchedness. A free spirit destroyed.* She seemed eager to repeat the words *'not a pretty picture is it'* at every opportunity. *'Swift clean cut'* became her mantra. If she wasn't dead I would have killed her.

Zee winked at me over his book and sent my reserve fluttering to the ground. I must have looked blue because he made a crazy face as if he'd heard Jakobina's prophecy.

"Sacrifice sucks," I said in my head.

"And fate stinks," Jakobina countered, sounding remarkably modern. "But we do what we must. It's your choice. Your children will visit their shell of a mother in a depressing prison and keep the curse alive or you can end it. Only you can stop the madness before it's too late. Only you. Right now. Feed the demon or kill it."

"Martyrdom bites."

She gave a deep sigh. "Sacrifice has its rewards."

"Please. Spare me. There's no need to plaster any more bumper stickers of 'FREE ZEE' over my life. I get the picture. And it's no Vermeer. It's more like Munch's 'Scream' painted across a crazy sky."

Jakobina gave a grunt of approval. "There it is. The choice is simple. Pure and simple."

"Purity is a pain in the ass," I countered.

Her eyes narrowed. "No no no. Purity is a virtue."

I glared back. *"Simplicity is overrated."*

Our conversation went on like this for a ridiculous duel of parry and thrust to no one's advantage. We were supposedly on the same side – to find the best solution for three people. But regardless of how near or far crazy was, I was on a one way trip to the shadowlands where Zee's love could never reach me as hard as I knew he would try. My journey would end at a crossroad with two signs: this way to Selfish... that way to Sainthood.

Two months ago, in this room, on this table, was where I showed Zee my find from an antique shop – a vintage toffee tin with a picture of Bodium Castle on the lid. I'd tapped the castle with the words "this is what I want. This is where I want to live. I've dreamed of a place like this. But a moat isn't good enough. I want the sea." I closed my eyes in bliss. "I remember the sea." He'd answered with his usual cheery 'No problem. When I'm a famous architect, I'll be able to build you one of those in my sleep.' I told him it was my go-to happy place. He'd asked me what I was going to use the box for, and smiled at my answer: to store my best memories and dreams.

Zee was unusually quiet walking me home and in parting he'd said: "I'm sure they won't all fit in there." I looked puzzled. "Our best dreams are too big to fit in your little box," he said. He gave me a quick peck on the cheek and left me glowing on the sidewalk outside my house. I was in no doubt we had a future.

My letter to Zee had been a challenge. As the winter storm raged outside, it weighed heavy as a stone inside my purse. I planned to find a time to sneak it into his backpack. I'd used my favorite mauve writing paper and the color of ink I perfected by mixing equal parts peacock blue with vermillion which made it a tad romantic for a letter delivering the devasting message 'goodbye forever'.

The storm grew wilder, clawing at my brain, and I fancied it blew the cobwebs from its fuzzy synapses, and for a moment I thought I was cured.

"You're living in Dreamland, Aurelia," Jakobina whispered. "You can do better than that."

The rain sluicing down the windows turned the library into an aquarium. I cherished the sanctuary of its walls lined with books and our banker's lamp that shed a soft green light over a terrifying future. The library was ours, but sadly, it was emptying. It was time to go.

Zee closed his book with a snap, got up from the table and stretched his arms above his head. "Race you to your happy place," he said grinning.

"I'm way ahead of you," I replied. "I'm already there."

*Execute every act of thy life
as though it were thy last.*
— MARCUS AURELIUS

chapter 6
EXIT STAGE RITE

The Winter Solstice
– December 22 –

The last three Sunday afternoons Emily had been sleeping when Jakobina and I arrived. Jakobina used the time for her lessons outlining the benefits of immortality against the grim reality of death by dementia. Sadly, I became more unstable as her confidence grew. Our fragile relationship progressed on an imbalance of personal powers, yet in spite of its absurdity, Jakobina's solution grew on me. She was that 'force to be reckoned with' one thinks they'll never meet.

We sat side-by-side on a floral loveseat. Emily's postcard of 'The Girl With A Pearl Earring' eyed me from her bedside table.

While Jakobina talked, I focused on a heart-shaped shard of garnet sea glass positioned on the postcard directly atop the Pearl girl's red mouth. I'd given it to Emily when she was still my mother, on our last trip to the seaside. It looked as though the postcard Jakobina was about to eat a strawberry.

Jakobina nudged me. "So, what do you say? Do we have an agreement?"

I needed more time. "Possibly, being wooed within the confines of a dementia ward is not the best place to summon the greatest picture of health," I said.

Jakobina pounced on my words. "Yes, yes. That's it exactly! That's what I've been saying. My portrait can be your 'picture' of health." She twirled slowly, showing off. "Look at me. I've been seventeen for three-hundred years, without becoming old and ugly. No medication.

No loss of memory. No disappointments. And your years will disappear too, after you take my place."

I played along. "What years? I'm only seventeen."

Her expression was triumphant. "Your *future* years, but the timing is critical, now. I assure you our pact will only be consummated after you've lived a long productive life." She shrugged her shoulders. "We can see how it goes."

I snickered. "Productive? You've got to be kidding."

"I have all of Delft to explore behind me. You will too. I didn't sit and watch life go by. You'd be amazed what one learns eavesdropping for hundreds of years in an art gallery. It's a quiet place where people meet away from prying eyes. They dropped all sorts of secrets in front of my painting."

"And into your prying ears."

"You may imagine, as with any *normal* ghost, that I frequent my past. The difference is, that while I may be limited to my past, other than being with you, I don't simply observe the movie of it. My mind continues to learn. *History* may not change but I *do*. My living years offer me a variety of seasons and landscapes to choose from. Even a Delft Winter is comfy when you no longer feel the cold."

I stood and paced the floor. It was easier to face her from a distance. "And then there's that prying mind of yours."

"Time may stand still in my world. It's always 1665 in Delft. But in yours, it never does. Delft came with its own advantages. I explored every home and street of it. I followed everyone until I knew all their secrets. I became adept at the mathematics of human relationships. I learned that things hardly ever add up. And from my perch inside a painting on a wall, a continuous progression of new language paraded by. Death is a school for me. Time is a door. Reincarnation is a window. I speak your language because I studied hard."

I faked banging my head against the wall. "Stop. I get it. Life is a big revolving door, spinning out of control at the speed of light, within the artfulness of time." I walked to the bed in anger and tucked Emily's blanket around her shoulders, careful not to touch her. "And some of us are cursed."

I felt the stirrings of a memory brush past me. "I had this weird dream last summer. I was in the cafeteria. Several of my friends from the Stargazy Club had aged. I mean, they were ancient, scattered among the tables, seated in wheelchairs. The details are hazy, but I think you were there."

Jakobina's expression froze for a heartbeat before she smiled. "I *was* there. Briefly. I've popped into your dreams many many times. Don't overthink it."

I blinked. "It's already gone."

Her eyes searched the air. "Now, where were we? Ah, yes, you mentioned being cursed." She gestured to the armchair across from her. "Sit. Be as sarcastic as you want. I understand that you're afraid. You're afraid all the time. But let me enlighten you about art and doors, sweeting. A painting is a secret door. A still-life painting is a snapshot of death. A painted landscape is a wider door. But a human portrait from life is a door marked private. Beyond that door there be dragons."

A familiar cold draught blew around my shoulders. Virgil's words came back to me: *'Disappearances can be revealing. Look around you. There will always be unlocked doors.'* I opened my mouth to speak but Jakobina silenced me with a raised finger across her lips.

"Every human life is a story. A story is a door. A fairy tale is a broader door. Death is a hidden door. Rebirth is the biggest door of all. Immortality is a corridor to…"

"Boredom," I whispered. "How about the door to a million years of boredom?"

"You love art," she said as if she'd suddenly thought of it. "Delft was teeming with brilliant artists." She paused, leaned close, and tilted my chin so there was no doubt I was paying attention. "And what about your recurring dreams? That river you dreamed of so often was a canal in Delft. The art studio you glimpsed was Vermeer's. The castle above the sea was in Cornwall. I died there. So, you see, your dreams are my memories. You've been expecting me."

In a weird way, I almost admired her single-minded slyness, a side completely devoted to her mission to live again. But it was all too clear that her mission was pretty much dependent on me.

I called her bluff. "I think what you mean is, if I entered your painting, I would be spared an undignified end, meet Vermeer, and watch him paint as an invisible spectator... I mean *spectre*. You're asking a great deal from a distant cousin."

She brightened. "Think what you would learn. The Dutch School was vast."

I sat there smiling like a stunned idiot. "Well, no problem, then," I said. "Let's go," and quoted a line from a nonsense nursery rhyme that popped into my head. "And the dish ran away with the spoon."

The rules of immortality were exacting and less than illuminating.

I steeled myself.

Jakobina settled herself across from me and grasped both my hands. I was suitably disturbed yet too curious to run. Visiting hours were over. "The laws of balance decree we must reach the same threshold of death," she said. "I lived to be seventy-two which means you have a lot of living ahead of you."

I did a quick calculation. "Fifty-five years. Fifty-five years without Zee."

"Without the guilt of ruining Zee's dreams."

"You don't know that."

"He's a dreamer, Aurelia. Zee worships outer space for a reason. He will thrive as a free bird. Give him that chance."

"Assuming I agree, how would it happen?"

"A man will come, shortly before your transition. I met him... after I lost my husband."

"Was I married?"

"You were a mother, Aurelia."

"Son or daughter?" I asked.

She slumped in her chair and for a moment I thought she'd given up but she tightened her grip on my hands with renewed energy. "This man was a brilliant leader. A healer. A mystic. A sage who promised to help me rejoin the world, settle an incarnation of me in my place, and close the painting's door – a portal between dimensions. Not to worry. You won't be ready. You won't know the day."

"This man, he spoke to you about me?"

Jakobina's eyes avoided mine, glanced off the floor and ceiling, and came to rest on the sleeping form of my mother. She was clearly uncomfortable because her voice came out high and trembly and she stuttered some senseless words in double-Dutch.

After a few false starts she finally managed "You called me in your way. And I found you, so *yes*, he spoke about you and the two of us together. Your… 'dish and a spoon' running away. In the painting and outside it as we've planned."

I corrected her. "As we are still *discussing*."

She conceded with a hesitant nod. "As we are still *planning*." She pinned me with sorrowful eyes. "You had a son."

I took a deep intake of breath, momentarily pleased.

Jakobina stared hard at me without blinking. "And like it or not, Aurelia, you still have a mother."

The day I said goodbye to my mother she didn't know me. She never looked up from the tattered postcard of Jakobina that had taken my place. I took consolation from the fact that she would never miss me. I left her a shopping bag full of M&Ms on the foot of her bed while she slept.

I left a goodbye note for my father who will, I'm sure, feel thankful to be relieved of his tiresome womenfolk and leave town to find a new life. I say, good luck to him. It's what I'm doing. But unlike my mother's cold pitiless farewell, my future must be clear of victims. Confused as I was, I felt it best to depart without ceremony. After all, I'd been underage, and, if reported missing to the authorities, I could leave no footprints to follow.

I'd excused myself in a letter to Zee by telling him a whopper of a white lie, that I'd gone away to an art school in Europe, naively, imagining that was the end of it. And it wasn't a complete lie because I did eventually take up painting and I had brave new horizons to conquer or at least, endure. If life was one big school, and it seemed likely that it was, then Zee deserved a chance for the highest education possible.

I convinced myself that leaving Zee was an act of love, and that eventually, we would each escape to better things from my sacrifice. For many years, believing this to be true sustained me through tough times and lean times and thoroughly bad times. But there was cowardice in it.

In any case, I lost my nerve. I sealed my letter to Zee in a stamped envelope and laid it to rest in between some family snapshots in the castle box.

New Years Eve
– December 31–

Christmas was a musical blur of red and green decorations set against a soundtrack of shmaltzy good cheer – an annoying background noise that whipped my torment into an endless nightmare of frozen smiles, mindless prattle and cloying eggnog. I thought it would never end. I dreaded that it would end. Christmas break meant breaking up with Zee.

On New Year's Eve I ran away from Zee, dementia, and my home, in that order. But for the life of me, I couldn't shake my soothsayer with a pearl earring. I found a series of brain-numbing jobs for minimum wage and kept a low profile.

To punish myself, I left Felix behind. And due to the chilly weather, and in an uncharacteristic deference to nostalgia, I donned my mother's fur coat. The coat I'd named Sophie because Emily looked like a movie star when she wore it, and more importantly, because *I* felt like a movie star when *I* wore it. It was the fur I used to snuggle into as a child whenever I needed comfort. It had always made me feel protected. I imagined myself a bear cub and the coat was my mother.

I wore the T-shirt Zee gave me to rags, and fashioned my apartment after Vermeer's austere studio. On clear nights I visited the stars with my telescope. I tried once, to access my poetic gene by dabbling with my memoirs, such as they were, but ironically, my memories were all 'too clear' and capturing them on paper proved less than cathartic. I tore out the first page and used it as a coaster, rescued it, dried it in the sun, and buried it alive with Zee' letter.

I kept up with my art classes and volunteered at a local brain-injured society pretending to be of sound mind, using the art therapy techniques I developed to ease my own pain. I achieved this in spite of being companioned by Jakobina's continual haunting presence. I felt like a long suffering wife with a nagging mother-in-law. Jakobina kept me on my toes, waffling between angelic moments of compassion and the manic mood swings of a harpy.

I'd promised myself I wouldn't disappear from Zee without a goodbye, but I did.

My former mother had recognized me early on for the precocious child I was expected to be. She swore, as I have echoed ever since, that the women in our family contained an erratically poetic gene – the life's blood and mixed blessing of artists everywhere.

It seems we are programmed for eccentricity, that leads, in due course, to higher truths. One came to me upon waking and I wrote it in my diary:

Dementia arrives the way a swan enters the water without so much as a ripple.

Until I met Jakobina, I'd never considered drifting into the promised wasteland so completely or so soon. But now, it seems I have a confession to write before I glide away on the back of a swan.

THE CASTLE BOX

FOR THE LIFE OF ME

I awoke from a pleasant dream with Virgil shortly after my ninth birthday when my mother disappeared into hers. I remember the first time she forgot who I was and I discovered that reality was pain and suffering and the loss of love.

I no longer believed in happy-ever-after. There would be no prince for me. No true love's kiss. Childhood seemed a complete waste of time.

Magical intervention hadn't saved my mother or comforted my bereft father, nor was it likely to protect me from the evil curse that haunted the women in our family.

When I was fourteen, a series of recurring lucid dreams began where I wandered through the stone ruins of a castle high above a wild sea. A mermaid called from the rocks and I found myself transported to the banks of a frozen river.

I followed its course, drawn towards an artist's studio, driven by a sense of belonging.

I became obsessed with castles, harbored a dream of living by the sea, and decided to devote my life to unravelling why art touched me so deeply.

Shortly afterwards, the visions and headaches came. And then I did something completely selfish. I fell in love with my best friend, Zee, and ran away from home.

ONCE UPON A TIME-SLIP

In my beginning is my end.
In my end is my beginning.
— T.S. ELIOT

chapter 7
SLIPPING AWAY

Castle Island
– May 8 –
2019

It took me a lifetime to learn how to be a child, and now, the restless girl in the painting is teaching me to be old. As time flies, Jakobina has been with me over fifty-years. Our 'arrangement', such as it is, remains a transparent power play for immortality. When the time comes, I've more or less promised to take her place. The debate continues.

I call our pact tentative. She declares it a binding contract. And since there are no hard and fast rules to being haunted or being held to adolescent promises made under duress, we live in a state of meaningful uncertainty. For duress it was. I see that now.

There are decisions made at seventeen that are impossible to keep. Instead, Jakobina and I keep up the pretense that we're both right, and muddle along from day-to-day, waxing and waning like twin moons in a collision course with the sun.

And so I've discovered with the contrary forgetfulness of old age, that while small matters fade, my biggest mistake haunts me more than any restless spirit.

My old life is a distant memory inhabited by the ghosts of stillborn dreams. It's where I abandoned the one I loved most, and the ones I should have loved, and the ones I failed to love.

There are nights I believe I deserve to forfeit the safe harbor that Jakobina offers me. If there's such a thing as karma, it would be a fitting atonement if I died the death I once feared more than love itself.

. . .

Jakobina had been relentless in 1965. I'll give her that much, and she'd been right about one thing. Metaphorically, I started to disappear not long after we met. But it was a subtle form of depression.

I likened it to standing in a puddle of bleach. One morning, my colors faded from the toes up, even though my molecules still existed. I knew this because I interacted with physical objects as well as ever. I just stopped caring.

But… each morning, after a few moments of uneasy transition, there I was – the picture of health, materialized from head to toe in a full-length mirror, perfectly sound.

I dreamed up a fanciful notion that an artist repainted me overnight and that one day all that would remain of me would be a pair of rose-tinted reading glasses floating in the breeze.

My disappearing act worsened with age. Everywhere I went, especially hailing a waitress or a taxi, I was overlooked. But in spite of this, I've defied the odds and journeyed full-circle to live by the sea and write a second novel for the first time… or to be more precise, to pen a first novel for the second time.

Bizarrely, it's the memoir of two lives I can't quite remember. Mine and hers… Jakobina's – the girl in Vermeer's masterpiece with the pearl earring, his 'Mona Lisa of the north'.

According to the laws of metaphysics, and why should they be any less sound than the others, I'm dissolving into Vermeer's painting as Jakobina is venturing out. A prospect infinitely more appealing than dying like my mother, one brain cell at a time in a hospice.

I humored Jakobina and accepted my situation because, in my state of mental and molecular confusion, facing the inevitable is all there was. The spontaneous moments when I found myself inside the painting looking out were disconcerting, but if anything could be called real in my life, I considered those visits dress rehearsals for the real thing.

By my reckoning Jakobina has one full year before my mental 'earthquakes' consume me and I vanish completely, because although I still cast creative aspersions from time-to-time, as my memories evaporate, there are days I feel as if I no longer cast a shadow.

Our island retreat, Tintagel Cottage, as Jakobina renamed it, is a miniature castle planted on a windy point, on a relatively low outcrop of flat boulders that blend seamlessly into a stark garden of sand dunes thatched with beach grass. Seaweed catches in the teeth of its sagging fence of large toothpicks sewn together with wire. I can't imagine living anywhere else.

Nevertheless, there's a reason why the universe rhymes with perverse. And since I've never fully trusted providence, it was hardly a surprise, a week ago, when something unsettling arrived on the tide to square paradise. A tranquil walk on my private beach delivered more than my morning's gift of sea glass. It was, profoundly enough, the first of May, a gentle date I'd always associated with Spring flowers and traditional images of May poles festooned with ribbons, but my lighthearted air of celebration was overshadowed by an eerie feeling of being watched.

I shivered with goosebumps, blindsided by a distinct threat.

At first I was too angry to be afraid. An ominous stranger had destroyed my growing contentment of isolated bliss. No small thing. I'd become relatively accustomed to supernatural anomalies, but this was different. It had the air of stalking about it.

We'd been visited by a freakish trespasser worthy of a 'May Day' alert. No ordinary intruder could drop onto an island unannounced nor leave without a trace in the sand.

I sent a mental S.O.S. distress signal into the universe, hoping for a rational explanation. It was the only thing I could do. Considering Jakobina was beyond bodily harm, saving two souls was never the issue. I needed to save my own.

Although, I have to say, Jakobina didn't seem overly concerned about my safety. She was much bolder than she used to be. In fact, ever since the incidents on the beach, she appeared happier than she'd been in weeks.

She became pixilated. Her eyes were brighter... almost feverish. I met her in my own reflection in the darkened window over the kitchen sink when my hands were deep in soapy water.

Apart from the Felix clock with its pendulum tail and roving cartoon eyes, the kitchen was one of her favorite hangouts... I don't like to use the word *haunts*, although I can confirm that pestering the living with requests is the essence of haunting, and, I believe, the primary inclination of apparitions in general.

Jakobina is more than a vaporous shell. She's family. We've been together ever since she proposed the pact to resolve our mutual issues of mortality. Jakobina wanted a second chance to live and I wanted to avoid death altogether. I was unbelievably young and naïve. Jakobina was incredibly motivated. It had seemed like a match made in heaven.

Jakobina passes me on the stairs, materializes beside me when I'm daydreaming, and peers into rooms with that frightened deer look she has. Sometimes, when I drive away, she waves to me from a window. She chooses different ones. The furthest she's ventured from my bedroom, where a print of her portrait hangs, is up to the widow's walk where I've set up my old telescope.

I tell Jakobina about the stars and she tells me about the artfulness of time.

Over the years I've considered what it's like to live on borrowed time. So much so, I've retired here to make peace with a double mystery. The sea holds a secret I need to remember and a promise she needs to keep.

It's said that all things, good or ill, appear in threes. In my case, a triple mystery on my stretch of deserted beach was too deep to ignore.

It was the third sandcastle that rang alarm bells.

I hit the sand running.

In the middle of the journey of my life,
I found myself within a dark wood
where the straight way was lost.
— DANTE ALIGHIERI
'The Divine Comedy'

chapter 8
A LINE IN THE SAND

May Day
– May 1 –
– *one week earlier* –

I must have been insane, listening to a cat clock. But then, I suppose Felix was part of my overall disintegration. The morning of May 1st began on the tail of a dream where Felix misquoted a famous line from a poem by Robert Frost to send me a message. *'You have promises to break and miles to go before you wake'*. Once more, he repeated his most fervent advice, that time was an illusion and insisted he was my ally. *'Remember'*, he said, perfectly serious, *'You can always count on me.'*

I woke with a real cat in my face and the echo of Felix's mantra. *'Go back, Aurelia... it's easy... you're already there.'* Today it felt more like a warning. Punch's ginger fur made me sneeze.

As was customary, I glanced briefly in the mirror to see how I fared. I was blurry but I stood my ground until I came into focus. I arrived, my colors robust, and so I scribbled a haiku in my journal before it, too, might disappear:

High tides anticipating
Battered hopes clinging
Dreams tumble into the sea

It was a mildly unsettling portent before walking the seashore for the day's harvest of sea glass, that, by the end of the week, beached a mystery of infinite importance. But that morning the sand was strangely empty of glass gems and overly rich in castles. As always, Punch accompanied me, appearing and disappearing as distractions took her fancy.

Camelot Revisited
the first sandcastle

A strip of mauve paper protruded, fluttering from the highest turret of a classic sandcastle like a royal banner. I pulled it out at once, like extracting Excalibur from the stone. It read: *"Dear Aurelia. I am yours til' human voices wake us, and we drown."* It WAS for me – a line quoted from T.S. Eliot, one of my treasured literary friends. How mysterious. How lovely. And so I overlooked the greeting, thinking it might be from Jakobina, although in all the years I'd known her, apart from our roof, she's never ventured a foot outside.

I drank in a lungful of sea air and sank to the sand, wriggled a comfortable hollow for my derriere, stretched my legs towards the surf, and leaned back on my elbows to savor the romantic spirit of the moment. Who was my secret admirer? I basked, eyes closed, salty sun on my face. Glorious.

Old T.S. had welcomed me home. Thoughtful. Perfect. Who was luckier than me. I had a secret admirer. An elemental, perhaps. Anything is possible if one's sanity is in question on a haunted island where time stands still.

Punch bounded from the grassy dunes, startling me by running headlong at the cluster of seagulls forever hounding me for scraps. It was a brave gesture, doomed to failure. In any case, it broke the mood and we pushed on.

chapter 9
THE GHOST OF A KISS

Bodium In A Box
the second sandcastle

The second castle had one side of its crude design washed away. It looked as if it had suffered a stroke. It's clue, for by now that's what the messages seemed, clung precariously to a squashed flowerpot shaped dome surrounded by a puddle of seawater. It read: *Aurelia. I think of you and "Days of hands that lift and drop a question on your plate"* I was intrigued. "Consider it dropped," I said to the sky. But not before peering around quickly to catch my prankster out. "HELLO," I shouted over the surf, "If this is a scavenger hunt, what is it you want me to find?"

A seagull swooped at Punch, already slinking defensively low to the ground. I knew the feeling.

Thankfully, I was spared the shock of a possibly masked and cloaked humpbacked beasty-man leering at me from behind the high dunes. "Thanks Eliot old chap," I whispered. I made a display of folding the note in four and pocketed it with some show of ceremony. "This goes in the collection," I said, loud enough for any phantom in the vicinity to hear. "I thank you, but enough is enough. Okay?" It was clear, the notes were *not* from Jakobina.

Back home, I smoothed the papers and trapped them under a heart-shaped granite paperweight.

Jakobina placed a bowl of oatmeal in front of me and moved the sugar bowl out of my reach. "I've had an encounter," I said, retrieving the sugar. I cleared my throat. "*Two* encounters."

Our game of sugar chess continued. Jakobina deftly moved the sugar to a cupboard and steadied her forehead on the door. Her voice shook. "And this means?" she said with her back to me.

Big sigh. I counted to ten. "It means we have a visitor on our island. It would seem a builder of sandcastles."

She wheeled, her eyes wide with hope. "Oh Aurelia, do you think it's him?"

"There is no 'him'. I'm only seventy-one. It's far too soon. I have one year left. Besides, I'm not ready. Our intruder is someone else."

She clasped one hand to her neck. "Were there footprints?"

I felt a warm surge of excitement as I visualized the beach and spun 360 degrees for the fullest memory picture. A blank canvas of sand stretched in all directions. I shook my head. "Nope. Not one."

Aurelia sank to the floor, a crumpled queen on a black and white linoleum chessboard. She drew her knees to her chest and rocked slowly, emitting the unearthly moans of a creature in pain. I knelt and put my arms around her. Her shaking penetrated my body, but the moans subsided and she slowly uncurled, her face radiant with tears. She grabbed both my hands and kissed them wildly. Her voice was strangely triumphant. "I remember. I remember everything."

"You are unsettled," I said. "Come. Help me look for something. It's in the bedroom. At least, that's where I last saw it."

"The castle box," Jakobina whimpered. "It's in the linen chest. Please don't open it."

"Ah yes, my sad little hope chest," I countered. Among its contents lingered the emotional clutter of abandoned romantic aspirations squashed between winter woolens, linens folded with sprigs of lavender, and a few fossilized sketchbooks from art school.

Like cats everywhere, the squeaky hinge of a trunk lid alerted Punch to an adventure. I was aware Jakobina tolerated Punch to humor me but I refused to indulge anyone's intolerance for cats. Jakobina faded into her portrait as, with Punch's assistance, I rummaged through blankets and sweaters. My hands encountered a worn T-shirt, and a scented floral scarf. I pulled away as if burned. The pain encouraged me.

I found my old treasure box wrapped in a quilt at the very bottom – a battered toffee tin with a picture of Bodium Castle on the lid. The contents – a time capsule of high school memories, had been left stewing for fifty-years. The psychic heaviness of teenage secrets rattled inside.

"They're still alive," Jakobina called from her portrait. "Be careful."

I mumbled something about Pandora and worrywarts that silenced her.

Jakobina glided from the painting to materialize behind me, her hand on my shoulder, her anxiety infectious. "It'll be all right," I said, patting her hand but I was disquieted. When an abandoned box of memorabilia calls it's always an omen with a double-edged invitation to face unfinished business. The lid took some effort to open, and unstuck suddenly with somewhat of a melodramatic pop. I stopped breathing.

The scent of Chanel # 5 and the disturbed ghost of a high school ring, long since lost, floated out, screaming past me. I recognized a silver snap stamped with the word Levi from Zee's denim shirt, a twist of greying paper containing two black buttons, and a worn Pink Pearl eraser with the initials A and Z drawn inside a heart in blue ballpoint ink.

Jakobina gave a choked cry and disappeared. Why was she so distraught about unleashing my memories? Then it dawned on me that she'd been there. It was where we met.

The gauntlet was down. It was up to me to stay or follow a nervous thread into an age-old labyrinth I'd only vaguely acknowledged that I'd come to find by the sea. According to Jakobina's original prediction, I had one full year before a timely deadline would force my surrender and her deliverance.

I hadn't entirely known what I was searching for until a hard object slid with a clunk from under a wad of paper clippings, including a faded blue leaflet that surfaced with the word DREAMS printed on it in bold white letters. Angry bees stung the inside of my stomach. It was a talisman from my best friend, Zee – a smooth green bloodstone – a worry stone kept under my pillow at night and carried close during lapses of loneliness and fear. The cold weight of the Zee Stone in my hand quickened and unleashed a guarded crush on my best friend, now an old man or quite possibly, dead.

I heard myself laughing in sobs. Zee had been much more than a best friend. The floor met me halfway, its hardwood bruising my knees. My thumb found the well-worn depression on one side of the stone. Warm electricity flooded my hand. I felt the urge to runaway to sea and I realized with a wry shock that I had. I felt a strong urge to prevent a circle from closing. At least one that would leave me on the outside. I felt an irrational need to hold open a door that wasn't there.

Punch pawed my face fussing for attention and purred loud enough to stir me. I hungered for sugar.

Jakobina evaporated and manifested in a state of agitation several times in various places throughout the room, finally ending back where she'd been before her lapse of molecular control. "What can I do?" she murmured to herself, wringing her hands in a somewhat ghostly cliché.

I cuddled Punch like a teddy bear and managed to order sweet tea as a dying woman might make a last request. "Please make it very *very* sweet," I instructed. "And strong. Three teabags."

"You're in shock," Jakobina chastised, somewhat accusingly. "Be careful. Please."

"I intend to." I said. "Sweet tea was how Londoners coped during the blitz. It's the first line of defence against trauma. The British knew the power of sugar during rough times. And if I'm in for the war I think I am, I need to perk up. My soul is in tatters. I think I'll take a cat nap before supper."

"But the doctor…" she changed her tack. "Aurelia, please put down that dreadful box." She reached out to take it, her hands shaking.

I kept hold of it and evaded her grasp. "Hang the consequences. You and I are already victims of an *old* war. Assuredly, this *new* one won't be a fair fight. Be an angel. Make the tea strong enough to melt a spoon and inhumanly sweet." I dismissed her with "please and thank you."

I counted slowly to eleven and stood with Punch in my arms. The colors in the room vibrated and hurt my eyes as I took a turn about the room. I ignored Jakobina's portrait but in peripheral vision I could see that its frame held a void of white space that crackled with sparks. Punch hissed at the painting, struggled free, and leapt to the windowsill, her fur plainly in a huff.

Jakobina sidled past Punch and melted into the bookcase across the room with the words "I'll put the kettle on." I blinked. It was always a bit of a shock when she played up the ghost thing. It was happening more often. Like I needed a reminder. I followed a distinct humming noise that came from a book jutting oddly from the shelf. "Once more into the breach," I said to the spine of a familiar volume. I pushed it back. "More like, into the *beach*." I chuckled without humor. Shakespeare was, as usual, dramatically correct.

While I sipped a second cup of tea, Jakobina pulled a faded polaroid photograph of Zee and me from the muddle – a pair of smiling faces, innocently pressed together, close enough to be intimate. "I remember when this was taken," she said, her voice softening. "When I traipsed after you, hoping to be seen."

I touched my cheek. My fingers met the shadow of Zee's lips and stirred the muscle memories of first love. He'd kissed me after the shutter clicked. The palest kiss. Innocent. Soft. I'd been completely happy.

"I'll leave you two alone for a while," Jakobina said. "I know all about memories. They're terrible things." She squeezed my shoulder and was gone, leaving a faint trembling sensation in the air. The sugar bowl was nowhere to be seen.

I pocketed the stone and closed the box. There was a letter in there I didn't want to see. My hands shook as I lifted the teapot, poured cream, and stirred.

The third cup of tea unleashed fifty years of tears and regret. I returned to the linen trunk alone and retrieved the T-shirt Zee had given me – one of his own that I once wore as a hug. And wear it I had, for months after my untimely exile. I held it to my face and used it to dry my tears.

After a time, I slipped it on, stumbled to bed, and retreated into the shadows of 1965.

chapter 10

A COLD WAR

After supper, I returned to the bookcase to find my copy of 'Morte de Artur', and drifted off into the pages of a Camelot that never was. I imagined invisible elementals gathering close behind my eyes, whispering words of encouragement. *Come with us Aurelia, time's a wasting.*

I hummed dreamily to the crashing surf and sang an insistent line of lyrics stuck on replay, looping inside my head. *'Mister Sandman, bring me a dream'.*

Jakobina heard me and materialized without ceremony. "Mr. who?"

"Thanks for dropping in," I said, without opening my eyes. "Well, Miss Eavesdropper, if you must know, the Sandman is a keeper of dreams who drops a grain of sand in our eyes to make us sleepy." My face crumpled. "Oh my god, I've had Virgil's eyes all this time."

Jakobina gasped. "It might be *him*. My stranger was a dreamer. That much I know." She pursed her rosebud lips, covered her mouth with her hand, and turned away. "Sorry. That's all I'm allowed to say."

I stretched awkwardly as only one *can* stretch in an armchair and gave her an impassive stare. "Okay, Mister Dreamer," I said to the ceiling, "after this day of castles in the sand, which by the way, Jakobina, is a metaphor for impossible dreams, I could use a romping good tale of chivalry and valor." I managed the line *'please turn on your magic beam'* before the weight of sadness sank me a few miles beneath unconsciousness. I zoned out to the bottom of a warm sea, rubbing the Zee stone like an Aladdin's lamp and fell asleep with it in my hand, dreaming of a lost boy I knew in school.

The day's jousting was over. The great hall echoed with revelry. The King and his knights nursed their sore muscles with feasting and drink in an aftermath of camaraderie. They listened, enchanted under a minstrel's spell, immortalizing the day's triumphs in song. After each verse, the hall erupted with the din of appreciative table pounding, and as the harp strings silenced, the castle exploded in triumphant shouts of victory and homage to the king.

The King's fool rattled a cymbal at the palace dogs snarling under the table over the best scraps.

I served mead at Arthur's roundtable, slipping silently over the rushes in a luminous shift of forest-green silk. Servants in colorful livery stood back from their masters like sentries. Ladies bound into insanely corseted gowns retired to the shadows to sip mulled ale by the fire. I kept my eyes on Lancelot's glorious profile. As my champion, he'd begged a silk favor from me. The memory was as fresh as the tear in the gold fabric of my under-sleeve showing it's recent sacrifice. Grief overwhelmed me. 'Don't have nobody to call my own' a voice sang.

The great hall echoed with the sound of heavy goblets toasting a fair land, safe from prophecies of a winter blight. I moved forward to replenish the King's wine but sand poured from the ewer's spout, filling his chalice with golden dust.

Arthur closed his eyes, recalling his memories of an old wizard playing a harp in the firelight, and himself, an untried boy named Wart, his eyes shining, listened to the minstrel singing of a holy grail and the promise of a boy king to out-king them all. 'please turn on your magic beam,' he sang. 'mister sandman bring me a dream.'

Outside, the wind howled into a nightmare. The north gate buckled as a wave of grey seawater crashed through the courtyard. I tried to warn them. "The castle walls are breached," I yelled. "You'll be washed away." But no-one could see me, and the knights were too enthralled with the performance to care.

A dog barking frantically woke me with a start, and I shouted "Mordred, save him." Angry storm clouds raced across the sky turning the Spring night to Winter-dark at six o'clock. Weather, caught out of season, had closed down the day.

Punch pawed my arm, one claw catching on my favorite gold sweater. I petted her to relieve my anxiety. "Are you hungry, old girl?"

Jakobina, seated beside me, clumsily detached Punch from my sleeve pulling a golden thread with her. She tried to minimize the damage without success. "I fed her while you slept." She brushed cat hair from her dress with obvious distaste. "Who's Mordred?"

I locked out the chill and lit a fire. "Mordred was King Arthur's estranged son who plotted his death. A jealous murderous child conceived through enchanted incest. Talk about your dysfunctional royal families. Did you hear a dog earlier?"

Her earrings flashed white sparks as she shook her head.

Returning to my book proved hopeless. All I could think about was an ethereal Sandman who knew my name and the name of my favorite poet.

Punch scratched at the door eager to be off on her night prowls but when I opened the door she hissed into the darkness, turned tail in a fit of feline grumbles, and retreated under the couch. Maybe a dog *was* out there. A rogue breeze, all that was left of the storm, sent drifting sand over the threshold, covering the toes of my slippers and suddenly returned full force. It was the first tangible sign of something untoward casting a net around us.

Jakobina did what she usually did at bedtime, fussing around me. The ritual of hot milk brought some normalcy to the house but not enough to push old scores and the threat of war from our thoughts. We sipped together in silence, letting the storm beat the windows and stared at the photo of Zee and me, symbolically propped against the mantle clock that ticked like thunder.

The flames acted as a scrying bowl. Familiar faces came and went. Emotions churned white hot. The seconds of fifty-years stretched back to a memory I couldn't remember because I didn't want to remember. Something had happened. A bumpy secret had been left under a careworn carpet.

When the clock chimed ten, I leaned my head on Jakobina's shoulder. "So much for the good old days," I said. "They're best gone." But the box had been opened and lightly-scented ghosts refused their open cage. Jakobina took my hand and pried open my fingers. The Zee Stone flickered in the firelight. Her thoughts echoed inside my head. "Yes, Grootmoeder, I know. You will remember soon. All in good time, yes?"

chapter 11

THREE's THE CHARM

The Legend of Tintagel
the third sandcastle

The third castle was a simple affair, appearing after a lapse of several days. A childish ring of sand inside a single row of shells. A familiar mauve message flapped in the breeze. It read: *Why is it, Aurelia, that it is impossible to say just what I mean!*

"Is it hell! Who are you?" I shouted to the seagulls, saving Punch from yet another attack. "Why are you doing this?" I remembered a line from a childish game of hide-and-seek and gave it a feeble try. "Come out come out wherever you are." A gull, or was it a banshee off course heading for Ireland, shrieked "And shite to you too, Missus." To be sure, it had to be a banshee with that kind of potty beak.

"Nice people don't play games," I shouted with less conviction. To make my point, I crumpled the paper into a tiny pill, flicked it in the air, and ground it into the sand where it landed with some degree of melodrama. I kicked the castle senseless, brushed the sand from my hands, and headed home. Punch hared off ahead of me and greeted me, tail up, on the porch. For the first time, I wished she were a dog.

I sank into an armchair, too annoyed for tea. Jakobina failed to answer my call, so I closed my eyes. I heard the hum of a mental projector and the clunk of a slide carousel loaded into place. The show began with images lasting ten seconds. But once the cycle finished it began again, this time each slide moved more rapidly, until on the third round they became an animation of images knitted together: the statuesque ruins of Tintagel Castle perched high on a Cornish crag, a fortress battered by killer waves, knights slaying dragons, and a secret lover shadowing My Lady Ygraine. Snapshots of treachery and betrayal came forward. A cuckolded husband dying on a battlefield. A changeling birth. An old woman trapped in a crumbling tower, staring out to sea, throwing something into the air that sparkled like white stars. A special boy, crowned and dethroned. I watched my prince run with the stags. A priestess sacrificed his blood to the goddess, and I woke with nerves shredded to coleslaw. I'd been there before.

I was certain, now. There had been no footprints. The sand had been combed smooth around all three castles as if they had descended from the sky. I drew comfort from the phantom of a grey dog that shadowed me wherever I went but I knew I needed a real dog to run guard on my beach.

I had a secret admirer. Correction. I *may* have a secret admirer. But dark-sky-thinking informed me I could be the random prey of a creative stalker.

But darker still, were my thoughts centered on a battered tin box with a castle on the lid. I'd cheated love, that much was clear. Perhaps I deserved to slip into dementia, ironically forgetting the days I never lived.

My head throbbed with shame. Felix watched me. "Doesn't living fully mean dying fully as well?" I asked him.

"It most certainly does," Felix purred. "Haven't you heard that immortality is a fate worse than death? *tic toc...* detri-*mental.* One might say its contrary sanity. You're still young enough to get it right. There's plenty of time. *tick tock...* Oodles. An excess of seconds, *tick...* Copious hours, *tock...* An overabundance of days *tick tock...* a plethora of..."

"Okay okay, point taken." I cooled my face on the enameled kitchen table. The loud screech of a fighting cat peeled my face from its hard pillow. I was alone but Felix's eyes had not only stopped moving, his thin feline pupils had widened into black circles. He wasn't finished with me but I was too tired to discourse about the nature of time running out or standing still, and most of all, time-slipping randomly off the beaten track to heaven knows where other than it was never what heaven was cracked up to be.

Felix stared at me and performed the impossible... he winked. "Finally, I can see what's what," he said.

I whispered *Et tu Felix* and rested my head on my arms. My thoughts were all about keeping my cowardly promise to Jakobina. In spite of my growing hesitation, friends should keep their promises. She'd saved me from a fate worse than… I chuckled. Nothing's worse than death. Well, she'd become a true friend. I owed her.

Felix meowed from the depth of his clockwork heart. "You can always count on me," he said inside my head. "This kitchen is your sanctuary. But consider this: Life is precarious – a time bomb with a short fuse, and immortality is overrated."

"Good to know," I said, muffled by my sleeves. "Why does Jakobina hate you so much?"

"Time will tell," came his reply. "Cats rarely comply. By the way, she isn't overly fond of dogs either. It's a ghost thing. Apparently barking ruffles their molecules, such as they are." Felix sniffed. "Hence the term barking mad."

"If that's meant as a slur directed at me, thanks very much," I replied. "I'm quite sane."

But something was terribly wrong. I had to face my past before my mind turned to jelly. In the meantime, a stone, two buttons, a fading photograph, a crumpled pamphlet, and an unsent letter, were stale breadcrumbs leading me back to the ghost of Zee.

Three intrusive long narrow slips of mauve paper that looked as if they came from a fortune cookie hastened me towards an animal shelter to adopt a sweet old-lady-dog for protection.

chapter 12
CANARY

I named my dog, Canary, after the feathered 'security guards' miners once carried down the mines as early warning detectors of poisonous gas. She's my canine litmus test against unwanted flesh and blood visitors – a gentle long-legged angel made of grey shag carpet.

The first day we met we were a couple of vanishing energies, dismissed as 'done' in the eyes of the world. I know this because the staff at the shelter never saw me arrive or either of us go.

– May 6 –

The day and I had been fractious. I was too keyed up to meditate and drove to the Vancouver ferry in a state of nervous tension transfixed by my fear of highway driving.

Felix's last minute advice cautioned me to remain calm. 'stay focused on your mission and the roads will clear,' he said. He'd warned me not to get cold feet, so naturally, to be headstrong, my wilful feet turned icy cold.

I endured the voyage slightly seasick, absorbed with my stalker problem. But Felix was right. Once on the mainland I pushed the speed limit with a determination that bordered on self-hypnosis, and magically, the traffic appeared to move in slow motion as if I was in a movie where the soundtrack ran out of sync with the action. I was there and not there. I was me and not me.

All the way to the animal shelter I heard the tinnitus of a ghost dog whining in the empty backseat of my car. I suspected the phantom dog from my beach.

.   .   .

I parked the car, relieved to turn off the ignition, and suffered the gravel of the drive through the soles of my shoes. My heels *click clicked* up three concrete stairs, echoing like tap shoes.

A jangling bell announced me like fingers down a blackboard. It irked me that the shadow of my body strobed as I walked lightheaded with feet of lead. I chided myself for missing breakfast. The nightmare sensation of wading through Jello made me queasy. Part of me hoped I was back home in bed, dreaming. The rest of me forged on. I was momentarily comforted as the word 'doggedly' flashed through mind, but the wall of fetid air inside was sobering. I couldn't wait to be away.

I marched over a worn carpet to the reception desk. Even so, my footsteps resounded like the rapid-fire trigger of a paparazzi's camera's. A notice in a plexiglass holder sat next to a brass bell. It read: Please ring for attention. I ignored it. The last thing I wanted was attention. I turned it facedown to make a point, and brazenly entered the door marked 'staff only'.

I met a damp pall of antiseptic and followed the terrified call of a broken heart. I wanted to howl at the moon but I sent a mental message. *I'm here. Hang on little phantom.*

I had the impression of entering a labyrinth, hand-over-hand on a thread into strangling fear, taut as a bowstring. *What kind of monster had done this?* The terror was palpable but it was not mine.

The inner sanctum resembled a row of dank prison cells formed of musty concrete and neglect. The staff were preoccupied elsewhere. I heard their clanking busy-ness, sluicing the outdoor kennel runs in the yard.

I silenced my shoes with a wish and shuffled along, invisible and muffled, an old thief in carpet slippers. At the far end, a cage door hung open, left unattended. *I'm coming. Where are you?*

The oppressive door rusted before my eyes and disintegrated into red dust. That changed everything. I straightened my shoulders and proceeded with the confidence of a dragon.

Inside, a downcast Irish wolfhound, who'd seen better days, observed me woefully through scab-encrusted eyes from the corner. A kindred spirit. Her head came up when she saw me, and she whistled through her nose. She knew me. I knew her.

The warmth returned to my feet. "Hello beautiful," I said. "I've come to take you home."

Her ears perked up. I continued in a honeyed voice although I wanted to howl down the moon. "What's say you and I get the hell out of here?"

I patted my knee. She limped over and nuzzled my hand. "Almost home sweetie," I whispered.

She held up a paw covered with livid sores. I shook it gently and knelt down laying my forehead against hers. "Oh, baby girl."

I called out of contempt to the minotaur. "How much for this one?" in the direction of spraying water. The uninterrupted sound of activity informed me I hadn't made an impression. I only asked once. "Don't make me breathe fire," I muttered under my breath.

"Come along old girl," I whispered, ruffling her ears. "Let's see if anyone gives a monkey's if we go AWOL, shall we?" She kept to heel without urging or a leash.

We moved swiftly. Peter Pan and his shadow, sewn together for all time.

The air stilled. We distanced ourselves from the minotaur and reached my car, now hot as a greenhouse. I opened a passenger door and a matted grey dog bounded into the backseat cooled by a sea-blue blanket. The sound of the driver's door slamming, startled the rosebushes. Their buds opened, releasing a sweet breath of perfume. A patch of sunflowers turned lazily to follow us. From far away, I heard Felix, cheering us on from the kitchen. "Time shakes itself like a wet dog," he said. "Bravo."

The song lyrics about mining for a heart of gold washed through my skull. That broke the tension for me. Life was surreal but it was *my* life and I hoped I still ran the show.

Sounds intensified: The squeak of leather upholstery, the zither of a seatbelt harness, and the metallic click of its burning hot clasp. My keys swung from the ignition jangling like windchimes. The electronic windows opened with a satisfying hiss letting in a fresh blast of freedom.

Canary panted behind me. I caught a glimpse of her lolling pink tongue in the rear view mirror. The car quickened and made a comforting crunch of tires on crushed stone.

I glanced at Canary in the back seat and giggled like a kid with a secret. *Atta girl.* And I meant me as much as her. *Wheee! Look at us.* I was completely giddy as we headed for the sea – the pair of us captured forever on light-sensitive paper by a hidden camera.

Canary crouched low as I drove coolly out of the parking lot. Down the road a-space, she sat up and smiled at the passing landscape. She sniffed blissfully out the open window and sneezed.

"Wait 'til you see the ocean, girlie," I said. "I hope you like cats."

I'd given Punch, a similar pep talk. *I hope you like dogs*, I'd said, and told her I was bringing her a canary.

THE POWERS OF NOW

chapter 13
BREACHED

So, here we are, residing off Windmill's Point – a commune of three old ladies and the shadow of a painted girl, all given second chances to shine. And if no-one else can see us, it's their loss.

I am well-served. Punch, is a first-alert monitor for ethereal vibrations and undesirable things that creep in general. She stares into empty corners and hisses away all manner of lurking insubstantials that thoroughly disquiet the human soul.

Companionship is delightful. At midnight, my best friends are a cat who dispatches persnickety eight-legged demons with zeal and a dog who thinks I'm nothing less than the triple-faced goddess of love, food, and shelter. Which is lucky, because I swear I'm the victim of a more sinister visitation than a sweet girl who wanders in and out of her portrait. Perhaps the eccentric ghost of a levitating beachcomber. But where would a ghost find mauve paper?

I've discovered my truth. I am becoming authentic at last. The me I'm almost proud of. Sometimes, accepting the passage of time even numbs physical pain. White hair doesn't mean a bleached mind. Wearing comfortable shoes is a smart concession to comfort, and reading glasses deliver an all around clarity of sensible perception: Hear no evil, Speak no evil… See no age spots.

Other than cobalt glass I've shed the intense blues, reds, yellows, and lime greens that were too bright to keep.

The color of an aquamarine jewel held up to the sun defines me. I'm at peace with my failure to succeed. And thankfully, when you're the color of seawater in a Turner painting, there are no boats left to rock.

I've lived a pale life to perfect the art of slipping away. And now I live inside a grand seashell of sorts. The castle's eccentric designer must have known me in a past life. He had indulged my craving for a hive painted in pastel seaside colors: a creamy palette of rain-washed pebbles, gull-grey, and sun-bleached driftwood. My castle's robins-egg-blue walls are offset by brilliant white woodwork. Soft wool rugs the color of sand lie scattered over pale birchwood floors. Snow palace archways with delicate lacework webbing connect a honeycomb of rooms. I sleep snugly under a domed bedroom ceiling, painted as the night sky while sea breezes trying to be hurricanes rattle the windows.

Down by the pier, a whitewashed boat shed with a peeling blue door reminds me that aging is a work of abstract art. I celebrate its several weatherworn incarnations of sky. Vibrant flecks of sapphire, golden yellow, and crimson, reveal the onion-skin of life. Patina takes time. A fact Jakobina's portrait knows only too well.

I didn't retreat here. I *ran* towards the water – a fox chased to ground by the internet and traffic jams. And, if the whole truth be known, the futuristic nightmare of being treated like an imbecile by staff in a care home.

At last, I'm free to explore in the rarified air of choice. Away from the battering storms of social small talk and gossip.

Better late than never, I'm experiencing a transcendental shift. I almost believe I imagined my fairy-tale castle into being. By fictional accounts, the best dreamers travel by unconventional tornados, and rabbit holes, so, if Dorothy can fly over the rainbow and Alice Liddell can escape behind a looking glass, surely, if I wanted to, I could evaporate into a painting. The thing is… I don't want to.

And this I've learned about mirrors: One's reflection is an innocent doppelganger. Twin entities sharing an optical illusion. And although poets claim eyes are the windows of the soul, and painters cite them as repositories housing the life-force, it's dodgy to stare overlong into one's reflection in a mirror for answers to impossible questions.

chapter 14
SALTY TRUTHS

At first light, I pad about over salt-encrusted decks in felt slippers, drinking tea, anticipating a post-storm walkabout to find what small shipwrecks of sea glass have washed ashore.

Gems of polished ultramarine are the best finds. I attach an unashamedly superstition to them. Akin to the rhyme *Blue sky at night, sailor's delight. Red sky at morning, sailor's warning.*

Believing in omens is too strong a delusion but I am willing to play a harmless divination game with signs. But I've collected vintage cobalt glass for years, so it's something rare to aim for, and after the castle manifested, I knew my psychic aim was true. Cobalt blue is the color of exceptional fortune. Ruby is a disturbance... not necessarily bad, but the dark red of garnets signals danger. Amber means it's going to rain. Olive green heralds blowy weather. Sage green, and I will see seals. Frosted white is a gift from the sea to stay calm. I can spot a shard of blue sea-glass from a mile away.

Punch accompanied Canary and I on a blustery day excursion. We take a path on higher ground, distancing ourselves from the water which was rough today. I don't want Canary to challenge the waves and chase them. It isn't worth the hassle of bathing her later. I keep her on a leash and let her run when we leave the dunes behind us.

On my glass foraging expeditions down the coastline, I walk the morning pebbles in wellington boots, looking back occasionally, to make sure my own castle is still there. The beach looms long and straight before it curves, so other than fog, there's no need for home to be out of sight. Someday, I promised myself, I'd explore further, and maybe convince Jakobina to venture outside.

Tintagel Cottage clings to a rocky platform with invisible claw-like tentacles reminiscent, I liked to imagine, of the baobab tree roots that threatened to engulf the Little Prince's planet, B-612. I still read this book to Jakobina. She's loved it for fifty years and it comforts me to have one perfect thing from my childhood.

As we turn for home, a sizeable chunk of garnet sea glass glints from a clump of brackish seaweed left high and wet on the beach. It stops me in my tracks. Punch toys with it as if it's alive. Canary gives a warning whine through her nose. I watch the glass shard sink under the soggy goo. Punch stares at the space it used to be and digs gingerly until she reached sand. Finding nothing, she makes practical use of the hole for a bathroom break, and in her covering up process, the red warning reappears.

Unlike me, Punch is oblivious of its fanciful ominous significance. Its unmistakable heart-shape means nothing to her. In any case, she buries it under the sand and I have no wish to unearth it. Red glass at morning… beachcomber's warning. Blue glass at night… dreamers delight. Besides, I've known this shard before. I'd last seen it with Emily, the day of my leaving. It shouldn't be here.

I ignore this new shadow hanging over us on an already stormy Spring day.

Canary stays close unless something grabs her attention. Today, mother crab, skulking back to the water sets her off.

"Settle down old thing," I tell her. "She's a friend."

I feel safely anchored, resigned to aging into the sunset. Hankering with grace… not *after* things but *because* of things.

I'm taller on the inside, now, not yet old enough to sit under the stars and knit a scarf longer than time, but too young to give up the ghost. *Hmmn…* now whatever made me think such a thing? I knew without a doubt I was the perfect age to give up Jakobina.

I listen for an answer in case one of my muses cares to enlighten me. Silence. I am alone.

There's an art to slipping away unnoticed. Sometimes it takes years. First, you change your address a few times and cover your tracks with a broom the size of a snow plough. Internet footprints dissipate on their own after you forswear social media. Emails are answered less frequently, and then, not at all. Telephones devolve from landlines to unlisted numbers and the portable lifeline of a smart phone you're not smart enough to use as a camera and never intended as an arcade of pointless games. And then, your memories play the ultimate game and you forget where you live. You've slipped away from yourself.

But the happy day arrives when you rediscover a ghostly lover kept in a tin box. After that, taking leave of one's senses is a matter of course.

And when you rediscover lost love in a tin box, time spins tantalizingly out of control.

I sing the body electric…
The thin red jellies
Within you or within me,
The bones and the marrow in the bones,
The exquisite realization of health;
Oh, I say these are not the parts
And poems of the body only,
But of the soul.
— WALT WHITMAN

chapter 15
THE INNER SANCTUM

Lately, I've been dreaming in clusters – a dream within a dream within a nightmare, and wake disoriented. I'd given myself an assignment by writing a special dream diary to keep myself in the subliminal loops that sometimes evaded me. Messages were everywhere if one cared to look.

I always read a poem from Whitman's 'Leaves of Grass' before turning out the lights. Long after I close my eyes his poems describing the body's exquisite tortures of passion haunt me like the lyrics of a song. Cleaving and clasping. Quivering and undulating. Time erases fifty years. Fluid bones with orgasmic marrows of pulsating red jellies screaming the body electric are the last thoughts I remember as I glide into a delicious fantasy.

The First Dream

The 'Outer Limits' brings Zee and I to the tipping point. It's 1964. The television screen shows flickering static with wavy lines as a voice announces: *please do not adjust your set.* We cuddle on the sofa, me pretending to be scared so I can huddle under Zee's skin before the show starts, and he can play up as my protector and hug me as an excuse.

Zee's musk mingles with the scent of Christmas pine and jumpstarts flirting with purpose. I stare at the open collar of Zee's blue jean shirt. We kiss. At the moment our lips meet, the image of a button on Zee's shirt fuses with the 'Outer Limits' theme music – an eight-count of devilish notes played on a piano. That, and the sensation of falling in slow motion, creates a questionable imprint of the birth of love. It's a Monday. 7:30 p.m. on a school night.

The show begins. It's as if I've taken a high dive into a bathtub of love potion #9 followed by the narrator's *welcome to the outer limits.* In the opening scene, a radiant bride-to-be is shopping for the perfect wedding dress. She is spoiled for choice as one gown after another is paraded out for her inspection. Her young daughter notes each one with a shake of her head. The woman holds a dress under her chin in the mirror. "This is the one."

The girl brightens. "Can we go home now," she says. "I want to play."

The narrator sets the story in motion: *Pearl Harbinger was a daddy's girl until the car accident. And now, her widowed mother is getting remarried. Pearl likes her stepfather-to-be. He's a kind man. But loyalty eclipses kindness. And a marriage is forever in the outer limits.*

The close-up of childish hands manipulate marionettes in a toy theatre. The camera pulls back to reveal a young girl playing with bride and groom puppets. The groom kneels. The girl cuts the groom's strings and he falls to the ground. Pearl looks up, smiling. "Daddy," she calls out. "I did what you asked."

"That's my girl," a disembodied voice replies.

Pearl's mother answers the doorbell. Two officers break the news. There's been an accident. She turns from the door and collapses in tears. Pearl runs to comfort her with a smile on her face.

The Second Dream

The scene changes into a second Christmas. I'm sixteen. Zee and I hold hands, vicarious students of love, in a dimly lit movie theatre where larger than life romance plays out our intimate fantasies. Zee involuntarily squeezes my hand as we mature in that dark tunnel of love. We watch and learn on the backs of actors directed to contort their bodies into a single gyrating shape. We watch and remember. And as we remember, the actors on the screen fade out as we take their place, eclipsed by lifetimes of intimate experience.

We race home to the sofa on shy conversations. Did you feel that? What just happened?

Zee's eyes reflect what mine have been asking for over a year. He strokes my wrist in that way that says we're talking in disguise about our dreams of being together. Drunk on boyfriend power, he nuzzles my ear and massages the nape of my neck, gently pulling me closer. Dancing pheromones spin us into a lost cocoon.

We take the stairs two at a time and tumble into the whitest of cotton sheets, cool against the heat of young passion. Adolescent clumsiness disappears into deft moves of limbs and tongues as the muscle-memories of past lives engage.

Zee is my leading man. The expert lover I willingly follow. I could sleep like this forever but

a dog barks frantically as I lie there, complete. I wake, alone on a beach walking by the sea, a giddy schoolgirl desperately in love with Zee. Stinging sand swirls up to my knees like fog.

A faceless witchy figure blocks the moon and delivers a lecture on the benefits of long term sacrifice to override selfish gratification. It's not a clear cut argument until she drops Zee and I into the equation. She paints a dark picture of mental deterioration and endless responsibilities. *'Your love is doomed to inevitable failure,'* she says without sympathy, *'and it's your fault.'*

There is no anesthetic to offset the future but like a good fairy countering a curse, she offers a time-sensitive loophole of compassion. Her fairy godmother's pronouncement comes with a karmic reward for being selfless. She throws me a rope into the mix of fear and shame – a surprisingly humane escape clause.

The choice is plain, my decision, swift. Anguish is not an option. I want to spare the love of my life inconceivable pain and suffering.

The Third Dream

A third Christmas. A different, future bed. Thick snow isolates the world. The wind is lazy, playing ping pong with helium snowflakes. Flannel sheets lie warm against the winter bliss of experienced lovers.

I wake up alone in the center of the bed, mourning for my lost love, wondering if Jakobina is a witch. It's raining hard. The rain my mother called cats and dogs. I scribble the gist of my dreams in list form and trundle downstairs to rustle up tea and chocolate biscuits, diary in hand. I need sugar. The shushing sound of the downpour transforms the breakfast room into a comforting isolation tank. I stare dreamily at a tall shelf displaying my collection of cobalt glass bottles while the kettle boils. Water cascading down the window distorts the wall into hypnotic blue ripples of living glass. "Do not adjust your set," Felix says.

"You're very catty this morning," I reply.

He hisses. "All the better to teach you by, Miss Riding Hood."

I feel as wobbly as the glass even after several biscuits. Felix suspends his ticking as I run my diary notes by him. "First of all," he says, after a long pause of silence, "Bravo. You've giving yourself an axiom to live by. There are no *inner* limits."

Extra loud ticking resumes, filling the hallowed space, making me feel as if I'm inside a clock. Felix interrupts. "And what precisely have you discovered?"

I answer from a cobalt trance. "No wonder love terrifies me. I was a mess." The joys of first love had been embedded within my psyche, cloned onto a musical intro that had become the default signature for spooky paranormal events everywhere. How appropriate I'd met

Jakobina's ghost. How dysfunctional. "How out of this world," I say aloud.

"Not to dwell," Felix announces, "but love is and always has been, the mindful act of disappearing into another completely."

His ticking reminds me of an S.O.S. message in Morse code. "Then it's kind of ironic that my death will be a conscious act of disappearing into a painting without a trace."

"Kindness doesn't enter into it. A witch, an obsessed girl, and a puppeteer wielding scissors. *Hmm.* Let's think. Who do we know that answers *that* description?"

I stare at the top of the page as if it's an assignment about to be graded by a teacher in a tetchy mood. "You don't like Jakobina much, do you, what's with it with you two?"

"Wrong. We don't trust each other. You lose points. There goes your A+," Felix says.

His comment sends a pleasant déjà vu shiver through me.

Felix's tail swings erratically and falls to the floor. It stares up at me like a black exclamation mark. When I reattach it, the clock casing vibrates in my hands with a gentle shock. Felix and I are literally face-to-face as I straighten him on the wall. "My dearest child," he says. "Pay close attention. Remember. Important messages arrive in mysterious ways."

Impulsively, I kiss his forehead. "I will. And thank you for all your help."

I stand back to make sure Felix is level. In spite of his dire warning, he purrs contentedly and winks. "Listen," he says, his eyes paused to the right. "It's time to face the music." His ticking becomes more melodic.

Felix is singing.

The companionship of even a hapless spirit takes the edge off my solitary confinement. Jakobina is, and has always been, a dour confidante. But now that she's cheerful, why do I feel anxious?

Jakobina says I called her and that our fears brought us together for a higher purpose. But that was the sixties when such New-Age notions were accepted without question. In any case, her fears were trapped under the dull varnish of immortality, and I'd been trying to sweep mine under a wall-to-wall carpet of doom with little success.

I'd surrendered quickly and we were like sisters. Then, for a time, I mothered her. Now, she's taken on the role of a granddaughter, looking after me, treating me, most days, like a senile halfwit.

Switching our positions from life to art is tricky. I've never worked out how Jakobina plans to accomplish such a mastery of physics, but if she *is* more than an elaborate hallucination able to leave her painting at will, I imagine she will take my hand, lead me in, turn around, and wave goodbye without a backward glance.

That said, fifty-ish years has somewhat paled my romantic take on metaphysics. And so, despite evidence to the contrary, I believe, in my heart, that the afterlife is a dream sentient lifeforms invent to take the sting out of human osmosis. The wistful notion of 'going home' by melting into the fabric of the cosmos seems a tad embroidered.

I suppose it's possible that my life with Jakobina has been an elaborate fantasy. But I didn't dream high school. I didn't dream my first love. And I didn't dream running away. I'd only suppressed the why of it, so that the memory *felt* like a dream. When the ghost of a girl tells you you're crazy enough times, you tend to believe her. And I most definitely haven't invented the disturbing messages left by a stalker, nor imagined Jakobina's giddy mood swings that have her disappearing and manifesting erratically in a merry tailspin at all hours.

In any case, while we still have time on our hands, Jakobina wants her story documented and I have the wherewithal to use a tape recorder and a keyboard. I remain hopeful that living by the sea in a whimsical dream cottage will be my solace, writing will ground me, and that the salty sea breezes will dislodge the cobwebs muddling my brain.

In any case, I've earned the right to indulge an old woman's fantasy. By and large I approve of quirky obsessions. Heaven knows life would have been dreary without at least one.

Tonight, my head is a radio. My brain is picking up intermittent signals of song fragments on an unstable frequency that spontaneously break into my thoughts at odd moments. At least, I assume they're random until I connect the dots and discover a faded map of messages and signposts. A pathway of flimsy clues that lead back to high school.

Jakobina is becoming more elusive, escaping into her painting more than usual, so Canary is my confidante of the hour. "It must be a muse that's stalking me," I tell her. "What do you think?" She shifts her shaggy head to the side and grins. "So, why won't it show itself or herself or himself?"

The answer arrives in a wave of static. This time in a female's honeyed voice behind me. *"Because if you saw him too soon it would ruin things. Sometimes events run on a strict timetable. Timing is everything. It's not his intention to alarm you. He's here to prepare you."*

I hang on to Canary's collar in case of trouble. "For what?"

"For whom," she replies with a hint of arrogance. *"You're a strong-willed woman. I sing to you for your own good."*

"You're the radio."

"If that works for you, yes."

On cue, a song breaks in to assure me. *"Stars linger but I'm dreaming on, dear…"*

"I know this one." I hum the familiar tune and join in… 'dream a little dream of me'.

"Still dreaming of your kiss," she sings.

"I dreamed about Zee last night," I volunteer.

"Quite. Songs are subconscious messages not dissimilar to dreams. Think of them as sendings. Heed them. No need to puzzle them out. The message is subliminal… seamlessly understood. Your brain doesn't

need to catch up. In fact, you're brain is too primitive to catch up. Nothing personal."

"None taken."

"... sing nighty night and kiss me... just hold me tight and tell me you miss me... sweet dreams till sunbeams find you..."

As I dry the dishes, I find myself gyrating and humming another song I'd heard as a teenager. Canary is suitably enraptured when I look into her eyes and sing *'love is kind of crazy with a spooky little girl like you'*. My internal jukebox's base thumps so high it vibrates the dirty dishes. More plates clatter inside their cupboards and the lyrics subtly change. I hear a refrain in my head: *'love is kind of crazy with a spooky little BOY like you.'*

Ever since that night when my muse sang out of turn, song popping has become a regular event.

Later, when I'm tucked up in bed, reading, Jakobina paces the room. Tonight she's distraught but there's a gleam in her eye that belies her displeasure. Canary, a throw rug over my feet, has grown bored with her melodramatic performance and ceased watching. There are dream rabbits to chase. Punch is making her rounds of the skirting boards and corners. She pounces on something and I slink lower behind my book, happily ignorant of the details.

Jakobina passes out of my peripheral vision, and I keep my eyes glued to a page that has grown dull from reading the same sentence too many times. Jakobina unexpectedly wheels on me in a flash of blue scarf. Her earrings swing wildly as she admonishes me. "Pay attention, Aurelia. There is no time for books. Please. Your mind sees further than your eyes. Further than your years. Haven't I always told you this day would come. Listen. He is at the door. He is here."

I am exasperated but I control my temper. "I am here. You are here. And I've made a decision," I announce.

Jakobina's eyes never leave mine as she backs into her portrait. I have frightened her. I tell myself it's for her own good but it's really for my own peace of mind.

"I've decided to record what's happened on tape," I say to her picture frame.

Jakobina's voice emanates from a square of thunderclouds that have replaced her face. "Why? Let's not upset him."

I face a solid black square. "Because, I hardly believe what's happened, myself. So much so, that I need to hear it. Besides, it's reference for the creative writing stage later when I add in the juice. Whoever *he* is, he deserves to be upset. I've made up my mind."

The eyes in the painting appear momentarily and fade to black. Jakobina appears behind me at the foot of the bed wearing a trembling red smile to humor me. I can see it's forced. "I will help you," she says in a shaky voice. "Forgive me. You know what's best."

She drifts off in true ghostly fashion, the way apparitions do after they've delivered a time-sensitive message.

Canary nudges my hand to remind me she's there… on guard. She and I are roughly the same age. Canary, in dog years; me, the usual solar calendar variety. I am her Queen. She is my seneschal. I love how the word canine carries a reassuring echo of canniness, another attribute I admire for survival. My animals and I crowd together at night on a double bed – snoring and purring heads to tails. The strains of a song arrive in a lullaby: *younger than springtime are you, older than starlight am I…*

I hug Canary and whisper into her fur so the muse can't hear. So Jakobina won't hear. "I miss him. I miss Zee. I was such a fool." Suddenly, immortality terrifies me. I choke on a flash of certainty knowing there is no possible way I will keep the ridiculous pact with Jakobina.

The chapter Jakobina had hinted at and pined for has come. Haunting dreams of stalkers ratchet up accordingly. I don't begrudge Jakobina her future, but it isn't lost on me that the autumn of my life is nearly over and that Autumn is appropriately named 'THE FALL'.

Life is a tale told by an idiot,
Full of sound and fury,
Signifying nothing.
— WILLIAM SHAKESPEARE

chapter 17
GHOSTWRITER

– June 1–
2019

Canary's canine instincts had tuned in to my wavelength the moment we met. We go way back… almost four weeks now, but then I can dream a lifetime in a few minutes, so time has little to do with our relationship. She turned out to be a natural therapy dog, able to read my body's personal 'earthquakes', moments before I 'go-a-wandering'. Her uncanny presence grounds me for fickle time-slip anomalies in the future… and by that, I mean the past. Who knows where time will take me or why. But having a brief warning is comforting. I grab Canary's collar and figuratively, let go.

I open the recording session with a spontaneous sneeze. There's no denying a destiny sneeze that has passed its best by date. I was taught that sneezing for no earthly reason was a good omen. It released ominous thoughts that had festered for too long. Be it shame or guilt or fear.

Opposite me, in her favorite chair, Jakobina is nervously plucking a thread in the upholstery. Her expression informs me my sneeze has had a negative effect.

Canary, is as close to me as she can get with her head pushed hard against my feet. She's on high alert. We all are. The tape recorder awaits.

. . .

Jakobina motions for me to stop. "What's up?" I ask her.

Her smile is not encouraging. "Tell the people in there that you're crazy," she says, nodding at the tape recorder, but she stops mid-sentence and looks askance at me. "Was that one of those *bad* sneezes?" She's a bit of a hypochondriac, and in her mind, a sneeze heralds plague.

I take a few cleansing breaths and flex my fingers. "Will do." *Like I'm going to forget.* I stretch my legs on the sofa, look up and to my left, the spot where my current muse has parked itself behind my eyes, and listen. I say current because I recognize more than one voice. Sometimes it's a shrill female, at other times a sympathetic gentleman with an Oxford accent, or several other incarnations of wisdom and refuge, including my Felix clock who sees right through me. I have a veritable company of muses. All of whom, are on my side, even when they rant with disturbingly foul language.

Click – I pause the cassette in my vintage Sony player and stage a sneeze for Jakobina's amusement, and narrate with my eyes closed to be sure I'm telling the whole truth.

"Recording tape one… testing one two three… here goes." My voice sounds far away.

Click play – I'm on.

"This is the story of a painting and a girl trapped inside it but first let me introduce myself, her narrator.

My name is Aurelia Marcus, so named in homage to my mother's literary hero, the Roman Emperor Marcus Aurelius who believed that obstacles were the prime ingredient to a successful life. The year I was born, Aurelius had been dead two thousand years as the crow flies. He was a philosopher and warrior, not always in that order. Briefly stated, he deliberately embraced any obstacle by running into its teeth with undisguised gusto. It was, he taught, the way to victory. The *only* way. A concept I never fully understood until this year.

It had never occurred to me that my mother had courage. Maybe it saved her in the end. I didn't witness her death but its eventuality had never seemed much like an approaching victory to me, but maybe death never does."

I glance nervously at Jakobina. Have I gone too far? But no, she seems fine. Even serene.

"Or maybe it *always* does. Like mother and daughter, we were DNA close, except when it came to the crunch, I chose flight over fight. And, in hindsight, so did she.

Suffice it to say, there are degrees of batshit crazy in my family. I 'dropped my basket' at least once a month but I never considered this an insurmountable problem.

Metaphorically speaking, I disappeared into my overactive imagination most of the time, anyway.

I get that conversing with a painting is utterly irrational to most people, but I've done so since I was three. It's no different than believing Christopher Robin lives next door or having an invisible friend who lives in your pocket. My mother always called it daydreaming with attitude. She said I came by it honestly and that it would be the making of me.

Like everything else, only time will tell. Two more years should be enough."

Soft ticking sounds encircle my head like a swarm of clockwork bees – the Felix clock is timing me, all the way from the kitchen. Canary issues a whine and lifts her head. I grab her collar tighter, just in case.

"As near as I can tell, none of the ways we mortals leave the planet are particularly gracious. I've always pretty much assumed I'm headed for the exit marked doolally.

Nevertheless, sometimes I look forward to 2020, my predicted year of 'departure', which is ironic because I dream in perfect hindsight, even if the years *are* out of order.

In agreement with the physics of storytelling, this may be the only way to unravel who I am. Who I *was*. So, in the spirit of planting a flag on my wildest dreams, I vow to ride out the waves of new beginnings with style, but this time, in the pretext of second childhood, I've decided to be beautiful."

Click stop –

Jakobina smiles inwardly into her past at this piece of yesterday's news.

She's inside a happy memory, as yet unexplained sufficiently to me. I only know she enters a zone where time stands still and she reaches for a person I can't see, even though I know it's her husband, Piet. Seeing her absorbed and clearly in high spirits, *pun intended*, warms me. She deserves to be in love. She's been a long time sad. She is perhaps, the most patient person I've ever met. But by patient, I mean longsuffering. Her eyes search mine. She wants more. I breathe easy and release my grip on Canary's collar. Canary grunts and flops back down – a loving blanket for my tired feet.

I sip tea grown lukewarm to clear my throat and resume.

Click play –

"I learned early, that entertaining oneself is a vital occupation. Denying oneself creative play is sacrilege for any adult with an unspectacular nine-to-five life.

I'm nearing the event I like to call 'The Age of Incandescence'. That wily season when it's time to luminesce from within and spiritually bleed out.

Any fight that's left in me is channeled to the writing at hand… the story where Jakobina and I have met daily for fifty extremely odd years. I focus to stay ahead of the grim reaper, an entity I euphemistically refer to as the 'dogcatcher'.

It's the limbo life of a painted girl for me, otherwise, I'm bound to follow my mother down the road to dementia, as her mother did before her.

There's simply no point in fighting fate. It's written in the stars."

Click stop –

"How was that?" I ask. "Crazy enough for you?"

Jakobina is near to tears. She plumps down next to me making the sofa bounce. Canary is displaced. "Why will you have to fight? We never fight."

I try not to look smug. "Whatever it takes, little one." Her form starts to dissipate, so I grab onto her sleeve. She surrenders and stays but her sweet face is a picture of concern.

"No Aurelia. No. You must *not*," she says. "I never meant to cause you pain. You must believe me. That is not the reason I'm here."

I squeeze her arm and tuck it under mine to keep her solid. "Jakobina my dear, if you're going to be a muse you're going to have to toughen up. Life is pain. Life's stories are painful. That's… just life."

She absorbs this for a moment and takes herself off to sit on the floor next to Canary. She ruffles the dog's fur and when she's settled, she nods for me to continue, eyes closed, her chin resting on her knees, her slender arms wrapped around her long skirts. Her happy place is three-hundred-and-fifty-years away in Delft.

Click rewind – the whirring of passing seconds – 'second-hand bees' tick louder towards a full minute.

I close my eyes and picture the bulbous cartoon eyes of my Felix wall clock, roaming from side-to-side, keeping time with it's plastic tail… marking time.

After ten years, Jakobina has never warmed to it. She called it a demon when first confronted with it, but then she thought the same of television, telephones, cars… and especially the microwave.

"You need to eat something," Jakobina says with the insistence of a vexed mother hen. "Your blood sugar is low. I can feel it. Come, it's time for lunch. I will make. You will eat."

I feel like a blank tape, seduced by patterns of sound. The whirring of the cassette pulls me in as a pair of spools juggle words back and forth. A tape recorder on rewind is the perfect metaphor for my life. Like me, its inner workings are searching for its starting point. I begin most days as a blank canvas.

My mind follows its drone, spinning backwards, whizzing past the day fifty-five-years ago when Jakobina and I met. We'd been seventeen. Now she calls me *Grootmoeder,* grandmother.

The sound whirrs higher, whining like a dog as the tape approaches its own tail. Canary barks once – an ear-splittingly sharp exclamation mark. I reach for her and startle when the machine shuts off with a loud judder. My left hand grips the sofa cushion. For a sick moment I'm not there. "What did you say?"

Jakobina is already heading for the kitchen, "I *said,* it's time for your pill."

I take a few deep breaths to center myself. "I just want to play this back first."

"What do you want for lunch?"

My present muse is not amused. I sense it tapping its foot. *"Art is food for thought,"* it moans. *"Choose. Write or eat. Keep in mind, the universe requires sacrifices. Especially from its star citizens."*

I know better than to take a break when I'm riding the alpha waves of subconscious daydreaming. "Give me a minute," I shout to Jakobina. "I don't want to lose the moment. A story is a delicate anticlockwise dance that must give the illusion of flowing clockwise. It's trickier than it sounds. Our story is complicated. Fractured."

"Fractured?"

"A broken timeline. Timing is everything, and my earthquakes are never in a straight line. They're trickier than you can imagine. I have to pay attention. Do you see?"

"I'll throw a macaroni cheese in the microwave," she calls back. "You take a break."

"*Perfect*," Emperor Felix snickers. "*Brain food with zero nutrition. Bring on the sugar rush.*"

Jakobina puts her lovely head round the door. "Instant food isn't good for your diabetes," she says.

Was I ever that young? "I don't *have* diabetes," I reply, miffed. "The doctor said I was maybe on the cusp. Maybe. And I don't intend to play hide and seek with food at this stage of the game. Rules bore me. A true artist doesn't live by bread alone... or so I've heard, besides, I'm a star citizen." *I'm almost sure I was sixteen once upon a time.*

Jakobina makes the usual busying noises that involve ripping open a cardboard package, clunking the door of the microwave, and punching the timer. In seconds, I smell the nauseating aroma of fake cheese wafting from the kitchen. Canary leaps onto the sofa and presses against me, whining. I grab her around the neck and bury my face in her fur. "Good girl, stay. It's all right." Something compels me to look at the tape recorder as a lone seagull cries past the open window.

"Hang on," Felix shouts. The microwave beeps three times.

In plain sight, the tape recorder pops like a balloon on the last beep. In its place is a blue paperback with a familiar white shape on the cover.

The word 'living' in the title pulsates with light and flares into a starburst inside my left eye.

I have received divine aids in dreams.
The Gods watched over me.
For I fell not into the hands of any Sophist,
Nor sat poring over many volumes,
Nor devoted myself to solving syllogisms,
Or star-gazing that all these things
Should so happily fall out.
There was great need both for the help of fortune
And for the aid of the Gods.
— MARCUS AURELIUS
Roman emperor c. 170 A.D.

chapter 18
STARGAZY HIGH

Monmouth High School
The Summer Solstice
– June 21–
1965

Students to my immediate left shimmer and disappear like they're transporting from the Starship Enterprise. I am terribly lightheaded. The crowded high-school cafeteria at high noon ripples underwater as a migraine aura arrives full blast. A wheel of spinning light obscures the right side of everyone. It's as if the world has had a stroke. Maybe it has. Somehow I know it will dissipate if I ignore it, so I rest my head on my book and wait out the ten minutes that seem to last forever.

A deejay is pumped from his melodramatic countdown of the top ten hits of 65' over the loudspeakers. One wall displays a prominent gold and black sports logo of a tiger leaping through a hoop of fire with the slogan 'Go Wild Cats' in a banner beneath it. The special lineup for 'fries only' goes on forever, but it moves so swiftly it defers no-one from waiting for a heart-stopping assault of greasy calories on a plate. Fast food has to be extra-fast here. It's an eat and run world.

Lunch hour has to allow for loitering time in the parking lot to check out who's who.

Two hundred growing teenagers require immediate sugar and fat to offset the 'wholesome' breakfast of frosted cereal they skipped. These are my people. I am seventeen.

At my table, 'Sam the Ham' is hitting on a willowy blonde, who, if she isn't a cheerleader, she's missed her calling. My best friend Zee is wiping ketchup off the corner of his assignment. He looks up with his irresistible lopsided grin. He's known for getting food on everything. He smiles and dips a napkin in his water and wipes the paper until it's stained pale pink. He steals one of my napkins and blots it dry. His wink sends a delicious flutter through me. "There goes my A+," he says.

Giggling girls held together by hairspray and white lipstick dominate tables scattered like islands of silliness – shrill pink birds, heavily defined by eyeliner, share makeup tips in a room of serious eaters. The radio muffles into the calliope sound from a carnival. The scene slows down into funhouse mirrors.

I close my eyes. I have enough milk left to down a couple of Aspirin, my go-to helper against the headaches from limbo. *These white pills are the wrong color and shape.* Zee watches me staring at the pills. "Is it one of your long headaches?" he asks touching my hand. "Does it look as if I'm melting?"

"Yes," I reply. "I can only see half of your face. No big. It will pass. Just give me a second. You're still a bit blurry."

Music circles me in a tornado of doowop. After a brief tango with nausea, I materialize back into a drunken Van Gogh landscape where Vincent's kaleidoscope skies enslave me. Zee's face looms in front of me, whole, and sweeter than I remembered. I close my eyes. I should be able to hear the surf. My fingers search for a dog's collar but there's no dog, no ocean. There's Zee and me and a surreal feeling of solidity. There are hard plastic chairs, a large pedestal table, and a boy who makes me feel like a princess in a fairy tale. Any minute now I will wake up. Except I've never been more here and now.

A new food smell assaults me that makes me open my eyes. The cafeteria is still there but a few isolated kids are wearing bibs and their chairs have morphed into wheelchairs. I can't identify which kids because their trendy clothes are now generic blue or pink terry towel bathrobes. A few grey-haired or bald heads bend over pale gray broth. I know this soup and the hospital-fare stainless steel bowls a little too well. These are my people too. By the look of them I should be seventy.

The nearest woman looks up from her soup with a vacant expression. I get the impression of wrinkled despair. If vacancy is ever pure, she is the embodiment of it. Flora's eyes focus when she recognizes me. She smiles weakly and lifts a hand, transparent skin mottled with age spots, taut as a drum. She tries to wave but the effort is too much. I hear her thoughts. I feel her pain. If she had the energy, she would cry, but instead she closes her eyes and grips the side of the table until the skin on the back of her hands resembles blue-veined tissue paper.

I send her a message. *No worries. Hang on Sloopy* – a private joke between us about living on the wrong side of town, and count to eleven to block out the crazy.

The surreal clatter of ghostly plates and cutlery and the piped-in golden oldies return. Brian Hyland is singing 'Sealed with a Kiss' over the loudspeakers. The lyrics wash over me: *yes, it's gonna be a long lonely summer.*

The music muffles into tinnitus but I have a more intense definition of a 'golden oldie'. The author Richard Bach called it being marshmallow helpless. It's the summer of 1965.

My disappearing act is real. I'm here. For better or worse, I'm awake. My island is somewhere in the future with sandcastles and strangers and a dog named Canary.

The paperback I've been absorbing for an intoxicating week stares up at me, its dark blue cover with a white seagull reminds me I have to return it today. It's a copy of Bach's 'Jonathan Livingston Seagull', a runaway bestseller that's being passed around the astronomy club, of which I'm a card-carrying member alongside my fellow outcasts of choice. Astronomy is deemed uncool by the in-crowd. They know nothing.

It's Zee's turn for the book. I push it across the table. "Have fun," I say. "It's crazy enough to be true."

Zee winks. "Like you," he says. "Thanks for the heads up."

I tap the cover. "If you think *I'm* a bird-brain then you'll love this."

Zee grabs the book and taps it on my head. "Hey little birdie, I'm crazy about your brain. And if the absolute truth has no crazy in it, then someone is telling a lie."

Brian is bringing his song home: *But I'll fill the emptiness... I'll send you all my love, every day in a letter sealed with a kiss.* I wish. If only.

I adore Zee. When he calls me Aura I feel like a princess in a fairy tale. That classic feeling of a lump in the throat when you're in love is real. Even the sight of the pulse on his wrist sends tender stirrings of arousal into my nether regions. All day I squirm with desire, daydreaming of our future in a blissed out fog. Like most girls I know, I harbor intense longings inside while it seems boys focus on cars and sports.

With Zee, it's astronomy and chess.

I have no intention of freaking him out. My body simmers. I'm content to percolate for the time being. Desire grows exponentially until there are days I feel like the birth of a star about to shatter the night sky. It's a long lonely summer but waiting is a powerful aphrodisiac. I'm so lucky to be seventeen again. This time I must do better.

Zee and I promised to never lie to each other. Other than my secret infatuation, I tell him everything. I almost confessed once, but it's best not to rock the boat.

Zee's soiled assignment is curling up at the corner. Its remnants of ketchup-past remind me of a bleached bloodstain. A soft voice in my head says *'welcome back. It's about time.'* I scan the surrounding tables and then I see her. Jakobina is in the cafeteria, a distraction, waving at me from across the room.

Zee snaps his fingers close to my face. "Aura! You haven't heard a word I've said. I got you your favorite mac and cheese." A dark cloud forms in his eyes. "Oh god, I'm sorry. Are you okay? Is it one of those episode things? Should I call your dad?"

I grab his arm. "Absolutely not. Please don't. He's got enough on his plate. I mean, No. I'm fine. I was far away, that's all. You know how I get."

"Well, I'm taking you to the nurse, then."

I jump up, panicked. "No more goddam nurses. They're nasty evil... they'll punish me!"

"What're you on about? There's only one school nurse." Zee's expression registers surprise. "You look as if you've seen a ghost."

I fall into my abandoned chair, embarrassed. "What? Yes, only one. Nurse, that is. I was daydreaming about a nightmare I had last night. I was in this... hospital... hospice place... and couldn't get out. The nurses were less than compassionate. Quite unlike my mother's."

Zee's eyes remain frantic. "You're having a lot of nightmares lately. Something's up." His words float from across the universe from Planet Zee. "Aura? Are you listening to me?" He snaps his fingers in front of my face, again. "Come back. Follow my voice."

I flinch from the static of light years – my brain is a receiving dish from inner space. "I'm here. No worries. I wish you wouldn't... please don't call me Aura."

"You were *definitely* somewhere else. This obsession you have with dementia has to stop. You are *not* your mother."

Jakobina floats towards me. She positions herself behind Zee and stares at me. "Leave me alone," I say to her. "Please go away." She places her hands on Zee's shoulder. He flinches and shrugs off a girl he can't see.

Jakobina evaporates and reappears at my side where she's easier to ignore.

Zee raises his voice to a rare level of irritation. "I'm not going anywhere. Where's the stone I gave you? This is one of those times it's for. I promise not to call you Aura. I thought you liked it."

I turn and glare at Jakobina. She vanishes with a sigh as I pull the Zee stone from my purse and lay it on the table. I shudder, suddenly cold but I am released. We're alone. Zee picks up the green red-speckled stone and places it back in my hands. He cups his hands around mine, rubbing warmth into them. "This bloodstone is the only medicine you need. When I'm not around, it's me. Pretend it's me. Hang on to it, Sloopy, and think of me." He nods enthusiastically. "Call me, okay? Remember."

I try to smile. "Now who's crazy."

"That's not funny, Aur… Aurelia. I put my heart and soul into that stone so you wouldn't feel afraid when… you know… you kind of… disappear into your bad thoughts. It will bring you back. It's a mind over matter thing. It works."

The stone vibrates like a heartbeat and I stare into Zee's beautiful eyes. His concern rivets me back to fear. The fact that he's close to tears saddens me. I am overcome with love. It's my turn to comfort him. The Zee stone purrs like a cat, and I know what I must do, and then Zee surprises me.

"I love you crazy girl," he says. "Don't you know that." He grips my hands tight. "Whatever happens, I will take care of you. You're my girl with kaleidoscope eyes."

Jakobina touches my shoulder, all the way from 2019. "Aurelia?" she says. "You're daydreaming. Don't let your food get cold." She's holding a glass of apple juice in one hand and two turquoise gel caps in the other. "Swallow these. Your dizziness will pass after you eat something." The color and shape of the pills is right.

And Jakobina is right. I'm lightheaded. My head is about to float off my shoulders. I'm supposed to remember something. I know this because I've squirted a large ketchup question mark over a plate of macaroni far too yellow to be healthy. "I should have told him," I blurt out, but my voice sounds like someone else.

Bright colors assault me from the table. Turquoise pills and a red message.

Jakobina's form flickers slightly as she retrieves my uneaten glop. "Oh, Aurelia," she whispers, looking nervous and happy at the same time. "Look. You have dropped a question on your plate."

The woods are lovely,
dark, and deep,
But I have promises to keep,
And miles to go before I sleep.
— Robert Frost
'Stopping by Woods on a Snowy Evening'- 1922

chapter 19
OUT OF BOUNDS

It's not easy to brush an hallucination under the carpet, but there's no advantage to letting Jakobina know I've had an 'episode' other than on a need to know basis. After all, she's only witnessed my queasy reaction to lunch, which is normal enough since I've cited erratic blood sugar levels more times than the boy who cried wolf. She's too preoccupied, fussing about, opening windows to exorcize the cooking smells, to notice Canary cowering in the corner.

Besides, it didn't seem like an hallucination, which leaves me with the quandary of how I left 2019 and materialized in 1965.

Jakobina's already expectant to the point of ghoulishness. Every time I flounder, her eyes ask "Is it time? Is it now?" I answer sharply that I am *not* ready and that I will *know* when I'm ready and not one moment before. Lately, I've juggled with the logistics of our pact. How will it be? Will I walk effortlessly into her painting the way she casually walks out? Could it be that simple? It begs the question… do I really want to go?

By reputation, ghosts do tend to hover, and lately Jakobina is intruding the way she did in the cafeteria. It's unnerving to be under constant scrutiny by someone who may not really be here. But like it or not, these are my days. I juggle my time between catnaps, writing, and collecting beach treasures during the strolling variety of walking. I feed the gulls, and imprint the sounds, smells, colors, and textures of the landscape. Life is full when you have no serious calendar. It's even fuller if one can time travel in their daydreams. I live in hopes that the tenderest dreams can come true.

But yesterday's trip unhinged me. I recognized the all too familiar momentary lapse as a wake up call bigger than a fourth sandcastle. I'd been with Jakobina in Vermeer's studio again.

An even stronger memory blindsided me. Why had I suppressed a perfect summer, sealed with a kiss. Zee loved me. He'd said so that nightmarish day in the cafeteria. The day of the bright macaroni and faded ketchup stains and the visions of wheelchaired 'seniors'. He'd cornered me after school and given me his high school ring. We were, as the ritual implied, 'going steady', which was the precise moment I embarked on my spectacularly unsteady decline that broke both our hearts. Why hadn't I told Zee that I loved him, too."

THE FINDING

Vancouver
– January 1–
2019

My rented castle was found, not entirely by accident, according to a blue leaflet handed to me on a street corner by an earnest young man with stars in his eyes on New Year's Day, 2019.

The Vancouver streets were slushy with grey porridge. Street people were dealing in dark corners and the homeless huddled in storefront doorways. I could not, *would* not, insult him, and so I smiled and stashed his leaflet 'THE ART OF DREAMING – subconscious wish fulfillment' into a canvas shopping bag to be polite, with barely a glance, dismissing it as religious tosh.

"You look familiar," I said. "Have we met before?"

He doffed an invisible hat. "I'm here every day, Missus."

"You're very young to be so dedicated."

When he flashed a charismatic smile I realized how truly handsome he was. "It's an obligation, actually. I always work this corner. I'm helping out a friend in trouble."

We exchanged seasonal greetings. "I hope things work out for your friend," I said as he drifted towards a likely customer, and I moved on, seamlessly into the New Year.

I read the dream leaflet aloud on the rainy evening of January 13, 2019, trapped in the dead concrete of a city that had abandoned me, with Jakobina massaging liniment that reeked of camphor into my toes, fussing over the precarious state of my circulation. The smell was oddly comforting. It conjured the scent of linseed oil from an artist's studio.

The soles of my feet felt like they were calcifying into bags of gravel and flexing my toes was an odd sensation – a strange combination of heightened sensitivity and numbness. In many ways, Jakobina wasn't far wrong when she quipped she was rubbing the life back into my soul/sole.

A big-band rendition of 'Mr. Sandman' was playing on the radio. *'Mr. Sandman, bring me a dream,'* the female vocalists sang. *'Please turn on your magic beam.'* Broken lyrics flapped out of order *...'someone to hold'...* *'...before I'm too old'*. Thunder crackled and dispersed the song into static, a heartbeat before the lights went out.

I lit an entire box of utility candles, and at Jakobina's insistence, I closed my eyes and played the manifestation game. She linked her hands in old-fashioned prayer while I placed an absurd order with the universe: "Okay, Universe, I'll bite. Please provide me with an affordable 'dream-castle by the sea', forthwith, if you will – a sublimely-situated, fully-furnished haven, a solitary retreat away from the moving herds of texting robots, shrieking sky trains, flashing neon, and rush hour."

I sent Jakobina a look that said, *how was that?*

Her answer came as exasperated eyes lifted to heaven. My list had shocked her.

A renewed torrent of horizontal rain sluiced the apartment window into a funhouse mirror. "Oh, yes. One more thing," I added with a sly glint. "Please make it remote enough to be isolated from neighbors... the physical ones, but near enough to civilization to buy lightbulbs and chocolate. It must have 'weather'. Wind and storms are acceptable, as is an uninterrupted view of the stars. Keep the snow to yourself, thank you very much. Oh, and please help the charming young man from the street corner to resolve his friend's troubles. I guess I'm done. Over and out."

Jakobina's face glowed in the candlelight. "So... you're finally going to retire," she said. "It's about time. That job of yours in the supermarket is awful. Look what it's done to your feet. You shouldn't be standing up all day at your age." She fussed around me, straightening the blankets until I was comfortable, dislodging Punch in the process who meowed in protest.

I moved to get up. "Damn, I forgot to feed Punch."

She gently pushed my shoulders down and swaddled my feet, snug as a bandage. "Aurelia, no. You stay there. I'll feed her." Her doe eyes crinkled with humor behind the candle. "And *furthermore,* you can make an appointment with a 'doctor of the feet', tomorrow... *forthwith.*"

She flickered towards the kitchen inside the candle's yellow halo. A vision of a lovely young woman sashaying in a sweep of long skirts, her blue turban turned from cobalt to dark green in accord with the mystical laws of the color spectrum. She turned and smiled, a masterpiece of Dutch chiaroscuro, framed in the doorway, as the lights snapped on. *Was I ever that young?*

For a moment it looked as if she'd blinked out, but it was only an optical illusion when the science of electricity eclipsed beeswax-technology.

Jakobina's ruby lips puckered into a rose and blew out the candle.

Shakespeare's words: *'Out, out, brief candle. Life is nothing more than an illusion'* flashed through my mind before the entire passage came at me full-on in a flood of remembrance. *'Tomorrow, and tomorrow, and tomorrow,'* I recited. *'The days creep slowly along until the end of time. And every day that's already happened has taken fools that much closer to their dusty deaths. Out, out, brief candle. Life is nothing more than an illusion.'* William knew his stuff.

"Goodness," I shouted to Jakobina. "I'm a bit morbid tonight. That's not likely to endear myself with the Universe."

Jakobina's voice floated from the kitchen. "It's not morbid. It's the truth."

I looked out the window and up into the black hole of heaven and found a likely looking star. "Star light star bright," I recited, "first star I see tonight. I wish I may I wish I might, have the wish I dream tonight."

"That young man was extraordinarily handsome, wasn't he," Jakobina said inside my head.

Vancouver
– February 1 –
2019

The glass door marked Podiatrist opened into a closet-sized waiting room with end tables offering tidy stacks of reading material. My hand moved past a grisly plaster model of a foot cut in cross-section to the home décor pile. The castle magazine was at the bottom of pile three.

The moment I saw it on the cover of 'Architect Quarterly – special 300th edition', a gear shifted in my solar plexus, flooding me with what felt like warm helium. I covered the lower half of my face with the magazine, counted to ten, and peered over the top to check the faces in the room in case I'd cried out.

Nothing. I had done nothing unseemly.

An otherworldly voice whispered *"page 33"* in my ear. A tender kiss brushed my cheek.

I opened the magazine in a trance. Blocks of text and colored squares blurred by until the same voice said *be prepared… just breathe*. I checked the number at the bottom of the page. It was 32. In spite of the ethereal advice, I held my breath and turned it in slow motion with the sound of waves crashing in my ears. Page 33 did not disappoint.

A mauve-tinted image wavered under the banner heading 'BEACH HOUSE SANCTUARIES'. I gasped and said *Mother of God,* loud enough to draw stares. A mystic designer had reached into my dreams and taken a snapshot before I woke up.

It stood, a picturesque silhouette, designed by a whimsical architect for an eccentric client – a Victorian folly built of stone and slate with a flat crenelated roof. Clearly, it had defied the salty elements that had weathered every sharp contour into a modern ruin for quite some time. I hungered to live there. The fragment of song lyrics brushed past me, sung by the same ethereal voice. *'someone left a cake out in the rain… I don't think that I can take it.'*

Tearing out the page sounded like ripping a shirt in half but the receptionist remained absorbed in her monitor. I hated to fold it but my handbag was the size of a change purse. There was nothing for it but to crease it tenderly, and hope for the best.

I stowed it flat, closed the magazine, and rose with the intention of bolting from the room, mission accomplished, but sharp pains stabbed my feet, reminding me I was there on a different mission. I dropped back down, pulled my innocent coat over the crime scene, and continued reading with my leather purse pulsating against me like the beating heart from one of Poe's Gothic horror stories.

My stealth paid off. The article went on to give the location and name of its designers – the firm of Zygmont & Carter, Vancouver, and a telephone number that I hastily memorized.

An hour later, after being given an appointment card for an x-ray, and emboldened by destiny, I rolled up the magazine and strolled out of the office with it under my arm, bold as a crow.

chapter 22
JUDGEMENT DAY

Valentine's Day
– February 14 –
2019

I couldn't help but confront the castle's reality a dozen times a day. Jakobina insisted I clamp its photo to the fridge with a magnet, carefully calculated to greet me at eye-level. Whenever she touched it, she claimed she heard a man calling my name. Whenever I touched it, I heard seagulls.

'Cornwall House' on Castle Island, off Salt Spring, whimsically referred to as the 'Mermaid Observatory', had been built for an astronomy enthusiast who never lived there. It had remained on the books of Zygmont & Carter's property management department since 1982 as a showpiece too precious to rent and too sentimental to sell. And, as I came to understand it, the pet project of one of the partners who kept it for his eventual retirement.

I held my breath for a week while my initial seven page letter of inquiry, written with an old fountain pen on my best paper, snailed its way across downtown Vancouver and scaled a skyscraper.

I was summoned from on high within the week, to an impromptu meeting where a young receptionist led me down a plush corridor to a boardroom flooded with sunlight, high above the city.

"Please make yourself comfortable," she said. "I'll be right back with… tea isn't it?"

"Yes, please. That would be lovely," I replied, yielding to vertigo by keeping well back from the panoramic view.

An expanse of floor to ceiling windows overlooked an organic entity that looked strangely mechanical – a large computer chip populated with ants that I had once euphemistically called home.

Eventually, out of curiosity, I craned my neck forward, but remained firmly planted. Laid out far below was an animated road map where I didn't belong. It sickened me that I could pinpoint the network of crossroads where a box of cement served as my current address. Down there, the stagnant lifestyle I wanted so desperately to escape for sand dunes and rough weather, festered.

I shook my head in disgust. *It's long past the time for Rome to fall again,"* I whispered under my breath in case someone was listening.

Curiosity bid me step closer at something out of focus. I moved forward and placed my hands on the window, straining to see past the city centre to the island coast where a future, happier me, unpacked her belongings in a white room.

The plate glass was cold to the touch. Eyes closed, I willed Cornwall House into view and sent the words: *wait for me.*

The castle, scaled down to cottage proportions, materialized, front door first. I saw myself shaking a blanket in the garden. A good domestic omen.

Wispy tentacles of energy stretched across the Georgia Strait, reaching out to a future me. Instinctively, I backed away, returning behind the line I'd drawn in the carpet for safety, and retreated to a chair at the head of the long conference table where a carafe of ice water and two glasses had arrived in silence. I dried my hands on my dress. They shook as I poured half a glass and then another. Visualization was thirsty work, and now I needed hot tea to warm my frozen hands.

Seeing downtown in graphic perspective increased my anxiety. Too long I'd floundered in that selfish jungle of traffic, elbowed by upwardly mobile go-getters and street beggars. A police siren wafted up from the streets like chimney smoke. I was trapped – a butterfly caught in a high-flying web.

I clung tighter to my purse and the picture of Cornwall House it contained for comfort, opening it briefly to peer inside as one would consult the photo of a loved one in a locket. I touched the corner of my 'amulet' for luck and then chided myself.

The photo had become a 'go to anchor' in moments of doubt.

And now I doubted this place. Was I being observed by someone unseen? The thought was accompanied by a prickly sensation as if a new ghost had laid its hand on my shoulder.

My imagination bubbled out of control as I scanned the room. Maybe there was a peep hole in the seascape painting on the wall. I controlled my instinct to wave at it by gripping the back of the nearest chair and deliberately smiled in it's direction to make a good impression.

The seascape blurred into soft blue and yellow bands of water, sky, and sand. A frothy border of animated white lace picked out the shoreline. I visualized myself on the narrow strip of beach looking out to sea, and while there, I sent the Universe a thank you note. It responded with a gentle breeze that stirred the room, brushed the hair from my face, and left the taste of salt on my lips.

After a time, the skyline of Vancouver materialized on its horizon. I searched for, and found, the building where I now awaited tea and the decision of a stranger until, in my mind's eye, I saw myself, another me with eyes closed, forehead pressed against the very window behind me.

And then it happened. I spontaneously floated out-of-body, rising higher, weightless until the 'microchip' of downtown Vancouver morphed into a motherboard sprawling in all directions – a vast country of predatorial circuitry inhabited by human viruses.

It was sobering to be, quite literally, beside myself, a rebel furious with history, thoroughly disgusted by a non-local mind cruel enough to engineer a food chain of chaos on purpose.

Vancouver lurked below, a humming timebomb of poverty and toxic wealth, crouching like a spider, a sentient predator feeding on human dreams that sucked in money and breathed out poisonous debt.

The room spun counter-clockwise, and when I looked again, earth throbbed in space – a vital organ with veins and arteries teeming with microbes, with me, a hapless embryonic host attached to the planet by a double helix umbilical cord of spirit, borne along for the ride.

I left the solar system as pure thought. Earth receded into its famous blue dot. Envisioned from space, earth's metropolises held hands forming a polluted constellation connected by greed and human industry.

The astronomer me, observed pockets of civilization flower and die on time-lapse film. In contrast, the primal intention rebirthed itself into a new jigsaw puzzle of carbon and hydrogen. Continents collided. Swamp smog lifted to reveal the bright blue shape of the Pacific hugging a jagged green coastline of vegetation.

My thoughts were lucid. *Out here I'm free. Castles and money mean nothing. Had I died? Was I dying? Was I manifesting an even wilder dream of death than being absorbed into a painting?* I toyed with the idea of cutting my puppet strings. Out here, in innermost space, I could escape the endless wheel of death by blinking out or blinking *in* to a singularity a moment before going nova. I held my breath as the universe breathed in and out.

I was about to embrace the end with nothing less than total surrender, when the tea tray arrived in a clatter. "Sorry to take so long," a voice said, jolting me out of my daydream. I whirled from the painting, embarrassed to discover my eyes had misted over. "That's a powerful painting," I sniffed, wiping a tear away with a bare finger. "I must have gotten a grain of sand in my eye. Painted beaches can be dangerous."

"That's the view from the roof of Cornwall House," the girl said, ignoring my humor. She hesitated momentarily, her brows raised, looked past me at the painting and carried on, professionally chirpy. "Yes, I prefer cities myself. Someone will be along to see you in a jiffy. Ma'am. Are you all right?"

My throat constricted. I pinched my arm hard and smiled brightly. "I'm fine," I said. "The sea always has a strange effect on me." I kept pinching for several painful minutes before letting go with a sigh.

Her return smile was brisk. Forced. She smoothed her skirt and straightened her back. "Yes, Ma'am."

Perhaps there *had* been a camera recording me. Perhaps it was my heartfelt display of genuine emotion that won the day. Perhaps the

Universe was feeling abundant. Perhaps it rewarded eccentric old ladies on Tuesdays. Apparently, my pleas struck a chord with the owner. I passed the tests.

Formal documents ensued in a flourish of signatures and legal stamps before a deposit for the first and last month's rent were accepted. I had a remarkably generous two year lease in my pocket without a hitch, and a livid bruise on my arm – a tattoo of self inflicted pain refusing to fade. The ease of the negotiations should have been a clue. Instead it was a surprise.

chapter 23
THE ISLE OF GLASS

Castle Island is a shard of rainforest adrift in the Strait of Georgia, owned outright, I learned post-lease, by my landlords Zygmont & Carter. Turns out it's a best kept secret with north and south poles — two locations, separated, and by that I mean *connected*, by an invisible force field.

Glastonbury, an old 'New-Age' commune clings like a barnacle to the northern shore proving the axiom that everything old is new again. It's a folksy time-slip retreat that prompts me to consider my side of the island is pretty much a counter balance new 'Old-Age' commune.

But Glastonbury is more of a concept than a commune, and by that I mean it harbours a select gathering of humans collectively seeking an underground seam of breathing space. The Vancouver ferry docks there twice a week bringing supplies and depositing pilgrims of one kind or another.

My destination, Cornwall House, is anchored on its fiercely private, southern tip.

Retreating appears to be Castle Island's sole purpose, which is why it called to me out of the grey of post-Christmas Vancouver. I picture it as a symbolic yin yang of two energies segregated by a snaky S curve that symbolizes duality and perfect harmony.

The first thing one sees approaching Glastonbury is a stone lighthouse modeled after a Saxon round tower. After that, one is primed for the unexpected.

A circular maze of painted stones on the beach greets automatons escaping false news, corrupt social media, and chronic psychic pain. It maps out a walking meditation pathway that sets the tone for the inner journeys restless visitors seek. Above it, a lone standing stone marks the top of a low hill known as the 'Tor' like a homing beacon.

The frustrated ingenious, innovative, and inventive introverts, approach Glastonbury, literally, as a last 'resort' of hospice for the terminally jaded – an actual life threatening condition for artists, in a bid to achieve nothing less than creative reincarnation. A revolving family of kindred foot passengers arrive without ceremony and depart silently in order to preserve its sanctity.

Wounded imaginations circling the drain, emboldened to detox from mainland burn outs, stay in 'The Keep', a habitat of seven designer cabins – state of the art 'isolation tanks' rented by the month. Restless and lost, they're driven to cloister in pursuit of impossible dreams, infuriatingly out of reach in plain sight. These are my people.

I meet their eyes on my shopping expeditions… vacant, haunted, mystified, and the rare few animated with pearls.

The universe had heeded my order. The Island had an abundance of weather, and 'The Quest', Glastonbury's greengrocer, is my go-to supplier of lightbulbs and chocolate. There's a café grill called 'The Grail' where, I'm told, organic quinoa and wheatgrass shakes fuse peacefully with heart-stopping sugary treats and lamb stew. I'll collect my mail at 'The Findings' - a veritable Merlin's cave, selling pens and notepaper, casual meditation attire, amulets, aromatherapy, herbal teas. 'Pen-Dragons', a copy service for visiting writers, is an unexpected godsend for printing my manuscript to be. And lastly, 'Fisher King's Second-hand Books' with its lovely history as the owner's parents, Mr. and Mrs. King had whimsically named their son, Fisher.

I've come to regard Castle Island as my personal Avalon – the legendary 'Isle of Glass', King Arthur's final hospice. Partly because the white beaches conceal a bountiful crop of muted sea-glass and partly due to the fabled references of a king healing in the aftermath of battle which I find suitably poetic considering I'm emerging from the wastelands of a small life, trailing psychic wounds. Arthur made his last stand at Camlann. It's fitting that I will make mine on an Isle of Glass.

Collecting sharp edges of broken bottles tumbled smooth by the waves connects me to the sea. It's a morning ritual that not only centers me but also delivers a gentle heads up divination akin to reading tea leaves.

After Glastonbury's initiation, I can't help but reflect on King Arthur. Symbolically, like the eternal snake whose bite meets its tail, Arthur's life completed a circle. He met his death where his sword Excalibur was born in the furnaces of white magic.

I know all about interrupted circles since opening my time-capsule of broken high school dreams. The door to mine will slowly close if my resilience fades.

Castle Island is where my suppressed memories may come home to roost. Dredging up the past may expose a field of cruel leg traps or the repository of my highest truths… perhaps both, and so the island holds a challenge that's bizarre, even for me. Dipping into unfinished business is definitely no place for sissies.

My terrifying secret still hesitates on the cusp of here and there. Will I remember in time or is it time to let it go? I have two choices. The easiest course is sliding into the future without a ripple. The hardest, is making waves by dredging up the past.

Tintagel Cottage is connected to Glastonbury by an umbilical road reminiscent of a long driveway to a stately home. The castle in the sand marks the boundaries where my old life ends and the world of shadows begins.

THE MOVE

I must go down to the sea again,
For the call of the running tide
Is a wild call and a clear call that may not be denied;
And all I ask is a windy day with the white clouds flying,
And the flung spray and the blown spume,
And the sea-gulls crying.
— JOHN MASEFIELD
1902

chapter 24
POSSESSION

Tintagel Cottage
The Vernal Equinox
– March 20 –
2019

Moving Day

The muse whispered in my ear: *call it, Aurelia, it's all up to you. Heads or fairy tales?* Its voice was male. Hot dice rattled inside my skull. Someone threw my brain down the length of a craps table and cried out snake eyes. "I should have taken the Ibuprofen before we left, when you told me to," I remarked to Jakobina.

Moving boxes littered the floor. Jakobina was already intently rummaging through a linen trunk, muttering to herself in Dutch.

My mental earthquakes were stabilizing by degrees with every moment beside the sea but my nerves were frazzled. I intended my brain's seismograph needle to settle on zero and stay there.

"Whatever you're looking for, leave it till later," I snapped. "The movers will be gone soon." I could only hope my snarky muse would be gone as well.

Jakobina straightened, stretched her back, and threw a pillow at me. "Heads up grumpy!"

My high school education was not lost on her. Nevertheless, her use of modern expressions still caught me off guard.

I caught the pillow after it bounced off my face.

She frowned without a trace of anger. "You *do* know the movers can't see me, right?"

I plumped the pillow with returning energy. "They might. This place has a mind of its own. People have spontaneous psychic flashes. But I'm fairly sure they'd notice a projectile floating through the air. What were you looking for so earnestly?"

Jakobina's lips pursed in anger. The faint white scar tracing her jawline twitched and reddened, prominent as a fresh cat scratch.

"Why are you upset?"

"Who says I am?"

I reached toward her face. "That hairline scar of yours pinks up when you're in a snit. You've never told me what happened there."

Jakobina recoiled, stopping me from touching it. She rubbed her chin. Her eyes narrowed at Punch. "I had a run in with a cat."

I had noticed Jakobina's nervous reaction whenever Punch leapt on my lap. "Well, that's what it looks like. It's a bit of a handy signpost to your mood swings, for me."

Jakobina made a display of dragging the open trunk to the window. "I've tried to like Punch. But cats are…" She inched away from Punch. "They aren't overly fond of ghosts. They disrupt us. It's most unpleasant." She straightened, clearly vexed. "My moods do not swing. And you have too many books and pieces of glass. You collect too much. It's not healthy."

"I love my cobalt glass. It soothes me."

She giggled. "We'd best unpack it quick, then."

The sun was painfully bright but I didn't want to draw the curtains printed with a pattern of Dutch windmills over the glorious view or block the salty breeze reviving me. It passed understanding how I'd denied myself this dream my entire adult life.

The sound of men's voices on the stairs alerted Punch. She jumped into the trunk and massaged the folded bedding with her paws. Jakobina wiggled her fingers under a blanket to make her pounce.

An overstuffed loveseat upholstered to match the curtains entered the room on a dolly. Two men followed it. "This the last of it," one of them announced cheerily. "Where's it to go?"

"I see your cat's already settling in," the other said, interrupting Punch's game by scratching her ear. "Whatcha got under there, eh? A wee mousie?"

I sent Jakobina a defiant glare. "There are no mice in this house. Cats can see things we can't," I said out loud but meant for her.

She stared back at me, smugly, her arms crossed. "Magic is lost on mere mortals," she said.

The men shifted a few of the heaviest boxes at my direction and left.

I waited for the sounds of the truck to evaporate before I joined Jakobina at the window. My new front yard was a glorious windswept beach.

The sea glistened, slick with sunbeams, heaving and sighing. My personal therapist.

I am perfectly content to die here but not until I unravel the secret I came here to remember.

chapter 25
SANDMAN

The first day home, much to Jakobina's disgust, I rescued Felix from under the bed where she'd hidden him, and installed him in the kitchen.

The second day, I created a wall of cobalt blue glass in an east window, transforming the breakfast room into a vibrant sanctuary of sky and rain and seawater.

The third day, I lounged there, bathed in glorious blue light with the restful sound of Felix ticking from his new place of honor. Ten days of bliss passed before the first of the shenanigans appeared.

Fools Day
– April 1 –

An old song ran through my tea making ritual. *Mister Sandman, bring me a dream.* I filled the kettle. *Make him the cutest that I've ever seen.* Click. A friendly cobalt blue light popped at the base of the appliance showing it was good to go. *Give him the word that I'm not a rover.* I took cream from the fridge. *Tell him that his lonesome nights are over.* I sashayed a blue cup and saucer to the table. *Mister Sandman, I'm so alone. Don't have nobody to call my own.* I warmed the pot and tossed in an extra Earl Grey teabag for luck. *Please turn on your magic beam.* Poured boiling water and inhaled the steamy lavender facial. *Mister Sandman, bring me a dream.* How had I known the lyrics from a song I hadn't heard in fifty-years?

No, wait. I had. Somewhere not that long ago. But where?

This musical interlude business was getting to be a regular occurrence. Song byte birds, flew in and chirped on my shoulder at all hours. And thanks to Felix, Jakobina abandoned her usual place, haunting my shoulder, and left me to brood alone in my blue sanctuary.

I sipped my tea and drifted lazily into my new life. Felix's cartoon smile widened and his hypnotic ticking grew into the sound of crashing of waves.

I woke from the spray of saltwater in my face with my toes in the sea and an empty teacup in my hand. Felix's eyes watched me from the sky. "Is this going to be a regular thing?" I shouted. "Am I a sleepwalker, now?"

His answer mutated into the cries of gulls, overhead. "No need to thank me," he called out, evaporating fast. "Silly girl. It's your un-birthday… spiritually speaking."

Felix's eyes faded into the clouds and I walked back to the house in a bubble of peace. I was Aurelia in Wonderland with my very own Cheshire Cat.

May Day
– May 1 –

The day of the first sandcastle had been perfectly innocent. In true 'first of May' tradition we filled the cottage with spring flowers. By midnight on May 5th I required help. I sent out a mental S.O.S. for reinforcements, and on May 6th I found a Canary that could bark away the shadows.

An aged man is but a paltry thing,
A tattered coat upon a stick, unless
Soul clap its hands and sing, and louder sing
For every tatter in its mortal dress,
Nor is there singing school but studying
Monuments of its own magnificence;
And therefore I have sailed the seas and come
To the holy city of Byzantium.
— WILLIAM BUTLER YEATS

chapter 26
NIGHT & DAY

The Summer Solstice
– June 21 –
2019

The morning of the Summer Solstice matched my misty mood. I heard the sea but it was lost in a low fog. Very beautiful, but fog has its drawbacks. Canary needed her walk and I didn't want to get us lost or for either of us to break a leg. It was unseasonably cold. Looking back, the 'May Day phenomenon' seemed eons away and yet it's ghost was always stalking me. The tension of waiting for the clouds to break took me by surprise every time.

I called up the stairs to Jakobina for the hundredth time. "Come with us." As always, she peered over the railing, dismissed me with a wave and vanished through the wall in true ghost-like fashion to make a point.

I bundled up in Sophie, my mother's vintage fur coat, muffled in a wool scarf long enough to cover my head and wrap around my neck twice. I grabbed Canary's leash but it was me who needed one. I tethered myself to the porch with a blue nylon rope that played out until the house disappeared.

After a quick pee, Canary hared off. Giving the ocean a piece of her mind was her first formal duty of the day. I heard her barking at the surf on a distant planet. I was left alone with my thoughts.

I gave the dear creature her freedom for twenty minutes or so and hunkered down inside Sophie to meditate – a human bear in hibernation. At the risk of sounding maudlin, it occurred to me that wandering in a colorless world surrounded by the extraordinary clarity of smells and sounds was perhaps the Universe foreshadowing the nuances of serious memory loss that will invariably come. I'm told dementia will progress by degrees. A series of false starts at first, and then, oops-a-daisy, the big drop off… and cruel fog.

Even though I couldn't see past my outstretched arm, I closed my eyes to fully appreciate a refreshing facial of salty spray, the sound of crying gulls, and the crashing of strong waves against the rocks. No gentle lapping today – the sea was wild. Definitely not intimidated by a frenzied dog.

I was accompanied by a heavily-breathing wind that reminded me my stalker, never far from my thoughts, might be within a few feet of me. To rally, I pictured my future self drinking hot chocolate in the breakfast room, with Felix, my feline metronome, ticking pleasantly.

Time was relative in my pocket of solitude, but after a reasonable wait, I recalled Canary from her mission to hold back the tide. "Okay old lady," I called out. "Time's up, Princess Canute. You can try again tomorrow."

I made it home, hand-over-hand on a lifeline and as the light on the porch emerged, it dawned on me how profound a walk in the fog could be. My time *wasn't* up. By all counts I had plenty of tomorrows. Felix assured me so.

This morning I had meaningful work to do, animals to feed, the chapter of a story to transcribe, and hot chocolate to make.

The castle materialized from a movie of itself. Being momentarily enveloped in fog and coming home to a house lit up with strings of pea lights was a grand metaphor to celebrate a disappearing and reappearing woman.

What else could a bizarre memoir such as mine and Jakobina's be if not a fantasy.

But my story was deeper than a quirk. It had been an obsession of mine since someone told me I bore a remarkable resemblance to the girl in Vermeer's 'Girl with the Pearl Earring' when I was seventeen. In my wildest dreams I has been her twin doe-eyed innocent. An equal opportunity doppelgänger with a luminous ivory complexion, and had, as the love songs like to eulogize, lips red as cherries.

It began harmlessly enough, as most obsessions do, and quickly progressed to in-depth research and musings. None of which have proved harmful, although the recurring lucid dreams of a ghostly lover have fizzled more than one romantic relationship.

What prospective beau could compete with an ethereal man who read minds. I knew only that the man of my dreams stood in the shadows, close to Jakobina's fiancé, Piet. We kissed in the dark so I never saw his face. I imagined I felt wings brush my face as he departed, and saw his silhouette against the moonlight a few times. It was never enough.

Jakobina has leaked the highlights of her life with due diligence since high school from snippets of joyous serendipity to ill-timed misery. She's had her fair share experiencing the exquisite agony of fulfilled love.

From the beginning of our acquaintance she made sure I knew Master Vermeer was *not* her lover. He was her lover's teacher.

Piet's apprenticeship had culminated in commissioning Vermeer to paint a wedding portrait of Jakobina, but something happened before it could be delivered. That's all she'd say. *'All in good time,'* she repeated wistfully whenever I pried.

The fog was an apt metaphor for her, too. She'd been happily lost, appropriately enough, in a 'fog' of desire, during the months of posing. I knew from experience that modelling for an artist was an undertaking where a mind wandered in order to survive backache, cramped shoulders, and boredom.

I recalled her exact words. "I was preoccupied, imagining Piet's touch and kisses, thinking of imminent marital bliss, flushed with feelings I barely knew what to do with." I'd chided her that she must have attended high school where such romantic dalliances dominate a large portion of a girl's frontal cortex. It was any wonder math and science makes a dent at all.

Jakobina couldn't get her head around the idea of a frontal cortex, but once, after I overwhelmed her with technical jargon, she silenced me with "I saw a mermaid once, and made a wish."

Castle Island
– June 22 –
2019

In the first moments of post-magic-consciousness, I touched my face and felt the craquelure of Jakobina's portrait as the surface of my skin. I was inside the painting again, looking out at Jakobina standing at the open window with gauze curtains flapping around her like diaphanous wings. She spoke facing the water. "It's only for a minute, Aurelia, don't panic." She reached a tentative hand through the window but stopped as if she'd hit a wall. "It won't take long."

I was trapped – an anxious woman with varnished wrinkles, hanging on the wall until Canary broke the spell. She bounded through the door and leapt on the bed. I woke up in time to see a bright light flash from a pearl earring on a background of solid black. For a brief moment the painting was an empty gold frame on the wall.

"Drink your tea while it's hot," Jakobina said from the foot of the bed. She was carrying a laden breakfast tray. "It's a blustery Christopher Robin day. The kind you like. You'll need all your strength."

I corrected her. "A *'Winnie the Pooh'* day," I replied. "The best kind for clearing fluff between the ears. You know, you might ask before you pull me into your 'prison'. It's disconcerting to wake up inside a painting."

She turned to me all wistful and ignored me with a smile. "I wish I could go outside."

I closed my eyes and clutched the bedclothes to confirm I was back in bed. "There's no earthly reason why you can't. You're able to join me on the roof."

Jakobina tamed the dancing curtains and secured them with a loop of braided rope. "There is. It's part of the promise I made. There are laws."

"Strange ones, if you ask me. You can drink tea and eat the same as me."

"You see what you want to see."

"Are you saying I wash invisible cups and plates?"

Jakobina frowned and headed for the closed door. "Perhaps," she said, exiting in classic ghostly fashion. Her dematerialized words "it is unclear to me" came muffled from the hallway.

I jumped out of bed and made a beeline for the painting to examine its surface. It was a museum quality print, smooth as satin, and yet I could feel the uneven shell of fine cracks beneath my fingers. The girl's lips felt chapped. I touched my cheek. It was pliable and warm. I was back.

I moved to my dressing table and applied a dab of rich moisturizer to my face and neck, taking care to massage it in until my reflection in the mirror glowed pink with life. My living portrait stared me down, reminding me of Dorian Grey. I had an urge to smash the looking glass so my image would match the craquelure of Jakobina's portrait.

The morning window temped me to open the curtains. The swish of the curtain rails startled Punch. She burrowed her head under the bedclothes. The island was bathed in wholesome light that dazzled over calm waters, the polar opposite of blustery. Ripples of liquid gold played in concentric circles as if a mermaid was about to surface. For a moment I imagined her tail breaching the surface. It slapped a friendly hello and disappeared. Temporal anomalies aside, I lived on an island of appearances and disappearances.

I've examined Jakobina under the forensic microscope of daylight, studied her moods under every phase of the moon and in the brightest sunlight. I've dived with her into the emotional abyss only a tormented woman can know. She's not a complex creature but she's a tenacious one, and her darkest contemplations are truly terrifying.

I've learned to be discreet. Ghosts shrivel under a magnifying glass. She and I have stirred our joyful memories together but she wielded her biggest secret over me like a blunt instrument she's not afraid to use. You wouldn't credit her moxie from her doe-eyed portrait, but she's lived a long time to come by her temperament honestly. And when she told me her biggest truth it resonated as if struck by a tuning fork. It unfolded at night whenever she urged me to bed down early. On those nights, she delivered nightcaps of hot chocolate with an expression she'd learned from me. "Gird your loins," she'd say, thinking to amuse me. The first time she said it I laughed at such a phrase coming from a seventeenth-century girl but the future was no cause for merriment.

We lived vicariously through each other as if our own experiences were too raw to bear alone. We're sisters born over three-hundred-years apart.

I love her in my way, somewhat distractedly, but in a twisted blip of fate, she is literally charged with loving me to death.

chapter 28
THE ART OF SITTING

– June 23 –
1965

Delft

I was sleepy. Close to falling over that nocturnal line in the sand that beckoned *beyond here be your wildest dreams*. The 'Girl with a Pearl Earring' hung, as if illuminated from within, on the wall across from my bed.

Rather than count sheep, which has never worked, I followed the lazy fingers of moonlight as they traced the outline of Jakobina's sweet profile. The corners of the gilt frame flashed with sparks as the man-in-the moon cupped her sweet face with light, tenderly as a lover. I closed my eyes on the edge of the abyss before I fell.

I've been sitting on this uncomfortable stool for hours but Punch is with me. I shift slightly and her claws automatically splay to stabilize her perch. I feel her slipping so I raise my knees to stop her from falling and make a fence around her with my arms.

A tall man with his back to me stands before an easel painting a girl. A younger man with his arms crossed studies the artist's every move. The girl's eyes momentarily flit towards me but she remains immobile. She's visibly nervous. But her gaze is directed at Punch.

Words in a language I don't understand pass between the two men. The young assistant strides the distance between artist and subject and whispers in the girl's ear. He playfully taps the pear-shaped pearl dangling from her ear and sets it quivering. She blushes but continues to steal a few furtive glances in my direction with distrust in her eyes. She's wary of Punch. I seem to pose no threat. I pick up her fear of cats. How silly.

Not overly fond of silly girls, I tease her by repositioning Punch into a cuddle and make a display of rubbing her ears. Punch preens and is clearly about to jump down. The girl's mouth opens in response. She wants to run. I'm almost sorry that I played cat and mouse with her. I feel her tense, and tighten my hold on Punch.

Punch settles back into a round harmless shape but the girl's doe eyes remain hesitant. I send her a mental message "It's okay," I tell her. "Trust me. She won't hurt you. For goodness sake, there are worse things in the world to worry about than cats."

The sharp scent of distilled pine oil acts like smelling salts, and my nose awakens me. I'd been daydreaming. I'd dozed off, left my bedroom so to speak, and crossed the boundary between waking and sleeping. My breath was even now that the cat was gone. Posing for hours was tedious business. I sought Piet's eyes. He smiled and unnerved me with one of his devastating winks. He knew how to reach inside me and squeeze my heart. I glared back but defiance wasn't possible. I wanted him as much as he wanted me. And who could hide a fire like that. Certainly not me, and he never has.

Master Vermeer chastised me. "Ah, you're back," he said. "At last. Now we can finish your eyes."

Piet nodded his approval to center me. As an apprentice under strict rules, he stood behind Vermeer – an actor on his mark. Two paces to Vermeer's left or right and no closer, to his master's back.

Vermeer addressed Piet, without pause. "Never paint the light in a subject's eyes until you stand before the presence of their soul," he admonished. "Your fiancé's soul has been wandering. Daydreamers can ruin a good painting." His expression was a stern mask that he turned towards Piet. "NEVER paint empty eyes!"

Piet glanced at me and frowned. "You must not woolgather, Jakobina. Did you hear Master Vermeer? Your presence is vital."

I lowered my eyelids slowly as an apology.

Vermeer shushed him with a raised paintbrush. "You will know the exact moment. But for this you must wait. Use the time to polish the drapery. In Jakobina's case there is also an abundance of life in her lips. Choose each moment with care. Lifeless lips and dull eyes abound across dinner tables and in the streets. A portrait is not real. It is a critical moment above time. Between life and perfection. What your little butterfly reveals to us is her desire for you. We must catch it quickly before she flies away."

I blushed. Vermeer talked about me as if I was little more than a bowl of fruit, but ironically, his painting raised me from 'still life' to an amorous blushing woman, dizzy with love.

I'd been cautioned at some length to remain silent, instructed to ignore the content of Vermeer's blunt words unless he ordered me to move. I was to be the invisible made visible.

Vermeer chastised himself. "But you see? I have made her turn away with my words. Please, Piet, reposition her. You know her pose. Make haste and reassure her. We want her in a heightened state of feminine guile."

Piet hastened towards me, grinning. He touched my shoulder and I returned with a jolt from a daydream of rare passion. I tried to cling to my memories of love but Piet took my shoulders and moved me just so, angled my chin slightly down, kissed one of his fingertips and used it to tap my nose.

Vermeer chose a fine sable brush with a rounded tip. "We must capture her desire with zinc white, yes?" His voice snapped. "Jakobina, lick your lips. Do *not* move your head."

It was a command, and I obeyed because Piet's brief nod showed he approved.

"Talk to her, Piet," Vermeer said. "Tell her your heart's greatest wish."

Piet loosened his cravat with purpose, all the while holding my gaze. He straightened his shoulders and sent me a devastating wink. I felt the quickening of desire in my belly. He licked his own lips amorously, and began to tease me the way he did in private. I was drowning in the moment. A desperate need passed between us. He opened his mouth hungrily, and in response, my lips answered by parting slightly in anticipation of a kiss. Piet stepped back. My soul reached for him, Vermeer and Piet disappeared, and I opened like a flower.

Piet turned briefly to Vermeer. Presumably a private look passed between them. Piet shrugged without any guise of innocence and grinned. Vermeer's expression was one of amusement. He observed me. My face was hot. I was breathing faster. "Piet," Vermeer said. "I believe your little butterfly is ready."

Piet returned to his place as observer. He had shocked me by obeying his master over my shame.

"Watch carefully," Vermeer whispered. "She is a candle. Her portrait must illuminate the room. Her love is incandescent. It must rise from the common matrix of canvas and paint. We are painting a soul, Piet. You must always paint the soul. A woman in love is a lantern. Mere mortals will see what is infinitely possible reflected in her light."

His voice changed to a whisper. "You have prepared the magic white?"

"Yes, sir."

Piet held my gaze as he smeared a dollop of white paste on Vermeer's palette.

"We have been waiting for your bride to join us. And now she is here. Squint now, Piet, and tell me where the pearls of life occur."

Piet launched into the answer he knew by heart. "The shine in her eyes, the tip of her nose, the fullest part of her lower lip, the corner of her mouth, and, of course, the sphere of the pearl earring."

"And now you know why I dress my models in pearls so often. The highlights of all paintings are a series of perfectly-placed pearls. A lead white ground beneath the painting illuminates the colors from within. But more importantly, the final application of pure white pearls breathe life into art. This is why it is called magic white. Drops of white sunlight fall on every face we see and bequeath life. Jakobina will form a shape that will be recognized as an icon of desire. We will ignite her soul."

Vermeer rested his painting arm on a padded stick to steady his aim. A dot of white must be both slow and swift to be precise. "Good, her cheeks are brighter. She's primed. Reborn."

He struck deftly as a snake. His aim was true as he delivered the sparks of life. Without hesitation, Master Vermeer wiped his brush and refreshed it. He tested the pigment's fluidity on a scrap of prepped canvas. It beaded perfectly into a liquid pearl. A grunt of satisfaction escaped from Vermeer's throat as he struck again. Five times he applied a tiny pearl. I felt five pearls quicken my portrait.

In a parallel life, somewhere across my bedroom, Jakobina stirred within her finished portrait. She shuddered involuntarily. A barely perceptible pulse began to beat at her painted throat.

Vermeer stood back, surveying new life. I copied Vermeer and ceased to breathe as he applied a sixth pearl, and it was done.

The three of us exhaled. The sigh Vermeer had been holding in for weeks filled the room.

Piet's expression was intense from memorizing every move. His look was one of awe. He shook his head and smiled at the portrait. "You have captured my butterfly," he said.

The 'God Vermeer' held up his hand for silence. He reached for a cloth and wiped his hands. "Well done, my child," he said to me, "you are free to fly." There were pearls in his eyes that I'd never noticed before, and what he said next sent a shiver through me. "Welcome to immortality, Jakobina."

I closed my eyes, dizzy from the cloying smell of linseed and varnish. But more than that, the hot coals of lust buried beneath my skirts throbbed with flame. I dared not look at the finished portrait, but then I hadn't been invited to. I saw it months later, after it was dried and framed. For a few seconds it took away my breath, but then I breathed new life into the rest of my days. Being immortal has its consequences. I could do nothing but go on as if nothing had changed.

Piet convinced me later, Vermeer's declaration had not been an act of vanity. "A true master knows when he has surpassed himself," he said. "Vermeer has no guile when it comes to his art. His studio is his castle, perhaps the *only* place, where he is completely honest. He often repeats his creed that a true artist must see beyond a human subject to bequeath the gift of life to one who is barely alive. It is a privilege to serve him. He cautioned me from our first meeting that he could not *teach* this gift, but that I may *learn* it from him."

Piet's words ignited a dormant lust within me. I became exhausted with the wanting. After I woke I was breathless and moist between my legs, held hostage with the dizzying heat of constant longing. I ached until it seemed I would be consumed by desire, all the more heightened from prolonged deprivation. Jakobina had no choice but to wait.

Jakobina shared a mind memory with me. She recalled a sobering claim of wisdom from her older sister that refused to cool her fever. She'd been assured that a look of desire across a room may be fire but a kiss stolen too soon was cold water.

By nightfall I was exhausted with bliss. The stars mocked me as I crawled into bed and closed my eyes. It seemed I must cope with this newly awakened me and Jakobina must wait for her true love forever.

Castle Island
– June 23 –
2019

"Wait!" a star shouted. "Where are your manners?" A commotion of clattering and barking woke me. It was Jakobina giving Canary orders to heel. I must have drifted off.

My nether regions were tingling My body remained in full arousal from the kiss that never came. I must be fairly glowing in the dark. Punch was staring at me from the foot of the bed like a marble statue with fibreoptic eyes. The window was filled with stars.

The radio muse's words came back to me. *It's not his intention to alarm you. He's here to prepare you.*

I prepared myself for the ritual making its way up the stairs. Canary bounced in ahead of Jakobina, carrying a tray of cocoa and a tin of dog biscuits. She carefully placed the tray on the bed. Punch sniffed her saucer of cream.

The moonbeams had travelled to my dressing table where they caressed a bottle of perfume. The painting waited in shadows.

I wiggled my toes. Punch pounced. She'd been waiting too. A sharp pain informed me my toes haven't disappeared. I was warm. I was alive.

Jakobina balanced a dog biscuit on Canary's nose. "You do not deserve this," she said smiling. "Dogs that push in don't deserve such treats."

I acted coy. "You'll never guess where I've been," I said to her over my drink.

She glanced from me to her portrait and back to me with a knowing smile. "Was it fun?"

"I'll never know," I answered, smoothing the coverlet. I met

Jakobina's portrait eyes and studied the white pearl at the edge of her painted lips. "I was interrupted."

Jakobina handed me a dog biscuit. "Canary has earned all the treats in the world."

"Timing is everything," I said lowering my voice to serious. "Jakobina, we need to talk."

Jakobina flinched before recovering her composure. "I am still flying," she said smiling into her past.

I frowned into our future, showing Jakobina the calendar where I'd crossed off the days since May 1st. "It's been two months since the first sandcastle," I said. "And we're no nearer to discovering the identity of our intruder."

Jakobina's smile froze. "Then, perhaps timing *isn't* everything," she said glibly. "Perhaps it's destiny."

Castle Island
– July 1 –
2019

I walked purposefully with Canary at my side with the Zee stone in my pocket, and as has become my custom, nervously scan for castle number four. And there *he* is. The king of the castles. A figure in the distance. Just a man on a beach carrying his shoes, white pants rolled to mid-calf. My thumb rubbed the stone without being asked. A seagull swooped at Canary who was already running excitedly in circles around me.

Poetry fragments from T.S. Eliot intruded over the scene like the running commentary in a dreamy documentary: *'I grow old I grow old I shall wear the bottoms of my trousers rolled.'* The stranger sauntered through the surf and waved to me like an old friend. *'I shall wear white flannel trousers, and walk upon the beach.'*

"Be still, Eliot," I murmured under my breath. "I need to focus." I pulled the first mauve message from my jeans pocket and waved it but the wind snapped it from my fingers and we both watched it 'sail off to Byzantium'.

Canary fairly pranced towards our stranger like a show dog on hot coals. He stooped to pet her. *Hmmm. He's tall. Why does that matter? Who does he remind me of?* I shook off my muse, interrupting with its Jeremy Irons' voice and prepared to confront the enemy. My builder of castles. My sender of evocative messages. Who does he think he is? Does he take me for a complete noodle? I am ready for verbal warfare. I shall take no survivors. The Zee stone is hot with tension. I stopped fingering it and gripped it tightly so it slept in my hand.

"Turncoat," I hissed at Canary as she returned all smiles, reluctant to leave her new friend. She showed not the slightest remorse for her traitorous ways. In fact, she loped back and forth between us, drawing us together in a net.

Shoulders back. Calm expression. Deep breaths. Canary sniffed around the stranger's feet and gazed up adoringly. So much for dogs and loyalty.

"Hey girl," he said to Canary. "What can you smell, eh?"

I answered, trying to keep the irritation from my voice. "An escaped gas."

He looked up with a devastating grin. "How flattering."

I'd accused more shrilly than I'd intended. "You're my stalker!"

He seemed delighted. He clicked his heels and bowed from the waist. "At your service Ma'am. But I prefer to call it courtship."

Suddenly I knew who he must be. "Ah… you're one of those Glastonbury writers."

He winked. "Let's just say I dropped in from the sky like a *good* penny and leave it at that."

"You're a trespasser. I was assured I wouldn't be bothered here."

His response was meant to be charming. "Well then, I promise not to be a bother."

"You are disturbance," I send back like a ping pong ball, feeling rather proud of my bravado in the face of danger. I tried winking but my eye twitched into a spasm.

"Stand still," he said taking a step closer. "I think you have something in your eye."

The bravado evaporated. He materialized closer still, invading my space, enough for me to see he was even taller than I'd thought and too elegant for my own good. He was no beach bum and too well dressed for a pirate. But just to be sure, I scanned the horizon for a ship. The first real detail of note were his laugh lines. My mother taught me that laugh lines never lied. He was a man of good cheer. Rather lovely, I expected, in spite of his sandy crimes. A suntanned grey fox with a winning smile. Canary was a good judge of character. I should have given her the benefit of the doubt.

"I think *you're* lovely, too," he said, in a posh English accent with Shakespearean tones.

I froze. "Are you an actor?"

He bowed again. "All the time." His eyes never left my face. "And you, young lady, look like a Vermeer painting," he said. He raised his eyebrows. "So… you read my snippets?"

I opened cautiously. "Is *that* what they were?" But not being a chess player I silently made up a faux move to settle my nerves: *Queen's pawn to block Knight's Templar.* "T.S. Eliot," I replied sheepishly. "If you're trying to impress me, I have to say, you know what you're about."

"It takes poetry to catch a poet."

"Indeed."

He stooped to study my face. "I've upset you." Again, there's not a question in sight.

I scuffled my feet until the heel of my shoe revealed a patch of dark wet sand. I took a breath and sent him a defiant stare, hoping to appear fearless. It was his move.

"I don't have a hump," he said, breaking the tension. "I left it at home." He cleared his throat. "Back in Byzantium."

"You mean Glastonbury."

"I mean Byzantium."

I hid my smile. We were playing poet ping pong with Keats and Yeats. He had impressed me by batting a backhander to my Yeats' reference which was clearly his intention. I played it cool. "What?"

He grinned, innocent as a schoolboy. "I said, I'm not a phantom."

I made an unintelligible choking sound and stared into space for an eternity. My hand woke the Zee stone which had gone to sleep.

I didn't recoil when he touched my arm. "I think it's your move," he said.

I nodded. "You're a writer *and* a mind reader. So… a lot scarier than your basic phantom."

He extended his hand. "People call me Catcher, DC, or just plain C."

There was nothing to do but follow the social niceties and accept. One firm, warm, gentle shake sent a spark from the Zee stone into my solar plexus. I felt warm. Strangely safe, and the fear left me. He was not an elemental. A tingle passed between our fingers. "I'm Aurelia. What does the D stand for… dog?"

"The sand is fascinating today, is it not?" he said with a raised eyebrow.

Now he was Mr. Spock. "Okay, you have to stop… I mean, I guess you're not a…"

"A beasty-man? Not a *dog* catcher, either."

I stared at his bare feet. *Lovely toes. What the hell is going on?*

"Check," he said.

"Pardon?"

"Your queen. She's in jeopardy."

"Pretty much always, but good guess."

He won our mental game in two moves. He played dirty. First he winked. *Man, was he good. How did he know that was the one thing that always unseated me?* And then he said casually, as if it was no big deal and he'd only just thought of it, "You do know, don't you, that you can't get blood out of a stone."

I pulled the dark green Zee stone flecked with red inclusions from my pocket and exposed it to the sun. It lay there on my palm as expectant as me. "How the hell? It *is* a bloodstone. How did you know?" I felt dizzy but I had no chance to recover before he answered with a casual: "Ah yes, the Knight's Templar to front porch opening. I believe it's my move." He extended his arm, and natural as breathing, I took it, still clutching the Zee stone.

Somehow I felt grounded, walking home to Byzantium on a squishy chessboard made of sand.

A pot of tea on my front porch later, Catcher and I were almost friends. Jakobina hovered with dreamy doe eyes – an apparition in the doorway. She was clearly captivated enough to venture outside. She seated herself in the porch swing, causing it to move rhythmically with a soft squeak.

Catcher paid it no attention, but judging by his perceptions so far, it was unlikely he'd missed a chair swinging of its own accord in his peripheral vision.

"What high school did you go to?" I asked, hedging. "Because I swear I knew you before."

He looked up and to his right as if the answer was there in a speech bubble. "*Um…* The one where you were a cheerleader."

I snickered. "Not in this life. But I suppose *you* were a star quarterback."

He shook his head. "Good gracious, no. I was president of the astronomy club. So, a bit of a dreamy stargazer."

Nothing could have stunned me more. "Me too."

He stroked my wrist. His voice pulled me under. "I guess we must be soulmates."

I blushed like a schoolgirl. I was drowning. I saw Zee's face floating like a mask between us. I was melted chocolate. But there was more. He delivered another devastating wink and said "Checkmate."

I stared at his bare feet, dumbfounded. His sculptured alabaster toes and ankles and lower calves were encrusted with white sand, fine as salt, that made me anticipate the saltiness of his kiss on my lips.

"Of course, I wear my trousers rolled," he said out of the blue. "Soggy pantlegs encrusted with grit are surely the mark of a careless man. It's asking for trouble. One puts their best foot forward when meeting a lady… and the best impression a sandman can make is poetry and unflappable pantlegs, don't you agree?"

When the tea party was over, Catcher shook Canary's paw and stared into her brown eyes with mock seriousness. "You do have a license, don't you, young lady? Because I'll be coming back tomorrow to check." He looked over her head at me, and winked his trademark wink again. I caught a barely perceptible nod in the direction of the porch swing. "See you in my dreams," he said.

His third wink aroused my growing feelings of desire.

When he was out of earshot I said rather cattily to Jakobina, "He meant me."

THE MENTORSHIP

I grow old, I grow old,
I wear my trousers rolled.
I shall wear white flannel trousers,
and walk upon the beach.
I have heard the mermaids singing, each to each.
I do not think that they will sing to me.
I have seen them riding seaward on the waves
Combing the white hair of the waves blown back
When the wind blows the water white and black.
We have lingered in the chambers of the sea
By sea-girls wreathed with seaweed red and brown
Till human voices wake us, and we drown.
— T.S. ELIOT
'The Love Song of J Alfred Prufrock'

chapter 31
PROFESSOR C

Castle Island
– July 2 –
2019

Catcher hailed us with a wave like an old friend. "Ladies," he called out. "I was hoping I'd run into you."

By ladies he meant Canary, Punch, and I on our evening walk.

Punch swore and hared off into the dune grass. Canary whined and leaned heavily into my legs. Both of them were strangely antsy. I reassured Canary with a line stolen from 'Winnie the Pooh'. "Silly old bear," I whispered in her ear. "What's wrong with you? It's only Catcher." She licked my face wanting to stay close. "This is our beach. No worries," I said to her. Even though, yesterday, Catcher had awakened a long lost sexual need within me, I'd reset my dormant libido. He was interesting and nice but I couldn't help hoping he wasn't going to pop up on our beach whenever he liked.

When Catcher was closer, Canary sniffed the wind and was won over with "here girl" and a treat. The threat was over. Catcher examined Canary's collar. "I see you're wearing your license," he said. "That's my girl."

In minutes Canary was bounding ahead of us as we trod silently over a carpet of sand that reflected the coral sunset. As before, Catcher's pantlegs were rolled to his calves.

As for me, I'd been having too many senior moments and now I was seeing pearls everywhere – in sparkling water, on objects emerging from the shadows, and especially in my eyes in the mirror.

Photographers' light turned us young. I forgot my past and for an all too brief moment felt carefree... a glorious future loomed ahead bathed in starlight. The tide teased me, offering a push and pull of living foam so the shoreline glistened into the distance like a long pearl necklace. I inhaled the heady odor of salt, rotting crabs, and seaweed. I was home.

It had been an exhausting, exhilarating day. I still checked out my stranger, warier now that his male presence had disturbingly relocated my feminine drive. The iceberg of our relationship was barely exposed but once again my dormant body tingled in neglected places. Disconcerting. "You're a philosopher," I blurted out to break the silence and ease my discomfort. *Not the most subtle of observations.*

Catcher tilted his head to one side as if listening to the sky. "Among many other things."

"I quickly countered with "I mean, it's an admirable, if not a dodgy, pursuit of time." He pursed his lips. I had offended him. "Sorry," I backpedalled. "I didn't mean it to sound like an accusation." And then I asked what I really wanted to know. "You're here to prepare me, aren't you."

Catcher's sunglasses slipped down from his head onto his nose as he picked up a pebble of frosty white sea glass. He straightened and held it up to the fading light. "I call these beach pearls," he said over the rim of his glasses. He pushed his shades back onto his silver hair. "Happily, I can indulge what I love best. I go where my dreams call me. Your dreams called me because we are kindred. You are preparing *yourself.*" He met my gaze and winked. "And, here's something to ponder. Senior moments are hardly episodes of memory loss. We make room for memories that push in at random moments. We are meant to listen, and in doing so, the moment is given over. Trivialities no longer count at our stage of maturity, Madam."

"That's good because I forget an awful lot," I said. "You're reading my mind again."

He slow-clapped his hands. "Forgetfulness as the years advance is actually remembering what's important. Serendipity is an advanced art form. You, my sweet, are an artist."

I snickered. "Seems to me, you're being diplomatic. What you're really saying is it's time to get my affairs in order."

He grinned. "Literally."

"I don't understand."

"Your *affairs*. Love affairs to be precise."

"Ah, that would be love affair… singular."

Catcher spun around and walked backwards facing me. "All the more reason. It's now or never."

My blood heated up. I looked away and mumbled. "Or it's too late."

He spun again, arms wide to embrace the sea – an actor delivering a line. "'Tis is the age of meaningful coincidence." And then, as a stage whisper to me, "When you dream properly, my love, voila!... travel requires no tickets or luggage."

"*Um*, maybe not luggage but certainly baggage. Bags of karma."

"Dreaming is an art form where I come from. Quite teachable to a lifelong student like yourself."

"You make it sound positively heroic, but I *do* understand dream travel. It's…" I paused to consider a sane explanation but his face disarmed me. He'd turned golden as the sun dropped lower into the horizon. He looked taller. More majestic. I was captured whole. A small pilot light of passion flared in my entrails. I blushed. Damn.

"An obsession of yours," he interjected. "And if I may be so bold, here we meet on the same page. Like attracts like – a pair of philosopher beachcombers with dreams on our hands. Companions who have that magical ten-thousand hours to discuss what matters most."

He proffered his hand to shake as if we're meeting for the first time. "At last we meet."

I'd longed to take his hand again to feel the delightful waves of intimacy he delivered, and this time he didn't disappoint. When he removed his hand he'd left the newfound sea pearl behind. I was breathless but emboldened to say "I think we're going to talk well into the night." I had the distinct impression I'd been hypnotized. But I didn't care.

Canary dropped a stick at Catcher's feet. He picked it up and heaved it towards the castle. "Many many nights, *principessa*," he said.

I acted nonchalant through an emotional spike of joy. I was a *principessa*. His princess. Unlike most little girls I hadn't fallen prey to dreams of being a princess. Clearly, my internal fire was no longer banked. Canary ignored me in favor of chasing a stick, so, clearly, the 'spike' was not one of my 'earthquakes'.

By the time Canary bounded back to us, we were turning mauve in the first inkling of dusk. A slight wind whipped the sand over my toes. "It's past Canary and Punch's suppertime," I said casually. "I've seafood chowder on the go if you'd care to join us."

Canary raised her head when I mentioned her name and thumped her tail, swishing a furry arc in the purple sand. "I could rustle up a robust red wine too, if you're not wedded to the rules of white for fish."

"At our age there are no rules," Catcher said, throwing the stick ahead of us. "But I do believe there's an elephant on the beach. We can't philosophize until it's acknowledged. So, ask away."

I looked around half expecting to see a pink pachyderm. "Maybe after dinner," I replied coyly. "In a few days."

We advanced home stick-by-stick. Prince Catcher took my arm and Canary led us. I shuddered and Catcher wrapped his sweater around my shoulders for the last leg. I was enveloped in a cloud of well-being, heady from the intoxicating night perfume released by the flowers surrounding the house. But then, Jakobina waved from the roof and Catcher waved back. "I think it's time I met your friend," he said.

I recoiled, cruelly awake. I didn't want to share this moment with Jakobina who is young and beautiful.

Grow old along with me.
The best is yet to be,
The last of life for which the first was made.
— ROBERT BROWNING

chapter 32
A CLOSEUP TOO FAR

– July 4 –
2019

Mercifully, Jakobina kept out of sight for a few days – an uncharacteristically low profile considering her off-the-chart level of excitement when Catcher had merely been the merest blip on her radar.

Catcher greeted me on the porch with a hearty "What ho, milady? Time to break our fast."

"A man should be wearing a wide brim feathered hat to use such language," I replied.

"And don't think for a second that I don't have one, either," he countered. He looked eager to play. It was still my move after I'd been checkmated.

I sighed and stepped aside. "You may enter, sire," I said, curtseying.

He strode directly to the living room and stopped. "Well," he said, rubbing his hands. "Are you going to tell me, today? I think we've danced around your suppressed confessions long enough, don't you."

We stood, looking down at the 'Girl With a Pearl Earring' on the cover of a coffee table book about Vermeer – a couple in the hush of a gallery where one of us needed to step up as the tour guide. It fell to me. Catcher was right. I did feel the need to confess. "I have this fantasy," I said. "It's more of a conviction, really." I took a few cleansing breath before I could continue. I inclined my head towards the portrait and tapped the book. "That I've met that girl. I know who she adores and what she fears." I keep my eyes averted. "There's more."

He shuffled his feet, took a step closer to the painting, and peered into the girl's eyes, and then into mine. "*Hmmm?*"

"I used to have this special… *um*… night visitor." I hesitated. My throat was dry and my voice issued forth irrationally high-pitched. "A ghostly lover I met in lucid dreams.. I didn't need a husband after that. I was ruined for an ordinary man. Why am I saying all this. Forgive me."

Catcher said nothing. And then issued another noncommittal *hmmm*.

The pause made me restless and the restlessness made me brave. I made a small coughing sound. "Are you him?"

"Let's just say that, in your mind, I represent part of him."

"Doesn't that make me rather pathetic?"

"There you go. Thinking the worst about yourself. Maybe you're simply astute."

"Do you believe in reincarnation?"

"A version of it, yes."

"Is that….? Could you be more explicit."

"It's complicated."

"I have all the time in the world."

His spontaneous chuckle was not unkind. "You know, in a way, you do."

I bit my lip and dug a fingernail into the palm of my right hand for courage. "Look, contrary to appearing sane, my best friend…" I tapped the book again. "that is, my roommate, is this girl in Vermeer's masterpiece. Her name is Jakobina. She lives here with me. Ghosts don't age, so she's still seventeen. She's invisible to everyone except me. At least I can see her. She's been my ghostly companion since high school. But you saw her, too."

I took another breath and out came white hot anger. I was mad at both of us. Me for revealing Jakobina, and Catcher for his nonchalant dismissal of a difficult confession. I was humiliated. But I still dug for clues. "Jakobina told me you were… *um…* significant. She knew of your coming."

"Ah, yes. The girl on the swing who waved to us from the roof?"

I picked up the book and thrust the cover under Catcher's nose. "Yes, *this* girl. What does she know? Who are you? And what kind of answer is *hmmm?*"

"It means *yes.* You have the right to dream whatever you want. And so does Jakobina."

I took a step back, amazed. "What a heartless thing to say." But he hadn't flinched about my extraordinary relationship with a painting. Maybe he hadn't heard my whole truth.

"Not at all," he countered, reading my mind. "I merely offered you the truth of a finished man to an unfinished woman stuck in an ongoing truth, seeking an answer to an impossible memory. Have I got that right?" He stared hard into me, eyebrows raised, and delivered a crushing blow. "Aurelia, did you consider the elemental visitor wasn't visiting you."

He was teasing me. Testing me. Preparing me. "This painting… this girl, commandeered me from an art history class. She obsessed me for a while. I lost a good deal from our association including my sanity but rumor has it I never had it in the first place."

"Did you hear what I just said?"

I didn't want to hear him so I pressed on. "Jakobina asked me to keep her portrait in my bedroom so it would be the last thing I saw before I closed my eyes. Her face greets me in the morning. Sometimes it feels as if she's watched me all night."

He shook his head, sent me a sympathetic look, and held out his hand like a stop sign.

I ignored his signal. "The painting in my bedroom is a doorway."

Catcher took my hand. I was under his spell. He turned it over, kissed my palm, and chafed it as if it was a cold day.

"*Hmmm,*" he said. "Let's be very clear, Aurelia. You are perfectly sane. Do you understand?"

I was a child being chastised by a stern father. I nodded meekly but he grabbed my shoulders and stared into me. His eyes were ferociously kind. "Dream lovers aren't visitors. They're visitations. And, you're not the only woman living here. Do you see? Do the math."

Catcher positioned me into the light and examined my face.

I backed away. "Please don't. I prefer my age lines scrutinized from a distance or not at all."

He ignored me and stepped forward, staring closer. His right eye squinted like Sherlock Holmes behind a magnifying glass. He delivered his verdict. "My dear girl. You've been lonely in love."

I stared him down for a few seconds before I muttered "I have been in love", directly to the floor.

Catcher held my shoulders square and gently shook me. "Sweetheart, love terrifies you."

"I guess I'm a smart cookie, then. Loving leads to heartbreak. It's a horror show. I'm too old now, anyway. And for that I am truly thankful."

Catcher lifted my chin. He kissed the tip of his finger and tenderly touched the creases at the corner of my left eye. "Those laugh lines could be so much deeper. Do not disparage them, entirely."

I traced the skin near his eyes. "As deep as yours?"

He pinned my hand to his face. "Exactly like mine, yes."

I looked away. "I did my best."

He kissed my palm and closed it into a fist before he let go. "The best is yet to come."

I groaned inwardly. "So Robert Browning said, but it didn't stop the tragedy of his love affair with Elizabeth Barrett, did it."

"It wasn't an affair. They married."

"Excuse me… the tragedy of his *marriage*."

"I simply stated a fact."

I flailed my hands in his face as if I was erasing his words from a blackboard. "Stop. Do *not* go there. Please, spare me the 'grow old along with me' speech."

He shrugged. "Sorry kiddo, I can't help it if the best is yet to be. For everyone if you comply."

I kicked his shoe hard, lacking the courage to do some injury to his shin. Much to my horror, my voice caught in a sob. "The best *never* happened. Because I ran away."

I spluttered my apologies and searched my pockets for a tissue. But one was already waving in my face like a white flag. I accepted it from him and covered my red eyes.

He touched the bruise on my arm that resembled the shape of Castle Island. "Where did that come from," he asked.

"I pinched myself to prove I wasn't dreaming. But it disappeared weeks ago."

"Disappearances can be misleading," Catcher said. "They come and go."

I checked my arm again. The bruise was gone.

"My sweet girl," he said, "if I teach you nothing else, note this well: time is an illusion. At the end of the day, at the end of all of your days, an hourglass can always be righted. It never runs out of sand."

chapter 33
DIRTY RASCAL

– August 1 –
2019

Canary lay at Catcher's feet. From time-to-time he crooned love words to her. I felt a silly twinge of jealousy but Punch stirred in my lap to reassure me she was on my side. Jakobina clattered at the stove making a concoction of milk and eggs and spices.

It was surprisingly easy to fall in behind a stranger who'd pushed in. Catcher's proposal of mentorship grew imperceptibly each day. I found him a welcome diversion. He was good company, entertaining but a creative liar which was disconcerting. It became increasingly hard to remember he was acceptable only as long as he remained benign.

I relaxed into my chair, happily cocooned by nutmeg and cinnamon in a kitchen where steamy windows blocked out the darkness. Drowsiness lulled me into forming impertinent unasked questions.

Felix hovered above me like a full moon. "Seduction comes at a price," he purred. "You're deeply in check. Your next move is caution. Do nothing rash."

His words popped me out of my comfort zone. I kept my gaze riveted on my shoes.

Catcher studied my face, and Jakobina eavesdropped from the ceiling at odd moments just to be ghostlike.

In any event, Catcher read my mind and I breezed along behind him like a kite.

"There are stages of dreaming throughout life," Catcher began, pouring a heavy dollop of cream in his coffee. He raised the jug towards me. I covered my cup with my hand as a shorthand, none for me thanks. "Right now, at your age, let's call it the 'age of incandescence'," he said pointedly. "You are in your prime for dreaming. Consider this: dreams are your reward for a life of dedication."

Jakobina snickered unkindly and disappeared. Suddenly I had to inspect a fingernail. "To what?"

"To finding this place. Do you suppose it materialized for you? It did not. It's been standing here uninhabited for most of your adult life."

My face froze with embarrassment.

"You see, you do listen to the silence when it counts."

"Am I dreaming this? Am I dreaming Jakobina?"

"Not every dream requires sleeping. Moving here was a dream. Meeting me was another. What you dream tonight is something else again. You've been carrying an important dream around for years. It's in your eyes. That is to say, the pearls in your eyes tell me a great deal. For you, dreams are a vital part of your creative life."

"You can tell all that from eyes?"

"So can you."

"Is this your subtle way of telling me…" I stopped, my words took a right turn. "Am I going to die?"

"Sleep is not dying. It's playing. And you're not immortal…yet, so eventually, yes."

I leaned forward and stared point blank. "Are you? Sorry, I don't mean to be rude, but I have to ask. Are you Death?"

Hot milk hissed down the side of an unattended saucepan behind us. Jakobina was gone again. I moved the pan and turned off the burner. The comforting smell of scalded milk filled the room, innocent as childhood. Milk made the kitchen safe. Thoughts of death evaporated. It occurred to me that the hiss may have come from Felix.

Catcher leant back to re-establish the optimum space between us and assessed me. At least he didn't laugh. I imagined he was looking me over for signs of guts or fear before he answered. There were things about him that I found endearing. Diplomacy aside, he was going to tell it to me straight. I could be rattled afterwards. Right now, saving face was my best case scenario. "It's okay if you are," I added quickly. "Someone has to be."

"You'd think so, but that's not the way it works."

"Another ghost then?"

"A ghost who seduces cats and dogs and goddesses in the light of day." He tipped an invisible hat. "Pleased to make your acquaintance."

I didn't care for his tone. "Tosser."

His grey head dipped in deference. "No, it's Catcher."

I was a willful child being reprimanded by a kind uncle. I inclined my head as gracefully as I could and checked the ceiling for ectoplasm. It was clear. "Touché"

"I have a question," I whispered, nodding imperceptibly to the ceiling. "It's sensitive. Rather tricky if we're, you know, not alone."

Catcher checked the ceiling too and shifted forward in his chair. "Ask away, McDuff."

I stared at his chin, coward that I was. His eyes were too… pearly.

"I'm on the edge of my seat," he said looking remarkably calm.

"Do ghosts sleep?"

"All the time."

"Is it possible to wake them up?"

"They are the quintessential embodiment of lucid dreaming."

"Is that a no?"

"They pretty much wake *you* up."

"Will you be leaving soon?"

"Maybe I'm not really here," he said.

"Maybe this island is the Bermuda Triangle of lost causes."

Catcher grinned. "Now you're thinking with your heart. Well done, but it's lost sheep, not causes."

"I had a nightmare last night where I was being assimilated by the Borg. You know, those cyborg things on Star Trek."

"I know Star Trek well. It's always a good reference. Did you think to ask them why?"

"Never crossed my mind."

He scratched his chin and lifted his eyes to the empty ceiling. "Let's see," he said acting coy. "The Borg travel in a cube, do they not? A cube can also be a box. Have you opened a can of worms lately? A box, perchance with a castle on the lid?"

"Jakobina told you."

His shrug said of course she did. "Aurelia, always confront the Borg. They're creampuffs in scary clothing. Call their bluff. And continue to think with your heart, Bo Peep."

I shivered and reached for Canary's collar. Felix issued a faint hiss that sounded like another overflow of hot milk. The lingering smell of burnt milk comforted me a second time.

"You've gone quite pale," Catcher said. "It's no use crying over spilled milk."

"Are you assimilating me?"

He grinned his most devasting grin. "I thought you'd never ask."

I risked looking a fool and revealed a truth while we were alone. "I've always been afraid of dying."

Catcher patted my hand like a grandfather. "My dear sweet child, you've been afraid of *living*."

Pow! A low blow to the stomach.

"Dreams will take you," he said. "Deposit you. I predict you will experience extrasensory dreams as you 'open' your mind. Not to worry, they're teaching dreams. My advice is to, quite literally, rest assured. Close your eyes on a well spent hour. Shakespeare was right: *'For in that sleep of death what dreams may come.'* And now I must head off into the…" He looked at his bare wrist as if a watch were there. "Well, it's way past sunset, so a starry walk. My car is down the beach a ways at Mermaids Point." By now he had long since unrolled his trouser legs and donned his shoes. He pulled a grey windbreaker from his pack. "I came prepared," he said, shaking it out and holding it out for inspection. "But not usually for so delightful a surprise as meeting a kindred spirit."

I grabbed my coat. "I'll walk you to the beach." I felt like a wistful schoolgirl with a crush.

When we reached the last sand dune, Catcher sat down without warning. He patted the sand next to him as an invitation. "Join me," he said. "Sit. There's no need to be wistful. *Wish*ful is better. Wishful thinking is dreaming with your eyes open. Powerful stuff. Keep your castle box open and your eyes on the prize."

My voice was that of an insecure teenager. "Will you build me another castle?" I asked, unexpectedly shy. "Please," I added with a degree of cunning that embarrassed me.

Catcher rose and brushed the sand from his pantlegs. "Mi casa su casa," he said with a formal bow. "My castles are your castles, my lady. Thank you for supper… and by the way, I'm not a hypnotist, or at least I try not to be."

Canary followed Catcher a few yards down the beach before loping back to me. "Goodnight sweet prince," I called out and wondered at my audacity, thankful the darkness covered my mortification. *For heaven's sake. Get a grip.*

I felt Catcher smiling in the dark. "May flights of angels sing thee to thy rest," he called back.

My mind was a beehive of questions. He'd lied. There were no cars allowed on this island apart from mine.

"Careful," he shouted. "Thoughts can sting."

"When will I see you again?"

Catcher was too far away to see me turn for home but his answer arrived all the same. "You'll see me in your dreams," he whispered inside my head.

"Immortality is overrated," a different voice said accompanied by ticking sounds. It was my old friend, Felix. "Nice job being cautious."

I made my way home, absentmindedly brooding about the ways a human may be stung.

Jakobina's eyes were wider than usual when she saw me. "What's wrong?"

I hung up my coat and headed for the bathroom medicine cabinet. Jakobina met me at the head of the stairs. Without thinking, I walked through her.

"Aurelia? I asked you a question."

I wasn't surprised that she stared at me from the mirror over the sink. She was behind me, but when I turned around she'd already moved into the hall. I rattled a bottle of pain killers in her direction, and pointedly walked around her in a wide curve. "You needn't look so worried," I told her. "I have a splitting headache, that's all. I'm going straight to bed."

chapter 34
RAGGED CLAWS

The dream arrived the moment I closed my eyes. The ocean at midday shimmered with heat. The sand was too hot for my bare feet. Catcher stood, backlit by the sun so his voice issued from the center of a halo. I remembered his advice about the Borg and confronted him directly even though I couldn't see his face.

His voice echoed around me as he misquoted T.S. Eliot to make a point. "And so we speak then, in *ironic* pentameter, you and I, traipsing the beach – *a pair of ragged claws scuttling across the floors of ancient seas.*"

Jakobina appeared at my side. "Jakobina," I said. "This is Catcher. Catcher, I'd like you to meet Jakobina."

"Charmed," he said, winking at one or both of us. But it seemed it was for Jakobina who squirmed beside me, bubbling with joy.

Catcher's eyes found mine. He raised his eyebrows. "Shall you continue to measure out your small life with coffee spoons, Aurelia?"

I folded my arms and widened my stance to appear confrontational. "Okay, you can stop now. The T.S. Eliot ploy is getting a little old." The sand burned my feet.

He smiled at me with great sadness. "Say it. Ask it. You know you want to."

The sand was blistering. I tried to copy Jakobina's innocent expression but my eyebrows arched of their own accord in pain. "Well?"

"Tell me," Catcher demanded.

I stood my ground. "There's no need to bellow."

Catcher was suddenly beside me, and we three unlikely friends walked arm-in-arm towards the castle. He nudged my elbow. "C'mon, woman, a stranger appears on your doorstep with all the bells and whistles of a god and you have no questions? At least be honest with me."

I stared madly at nothing and everything. I felt like Felix, my eyes bulging, searching the beach for an escape.

"Let me help you, then," he said in a conciliatory tone. "Who am I? Why am I here? What's going on? Are you safe? But that's not it, is it?"

"That'll do," Jakobina said. "She doesn't have to know everything at once."

"Aurelia," Catcher said. "You're safe as houses… safer in fact. You're safe as castles. Safe as a library on a rainy day. I'm here to save you because I know your future and if left to itself it's a tad grim. It's what I do. I'm here now because there's still time."

I dropped Jakobina's arm and dismissed her. "I need the beach," I said. "I'll see you back at the house." Amazingly, she complied.

I faced my inquisitor.

"Ready to spill?" he asked without opening his mouth.

"Ketchup," I said hoping to sound offhand.

He laughed. "Ah… the macaroni and cheese. You're referring to the question on your plate."

I turned my back on Catcher, faced the horizon, and asked the water what I needed to know. "Not long ago, I took a trip back to high school. It was spontaneous. Wonderful. Creepy wonderful. I was seventeen again. The friends from my old astronomy club materialized moments later as seniors in wheelchairs. And I don't mean high school seniors. They were ancient and feeble. I'd been home, and then… zap, I was there. It's going to happen again, isn't it? I'm going to get lost in the past. The dementia is happening. Am I right?"

Catcher took a long time to answer. I figured he was working out a compassionate way to say yes.

"Time-slipping runs parallel to dementia," he said. It can briefly intersect, but in your case it's a healthy time-sensitive gift. You are calling someone to make amends. It's a miraculous door that opens when …"

A sudden chill made me shiver uncontrollably. I saw the circle with its open door from the day of the box. "And the old ones? Literally, my *old* friends."

"They heard your call from the future. I don't want to alarm you, but the hospice where they await death is only two years from here. You are their teacher as I am yours, if, that is, you choose to do the work. Do you want to play? Do you want to honor your life?"

"And if I don't?"

"Your grief and guilt will consume your gift, you will join your chums, and deteriorate into dementia."

"Does Jakobina know?"

"Absolutely."

"So, then it's true. I *am* batshit crazy."

That night the universe sent me a dream of Zee. We were seventeen. I told him, as I never had in life, that I loved him, and as the song goes, we sealed it with a kiss. It was going to be a long lonely summer.

I wanted to play.

SCHOOL DAZE

To begin is half the work,
let half still remain;
again begin this,
and thou wilt have finished.
— Marcus Aurelius

chapter 35
REMOTELY POSSIBLE

– September 1 –
2019

Like the good old days, school term begins on September 1st. It's the first day of what I call 'Catching-Up' School.

Catcher chose my blue glass sanctuary as our classroom. He calls it Fishbowl University, and, to be curmudgeonly, I dub it FU for short. Felix audits the lessons. He's my study partner and, as always, a teacher in his own right. Jakobina flits around phantom-like, obsessed with Catcher.

Lessons end with a Q&A session Catcher refers to as housekeeping. When he assumes a meditative pose and closes his eyes, it's my signal. I wait for his nod that indicates the floor is mine.

I honor day one with a blunt question. "What's all this time slipping for?"

Catcher opens one eye. "Consider it a birthday present," he says and closes it again. "You asked for a second childhood. Now, I have a follow up question. What are you going to do with your gift of time?"

Disconcerting as it is, I address a pair of closed eyes after I make a rude face. "Just to clarify, by second childhood, I meant being seventeen and falling in love with Zee again, but with an added happy-ever-after clause."

Catcher opens both eyes and looks skyward with a sigh. "Aurelia, if I've been vague, forgive me but I've intervened at the eleventh hour of your life to awaken your senses for a far greater purpose than regret. Wishing isn't magic. You made a conscious wish and were put out because it didn't appear exactly as ordered. Disappointment is the essence of wishing. No wish comes true in the way one hopes. Dreaming is different. Dreams are active creations where the outcome is yours. I hate to burst your fairy tale, Aurelia, but if you don't know it already, may I remind you that I have a low tolerance for whinging."

"I was merely restating my case."

"As for childhood, may I also remind you that you were far too intelligent to fall for nonsense. You were above such rot as happy-ever-afters. Time slipping is not a game. You are not a *case*."

"Jakobina has played with my mind for years."

He pinned me with a cold stare. "I won't coddle you and I will only drag you so far. Make no mistake, the success of your mission rests entirely on you. If you don't believe me, believe in your namesake. What would Aurelius do? Mourn the past or embrace the future, warts and all?"

"You seem to forget that I've watched Jakobina obsess over her past for fifty years."

"Jakobina singled you out against the rules, and she's paying for her mistake. It sometimes makes her… short tempered."

"Sometimes?"

"Prattling about lost love is your prerogative but it's a waste of time. It's a luxury you can no longer afford. Feeling sorry for yourself is unworthy of a warrior. Walk back from failure because there *is* a way back. There is a window. I'm here to give you that chance. It's not complicated but it will take perseverance. The truth is, all you have to do is dream. Seven words to live by. Please memorize them."

"I'll need more than one window," I say in a huff. "Virgil used to say there were always doors."

Catcher checks the clock and dismisses me even more coldly, like a master to a servant. He stretches back in his chair, arms behind his head, and closes his eyes. "That's it for today." He waves an arm in my general direction like a king in a carriage. I curtsy well out of his line of vision.

He's not done. He disarms me with another casual one-eyed glare. "Be a dear and make us a pot of tea and a plate of sandwiches before you go live your dream. Black Forest ham, I think. With mango chutney and a couple of devilled eggs. And there's no need to curtsy. You're not invisible. Are there any strawberries left?"

Day two. Fishbowl University is in session.

Catcher and I sit facing each other across the breakfast table in wicker peacock chairs. My chair dwarfs me. Catcher should be wearing Jakobina's turban because he resembles a grand poohbah, in his.

Sunbeams filtered through cobalt glass dapple the walls and floor with blue patches of moving light that resemble the living surface of the Pacific Ocean. Canary lies sprawled on her side, snoring on a tile seabed.

Catcher stares into me as if I'm a crystal ball. His voice dips low. "You have to dream with a purpose. What do you want? Don't tell me your hopes. Give me your dreams."

His question is charged. I feel a frown forming and bile rising in my throat. "No pressure," he says. "There are no wrong answers, but there *are* slipshod ones. Don't overthink, Aurelia. Trust yourself."

I can't be sure if it's Catcher or Felix speaking. I am face-to-face with an impatient genie, fresh out of his bottle where every word counts as a gold star or a landmine.

I hold my breath and search the blue glass wall for the best answer. The wicker creaks as I shift in my chair. Canary whines.

The room drops like an elevator. My voice stays stuck to the ceiling as I fall. This may be death. My words float like lazy soap bubbles and break one by one. "I want to make it right with Zee. I want him to know that I left to save him from my future insanity. I want to die a natural death when it's my time. I want to be freed from Jakobina's selfish curse"

Canary's bark breaks the silence like a gunshot. Felix may have gone mad because he cuckoos three times. In the silent aftermath of a crowing clock the laws of gravity connect my body and brain. I am emboldened to eclipse Catcher's pearly eyes with renewed purpose. "And I absolutely *don't* want to disappear into a painting. Ever."

Catcher's creaky chair echoes mine as he leans back and presses his fingers together. He looks as if he's praying. He clears his throat. "Aging is threefold and then some," he begins. "There's intellectual aging and psychic aging. Some of these touch the nuances of maturity. Your biggest hurdle is love and guilt. Physical aging is a third dimension. Your mirror is your guide in that department."

"There are departments?"

"Classrooms… fields." Again, a wave of his hand dismisses my ignorance. "Experiences in which to absorb the basics of human chemistry. When I was a student, I majored in human chemistry. Love, for example, is a simplistic chain reaction. For our purposes we will consider it purely chemical. It's a lot like aging, only faster."

As he speaks I doodle hearts and the name Zee in my notebook like an adolescent girl. "And to think you caught me with poetry. So, what's *my* major Professor Hydrogen?"

"Extracurricular activities. Fishbowl University could be a rejuvenating spa if you avail yourself."

"Perfect. Maybe I'll learn how to cure my insomnia."

"Counting sheep never works. Sleep counts you. Ask Felix."

My pen spins to the floor where Punch pounces on it. I'm betrayed. "Felix talks to *you* about me?"

"No, but you record your conversations and turn them over all day long as if they were compost… which in fact, they are."

I check the wall. Felix's eyes are closed in meditation. His tail is still. He's smiling, Cheshire-like.

"My privacy means nothing, then. I'm an open book to you."

"You need to be mindful if you want to keep secrets," Catcher says. "Don't play me, Aurelia. You don't have insomnia. Now, please retrieve your pen and open your mind to page one."

.   .   .

Catcher approaches from the boulders at the end of the beach. Even at this distance I can tell he's striding purposefully. I imagine a huge question mark hovering over his head. There is no cheery wave hello. He stops abruptly, five feet in front of me, feet apart, his forehead creased, laugh lines erased, his arms crossed. There's no lovely-to-see-you hug for me. No ear ruffling for Canary. He removes a tiny earbud from his ear. The strains of a sixties love song drift into the sunshine: *'whenever I want you all I have to do is dream,'* "You have a question for me?" He delivers it like an accusation. His eyebrows raise the stakes. They clearly message 'go on then, I haven't got all day'.

"Nice to see you, too."

"What's up, Bo Peep?" he opens testily. "Times a wasting."

"I didn't see you in my dreams last night. You lied to me."

His smile is dismissive and lasts only a second. "It doesn't matter. I saw you." His smugness widens into a grimace. "Sometimes, to be effective, a teacher has to lie."

"You can be a right bastard."

He shrugs, "no need to thank me." Canary barks once. A sharp reprimand of her presence engages Catcher's 'dogs first' protocol. "Hey, little bird," he sweet-talks, bending down. "How is my favorite gas detector this morning?" He fishes an evil smelling dog treat from his jacket pocket. "I didn't forget you." He looks up at me as Canary wrestles the chewy treat down her throat. "Fake bacon," Catcher says with an apologetic shrug. He waves another dog treat at me. "I haven't had breakfast yet, you want some? It looks like beef jerky. Maybe it's tasty." Canary snatches it before I can say F.U.

Catcher is my friend again but he's clearly vexed. "You kept me up all night," he says. "Spill."

I think better of complaining, so I straighten my back and address him as if reading the phonebook. "Am I an ancient teenager or an infantile crone? Or simply some retrograde adult you feel sorry for? If I want you to go, will you go?"

Catcher claps his hands. "Bravo, my child. My little rising star. My ancient newborn wunderkind. I'm pleased you're now on your toes and reaching for the stars."

My response "Will I grow up to be a swan?" erases his smile.

"You're asking me, yet again, if the world is safe."

"This ride we're on, traveling at the speed of dreams… is it just me? Or have I gone completely doolally? Will I require a special pair of straightjacket pyjamas?"

Catcher licks his index finger and tests the wind. "You're okay for a little while longer."

Says the headmaster dripping with sarcasm. I say to myself. *Throw that teacher an apple.*

"I simply meant to reassure you, Miss Wise-apple, that your hands have never been, nor will ever be, tied."

"I told you I want to play."

"And I heard you, but next is a relative term. We're leapfrogging. Surfing." He stares at my blank expression. "No need to thank me. It's an inexact science. It's a threadbare ride on a bumpy carpet."

I return, eyes narrowed. "Not even a hint?"

Canary's overexcited yapping at the waves distracts us. We both turn to watch her attack the sea. Catcher remains focused on the sea battle and delivers a sideways comment from the clear blue sky, clearly meant to shock me, and it does. "By the way, Zee sends his regards."

"You're full of surprises," I reply, hoping to disguise my surprise. "I dreamed of Zee last night. So, technically, I only just left him… relatively speaking, that is."

Catcher's next accusation is almost drowned out by the commotion of several seagulls diving at Canary. He tosses his words out to sea, carelessly, on the back of a deep sigh. "Why didn't you tell him you loved him?" I heard his unsaid words skip over the surface of the water like a flat pebble. *Why don't women ever learn… learn…learn*

I fixate on Catcher's beautiful profile. "It was only a dream. And you're not to tell Zee about Jakobina." I tug his sleeve. "Promise me."

He waves his arms at the gulls like a magician without a wand. "Canary. Come here, girl. You can't outwit seagulls with a display of false bravado." He looks askance at me, all handsome with his hair flying like a halo and hits me with "Zee already knows. He's always known."

. . .

Canary sniffs the wind and races ahead of us to examine a dead crab. Catcher takes off after her at a sprint.

"Hey," I call out, "no fair, I can't run with these feet," but amazingly, I can. The wind in my face is bracing. "I think I can fly," I shout over my shoulder as I pass Catcher.

"I think you can too," he shouts, and we were airborne. My first thought is that I've died. My soul has ejected free of my body.

Canary is below, barking, mad as a dervish. We circle her once and descend like floating leaves in an effortless landing.

I bend over to catch my breath. "Omigod. What just happened!"

"That was daydreaming with style. By the way, you never left the ground."

Canary pushes into me and I hug her neck. It seems an absurd afterthought, but I link a finger in her collar to keep myself from levitating again. "Of course we did. Canary saw us. Didn't you girl. This dream stuff is addictive. If all I have to do is dream, then, as the song goes, I want to dream my life away and die in my sleep."

"That would be extremely wasteful," Catcher says in my head. "I didn't come here to waste my time. Or, Zee's."

How we arrive in the kitchen without walking or flying is a mystery.

Felix's face shows 2:22. I pat the teapot. It's still warm. "I'll make a fresh brew, shall I?"

Catcher opens his mouth to reply but the phone jangles loudly from the hall, and cuts him off. The ring is so insistent I picture its receiver hopping off its cradle like a cartoon phone. Catcher pushes back his chair. "That's my cue," he says. "Must dash old thing." He salutes farewell and dashes before the third ring.

The receiver tingles hot in my hand. "Hello?" The world turns. The word hello crackles down a tunnel. I stand inside an echo chamber of dizzying hellos. Canary whines and sidles into me as the telephone receiver dematerializes in my hand.

chapter 36
HOSPITAL CORNERS

I arrive in the year 2020. Catcher is there to greet me in Avalon – the care home of no return. "You're almost a ghost," he says waggling a finger in my face. "As much as you'll ever be if you play your cards right. There are other plans for you if you're a good girl."

"If?"

"Just behave yourself." He refuses to say more.

I may have been there an entire month or two minutes. In any case, I left my ankles and bunions at the door because I float pain free above my vaporous shoes. An astral body means I can travel anywhere, fancy free, no longer footsore, kicking ass, Casper style, to a teenage time when I was too shy to say boo to a bunny rabbit.

My astronomy club classmates struggle with their unruly wheelchairs. They don't need them in retrograde high school but they're fighting it. I repeat Catcher's lesson. "Let go. You're trying too hard. Trust the wind to push you where you want to go. Be a wee zephyr. Skip over the years and play."

It's *not* Zen. It *is* Zen. Life is absolutely *nothing* like a bowl of cherries. I'm living a triple life. Past, present, and future. Some of the time I waste away in a world of hospice where my invisible toes struggle helplessly under white sheets, trapped between hospital-corners tight as a trampoline.

'Homeroom' in the Avalon is a stark dementia ward where starched nannies come and go in sensible shoes. My companions and I are elderly 'babies', diapered and powerless. A fitting homage, I'm sure, to rebirth. One of my favorite authors, Richard Bach, once named it marshmallow helpless, but perhaps he hasn't written those words yet. Time is slippery stuff.

That I live out of sequence is an understatement.

There are no comforting friezes of Beatrix Potter animals hanging on the walls of the seniors' nursery. No fluttering mobiles to keep us preoccupied. No television. For us, visual entertainment is limited to theatrical illusions of light playing on the white stucco ceiling that turn the shadows of texture lumps and bumps into faces if we are so inclined to connect a few dots. It's like seeing animal shapes in the clouds or a wintry landscape in the crumpled folds of our standard issue white sheets. If we gaze at anything of interest now, it's inward to revisit our memories.

But we have our own guru living down the hall a space. The nurses call him Doc because he was a Jungian psychiatrist when he was, dare I say it, alive, because he's wasting away in lucid twilight sleep, assuredly hastening towards death. But even in his comatose state, Doc's advice is down-to-earth wise. He reminds me of my bear, Virgil. Some nights I wake to find him watching me from the chair next to my bed. During those private visitations he stays silent… so there is some ironic connection to the words *vigil* and *Virgil*. I return the favor and drop by his room to chatter, citing my present dilemma, and read him poetry. The word present brings a smile to his face, so I know he hears me.

Since my last visit, an anonymous gift has mysteriously appeared above my headboard in the women's ward. A cheery dreamcatcher now watches over me, trying to impart a message. Its concentric circles of colored glass beads remind me of something important – strangely, *not* the circles of Dante's hell, but a mystical 'Stonehenge' woven in wool, semi-precious stones, and promises. The outer circle forms a bright necklace of ruby red glass dotted with garnet gemstones interwoven with beads of deepest burgundy. In turn, their darkness, is diffused with a sprinkle of cloudy grey moonstones which give way to a dazzling innermost circle of purest cobalt blue. A starburst of seed pearls leads the eye to a large single white pearl in the center. Dangling from the frame is a single feather from a yellow bird.

The night nurse I call Mouse, on account of her squeaky shoes and timid nature, comes in to tuck me in under covers that already seal me into a shroud. I must look like an Egyptian sarcophagus, lying there bound with a mouth that still has the freedom of speech.

"That's pretty," Nurse Mouse says spying the wall hanging while checking my urine bag.

"Yes," I reply. "It's a present from Doc." I wriggle beneath stone blankets. "Could you possibly loosen my blankets a little."

Mouse continues her night bustling and scribbles something on my chart. "Sweet dreams, young lady," she says at last and squeaks out the door.

I wait until her shoes squeak their way to the nurses lounge, and sneak into Doc's room to thank him for his gift. "I know it's from you," I say. "I remember telling you that my dreams were all over the place."

"Always remember to move towards your center," he replies. "The center will hold true if you keep it in sight."

Surely one's winter years needn't end in a heartless wasteland. I can think of no better reason for mentally escaping into the past than the alternative of lingering in a nightmare of mortification with minds sharp as tacks. It seems excessively harsh punishment for the crime of living past one's agility while remaining sentient. And so my chums and I lay as inert bundles of thought, needlessly swaddled into shrouds of submission until lights out.

As callous as the hospital is, it's obvious I have to be here in order to comply with Professor Control Freak's agenda. The harsh reality of helpless dependency is a powerful incentive to follow his orders. Visiting hours are lax considering we have no visitors. I only go places during lights out for a reason. The cafeteria episode was a test run.

Catcher says I have to puzzle it out. And that each trip is a single pearl on a double strand necklace in preparation for a big trip. He calls it graduation. He chuckles to himself and says he loves the irony. I have to puzzle that out too.

I miss Canary and Punch and my island. I've never been less interested in seeing Jakobina. Perhaps she's been exorcised and I'm free of her bondage. I live in hope to honor Virgil and Doc. It dawns on me that the yellow feather on the dreamcatcher is symbolic. It's from a canary.

chapter 37

VISITING HOURS

Felix time is 2:23. I've only been gone one minute. The telephone receiver is lying on the floor emitting a hellish busy signal. Felix's eyes look demonic and I can hear a distinct growling emanating from his clockworks. Canary is frantically emitting yips and yelps. My tape recorder and a few cassettes now occupy pride of place in the center of the kitchen table. Jakobina is pretending to wash dishes. The scent of lemon dishwashing liquid is stronger than usual. Heightened senses are a side-effect I've discovered after time-slipping. Light hurts my eyes. Sounds are sharp and dry. Olfactory nerves are working overtime. Time is disconnected. A lot can happen in one minute. I grip the edges of the table to anchor myself. Canary's whining fills my head.

Catcher casually pours afternoon tea. The tea gurgles into the cups. He pushes the sugar towards me. There is no preamble. I can tell from Catcher's half smile he's prepared for war. I feel the need to stand and flex my muscles, and try pacing but it's a ridiculous theatrical stunt, and I flounce back into my chair after a few rounds stomping about the room.

"So," I blurt in my most demanding tone. "What just happened. Where am I? On the scale of insanity, for instance? And where am I going… physically mentally sexually? I mean, is there a graph? Because I feel 'off the charts' pointless right now. So thanks for opening a can of boa constrictors. Worms not good enough for you, eh? Now what?"

"Go fishing, Cherie. Your hook is bated with juicy worms. But be mindful that in dreams, worms represent death."

Jakobina crashes the plates harder than necessary and mutters *take your sweet time, principessa*. Point taken. She would have reached Piet had she been given my opportunities. I am getting punier, disappearing like a bar of soap that gets smaller by the day. She turns and sends me a pitying glance with spikes. We have crossed the line of friendship to become real sisters who spar. Gone are the pleasantries of day-to-day companionship. The art of supporting and championing is well over. Compatibility has disappeared. And then she does just that. *Poof.* She disappears in a flood of pique and I see the Felix clock nudged sideways by an unseen hand.

"Don't you dare," I shout. "I like that clock. Nothing here belongs to you. Take your huffy molecules to the beach or better yet… begone spirit," which is melodramatically witchy even for me, given my worst mood swings of late. Catcher is mildly amused but his face darkens and the moment hops back to his lording it as teacher vs student in a powerplay I can't win. Time for a report card.

"Feel puny, dream puny, and puny you shall be," he says disdainfully.

I launch into the age-old "I'm all dressed up and nowhere to go approach" for sympathy. Is he done with me?

He picks up a cassette and deftly maneuvers it through the fingers of one hand the way a magician shows off his dexterity with a single playing card. "You won't get very far in your present condition."

"Well, that's my point. What exactly *is* my condition?"

"You're pregnant."

"Oh my god!"

He shakes his head. "Relax. Pregnant as in emotionally charged up. You really *do* need to stay calm. Now, state your highest truth."

I snivel like a spoiled child. "I want to be with Zee."

"So, give birth." He snaps the cassette into my player, clamps the headphones over my ears and presses play. A golden oldie fills my head… *'Do you think I have a lot to learn… should the teacher stand so near, my love. Graduation's almost here, my love, teach me tonight.'*

For I have known them all already,
Known them all:
Have known the evenings,
Mornings, afternoons,
I have measured out my life
With coffee spoons.
— T.S. ELIOT

chapter 38
COFFEE SPOONS

The Grail Café in Glastonbury was a charming surprise. I expected the standard kitsch of 'bistro-by-the-sea' restaurants the world over: tasteless mermaid décor of fishnets tangled with starfish and anchors hanging on walls. But it was a chic French tearoom with pale lavender walls displaying a half dozen small antique tables painted white, set with Victorian tablecloths, scalloped lace hems and all. Place settings of my favorite Blue Denmark china and creamy flower arrangements of peonies and freesia adorned the tables. Paintings of castles adorned the walls. Every table cleverly captured a view of the sea and exuded privacy. It radiated elegance with the nurturing silence of a library.

Catcher tapped a coffee spoon on my nose five times. One tap per word. "Never...*tap* … let...*tap* … it... *tap* … fade...*tap* … away...*tap*."

"What? I don't understand. Let what fade away?" But I *am* beginning to understand his wry smile – an endearing cross between amusement and smugness. "A falling star," he said. "Catch a falling star. Never let it fade away. You know… the one in your pocket."

I buried my nose in a white peony and breathed in its delectable fragrance. "You spy on me."

"I don't need to. You think very loudly."

"Never let IT fade away. Don't you mean me? Are you're referring to my lack of molecular stability? Can you see me right now?"

"In *living* color."

The emphasis on the word 'living' gave me goose bumps. "It's me isn't it? *I'm* the ghost and Jakobina is alive. I just can't figure out if I'm haunting myself or you."

"You are and always have been a figment of Hydrogen's imagination."

"Are you in my dream or am I in yours?"

He ducked his head, shyly. "We're dreaming the same dream."

"How often?"

"Enough."

"Enough is a bullshit answer, Professor Hydrogen."

Catcher smiled in agreement. I either amuse him or he enjoys being busted. "Okay, a lot."

"Are we doing it right now?"

He shrugged coyly. Too coyly for Catcher. A boyish shadow played across his face and disappeared quickly. He'd gone 'dark side of the moon', so I couldn't tell if he was pleased with my brilliant perception or he was dismissing me as a child who asked too many questions. I expected him to tell me to go to my room for a time-out. Not a bad idea, really... under the circumstances. Maybe he considers me a sad excuse for a student. Maybe I think he's a too much of a smartarse for a teacher. In any case, there was an uncomfortable lull in the conversation.

"It's just a bit of moon madness," he said, serious now. "The moon affects the tides within us. But you know all that." He shook off his mood and smiled mischievously, his spoon poised in a question mark, over his newly arrived crème brûle. The lull dissipated with Catcher's enthusiastic foray into custard. The bright chime of silverware against china serenades us.

It was our regular Saturday morning ritual in Glastonbury. Rich desserts for breakfast followed by strong espresso. This morning, sugar gave me the Dutch courage to recount Friday night's strange dream fragments in the hope of a brilliantly logical explanation. Catcher seemed unusually remote, which I put down to his scholarly mind assessing the deep meaning within the dream that eluded me. I needn't have worried. "You should try this," he said, after his first mouthful, sidestepping my issue, "runs circles around that cinnamon bun of yours."

I licked sticky white icing from my fingers, exasperated. "CATCHER. For heaven's sake. I *dreamed* I was a *chair*. Or was I a pair of shoes?... Maybe I was Cinderella. I don't know. It's all a bit of a muddle. But it makes no sense."

He corrected me. "You mean you thought it was *non*sense. Dreams have to be nonsensical to break the barriers of human logic. Tis the nature of lucid dream-sharing. And... it depends what kind of chair."

I expected no less from a teacher who dropped puzzles on my plate before breakfast.

"Life is a puzzle," he said, dipping his spoon into the caramel crust. He waved it as he spoke. "When is a chair simply a chair? When is a chair something else entirely? When are you, you? When are you not you?" I followed Catcher's spoon with my eyes, deliberately avoiding his gaze before remembering that repetitive spoon swinging may be the ploy of a hypnotist. "Dreams make perfect sense if you know how to interpret them," he said.

I blinked and rubbed my eyes. "I'd have thought that would make them more difficult to understand?"

He shook his head at my ignorance. "Dear Bo Peep, your sleeping brain is a professor of poetry," he said as if I were a numpty. The spoon stopped and pointed at me. "Your mastermind is a genius philosopher."

"What? So, when I'm awake, I'm a dunce?" I clattered my cup a little too hard onto the saucer and slopped a dark coffee stain onto the white tablecloth. "Is that it?"

His forehead crinkled disconcertedly as I blotted the stain with a napkin folded into a fan. Slowly, he savored another spoonful of dessert, wiped his mouth with annoying meticulousness, and folded his napkin into a perfect triangle at right angles to his coffee spoon. "Yes."

I resisted the urge to growl. "Not even, *maybe*?"

A moment of silence stretched while he sipped his steaming coffee. "No," he declared over the rim. It reminds me of the stoic conversations between my parents. Dad behind his newspaper and Mum adding a spoon of sugar to her tea each time she was dismissed.

"Wait. I remember something. I *was* Cinderella but I turned *into* a chair."

His eyes closed briefly. It's hard to tell if he's still off in dessert heaven, experiencing the perfection of coffee and dessert at seven a.m. or being superior. I decide on superior before he speaks.

He pushed his bowl an inch towards me. "*Aaaah,*" he said, eyes heavenward. Is he commenting on sugary bliss, tempting me with an invitation to taste, or has he arrived at a satisfying conclusion? Is it all a tease? Is he testing me again?

I pretended it was an invitation, leaned across the table, and dove into the dregs of his dessert with my coffee spoon. "You're infuriating." The moment the sweetness hit my tongue I closed my eyes. Bliss. "Okay, you're not completely smug. And don't you dare…"

But he was ahead of me. He winked and tapped the side of a water glass as if to ask for quiet in order to announce a speech.

I finished my thought anyway. "…wink at me."

He waggled the empty spoon at me. "Go home, write your dream as if it's a short story. You must read it aloud so you can hear it. Then, we'll talk."

I ordered a crème Brule from the passing waitress for myself. "And what, pray tell, will that accomplish?"

"Two things. One: You will remember subsequent dreams more easily. And two: Your daytime poet will engage. Think of it as a writing prompt. Dreams are not only puzzles, they're muses. You dreamed an exceptionally important dream, Madam Peep. One too good to dismiss as the aftereffects of bad clams. And you have to decode it yourself."

I opened my mouth to contradict him. Always a pointless gesture. I've not eaten clams for a week. But he knows this as we eat all our meals together.

I patted my purse. "The deed, tis already done. It's in here."

"Well, what're we waiting for. It's performance time. But not here. A formal read requires the blue classroom." He waved to the waitress and ordered a cinnamon bun to make me crazy.

"FU," I said, delighted that my words made him choke on his coffee.

Gentility eclipsed, Catcher wiped his mouth and his shirtfront with a napkin. "Indeed," he spluttered. The coffee stain I'd made on the tablecloth was gone.

chapter 39
EXISTENTIAL CHAIRS

Back in the blue classroom I pulled a baby starfish from my pocket. "I forgot I had this," I lied, and placed it on the window sill.

Catcher pushed back his chair and stared past the starfish with his hands behind his back. "Read it to me again," he said. He scowled over his shoulder, briefly. "And this time be the listener and recall the images. Don't embellish or stop."

I glared at him, cleared my throat and began. "These are first impressions from me and not me," I said.

It's midnight. The moon is full. It hangs in the sky, ticking like a clock. It has eyes where the numbers eleven and two should be, and a black tail. Moonlight outlines an Adirondack chair at the far end of the beach, left by a parallel me. It sits like an oasis, calling from the desert. I have to reach it before the stars go out. I am exhausted. Thirsty. My feet are bleeding from wearing blue glass slippers.

I touched the cobalt vase nearest me. "This color," I said.

I cast them off and crawl. I have to wriggle, pulling myself along by my elbows. The chair's skin is blistered and peeling from previous lifetimes as burnt orange, canary yellow, lime green and electric lighthouse blue. I hear the words 'aging gracefully'.

I took a breath and checked Catcher's face for boredom. It showed. Even I could tell I was in a trance.

The chair has the look of well-worn humility… weather-wise from decades of unforgiving sun and sea. She wants it but more importantly, the chair wants her. An auctioneer's voice shouts going, going, gone – to the lady in the ruby slippers!

. . .

I shook off the trance. The dream was like a self-addressed postcard I'd sent myself. "Wish you were here," I said out loud.

"No," Catcher countered. "You wish you were somewhere else entirely. Where Aurelia? Where do you want to be?"

I ignored him and continued to read.

The chair has seen decades of unforgiving sun and sea. Then, my position changes, and I'm on a widow's walk, looking down at the beach from the crenellated rooftop of Tintagel Cottage.

I'm a giant. I reach down and pick up the chair. When I have it in my hand I return to normal size. The chair is a miniature, scaled for a dolls house. I scan the empty horizon, and find solace in the fact that my husband and his ship lie at the bottom of the sea.

And then, I'm back on the sand. Crawling towards the chair where another me, sits like a queen on a throne. A doppelgänger. All around her is a gathering of translucent people. Not milling, but waiting for me. Old friends. It's dark but a pathway of glowing starfish light the way. A voice says 'follow the 'yellow brick road. You know you want to '.

The throne is empty when I reach it. I heave myself to sit upright at last, melding the chair's creaking body to mine, with the sloping curve of wooden vertebrae slats supporting the physical weight of my body. My spinal fluids flow into the chair's dry back and tired posts and aching legs, nourishing us both, sending strong shoots down through wood and soil into the damp heart of earth's core. I lean contentedly, pain free, supported against its fan back, the shape of a wooden peacock's tail, and fall asleep.

A narrator says "A deep tiredness envelops her. The surf washes the bunions from her blistered feet. She sleeps the purity of sweet baby sleep in a cradle gently rocking in a swell of water, adrift in a tiny bobbing rowboat. A line of rope plays out to the castle like an umbilical cord tied securely to a dock. Anchored. Securely berthed."

.   .   .

I open fresh eyes and notice the vast distance I have come from the trail of bloodstained footprints ending at the bottom rung of a ladder to the moon – a clock face with roving cat eyes and a metronome tail, keeping time. It hangs in the sky like a constellation. Stars pick out the points of its ears, eyes, and tail. The chair looms mountainous. I am ant-sized. Love vibrates my atoms into jelly, disintegrating a choking tumor of granite into powdery sand particles that have clogged my throat as long as I can remember. A grain of sand lodges in each eye and I cry pearls. I click my heels together and disappear – a human star going nova. I hear the moon purring. The blackness of space is a welcome blanket. I curl my tail over my eyes and cat nap.

That's it. I lowered the paper and waited. Nothing. I rattled the paper for attention. The Felix Clock ticked slower than a melting glacier. I mentally counted the swings of his black tail to ten. His bulbus cartoon eyeballs moved from side-to-side giving the impression they were looking from me to Catcher in a game of slow motion ping pong.

"Eleven," I blurted out. "Hello? Earth to Catcher."

Catcher faced me, his anxious student in the front row of our fishbowl classroom – a professor with a window behind him in place of a blackboard. "The 'First Person' is you, but … whose is that second voice? Who is 'she' and 'her'? Who is the parallel you?"

"I'm guessing, Jakobina?"

"Dreams are like flash cards. You're in grade one, learning a new alphabet. The language of the subconscious is elementary. Guileless. Children are fluent. Adults not so much. The universe delivers messages in a gestalt of nothingness with meaning." He flexed his arms like a magician about to deliver a nothing-up-his-sleeves trick and counted on his fingers. "Let's list the elements, shall we: Slippers: ruby red and blue glass, two lost girls – Dorothy looking for a way home. Cinderella in need of a prince. Red sea glass equals danger. Blue sea glass equals what, exceptional fortune? Which one of you is Dorothy? Who made a wish? And don't guess."

"Dorothy. No, Cinderella. No, both. I can be two people at the same time in a dream."

"Who was united with her mate and devastated? Whose time ran out at midnight?"

"Cinderella."

"What does midnight signify?"

"The bewitching hour. The last hour of the night. One's final hour. A spell running out of time. The midnight of life. A final lifetime… a cat's ninth life… oh, a cat clock. Felix was the moon." Felix smiled. His eyeballs rolled up and disappeared in his head.

"Pay attention to key words: lighthouse, peacock, red, blue, canary yellow, distressed, aging. "Are you aging gracefully? Whose nine lives?"

He inclined his head to the right. "Dorothy dearest," he said, staring into me. He inclined his head to the left. "Milady Cinderella, the point is, what does going home, meeting a prince, having a chance to shine, marriage, blue glass slippers, ruby slippers… and plain old bedroom slippers, for that matter, represent to you?"

I stared down at my ratty house slippers that had seen better days. My answer was clear. "Comfort and unrestricted freedom. Home sweet home. My very own castle. My dream home."

"Two girls in search of home, who require rescue," Felix prompted in my head.

I repeated his words smugly. "And two girls in search of home, who require rescue."

Catcher snapped his fingers in front of my eyes as if to wake a hypnotized patient. "When something is you and not you the message holds double power. You need to think the first thing that pops into your skull." He glared at Felix. "And please use your own words."

Felix's tail twitched angrily.

I shook my head. "I wasn't asleep."

"I beg to differ," Catcher said. He faced me, resting his chin on a cradle of his interlaced fingers, and raised his eyes to mine. "And what do you surmise from these choice tidbits? Give me your first answer."

"That I'm older than God?"

He shook his head in despair. "Okay, your second answer."

I blinked myopically, drawing a blank. "The existential nonsense about a chair being a chair means nothing."

He snapped his fingers again. "But, what does a chair mean to *you*?"

I shifted in my seat. "Comfort. A place to sit. Sitting."

He tapped his pen in time to Felix's ticking. "Play it through, woman. What does one sit for? Expand your thoughts. See your dream chair. What comes next?"

I looked around. The stones on the table take my eye. "Sitting at a table. Sitting at a desk."

Felix's tail was a blur. The pen drummed faster. "Think girl!"

"Sitting down, sitting pretty, sitting for a photograph. Oh... sitting for a portrait."

Catcher nodded. "That wasn't so hard was it."

He took a deep breath. "Anything ring a few bells about a *pearl*? Cells animating? Anything? Do you recall the creature that symbolizes reincarnation? Hint... it's a bird."

"The peacock...oh!"

"And berthed?"

I answered with some hesitation. "Parking a boat?"

His expression was almost comical. "You've missed the boat, Princess." His eyes squeezed shut. "Listen to the *sound* of the word. Close your eyes and you will *hear* it." He waited while I sat with my eyes scrunched into a puzzle. "And berthed sounds like?" he prompted. "Well?"

"Birthed," I answered, pleased with myself.

His mouth hung open for more. "And reincarnation is...?"

"Being born multiple times... oh! ReBIRTH."

"Atta girl. As a prize, I dare to deploy a new word for your further enlightenment. You may want to stand back for this one. He opened the kitchen door and exited to the porch, crooking his finger at me to follow.

Catcher's arms opened wide and theatrically embraced the afternoon. His scarf flapped wildly as if caught in a gale-force wind. Clouds scudding across the sky, made my head swim. Strangely, the treetops and dune grasses remained still. "FRONTERFÜHRING," he emoted with gusto. He turned to me, beaming. "It's a rather grand four letter word, is it not?"

The world stopped spinning. I broke the silence with my voice booming. "I guarantee T.S. never used it."

"My Empress Aurelia," he said bowing. "He most certainly would have if he'd known it. It means the sixth sense for intuiting the decisive point in a battle, and when your personal 'Battle of Camlann' reaches its turning point, you will have a decision to make. Go or stay. Think hard. Will your strategy be fight or flight?"

"It could go either way."

"Tomorrow's homework assignment is deceptively simple," Catcher said behind a solemn mask of tragedy. "I want you to remember everything about the last time you saw Zee. Make a list. Be prepared, old thing. I'm not kidding around. Time travel is a bumpy ride."

FAILING GRADES

chapter 40
HOMEWORK

Canary and I were late for Fishbowl University but our chilly walk on the beach awarded us several shards of blue sea glass that I triumphantly place on the breakfast table in a circle with the Zee Stone in the center. If it's possible for colors to emit a hum, a definite cobalt vibe jumpstarts a pleasant buzzing in my solar plexus. After a slurp at her water bowl, Canary flumps onto a large cushion with a sigh and leans her head on crossed paws. I brew a pot of tea, arrange paper and pens in a neat pile, and hunker down under a cozy shawl.

"All set?" Felix asks.

Today, Catcher is off chasing his own dreams. Felix is my substitute teacher. "How was the homework?" he says. "I gather by the smile on your face it was easy."

I pour my tea. "It was." The cream swirls into a hypnotizing whirlpool. I have to look away before I'm sucked in. I boldly help myself to three heaping spoons of sugar. Stirring tames the vortex into a calm brown sea.

Felix yawns a leisurely cat yawn. "Beware of easy, kiddo. Due diligence requires burning the midnight oil. *Remembering*, otherwise known as *memorizing*, is hard work. And go easy on that sugar."

I choose one of the blue shards and hold it up to the light. It flashes a cobalt wink. "I've done the math and decided to play along with Catcher's 'ride'," I say rather too casually. "So my answer is flight *and* fight. Wheels up at night, fly to high school, and fight Jakobina's insane death-by-painting idea during the day. It's an absolute no-go. I've decided to die *au naturelle* in my sleep and then haunt this castle for good measure. Night school is a better place to learn, anyway." I replace the glass stone. "This decision thing is a doddle."

Felix emits the ghastly sound of coughing up a hairball. He's being melodramatic to make a point. "Woah. Hold on there, Empress. That was NOT yesterday's assignment. You're jumping ahead, skipping an essential step necessary for making that big fronterführing decision of yours. Whatever you may think, Catcher's plan is not a done deal until you officially consent. Lucid dreaming is not a free 'ride'. I assure you, time travel is no place for sissies."

"Well, at least hear me out."

Felix twitches an ear towards me. "Aurelia, it's later than you think. There *is* such a thing as a trick question. Catcher is a trickster for all his positive mentoring. I warn you. Use your cat senses. Sleeping is fine if you keep one ear open for predators. It's the cat's way. We cats are survivors. We don't have that nine lives reputation for nothing. We are also natural Zen philosophers."

I don't wait for Felix's consent. "This is my reasoning," I blurt. "Dreaming takes up a third of a human's allotted lifetime which means I can spend a third of my daily ration, content to be living by the sea (which, by the way, is already a done deal); a third, daydreaming romantic thoughts; and a third, feeling loved in the movie I create in my dreamtime. By my calculations, dreaming my life away makes for a full and happy death. Who needs consciousness when it only brings regret and fear. Retreating into the half-life dither of old age seems a natural choice. Maybe it's all part of a compassionate plan." I sweep my hands together. "Done and dusted."

The room acts like an echo chamber. Felix's black plastic casing glows red. His ticking cracks like thunderclaps. I have to cover my ears. Felix holds up a paw like a stop sign. He looks like one of those mechanical waving cats you see all over Chinatown. He yowls and swears. We're deep in a cat fight. "I hate to tell you this, milady, but you've been dreaming up the wrong tree."

I wave my pen at him. "You can get as pissy as you want. My decision is still going to be the same."

His eyes narrow. "Hold that thought, dear heart, but don't tell Catcher… yet. If you dedicate yourself to small tasks and remain on the fence for a while you will earn my thunderous approval."

I walk over to Felix and shake his red plastic tail. "Deal."

He purrs, obviously pleased, and returns to his natural black plastic state. "Take your seat, replenish your tea, and settle down," he says, his eyes noticeably more bulbous than usual. "Today's lesson is inspired by the diaries of your friend Emperor Marcus Aurelius."

I groan inside without tangibly protesting and throw Felix a radiant smile. Felix's chuckle tells me that I'm being punished in spite of his catty grin. "Perfect," I reply. "I know all about him."

Felix counters quickly. We are sword fighting… pen to tail. "And I know all about *you*, so this will be easy-peasy. But whether you admit it or not, you're more than a smidgen overwhelmed by Catcher, which is good. By running into the fires of burnout like Marcus Aurelius, you will discover a great truth. Please write it a hundred times in your mind: THE OTHER SIDE OF AN EMERGENCY IS PURE EMERGENCE – a coming into the light. And by the way, the name Aurelius and its derivative, Aurelia, are spun from the Latin *'aureus'* which means golden light. Time travel is your literal chance to shine. Your initiation… or in this sense, your graduation. Consider it your very own coming out party, Goldilocks."

I make a performance of stirring three empty spoons into my sugarless tea, and murmur softly to myself. "With a short guest list."

Felix's cat senses hear everything. "Quality over quantity, dear heart. But sadly, wakefulness is much tougher than merely being awake. Please believe me, I'm mindful of your present limitations, but sweetie pie, you're seeking a breakout into that suppressed inner light of yours. It's called a spotlight… and you're the star of your dreams. Stardom is a bitch, but there it is. And, not to put too fine a point on it, living forever can be detri'*mental* to one's health."

Felix's whiskers twitch with benevolent pink sparks. His voice is soft. He oozes empathy. "Aurelia, be a good girl and tell the class what you know about the Emperor Marcus Aurelius. Please stand."

I am the room's only student, but I assume Felix is in character as a teacher, so I rise to the occasion with the Zee stone in my hand only to discover I've shrunk, small as a mouse, and stand inside the ring of blue stones on the table, which is disconcerting enough, considering my teacher is a cat, but what issues from my mind scares the hell out of me.

Felix intones like a sorcerer. "Sorry for the theatrics, Alice, but it's time you grew up."

Pow! Zoom! I'm regular size again, morphing through Wonderland. I consciously note that Alice had a stoned caterpillar for a teacher and mine is a sentient wiseass clock. Touché.

"I prefer the attribute time-sensitive, thank you very much," Felix coaches from far away. "Follow the sound of my ticking. We haven't got all day. You're late for a very important date. By the way, have you been paying attention to my eyes? What did you notice?"

"They grew larger. You were excited."

"What grew ?"

"Your pupils."

"And a pupil is?

"A student."

"Precisely, dear student. Let excitement be your guide. You're embarking on a quest. Feel the power of that statement. Emotion is your road to Zee."

The Zee stone is alive. Electric. My newfound wisdom is truly beyond me. My voice is unusually robotic without jitters. Very un-mouse-like. I'm strangely outside my body and aware I'm accessing a possible 'divine source' – I feel like a human dipstick plunged into a pot of gold.

"Aurelia's visual connections are strange but creative," Felix says as if recording his assessments of my thoughts into a tape recorder. Oh joy… a midterm report card.

I feel regal as I begin my speech. "Emperor Marcus Aurelius, circa 69 B.C., welcomed negative events like a long lost friend. In fact, he revered problems and believed that facing obstacles was essential to a successful life. Challenges, he proposed, led directly to victories, personal, political, and spiritual. In fact, he celebrated them."

Felix turns blue-black in the light. "Finally. It's about time. Aurelius was mindful that the art of living is a tireless act of picking up gauntlets and dropping a few of your own for good measure."

Rarely have I experienced owning a room as I did now in an aura of confidence, all grown up, brain cells pinging inside a bubble of cobalt energy. I list an epiphany of personal obstacles, one by one: "I used to think that time was my major obstacle but it isn't. Fears of death, the future, and losing are bigger obstacles. Guilt and shame are extreme factors that mean acceptance and forgiveness are two of my heaviest obstacles. But most importantly, Jakobina is an obstacle I can no longer ignore. She has to go. It's long past the time to crush our irresponsible pact."

Felix nods. "Eons past."

"I've always backed down from a fight. It's evident, now, that the only way to Zee is by fighting for him. And paradoxically, fighting to the death will lead to life. I am refreshed and eager to charge into battle."

"And?"

"Wakeup calls define our lives," I say. "We can choose to embrace each day even if it's a rude awakening. *Especially* if it's a rude awakening. We get to decide. Aurelius was a ferocious warrior. He treated every morning as if entering a battle."

Felix's jaw drops ever so slightly and closes with a lopsided Cheshire Cat grin. "Very good. Very good. Please note that I asked you to speak to an invisible crowd so you would hear *yourself*."

I continue, undaunted. "When one is bone deep in crisis, every hour contains a decisive fronterführing moment."

I am unstoppable atop my soapbox. "For better or worse, surrender is in my blood. My namesake, Marcus Aurelius, practiced the daily art of surrendering in order to fight like a man possessed. He was tenacious. I must fight like a woman possessed by a greedy ghost."

Felix's hands whirl around his face several times and point to midnight. "Possession is nine-tenths of the law," he exclaims with obvious glee. He's ticking so fast I fear he may fall off the wall. "Bravo, Eliza. I think you've got it," he says in the accent of a British aristocrat.

Catcher's unexpected voice issues from the doorway and startles me. "And Bravo Professor Higgins," he counters doffing an invisible hat to Felix.

I am fired up, surprisingly proud of my namesake, and face my mentor with a stream of newfound confidence. There's no stopping me. "Aurelius's philosophy states the shortest distance between two problems is acceptance. That the human lot is to rise above suffering by consistently practicing the art of salvation. It is our greatest accomplishment to be forever salvaged from the perpetual wreckage of the human condition. In fact, the truest meaning of reincarnation is surviving small deaths and starting over while still alive. Multiple cycles of birth and death are our internal ghost's victorious dance."

Punch strolls in and curls up on my abandoned chair. I know the rules. It's officially no longer *my* chair.

"And 'feline domestica' takes possession," Felix says smugly.

"One's own ghost is always alive inside us," I hear myself say. "Our personal ghosts know all about materializing to optimize the moment. It's our conscious job to get out of their way. We need to possess ourselves." Phew! Who is saying all this? Surely not the old, shriveled pawn, me. It can only be the me-of-me I met in my chair dream.

Felix crows like a cuckoo clock and Catcher's vigorous clapping stops my sermon. A bubble bursts. I am back to plain old me, flushed from a victory I didn't even fight. I pick up Punch and settle her on my knee. Her purr fills me with love. Canary snuffles Punch's fur and sneezes. I sit, on a Peacock throne chair, inwardly triumphant. I think I just scored an A+.

"Empress Aurelia, my fairest lady, I kneel before you a proud physics professor. Now we can proceed, you and I, to justify the end you seek through every means at hand." Catcher waggles a finger in my face. "Mind you, negotiating that maze won't be easy."

"Tell her," Felix booms. "She has a right to know."

Catcher inclines his head towards Felix. "Aurelia, this animated cat clock is your highest consciousness. Being truly catlike is wisdom twined with grace. But I implore you to recognize feline agility from sheer cattiness. Be mindful. Curiosity killed the cat."

"And my right to know is?"

"Some days it's best not to listen to me," Catcher says. "Listen to your instincts. Listen to a clock if that's easier, but listen with your cat senses engaged. Listen selectively. Be alert for predators. Listen as if your life depends on it. Because it does. I can't explain why. It will be clear later, but for now, trust me when I tell you NOT to trust me. There are times I am compelled to lie." He shrugs. "Even I don't know when."

I nod, speechless, and turn to Felix for help. And while my head is turned, Catcher leaves. The screen door slams. I see Catcher striding purposely towards the ocean, arm-in-arm with Jakobina.

"What the hell? Interfering bizzom!"

Felix's tail snaps in a whiplash of anger. "Look away. What you see is rarely the whole truth. Human deception is rife. People lie. Ghosts lie. We're dealing with a castle haunted with multiple personalities, a few of which are your own. You must decipher which ones to believe. I'm sorry it's complicated but unravelling the past is tricky. Timelines are as curved as space itself."

I remember Catcher's words from the day before: *tomorrow's homework assignment is deceptively simple.* "I can't always make him out. Some days he's *for* me and others it's as if he wants me to fail. Is he playing me? Is Catcher mentally ill? Is it a situation of the blind leading the blind?"

"Oh, dear girl. You've already sidestepped Catcher's words of wisdom, *curiosity killed the cat.* However, in answer to your questions, let's just say, Catcher is not himself lately. It's more like the farsighted leading the blindfolded. Neither of whom are you, Empress. Catcher is compelled to act two-faced for a reason. Believe me, he's perfectly stable but his agenda is, well, conflicted. Describing it as byzantine would not be an exaggeration. He's fighting his own war. And regardless of how his erratic tendencies impact your life, they are not your concern at this time. Stick to your purpose. Sidestepping is no longer an option. Face Jakobina. Look her in the eye and never deviate from the straightway to Zee."

"Easy for you to say, Professor Dante."

"Catcher doesn't mean to be deceitful but he's caught in a compromising set of circumstances of his own making, which means he is responsible for setting the whole fiasco right. Not unlike your own predicament."

"Wow. You really know how to hurt a girl."

Felix taps his tail against the wall. I'm reminded of a conductor addressing his orchestra. "Stand up to CATcher when it feels appropriate. Remember, a genius is always calculating a few chess moves ahead of his worthiest opponent."

"And that's me?"

"Catcher's worthiest opponent is himself. Obsession is his greatest obstacle. He's trapped in a precarious position, fighting himself."

The sun goes behind a cloud and turns the glass dark and forbidding. I cuddle deeper into the wool shawl that has slipped from my shoulders. "It's chilly in here. I could use a hug."

Felix's hands move to a horizontal position at a quarter to three. "That's the best I can do," he says.

His purr echoes inside me. I soak up the feeling of being treasured, and drink my tea which has surely grown cold, but it's as hot as the moment it was poured.

"Time is contrary," Felix says. "Tea doesn't always follow the rules."

Just as I feel the tension easing, Felix lets out a surprising roar for his size. He's a tiger hunting for a man to eat. "Mary Mary quite contrary, how will your garden grow?"

I think hard in order to please him. I want to remain his star pupil. "I guess it could do with a good weeding," I say.

"An understatement, Mistress Mary, the matter at hand is your own learning curve," Felix says. "It's an uphill climb and there's no time to dally. We will negotiate this mountain together, one second at a time. Yes?"

"Yes, Sir."

"Fantastic," he whispers with dripping sarcasm. "We have a lot to get through, so, let's move on, shall we. Your new assignment is to study the ways of engagement to reach your highest dream. Grab that weapon-like pen of yours. You may need to write these down. There are several ways to connect with Zee, and we start right now." He demonstrates by literally 'ticking them off a list' with his tail moving in time to each suggestion.

"*Tick*, automatic writing. *Tock*, meditation. *Tick*, visualization. *Tock*, writing Zee's name like a mantra. *Tick*, staring at the eyes in his photograph. *Tock*, becoming one with the sound of the surf. *Tick*, stargazing." His tail pauses mid-swing. "There are more but for now, seven lives is a good start." He yawns. His ticking stops. "It's time for my cat nap," he announces. "Class dismissed. You have homework to do."

He turns droll. His ticking stops abruptly. "There's no time like the present," he says. "Reality is the stuff of dreams."

chapter 41

NEGOTIATING THE CATWALK

I'm desperate to ask Catcher what Jakobina wanted, but confronting requires pinpoint timing. I wait for the optimum moment as he recounts Felix's list, adding his personal brand of color as we walk the midnight beach. His instruction is less lively and more formal. He's reaching for something profound, teaching with his eyes closed as if he's channeling a star. Canary lopes ahead confidently, so I'm safe from the tremors of a prospective earthquake. I am still on a report card high.

Catcher's eyes open briefly to glare at me. "Creative concentration," he states pointedly with pursed lips. He goes silent and resumes tapping some internal source. He finds what he's looking for and comes back. "Gentle focus is required at all times. Monitor your thoughts. Automatic writing works wonders. Guided and personal meditation trains the mind to be still. Stillness is a virtue, have it and life will never hurt you. Visualize the movies of your life when you and Zee were together. Observe him and yourself outside your body as a fly on the wall. Actions speak louder than words. Body language is an artform. Write Zee letters and burn them under the moon. Fill a notebook repeatedly with Zee's formal and nicknames written and printed in different colored inks." Now he's overreaching.

"That feels a lot like writing lines in detention," I say to break the ice.

Catcher nods but continues undaunted. There's no reward smile for my outburst.

"Sing Zee's name as a mantra, lose yourself in the eyes of his photograph until *he* blinks, recall the quality of his voice rather than what was said. Resonance is key. Emotional pitch is a magnetic force. Silent concentration is essential. Cuddle a purring cat. Hold the Zee stone during all of these breakthrough pathways and follow the sound of the surf under moonlight before retiring, and my personal favorite, stargazing… the time honored fallback of 'wishing on a star' – a ploy that works when you believe a thing is already true."

"Will there be an exam?"

He grunts a heavy sigh and ignores me. "Think of that internal ghost you mentioned so eloquently this morning as an invisible genie. Your wishes are its commands but it's a trickster by nature."

I give him a lopsided grin. "Like you, then."

Catcher remains impassive, picks up a smooth flat stone beside my foot and hands it to me. "This a serious lesson, Aurelia. Pay attention. Power always lies at your feet. Where did you think the Zee Stone came from? Zee imbued it with love, especially for you. That was really something, so show some respect. Be on guard, Queenie, you are in jeopardy at all times. We are about to play but it's no childish game. Chess is war. Love is a battle."

"Cats sleep 99% of the time," I say feebly, standing there pouting, reprimanded, a blubbering child, staring at the plain beach stone in the palm of my hand like it's going to bite.

Catcher takes the stone back and pitches it sideways over the water. "Cats tell lies too," he says, as it bounces off into the horizon, skipping all the way. He takes my shoulders and leans his forehead on mine. "Now, I'm going to leave you here with Canary. Stay a while. Sit and listen to the water. Write Zee's name in the sand. Talk to him. Remember, it's a casual chat, not a request. Above all, do *not* whine. Ask the moon a question, go home, and get a good sleep – 100% of the night." He wags a finger in my face. "Feral cats are awake 99% of the time. I hope you're up for a fight. Tomorrow, we play for keeps."

I believe him completely. In answer, Felix calls out 'white lies, if you don't mind,' in my head.

I ask the moon to watch over Zee. My sleep is deeply satisfying. I dream I'm wearing a graduation cap and gown as I accept a diploma from none other than Jakobina. I search the crowd for Zee. He's there in the front row, applauding, beaming up at me, sitting beside the seventeen-year-old version of me, holding Felix. She dissolves into tears and disappears with Felix. I wave to Zee as if I'm hailing the last taxi on earth.

Happily, Jakobina evaporates and Zee appears on stage at my side, extending his hand. He's transparent as a ghost. "May I have this dance," he says.

High school field trips require a note from a parent, and in true mentor fashion, Catcher opens his wallet and slaps a square of mauve card on the kitchen table. It's remarkably similar to the color of the sandcastle messages. The words HALL PASS are emblazoned on one side with the expiry date of January 1st, 2020. My name is embossed in gold on the reverse. It's far too snazzy to be official.

"You'll need this," Catcher says. "Use it wisely. It has unlimited privileges apart from the limited ones."

My excitement mushrooms into entitlement. I feel cheeky and give Catcher a cheap shot Brownie salute as I pocket the thing. My confidence is off the charts. Felix's warning that lucid dreaming is not a free ride, fails to dampen my spirits. I'm going back to school. I'm a kid in a candy store. I'm a helium balloon.

The magic pass is only a stage prop that disappears within the hour, but its message sticks. There are rules of compliance and I'm guessing serious consequences if I screw up. But I'm not a sissy. "I'm going back," I declare, somewhat hysterically. "I'm going back for Zee."

Catcher's expression is one of pity. "All the clichés and all the king's men couldn't put humpty together again," he says, with disdain.

"No problem," I announce. "I will dream my way back to him and wow him with science."

"Unwise, Miss Cheerleader," Catcher says. "Time slipping does not mean going backwards. Even dreams of the past progress forward. You must press on and dream new dreams."

I crash into a puddle of goo.

Catcher pats me on the head. "Not to worry, daring darling one," he says. "Zee will dream them too."

Joy deflated, I ask the elephant-under-the-carpet question. "Okay, what *are* the limitations of the fake hall pass? Please instruct me. Be kind."

Catcher takes my hand and pulls me to the door. "I think we need the beach," he says. I comply like a docile sleepwalker. Catcher drapes his arm about my shoulders and steers me towards the water. "For one thing, you can't blunder into the past willy-nilly. You must scout about when you arrive to determine an optimum moment when Zee is receptive. Use your time wisely. That 'fools rush in' thing is a real problem for you. Unlocking the past is precarious business. Restraint is your strongest key."

"How will I know if… when…?"

"Zee will react to your presence. He will appear to see you, but he likely won't."

"If he doesn't see me, what's the point?"

"You're stirring his memories. Letting him know how you feel. If you're successful he will respond as if in a trance. He may even catch a brief glimpse of you. You will be as a ghost to him. The rest is up to him. You must trust him."

"I'm being punished, aren't I? You lied to me. Time travel is cruel and senseless torture."

"Only as much as you believe you deserve. You have the power to forgive yourself as much as the determination to torment your mind into crazy. Either way it's a conscious choice."

The beach is windswept but for a miniature sandcastle. The waves take it as we approach. It disappears without a trace. Perhaps I imagined it.

Catcher holds my shoulders tighter and speaks over my head as if addressing the ocean. "Dreams don't appreciate being trapped in a box," he says. "A letter is alive until it's destroyed. Why do you think so many humans keep old cards and love letters and receipts all their lives but burn them days before they die? And if *they* don't, why do their nearest and dearest appoint themselves as designated fire marshals? Come to that, why did *you* fill a box with mementos? None of which were earth shattering secrets. I tell you this: a toffee tin does not a coffin make. If you had truly wanted your memories to die, you should have burned that dear John letter and tossed the Zee Stone in the ocean." He lobs a pebble into the water to make his point.

I shrug myself loose and face Catcher. There are pearls glistening in his eyes. I am defeated. "What do you suppose Marcus Aurelius would do right now?" I ask.

"Marcus Aurelius's crusades were all about victory. If he opted for suffering it was because he understood that success doesn't travel in a straight line."

"That's so textbook."

"Shall I tell you why you saved a box of useless souvenirs for fifty years?"

"I can't stop you. Go ahead, kick me when I'm down."

"Because each one was an emotional milestone intended to be paraded out when the 'big fog' descended. That box was an insurance policy against a mind wiped clean. On a subconscious level, bittersweet touchstones jumpstart the brain from wandering. There's some comfort in that." He cleared his throat. "Emptiness comes, anyway."

"That's pathetic. It's a baby clinging to a scrap of old blanket. It's my mother's imaginary teddy bear. It's hiding the postcard of a ghost under your pillow."

"You want the pain of remembering because pain is stronger than letting go. Pain pushes you to act. Being retroactive counts just fine. It's all live action. You fought dementia because you didn't want to forget Zee. Keeping tender moments alive is subliminal time travel. And here's something else that you know full well. Bad memories are the best lessons."

"Maybe people burn things to avoid being judged or humiliated or hurt others left behind. Maybe they're dreamers."

"Peace of mind is a powerful placebo that tranquilizes the mentally ill. Dreams can do that. A worry stone can do that. A good fairy's counter spell can do that. A pillow can become a bear. A painting can capture a soul. Death can be commuted to an endless sleep." He stops and lifts my chin. He pins me with his pearly eyes. "Forgiveness has no expiry date."

I pull away and throw my heart into the water. Zee sings in my head. *Fairy tales can come true. It can happen to you if you're young at heart*. I refuse to cry. I dare the ocean to make me.

"Preserving time is an occupational hazard of human birth," Catcher says behind me, or is it in my head? It no longer mattered.

He goads me. I think he wants me to cry. "An old eraser marked with initials inside a heart is a moment," he says. "An event is gone forever if there's no physical evidence it happened. Touching an historic doodad delivers life. Pain or pleasure, it's all the same in the end."

My almost tears strain behind my eyes. "Wow. Ironic. I kept an eraser for fifty years so that a moment would never be erased."

"This is no time to get weepy. Listen to me, kiddo, killing time is a real thing."

I collapse on the sand and cry like a baby. "I am afraid to die."

Catcher makes a harrumph sound and pats me on the head again before delivering his crass verdict. "You're afraid to live, Babycakes."

I wipe my eyes on the back of my hand and stand up, straight as a poker. A deep intake of salty air centers me. "I'm going back for Zee. I *will* repair the mistakes I made." A lone gull hopping at the edge of the water tips his beak and laughs at me. Maybe it's Jonathan Livingston.

Catcher's voice rings over the sand and startles my gull friend. "THINGS TAKE TIME. TIME TAKES THINGS."

I stretch taller than my 5ft. 4in. "I will confess. I will declare my foolishness."

"You're asking my permission? Haven't I encouraged you to dream outside the box from day one? And you can take that literally. I say this for the last time. You are *not* your mother."

I shrink back to under five feet tall. "I'm drowning in too many memories. This time, I'm going crazy, for sure."

Catcher's smugness irks me. He kisses the top of my head, turns abruptly, walks backwards, and casually delivers his cutting words of wisdom. "Then swim, darling. Strap on water wings, dog paddle, tread water, and dive in. Learn to breath underwater."

— WALT WHITMAN
'I Sing the Body Electric'

chapter 43
LIVING THE DREAM

I spend the week in study hall mode backpedaling doodles, swatting for an exam. I doodled with style and intention. Detention with intention… that was me. I am a super doodler. A dozen notebooks runneth over. It was a punishment with a twist. In a way, it was rather fun. It fanned my ardor into a bubbling volcano. I was crazy in love, living the teenage dream. My assignment was pretending to be (without pretense) a young girl writing a diary. I registered my projected wannabe married name a million times, my pet names were petted to absurdity. I used my signature purple ink to make it authentic. I should have been wearing bobby socks and saddle shoes, except I wasn't a geek back then. I was odd, yes, and a bit of a headcase, but I wore fashionable shoes.

Catcher mostly left me to myself but occasionally looked in to check my progress. This time he was carrying my Vermeer book. "Goodness, it's hot in here," he said, grinning, so I knew it was a joke. "You look different. Feverish. Are you quite well?" he crossed his arms hugging the book, assessing me. He walked behind me and looked over my shoulder at my even script.

I waggled my purple-stained fingers at him like a kid in kindergarten.

For the moment, he was a proud teacher and I was his assignment smothered in gold stars and red happy faces, and the words well done written in bold letters, and perhaps, just this once, I had eclipsed his expectations.

He judged my emotional temperature as one would check a pie in an oven. "You're done," he said standing back to gloat at me. "Your eyes are alive with pearls."

I snickered but I was pleased that my outside appearance coincided with my internal excitement. I felt lightheaded as I tried to stand. I'd hypnotized myself, giddy.

"It's about time," Catcher said. He surveyed my expression closely. "No, literally, it is. Don't act coy. Now, tell me your intentions. Will you lose the moment by mooning about all day in a glow of dreamy-eyed make believe or are you going to use the moment to make it real?"

"I need some air. Let's take a break," I said.

Catcher slammed his fist on the table. " Momentum, woman! Carpe diem isn't just a flippant truism. It's everything. Seize the dream. Dreams are like the grains of sand in an oyster. The body worries them into pearls. A beautiful pearl left in a shell is a waste of life. Remember Marcus Aurelius. Remember who you were."

"What are you doing to me?"

"I'm doing what any mentor would do. I'm fanning the dying flames within you, hoping to burn you to the ground. I want you incandescent. Nothing less than a conflagration of human desire out of control."

Catcher plunked the Vermeer book on the table. "Feel the painting," he instructed.

Jakobina's face stared up at me. I remembered being inside her in the studio. Underneath her innocent expression seethed a barely controllable lust for her fiancé.

Catcher's words sizzled in my ear. "The painting is a door. You are there, in Vermeer's studio. Feel the breath catching in Jakobina's throat. Your pulse quickens. Your body-heat is rising. You're about to faint."

I am there in 1665, awake in every sense of the word. No more playing with fire. I *am* the fire. I am ashes. Time flies and it's 1965, on a school night. I am studying Zee's face, living a dream that couldn't possibly fit into a box. Time is no longer a speculative *what*-if but a definitive *as*-if.

I am with Zee.

chapter 44

CATCHING A FEW Z's

At first, it was easy to arrive in 1965. I stalked Zee in the halls, outside his classes, and walking home. He never saw me. I became bolder and grabbed his arm. He slipped through my net each time.

Now, it's harder to time-travel, and sleep is impossible. Daydreaming not withstanding, the lack of regular sleep translates to no dreams and agitation. I am overtaken by the possibility of permanent separation from Zee. And yet, from my new perspective, I watch my old world with growing frustration and fascination in equal measure.

High school is aptly named. The entire student body was high on pheromones that hardly any of us knew what to do with. No wonder we broke out in blemishes and wet patches of fear under our arms. No wonder we gibbered to the opposite sex like tongue-tied monkeys. No wonder we blushed and froze speechless in a constant state of emotional turmoil.

When I first met Zee I forgot how to speak English or control the temperature of my face. So many stillborn flirtations fizzled. Being buddies was easier.

I lurk in the shadows and witness the lusty high school mating rituals with longing. Everywhere there is brazen flirtation and starry-eyed lovers intent on possessing and consuming each other. It's immensely thrilling but ultimately heartbreaking.

Teenage growing pains mean living in a terminal state of love-sickness, living on the edge of consummation while being consumed at the same time. However did we survive? How did we find time and energy to study for exams? How did we ever pass? How, in any sense of the word happy, could this emotional turmoil be described as the happiest times of our lives?

I witness a population of adolescent boys as tomorrow's leading men unable to lead, and their girl counterparts as female starlets who can only follow their boys of choice in overexcited groups of giggling girlfriends.

Teens are awkward conversationalists, plagued by the clumsy choreography of unrehearsed moves and illiterate body language. So many intimate sparks across rooms were smothered at birth. It's a wonder the human species survives grade twelve.

I've confronted Zee dozens of times. I feel like a ghost, as Catcher said I would. Maybe I've died in my sleep and don't know it. If so, I'm so new to this ethereal state that my haunting abilities are wholly amateurish. I take small comfort that even death is a learning curve, and forge on under the premise that 'a professional ghost is an amateur who didn't quit.'

I press on. Zee remains out of reach. His form is solid but his mind is preoccupied with anger and surprisingly, guilt. Ghosts aren't mind readers so I never get the details. Perhaps that's a skill that comes with time.

Zee still frequents our library table. I sit across from him hunched over a book and nudge his pen with my finger. I refuse to do anything so crass as to levitate it. Nothing. I move it a few more times, an inch at a time. Zee remains absorbed in his pages. I feel the room evaporating. Familiar objects from my kitchen overlap the row of green bankers lamps. I memorize a last glimpse of 1965, but as I look back, Zee closes his book, and moves the pen to its original position.

I sought out Felix, thoroughly discouraged. "You're pale as a ghost," he said "but thankfully, very much alive, my dear."

"Being a ghost is easier."

"Cheer up," Felix said. "This was to be expected. Zee is a powerful energy. It will take time to, pardon the expression, *break* him."

I bristled. "Not by me. I was given to believe that finding Zee would be easy if I complied by the correct rules of engagement, which I have."

"Getting there is easy but it's only the beginning. After that comes the reaching part which is by no means connecting as you've discovered."

There was no mistaking I was playing to win. My dormant passions denied oxygen, awoke from hibernation with killer instincts. Thanks to Catcher, I now possessed the kind of courage that's lost on the young and naïve. I discovered that way past middle-age, a wallflower can bloom formidably. Surprisingly, I had old age going for me. And there was a compelling revelation: well into seniorhood, an unassuming homebody begins to accumulate eccentricity points that eventually culminate in the brazen unconstraint of a true curmudgeon. Without trying, I have become formidable.

Forgotten memories of Zee hatched, fully-formed, and played like movies on a screen whenever I tried to sleep. Desire sprouted like mushrooms from every dark corner where I'd stored it. The 'castle box' had a lot to answer for.

I cornered Zee, in his bedroom, exhausted after a run, too tired to fight me. He lay spread-eagled on the covers as I sang him a lullaby. *'picture yourself in a boat on a river'*

He dried his face with the towel around his neck but he heard something because he paused to listen. I was encouraged to continue. *'with tangerine trees'* "Zee," I shouted, waving my arms. "I'M RIGHT HERE."

He lifted his head and surveyed the empty room. *'And marmalade skies,'* I sang.

"I won't give up, Zee. *'Somebody calls you, you answer quite slowly'*

His mouth moved. He spoke the last line. "A girl with kaleidoscope eyes."

It was a breakthrough that lasted a millisecond before Zee pulled a pillow over his face and cried himself to sleep.

I spoke to his sleeping form. "It's me, Aurelia. I'm the someone calling you." And then I slipped away to 2019 and lay on my bed the same way as Zee, with a pillow over my face and slept soundly for the first time in weeks. Tomorrow replayed itself. It was *not* another day.

Waking without Zee was terrifying but he was still there when I closed my eyes. I called back down the tunnel of dreams. His face looked like a snapshot staring up at me – a freeze-frame of the only picture I took of Zee, framed in students elbowing their way to math and science, and me, frozen invisible in his headlights.

His name flapped at me until I reached out and caught it. Instantly, Zee's face animated in the parted crowd of a teenage herd moving in a mass from class-to-class down a hallway buzzing with testosterone and estrogen. I followed him to his class. He moved to close the door but paused, looked both directions down the empty hall for a long time, and left it open. Had he seen me? I took the open door as an invitation and entered.

I sat in the back of the room and willed him to turn around. Why was I invisible? I had been visible in the cafeteria. Zee had not only seen me during that first spontaneous slip to the cafeteria, we'd talked. More than talked. He'd told me he loved me. It was my turn to confess. It wasn't fair.

The bell rang. Zee stood and turned to where I waited, his eyes unfocused, staring through me.

I imprinted Zee's red bomber jacket with white leather sleeves, a felt school crest sewn on the left shoulder, blue jeans, and white runners. Tall. Blond hair. A clean cut lad who oozed gentle compassion of the heart-stopping variety. My Zee.

I ran to him, unsnapped his jacket, nuzzled into his grey sweatshirt and whispered I love you. His arms tightened around me and held me close. I felt a sob welling inside him but it was me who cried. We stood in unbearable sadness until the room emptied and Zee let go of me, and

I found myself back in 2019, a human puddle on the floor of my blue classroom, hanging on to a boy who wasn't there. But I wasn't alone. Jakobina was there, pouring tea as if she expected me.

"Death looks pretty good right now, doesn't it," she said pushing the sugar bowl towards me. "Two teaspoons or three? And then she evaporated in a melodramatic pop.

Felix's purr vibrated inside me. "Breathe, Aurelia," he coached. "Long deep breaths. I am here. I assure you, Empress, time is on your side. Victory is near."

I blubbered uncontrollably. "His pain was unbearable. I caused that. I abandoned him. I'm a monster."

"Good. It's all good, Aurelia. It's part of the journey that you feel the pain you suppressed. It's not exactly karma. But you won't be free to meet Zee without it."

"You might have told me."

"Words describing pain are feeble things. It wouldn't have prepared you for the whole truth."

I emptied my grief into a Kleenex and sniffed. "Which is?"

"You have to experience a victim's pain first hand in order to heal. The guilt is part of your comeuppance. No-one gets out alive. Especially ghosts. You're feeling Zee's pain. Better now than never. But that's what you get for suppressing your own."

Hatred eclipsed the devastation of excruciating loss. I spoke clearly to Jakobina who was no doubt able to hear me, wherever she'd vanished. "If you weren't already dead," I said in a steady voice dripping with venom. "I'd kill you. Twice. I hope you wallow in agony, bereft and alone in your damn painting until the end of time."

I calmed down long enough to vent the worst of my fears. Misspent youth, indeed. I had banked every scrap of emotion for a future I erased, and for the first time, I realized maybe Zee had done the same.

If Zee was still alive, he was a seventy-year-old man with a chequered past. But with my gift, he lived in a perpetual hallway and I knew the date, close enough to track him down. Near enough to stand and deliver – me, a brave old dear in a seventeen-year-old body, savvy enough to break the silence of fifty years. It would be me who had to roll an emotional snowball down a hill into a boulder the size of a snowman's ass. Together we would build the rest, carrot nose and all. Our woolen mitts would pill up with snow and our breath snuggle into white words that ended with a kiss.

I needed the library where a storm brought Zee and I together, and I needed Felix to tell me the truth he was hiding. But instead, I felt woozy.

Canary whined goodbye.

In the middle of the journey of my life,
I found myself within a dark wood
where the straight way was lost.
— DANTE ALIGHIERI

chapter 45
THE NETHER NETHER

I've gone AWOL again… to Avalon, that future of discontent where I'm old and decrepit, living a blessing and a curse, on wits a hundred times stronger than my enfeebled body. Canary had pestered me all morning, whining and pushing her nose into me, signaling an inevitable time-slip was hanging around the corner, but even so, I was unprepared. A famous old quote 'Old age is no place for sissies' hung like a sports banner over a day softened by rain. It's okay, though. I deserve to suffer after what I did to Zee. It's penance, pure and simple. It's karma. It's comeuppance in spades. I am humbled.

I have named our nannies. There are nine. Nine nannies who strut in and out of our nursery from dawn to lights out. Each one inspired a fearful nickname. Suffice it to say, a quick shout of Mouse or Grub or Baby is enough to herald an angel lacking mercy. Pity springs to mind. Angels of pity carrying trays of grey soup with demons of boredom perched on their shoulders, forever nudging them with toothpick pitchforks. If, that is, we'd been allowed toothpicks.

Nurse Clipboard – efficient, data, impersonal, head of section.

Nurse Hospital Corners – goes strictly by the book, OCD, military persona, emotionless stick.

Nurse Mouse – shy and unassuming, wears squeaky shoes throughout the night shift.

Nurse Lavender Britches – wears lavender scrubs, kind, almost humane.

Nurse Baby-talk – delivers humiliating moronic conversations, insensitive, mother complex.

Nurse Grub – delivers the meals. The smell arrives before the trolley cart of blue melamine plates covered in grey plastic hats. Ugh.

Nurse Biz – a busybody who chatters nonstop about meaningless trivia in famous people's lives via the latest magazine headlines.

Nurse Brisk – always behind schedule, checks her watch, in a dither, leaves things behind, including her patients. We are things to her. She misses details.

Nurse Blue – her baby blue eyes see no evil. Insightful, psychic, knows patients are 'in there', respectful, asks the right questions, understands, her eyes mist up. Sympathy vs empathy but, it can't be helped, we depress her.

An old song is playing on the hospital radio in the common room: *Catch a falling star and put it in your pocket. Save it for a rainy day.* The library window is crying buckets for the two star-crossed teenagers parked side-by-side in wheelchairs. Our clubhouse is a ward of Mad Hatter's, tucked into a cheerless corner of limbo. We diapered adults lie in seven beds – the universe's sick joke in a blatantly cruel reference to rebirth and Snow White.

Our friend, down the hall, sleeps in twilight death. He's a great teacher. All of us stargazers sit at his feet, figuratively speaking, for wisdom and practical advice, like children listening to a storyteller. I call him the sandman when I'm here but I don't always remember. Our conversations are dreamy recollections that disappear after I arrive home.

Thank hydrogen, the rainy season has arrived. Bliss. The sounds it brings evoke precious times of quiet peace on a slow day – of cream cakes and scones with fig jam and Welsh cheese, savored in a teashop.

I recall needle-rain bouncing off trampoline streets. Wet sparks prancing from the grey sidewalks of an avenue that flicker like grounded fireworks.

Mozart drifts softly over vases of white freesia and Blue Denmark china. I've been here before, but when? Paradoxically, life can reach no higher depths. Even a beloved historical novel, chosen well to respect the sanctity of a wet afternoon, fails to draw my attention. The real story is in the umbrellas all around me. All my life I've been a pluviophile… a lover of rain. Umbrellas unleash a part of me that finds life joyful. I need it here. Umbrellas are my thing.

Umbrellas are tricky things. An umbrella held like a shield or too high or too low shouts amateur. Only a few people can carry off this fragile accessory with panache. Such poise is acquired from love. I can put it no less, for one has to love rain and darkened skies with the same joy as a sun worshipper reacts to waves of summer heat.

If rain is not considered glorious, it's doubtful sloshing through puddles will deliver a sense of happiness. For such as these, wielding an umbrella is like watching chimpanzees work out the intricacies of folding a napkin into a swan. Water bounces of their simian foreheads like tiny ping pong balls as they try to unjam the spokes of a wet balloon that was once a tidy walking stick.

On dry days, umbrellas always single out the park dandies who would be lost without their probing device of choice. I've seen them cutting eccentric figures on perfectly dry days – flotsam inspectors brandishing their happy extensions of reach, turning over bits of this and that hiding under the leaves. And, rolled umbrellas come in handy for prodding a homeless person awake who's appropriated their favorite bench.

It occurs to me that perhaps I'm a figure on a movie screen. A shadow moving in two dimensions, longing to affect physical objects with the tip of an umbrella. These are the thoughts that ground me during the wee small hours on a rainy night in bed seven.

But, imprisoned as I am, rain has always been my touchstone. Each of the others has their own. If I can help them find it we will form a new club because once that's who we were – a group of wallflower kids who loved stars.

So, when the skies are grey, I am able to emerge like the sun. I remember Catcher's words and mentally scribble in the margin of my school notebook: *'emergence is the mindfulness that springs from the winters of emergency'*.

Contrary to local popular opinion, this does not make me a gloomy cuss. I was born in a wet climate and embraced it early. Rain imprinted within me – a willing sponge for its sensuous voices. It whispers and roars in equal measure and ironically, its companion winds howl *away* any wolves from my castle door. For me, it brings back the simplistic joy of my island neighbor Christopher Robin in yellow wellington boots, a red umbrella held low, tilted casually over his right shoulder, sheltering a bear of little brain. I miss Virgil.

Suddenly without asking, without ceremony, I am wheeled away from the afternoon's glorious underwater window. "Come along, orphan Annie," Nurse Clipboard says, "the sun'l come out tomorrow." She laughs at her cleverness.

Her voice fades out. Suddenly, Doc is there, pushing my wheelchair. He leans down and sings in my ear. "Just stick out your chin and grin and say, tomorrow tomorrow … bet your bottom dollar there'll be sun." The gentle ticking of a clock accompanies him like a metronome.

There had been Summer resort hamburgers and cokes slurped in squeaky red vinyl booths in diners with posters of James Dean and red Hollywood cars, there were yesterdays with vintage poodle skirts, fuzzy sweaters, hula hoops, and saddle shoes.

No matter. In a manner of speaking, we-seven can fly, as in Wendy Darling and her brothers levitating above their beds who arrive somewhere a little east of the first star on the right. Because we-seven noticed stars. Stars were our thing. And I'd like to think that maybe one star in particular noticed us.

Nurse Blue tries to reach me at least once a day by dangling a pearl earring on a string in my face. It swings from side-to-side like a hypnotist's pendulum. "Think back," she says… "how did you get here? Come on. Remember, sweetie. You're nearly there."

After several weeks of sufficient punishment, I arrive home before Jakobina knows I've been gone. The Felix clock tells me only five minutes have passed. Canary and Catcher are sitting across from me, waiting like a pair of guard dogs.

chapter 46

PROMISES PROMISES

Karmic irony has come home to roost. I wander the school halls like a ghost amongst the living.

Catcher arrived three months ago. It's the end of June in Zee's world. Broken promises litter my life. Summer vacation draws near for Zee. I've wandered, or is it squandered? an entire month haunting the school corridors, making endless loops past trophy cases, and water fountains, in a sea of sickly blue and yellow school colors. Felix's black tail disappears around corners and I follow him like a trail of breadcrumbs. Pennants and banners adorn archways. But there are no posters of a missing student bearing my face.

Felix shouts from somewhere above and behind me that the word penance is more appropriate. The art of meandering takes me to the cafeteria waiting in line with Zee. I whisper *mac and cheese* in his ear. I drift down miles of aluminum lockers, and up staircases. I am Scrooge slipping through the ghosts of students past. My presence may not be having an effect on them but being here is stirring up memories for me.

Can they feel my hand on their shoulders or hear me breathing when I shout *see me goddammit* in their faces? Pinning my thinness against the solidarity of a living yearbook on parade wears me out. A marching band of potential tinkers, liars, backstabbers, and gossips slip between my molecules. I am as insignificant in simulated death as I ever was when I left. Being half dead is not as much fun as I was led to expect. Mingling is a colossal waste of time.

My own yearbook photograph is fazing out. I am disappearing – a polaroid image fading into a white square. Emergence in reverse. Although I have to say, I'm loving the thought of becoming a clean glossy square where I exist as an imaginary memory. There's something poetic and fitting that I will become the scent of a face.

And then the image plays back, reverses and I materialize like a Klingon ship decloaking in slow motion. A girl in red Mary Janes clicks her heels together while the mantra *there's no place like school there's no place like school* plays over like a stuck record. I am a human dimmer switch, ratcheting up my brightness and volume controls until I'm apoplectic with concentration. Sustaining this level of focus can't be healthy at my age but then I remember with startling realization, that here in 1965, I'm seventeen and have all the time in the world.

Some things never change. I'm still one of the wallflower people with as much impact as a shadow puppet thrown against a wall.

In my old neighborhood stomping grounds I'm the trace of passing perfume on an empty street. Heads turn to sniff. No-one's there. But I *was* there. I am there, still. I'm trying so hard to be there. I stamp my feet to get attention. My shoes are mute as fluffy slippers.

An imaginary scene plays in my taxed brain. It's somewhere fifty-years ago on a Vancouver street. A five-star Chanel girl clicks a mad S.O.S telegraph on the sidewalk with her high heels: I'm running late...*stop*... please wait...*stop*... I love you... *stop*... please don't go....*stop*. I picture blue pavement sparks igniting the hem of her tailored skirt. And just as I think I've passed the point of doolally, Felix whisks his tail around another corner and I run to catch up.

"Catch up, catch me, catch him," he howls. "Catch Catcher out."

Catcher was right. My senses are highly tuned to Zee and the wistful crazy girl that was. I catch a whiff of history in the school library through a blur of study nerves. A yearbook lies open on a table. A rogues gallery of strangers with familiar faces fill page after page of mugshots with growing pains.

My mind travels erratically, too. It pains me when Felix reminds me of an important message that I suppressed the previous day. Felix is no fraidy cat. He's a warrior as fierce as any Roman emperor. I have selective memories so no wonder I quash the replay that Felix implants in me. My wise Yoda whose tail is a light sabre in times of trouble, wipes my internal blackboard at the end of my expeditions so I can sleep.

I overhear Catcher and Jakobina. "She will have to know sooner or later," Catcher says. "I may overstep my privileges, Sweetheart, but ultimately, I'm as confined by the rules of metaphysics as she is. And she hasn't even considered that Zee might want to escape into your painting with her if given the chance."

But there's an unnerving something more. Catcher pulls Jakobina close and kisses her gently on those ruby lips of hers.

Catcher deftly pours our ritual Earl Grey tea while staring unblinking into my eyes. "A prince dreams he's a frog," he says dreamily. "A frog dreams he's a prince." Catcher chooses a fancy blue bottle with an ornate stopper from the shelf and plunks it down in front of me as if it's a chess piece. "Your move," he says. "A genie wants out of his bottle. A girl wants out of a painting. An old lady wants out of a commitment. Souls are trapped in so many ways. You are in jeopardy. And, it seems your king is playing devilishly hard to get. Or is he your prince."

I countermove with my newfound piece of cobalt sea glass. "I found this yesterday." I plunk it down to challenge the bottle. "Take that, Spasky. Keep your mind on the game. Your little love queen jeopardizes us all."

Catcher hooks my eyes like a hypnotist and reels me in. He lifts his queen with great ceremony and uses it to push mine off the board. "You know, I could have left messages for you in bottles on the beach but I knew you appreciated poetry, so I chose sandcastles."

I hold the glass up to the light and peer around it to meet Catcher's empty eyes. "And what is this one's message?"

"It's not a message," he says. "It's a threat."

chapter 47
LOVE'S SWEET DROOM

The mugginess of pre-thunder frizzed my hair, I smooth it into a twist and mopped my damp forehead with my sleeve. Even the air was nervous.

Catcher paced the floor and checked the progress of the storm each time he passed the window. "Where is Jakobina?"

I didn't care for his tone. "How should I know, I'm not your girlfriend's keeper."

"Well, *I* have to be," he said under his breath. "Jakobina," he announced to the air in a normal speaking voice, "it's important that you join us, please." She was always in hearing distance.

I raised my eyes in mock disgust in keeping with my sneer. "Should I gird my loins? Are we to have an after-dinner lecture?"

Jakobina wafted across the room in a heartbeat, smiling sweetly. "This should be fun," she said which was the first time I'd known her to lie outright. I am so naïve.

Catcher stood before us like a put-upon father and heaved a sigh. He was snarky about something and I expected he was about to punish us for our own good.

He indicated to where I sat on the sofa. "Jakobina, please join Aurelia, there's a good girl."

Ooh, condescending. She won't like that.

Canary took up her post on my other side and I linked my fingers under her collar.

Catcher noticed and shook his head. "You're quite safe. You almost never physically leave the present time when you descend into another. But if it makes you feel better, by all means, hang on."

"It does."

"Hang on for dear life, then," Jakobina whispered in my ear, with a tad too much glee. "I think you're in for a shock."

Catcher pulled up the ottoman and sat across from us. "Please hold hands, ladies."

There I sat, one hand locked on Canary and the other in Jakobina's sticky paw. I raised my eyebrows in a question. She answered with a shrug, but she was clearly in on the lesson. She was compliant but fidgety. Her irritation echoed my own.

Catcher pressed his splayed fingertips together. Aurelia, think back to the day when Zee gave you the touchstone. Tell us how you felt. How Zee looked at you. Tell Jakobina as if you're telling her a bedtime story."

"No doubt, she was *there*," I said. "She never left me alone when Zee and I were together." I turned to her, vexed. "Yes, why was that? I mean, there's such a thing as privacy between lovers."

Jakobina scoffed at that. "You were *never* lovers." She turned to Catcher. "They were a pair of immature children."

"We were in love."

"We are about to leave privacy in the dust," Catcher said. "And age, as you well know Jakobina, has nothing to do with true love. But it would facilitate the experiment immensely if it could be undertaken minus the peevishness. The simultaneous clap of thunder erupted outside as he brought his hands together. He meant business. Punch sidled in and preened against his legs. It rather lowered the tension as Catcher acknowledged her with a playful tug of her tail. I silently thanked her. She, in turn, hissed, and scratched Catcher's hand with a vicious swipe. Jakobina recoiled and rubbed her cheek.

I close my eyes. Zee and I are on my front porch. The scene feels rehearsed. He wears his red bomber jacket with the white leather sleeves and a school crest embroidered on the shoulder. He takes both my hands to center me, rubs them as if they're cold, and pries opens my left hand. For a moment we sit there in a bubble of sweetness as my old friend, the intimate breeze, lifts a curl of hair on Zee's forehead.

Zee produces a green bloodstone like a magician's trick, kisses it, places it gently in my palm, and closes my fist around it. It vibrates there like an egg about to hatch.

Dreamy déjà vu visions of high school stream in a seamless montage behind my eyes: the library, my locker, the basketball game bleachers, the planetarium, the Tuesday night Stargazy Club, Thatcher's voice, the movie house, greasy hamburgers in a red vinyl booth at the Burger Baron, and the school cafeteria that made my posthumous dreams come true.

Canary barks. I am thankful to be holding tight to her leash. The slide show breaks with the sound of smashing glass. A pearl necklace snaps. Pearls fall in slow motion and roll toward me as an icy river and settle into a frozen canal.

My voice drones away into white sound and another takes its place. Shelves of cobalt glass evaporate. The room is whitewashed plaster, stark and cold even though there's a blazing fire. A man raises a beaker of wine to the sound of applause. His round face beams his pleasure at Jakobina. She holds a small box in her lap. Its lid is painted with a pair of swans. Piet stands behind her with his hand on the back of her chair. I feel his presence as if he's caressed my neck. I know the symbolism on the box, well. Jakobina had explained to me that swans mate for life.

I observe the scene as a ghost might but my point of view changes. I am inside Jakobina, feeling flustered. I have to open the gift, exclaim how wonderful it is regardless of my true feelings, and make a dainty acceptance speech. Neither she nor I are in our comfort zones. But I needn't have worried. The gift is exquisite. Two luminous pearl earrings nestled in ultramarine silk. My breath catches but I accept them graciously. It's a wedding gift to welcome me to the family. "I painted the swans," Piet whispers. "Do you like them?" The family closes around me to admire the gift. It's hard to breath. A dozen radiant smiles aimed at me, a frightened girl in an unwanted spotlight. I recall the 'deer in the headlights' remark I once used to describe Jakobina. She had blushed then as well as now. But now I am privy to the hot cheeks and wobbly tummy and my shy vocal chords choke into a ball of self-conscious nerves.

· · ·

Canary barks me home. I am rescued. I crave warm milk infused with nutmeg, beyond all normal reason.

Jakobina's earrings sit on the table flickering with firelight even though the grate is cold. The evening is sweltering. A distant roll of thunder grumbles over the sea. Jakobina is sobbing gently in Catcher's arms. He's settled his chin on the top of her head. His torturous expression speaks clearly of suffering. It seems natural that his mouth remains closed in a forced smile when he addresses me. "Zee misses you, too," he says. "Isn't that a shame."

The Autumnal Equinox
– September 23 –
2019

I stormed into the blue sanctuary to take my frustrations out on Felix and freaked out Punch snoozing in a sunbeam. "This won't do!" I shouted and proceeded to flail about, pacing around the table clockwise, I stopped, turned, and continued to stomp anti-clockwise while Felix lowered his eyelids. He allowed me to let off steam before he opened one eye, then the other, and addressed me the way a timeless sage hanging on a wall would, during a crisis.

"As I see it, it's about time you fought for what you want," he said. "If you have a scheme, do it. The hare-brained ones are the best."

"It's going to get me into trouble."

Felix's tail thrashed wildly. "Excellent. Dreaming one's life away is never a complete waste of time."

I tuned the radio to a golden oldies station and propped the kiss-sealed-in-time photograph from my castle box in plain sight. Timely lyrics swelled from the radio and washed over me like liquid honey. *'I'll send you all my dreams every day, in a letter sealed with a kiss'.* My disc jockey muse was working overtime. For the first time I heard the word muse within the word music. A wave of nostalgia surged through me as only a love song can. An image of the school cafeteria slowly formed. I heard the ghostly din of a hundred conversations and the clatter of dishes. Zee sat across from me. His wink breaks my heart. "Please come back to me," I whispered to the boy in the photograph. I know exactly what to say.

"The whole truth," Felix called out. "Make it count."

I wrote a love letter and left it in Zee's locker along with his old T-shirt worn to a rag.

September 23 - 2019

Darling Zee

In case you saw me the other day, I'm not a ghost. I'm alive in the year 2019, and I miss you. If you can, find me, I live on Castle Island in the Georgia Strait, off the Vancouver mainland. In fifty-three years you will be able to reach me.

I have no business to expect our dreams may survive what I did to you. Hindsight has a way of painting one's mistakes into corners larger than life, but now, chance has offered me a wormhole of hope. A few months ago I met a teacher. A scientist?... possibly. A mystical sage?... definitely. A mentalist? ... absolutely. And whoever or whatever he is, he's proved to me that time-travel is possible through concentrated meditation and lucid dreaming.

I've been practicing, trying to connect with you, compelled by regrets too numerous to mention and driven by a lifetime of guilt and shame. The adage that important things are better late than never, kept me trying – a little too selfishly and relentlessly as it turned out.

My need for atonement keeps me day-tripping back to you. But you can't see me. I sing to you but you can't hear me.

Remember my headaches when I couldn't see all of you and you nicknamed me, Aura? This morning, when I brushed my teeth, I couldn't see my hands. The toothbrush and toothpaste mocked me but it made sense to go through the motions until the underside of my tongue burned with peppermint. I tell you this because it serves to prove that my odd way of seeing the world is as sound as it ever was, and because it's true.

That said, my biggest truth is that I didn't see many things clearly in 1965, and as for 2019... some days I see me... sometimes I don't. Time is slippery. My eyesight may be dodgy but my memories are clear. I remember the lively debates about time travel we had in the Stargazy meetings. I can tell you, the delusional New-Age freaks we used to laugh at with their bizarre notions of 'out of-body-experiences,' were onto something. I have demonstrated astral travel is possible. I hope that the contents of this package go a long way to proving my fantastical claim.

I promise not to stalk you anymore. Even so, I am there with you, in spirit. Look for me in the shadows. Listen for my voice in the silence. Be happy. Forgive me. I'm here in the future, waiting. I hope you come. One day I'd like to explain what happened and why I chose to run away. Please believe me, it was for my love for you. *forever,* A

I hastened to 'The Findings' in Glastonbury and purchased the current edition of the Vancouver Sun newspaper, several science magazines, and a package of gold stars. And on a whim, I searched 'Fisher King's Second-hand Books' for a significant title. I found exactly what I was looking for in a yellowing dogeared copy of Richard Bach's 'Jonathan Livingston Seagull' with its many subsequent reprint editions listed inside. Zee was reading it the week I left because I'd lent him my brand new copy that was all the rage, sweeping the world as the latest international bestseller.

A lanky young man in 'Pen Dragons copy shop' was kind enough to humor me and my lack of computer skills, to download several front page images of the 'Vancouver Sun' circa 1966 from August to December off their archive website. I thought better of having a passport photo taken as a move too far, purchased an official prepaid overnight envelope from the post office, addressed it to Zee with a purple felt marker in large letters, and peppered it with star stickers and a dozen unmistakably fresh stamps.

I sat hugging my purchases by the ocean before enclosing everything, along with all the dated print receipts, and added a pinch of sand for luck. Lastly, I dropped in the Zee Stone cushioned in bubble wrap with a note that read: please return to sender and an excerpt from a poem Zee knew I loved:

There will be time, there will be time

To prepare a face to meet the faces that you meet;
There will be time to murder and create,
And time for all the works and days of hands
That lift and drop a question on your plate;
Time for you and time for me,
And time yet for a hundred indecisions,
And for a hundred visions and revisions.
— T.S. ELIOT

EXPULSION

chapter 49
DETENTION

– October 1–
2019

In the real world, a new school year is a month old. As for me, my school terms ends with an explosion. I've been expelled.

Amazingly, after my mutiny, the glass university still hummed with calming blue vibes. Canary sat under the kitchen table, whining and restless. I made a feeble joke for Felix's amusement, pretending to be a psychic leading a séance. I placed my hands on the table, closed my eyes, and spoke in a wavery voice to the room. "Is anyone there?"

Felix chuckled. "It's only a matter of time," he said, "Catcher's on his way. I doubt he'll have damage control on his mind."

I took a nail file from my purse and proceeded with a fake manicure.

Ten minutes ticked by before damage control burst through the door in the form of Catcher with a wild-eyed Jakobina in tow, her unkempt hair, flowing loose. Without her turban she looked ordinarily small and defenseless. She clung to Catcher's sleeve and stared at the floor, nervously chewing her bottom lip, clearly afraid.

Catcher fairly foamed at the mouth. His declaration was meant to be brutal. "It's over!"

I levelled him with a look of annoyance. "Doesn't anyone knock anymore? You don't live here." I focused on Jakobina. "And neither do you."

Catcher shrugged off Jakobina and smashed a blue vase to the floor. "You can't go back. Ever! Not after what you've done." Canary surged forward, hackles up. For a moment I thought Catcher might kick her but Jakobina had attached herself to his arm again and he turned to berate her. "Let me handle this."

I was ready. I restrained Canary with a pat. "Time travel was killing me," I said indifferently, and continued filing my nails. "And logic dictated if I died too soon, Jakobina would be monumentally screwed." I made eye contact with her as I blew nail dust in her direction from an extended middle finger.

Jakobina flinched as if I'd slapped her, which in a manner of speaking, I had. It was obvious my truth damaged more than her pride. She was near to tears.

Having the upper hand made her toothless and empowered me enough to shout "this is my house. Get out, the both of you." Canary flew into a barking frenzy.

"Reset the clocks," Felix said. "It's just beginning. Bravo, Aurelia. Defying the rules is an EMPRESS-ive thing to do. Old Marcus would be proud."

Damage control shifted to a pair of irate strangers pretending to be contrite. "We can walk back from this," Catcher said moving towards me. "Let's stay calm."

Canary barred his way and growled a clear warning.

The next few seconds rivalled bedlam. Canary snapped and lunged savagely at Catcher. Felix let out a bloodcurdling yowl. Jakobina recoiled, dematerialized hysterically and reappeared several times in various parts of the room, screaming.

Catcher's livid expression softened as Jakobina ran into his arms.

I heard myself hiss like a cat and spat my words. "Oh yeah, how far back? I have no intention of going anywhere, least of all into a poxy painting."

"You rather upset the applecart back there," Catcher accused through the curtain of Jakobina's hair. "Events are already set in motion."

Jakobina, her confidence returning, released herself from Catcher's embrace and sashayed over to Felix. She kissed her middle finger and tapped it on his nose – a gutsy gesture for her, but I recognized it for what it is. She was mocking time. Thanking any clock that marked a long awaited event. She thought she'd won.

Felix sneezed.

Jakobina's ruby lips turned a sinister shade of burgundy.

My brain shut down. *Zee will never be with me. I've been hoodwinked and good. But why?* And then a horrifying thought occurred that maybe Felix was in on the whole ghastly set up.

Catcher dragged Canary over to me and forcibly placed my hand on her collar. "Stay tuned," he said. "Don't say I didn't warn you." Canary bared her teeth and snapped at him.

I slipped anyway, falling into a career day event, circa a few weeks after I met Jakobina, my ethereal static-cling-ex-friend whom I couldn't shake, although I'd tried to ignore her. She's still invisible to all but me, and definitely a secret I intend to keep.

Our interviews are over. Zee's guidance counsellor was Mr. Thatcher, our Stargazy Club's supervisor. I'm collecting a sandwich and strawberry shake from the cafeteria line. Zee has saved our table, and is waiting. I look over and wave. My arm freezes. Jakobina is sitting in my place, solid as you please. She has Zee's full attention because he doesn't wave back, although he's seen me. He's definitely seen her because he recoils when she touches his hand and tells her to get lost. She disappears, and Zee nearly upsets the table in his haste to get away.

Catcher sits at the next table, observing. He turns into Mr. Thatcher and hails me. "Over here, Aurelia," he calls cheerily. "I've saved you a chair." It's my worst nightmare.

I run after Zee but he's disappeared. The entire school is empty. Garbage litters the empty hallways. The clock in the entrance hall has no hands. I run outside into a curtain of rain, tip my head back, and let the downpour wash me away.

Instantly, I'm home, dry eyed and remarkably stoic, standing where I left. Canary leaped up and licked my face. I made a point of ignoring Catcher and Jakobina. "It's okay," I said to Canary. "They can't hurt us."

"You only vanished for a heartbeat," Felix said. "You're quite safe, for the time being. And I forgive you."

I addressed Felix. "Betrayal kind of throws trust out the window. It made me kind of crazy. I'm sorry. Whatever happened back then, it's been over for fifty-years so there's no point in crying over it. There are better dreams to dream."

Jakobina flew at Felix with a strangled cry and made a move to swipe him to the floor, but her body, fluctuating in and out of solidity, proved ineffectual. Her hands passed through him and the wall. She screamed at Catcher. "Do something."

A teenage version of Catcher slumped into a wicker chair and stared at the broken vase. I can see through his form. He's a ghost.

"Well, that's me, exhausted," I announced, heading for the stairs. I shouted to Catcher-the-younger over my shoulder. "I think you've done your worst for one night. I'm going to bed. Close the door on your way out, whoever you are. And take your wacko girlfriend with you."

Catcher raised his head. "My name is Mattias." His voice is different. Sad.

Punch raced ahead of me and Canary followed.

Judging by the sound of broken glass downstairs, Jakobina must have rematerialized in a tantrum because she and Mattias continued to argue.

I tried not to think of my beautiful glass collection. My hands shook as I pressed play on my white noise machine. A soothing thunderstorm filled the room at full volume. Canary, Punch, and I cuddled on the bed – nerves and fur against the shush of rain and drowsiness. I reached under my pillow, forgetting I'd left the Zee Stone in Zee's locker back in time. I was too tired to chide myself for being foolish, and without a warning from Canary, I slipped off to the hospice of 2020, disturbed that Mattias's melodious voice was alarmingly calm.

chapter 50
SHA BOOM

The Avalon Care Home
2020

A clock meowed midnight. I woke to the sound of a fifties pop song playing softly in the dark from a jute box. Zee stood at the foot of my bed, his green hospital gown glowed transparent as a ghost as he hummed along with the melody and clicked his fingers to the snappy chorus. *"Sha boom sha boom."*

I smiled, sleepily. "Sweetheart." I reached out my hand. "What are you trying to say?"

He moved closer. "Free will has no expiry date."

"They say that time flies when you're having fun."

Zee shrugged. "Go figure." The tip of his index finger brushed mine, Michelangelo style… God delivering a spark of life. "We're barely half-awake at the best of times," he said. "So, should we wake up and marry?"

Zee pulled his hand away, took a formal stance, and recited my favorite poem: *"And would it have been worth while, to have bitten off the matter with a smile, to have squeezed the universe into a ball to roll it towards some overwhelming question?"* As he spoke, the light behind him shivered through the spectrum and subsided into a pale mauve halo. "By the way," he added with a wink, "The overwhelming *answer* is YES."

"Eliot had a point," I said, sitting up fully awake.

Zee blew me a kiss from 1965. "Life is but a dream, sweetheart," he said gesturing to the open window. "Come on, Wendy, Doc says it's time to fly."

chapter 51
OUT OF TIME

– October 31 –
2019

For too long, it's been Halloween every day. Now I have a clear task of exorcism to complete. I took the 'Girl With a Pearl Earring' print to the front porch where I turned Jakobina's face to the wall. Surprisingly, in the half-light of dusk it looked like an original painting. Jakobina followed me back upstairs. "He's my teacher too," she said. I turned my back on her without theatrics and firmly closed my bedroom door in her face. Her voice seeped through the door and trailed off in an echo as she limped down the stairs . "Did you think you were the only one… one… one."

Jakobina disappeared after I formally declared 'bring it on' but no matter how many times I shifted it, the portrait returned to my bedroom wall. I had Emperor Aurelius to thank for my battle cry, but my elation was short lived. I was jumpy. Disoriented. Neither here nor there, yet almost content to be alone. I dithered about stumbling into furniture and accepted the resulting minor injuries of stubbed toes and shoulders bruised from slamming into door frames as punishments for being a damned fool. I'd been expelled. I have been liberated and yet the aftermath of school *quitting me* is a physical shock. What on earth will I do with my freedom?

Canary mirrored my mood swings as ever, and I gave her what affection I was able to muster from the greyness that enveloped me. My brain tried to wrap itself around the year 2019 but my mind was determined to stay in 1965. Time remained my enemy. Too little too late. Time on my hands. It was my time to waste away.

I bumped into the kitchen table and slammed my elbows on the edges of things determined to teach me a lesson. My reflection in the darkened windows revealed anxious eyes staring from a pale face. I looked ghostly... definitely tormented. Even in the half-light there were noticeable dark circles under my eyes, red-rimmed and sore. I went days without bathing, slopping about aimlessly in robe and slippers in a slump of self-pity. I boiled endless kettles of water and made pots of tea, forgetting the teabags. The times I managed to perform a successful tea-making ritual, I left cups of it to get cold and drank orange juice from the container. I took to drinking black coffee, and when my hands weren't actually shaking from caffeine overload, they felt as if they were.

And then the letter arrived with its newsy headline. I could lose my home. It was a formal announcement of an inspection, next Tuesday, from my invisible landlord – a man I'd never met who'd pulled his puppeteer strings behind my rental agreement. A man I likened to the wizard of Oz in an ivory tower with minions to follow his orders. I hastened to the bathroom, motivated to become a human puppet worth keeping as a tenant, and then cleaned my world with a vengeance not unlike a battle for survival. My monster companions seemed to have deserted the island. I was thankful for small favors in those days of forced recovery.

In 48 hours Tintagel Cottage is ship-shape and I am its presentable Queen. Felix calls me beautiful. I can hardly wait for this obligatory assessment to be over so I can get back to wallowing in peace. But there's something about a makeover that takes the sting out of depression. Perhaps it means I can move on and read good books once again and listen to Mozart and take simple delights in sea glass expeditions. Next Tuesday will come and go. After that, a succession of ordinary things will follow and fade. I can't lose my castle or leave my sea.

· · ·

The first light of Tuesday leapt onto my bed in the form of a hairy grey Canary that licked my face with some urgency. It occurred to me that doggie bathroom breaks were the saving grace of becoming mired in black depression. I braved the outside several times each day, in defiance of my gloom, and true to form, brisk winds and sea spray worked minor miracles of therapy.

This morning, a white mist enshrouded the beach in a pearly luminescent glow. I tramped the shoreline under an umbrella of light mist with my mind engaged in the sound of rubber boots crunching over pebbles which became a walking meditation of mindful steps that led me to the water's edge. That, in turn, steered me to a stunning piece of cobalt sea glass that fairly jumped out of the wet sand and waved at me.

Canary's lighthearted leaping and scampering lifted my own. If I were a dog, I would howl at the moon, still faintly visible. I imagined it hovering over us with best lunar wishes. It was good to remember the bigger things of the universe were reliable and sustaining. A hearty breakfast was another. I was hungry… a new sensation. Things were looking up.

Tintagel Cottage emerged out of a mauve and pink fog like a Turner watercolor. My steps quickened. I craved eggs over-easy, crispy bacon, and buttered toast. I fell into the 'art of tea' mood, and with it came the dregs of old domestic bliss. How lucky was I. I lived there, in that misty painting of a castle by the sea, and no-one deserved my newly-polished silver tea service more than me. I would wow my landlord with it later over afternoon high tea and sponge cake.

Canary overtook me and skittered to a stop. Or rather she continued to lope in slow motion. For a moment I wondered if I was about to 'travel', but instead of worrying, I accepted the strange time fluctuation and relished it, Emperor style.

The mist lifted to rain light as salt from a shaker. I was no longer obsessed with the past. Zee was a lovely shadow of what was and I am grateful to have been his girl. But now is now, and it's good. I have a castle and fresh eggs and a dog named Canary.

Punch stretched and meowed when she spied us from her favorite window. Predictably, she would race to the door to greet us. All was right in the world in spite of it moving so slowly. *Because* it was moving so slowly.

And then, from far away, I heard the metallic clatter of a slide falling into place in a carousel.

Each thing is of like form
from everlasting
and comes round again
in its cycle.
— MARCUS AURELIUS

chapter 52
CLASS REUNION

– November 1 –
2019

Canary and I maintained a discreet distance from the landlord's fancy car as it came to a stop on the drive. Canary sneezed. I felt an urge to cry happy tears. We were ready. I smoothed my hair and pasted on the smile of a perfectly stable tenant. Jakobina snarled in my head with a snarky *'good luck with that.'* I was prepared to act humble when a man's voice called out, "WENDY!"

I heard Felix ticking from inside the house. It sounded remarkably like applause.

"ZEE?"

Zee strode the gap between us, reaching for a hug but I hesitated for an instant. My ever-present reading glasses hanging around my neck presented an uncomfortable barrier to a warm embrace. I removed them and planted them on my head. Instead of a classic greeting my first words were "Sorry, these bloody things have become part of me. I need them all the time, now. They're a damn nuisance."

Momentarily at a loss for words, I managed a feeble "this *is* a surprise" as if meeting the subject of one's recent temporal dreams was a regular occurrence. Considering that the object of my past and recent affections had materialized in an extraordinary show of courage and good faith, what I meant to issue was a string of words that would make a sailor blush.

Zee pulled me into a rough hug. "The name's Peter. Lucky for you, I can fly."

I melted into the scent of his warm shoulder beneath a flannel shirt and snuggled longer than was seemly. Not nearly long enough to bridge the past of estranged best friends. I wanted to stay there. He rubbed my back. I squeezed his arms. We smiled idiotically and linked arms like old times. "Can I walk you home," he said.

A door slammed in a fit of pique from wherever phantoms go to brood.

Felix resumed his ticking and released my tongue. "Go Wendy Darling go!" he cheered.

"What on earth?" I blurted. "How…?"

Zee feigned surprise. "I thought you were expecting me."

"I can say with absolute certainty, I was not."

"You didn't get my message. I told my office to…"

"I was expecting….Oh my god. Mr. CARTER!"

Zee bowed and doffed an invisible cap the way Catcher had when we first met. "Sigmund Carter at your service. Aren't you going to introduce me to your ocean."

We sauntered to the beach with Canary tripping us up.

I introduced the water with an expansive gesture showing off a prize in a game show. "Zee… ocean. Ocean… Zee."

Zee got straight to the point. "Do you honestly think I would hand over my treasure island to anyone? I built this castle for you. Well, with you in mind. But then you were never *off* my mind. And after that dear John letter… I got busy with my career. Thatcher pushed me relentlessly. I have him to thank for becoming an architect. You have reason to be grateful to him as well. If he hadn't been around, this castle would be a sand dune. And you never returned the calls I couldn't quite make to a number I didn't know.

"I never sent you a letter."

"Your ring pretty much said goodbye forever. And so, I did the gallant thing and moved on. I pretended there was nothing untoward about the timebomb you left in my locker. I convinced myself it was a prank and in order to safeguard my sanity I never followed such an unlikely premise to its ultimate conclusion for many years. I retired several years ago and was thinking of settling here myself when I met Catcher who made me his student of metaphysics. He was an interesting diversion to old-age and so I willingly paid attention for a lark. He's persuasive and I was flattered to be singled out for attention. A bit of a mentalist with a tricky sleight of hand, is old Catcher."

"He's a good deal trickier than an innocent magician with a captive audience. Captive being the operative word."

"Catcher asked to visit my office and I gave him the grand tour. My desk was littered with unanswered mail. I was desperately trying to disengage from the business but he went directly to the pile, flipped through it and handed me an envelope with the words 'you should read this'. It was your handwritten inquiry that had reached my desk, postmarked with the current date. Funny that, coincidences. Your petition arriving, right on time, when it would hit me the hardest. A day later and it would have been too late. Strangely, purple ink can move a mountain. Your damn purple ink. It threw me I can tell you. Catcher sat me down and gave me one of his lectures on the art of timing. I realized you didn't know you were writing to me, so, in the end, your heartfelt message jumpstarted the promise I once made to take care of you. All my old feelings flooded back. I forgave you. After that, I missed you too much to stay away. Catcher volunteered to keep an eye on you, and I hoped some of his magic would help you the way it helped me. I have an interesting New-Age pamphlet about synchronicity. I'll show it to you over a cup of tea," he said.

"*New* age… *old* age… it's all good."

"And, well, the rest was a done deal. I had a series of intense dreams about you. And here I am, to see how you're faring."

I squeezed his arm to guide him around an oyster spout. "Seafaring," I said, "is an art."

He inclined his head towards the cloudless sky. "There's going to be a full moon. There'll be some kind of stars tonight."

"Lucky guess."

He stared at the horizon. "I reckon I'll be sleeping on your couch," he said, as if the notion had suddenly occurred to him.

I coughed. "Well, it *is* your couch, so I guess I have no choice, Mr. Landlord."

He winked. "No worries, I'm booked into the B&B in Glastonbury."

"Always the gentleman."

"Then it's decided. A class reunion, a celebration toast, and a date for stargazing. There's a bottle of bubbly in my car, chilling between two bags of ice."

"Champagne loosens the tongue," I said. "We have a lot to talk about."

He changed the topic fast. "Oh, I almost forgot the roses. They'll be needing water, and I brought an old friend of yours to join us."

Zee placed his hand in the middle of my back and turned me towards the castle the way a dancer leads his partner in the direction he's decided to go.

Canary bounded ahead of us – a welcome guide through the quicksand of unspoken thoughts that lay ahead.

"An un-birthday party then," I said. "There's going to be some kind of stars."

Zee spoke as the castle appeared beyond the last sand dune. We stopped to admire it – a Turner landscape turning pink and yellow in the light. "Now, who's that girl waving from the window?" he said.

chapter 53
SPECIAL DELIVERY

My tea plans were happily scotched by champagne and strawberries. Zee placed a large gift-wrapped box on an armchair where it perched like an invited guest wearing dark blue paper dotted with silver stars. Punch pawed the flowing ends of purple ribbon, delighted as a child on Christmas morning.

I lit a fire. Small flames licked a pyramid of pine logs into an intimate glow. The scent of lemon furniture polish, Felix's gentle ticking, and Zee's white roses made the living room homey. The radio, permanently tuned to an oldies station, sent the perfect love songs to serenade us. If I hadn't known better, I'd think a matchmaker was orchestrating a romantic first date.

Apart from a pair of gleaming candlesticks, the silver was set aside. Canary positioned herself in front of Zee, gazed at him lovingly, and raised her foot to his knee for attention while I lit the candles.

Jakobina was thankfully nowhere to be seen but from the corner of my eye small objects moved of their own accord. Punch hissed at Jakobina as she sidled by and swatted her ankles that only she, Canary, and I could see.

Zee's head tilted shyly as he poured. Felix ceased his ticking. For a lovely moment the only sound in the room was the fizzing and gurgling of champagne filling a pair of elegant glass flutes. The boyish grin of Zee-the-younger slowly materialized, slightly embarrassed and devilishly smug at the same time. "Champagne does loosen things," he said. He waggled a baby finger at me, slid off his pinky ring, and dropped it onto a china plate with a metallic clink.

I recognized it at once. A standard issue school ring with an enamelled crest. "My ring! How did…?"

"You didn't have to return it, you know," he said sadly. "It was over the top. I mean, I understood how you felt from your letter. Typing it was a little cold, though." He pulled a crumbling slip of folded paper from his pocket, worn to felt. "I've kept it all these years."

"But I kept the letter I wrote to you. I never sent it. It's still in the castle box, unopened. I reached for the scrap in his hand. "Let me see that."

Broken font alphabet letters from a vintage Remington read: DEAR SIGMUND - AURELIA SHOULD NEVER HAVE ACCEPTED THIS. SHE CAN'T KEEP IT. YOU DESERVE SOMEONE WHO REALLY LOVES YOU. SHE WISHES YOU WELL. SHE REMAINS YOUR FRIEND, FONDLY – A

"She used all caps. She must have been upset. And when have I ever called you Sigmund."

Zee ducked his head and winced. "Please don't. You of all people know how speaking of yourself in third person creeps me out."

"I *didn't* is my point. Because I *do* know you hate that. Someone else wrote that letter. There was a third person all right. You met her."

"Is she the ghost whose been moving things while we've been talking?" he asked with raised eyebrows. "Because she's really getting on my nerves."

GIVING UP THE GHOST

chapter 54
WARRIOR PHILOSOPHERS

It was wakeup time. I took a deep breath. "The ghost of a girl lives, well not exactly *lives*, here. Her name is Jakobina. She's trapped inside a painting. But for the moment, if you will indulge me, I will explain later."

"I await your pleasure," Zee said. "We shall let the childish poltergeist have her fun for now. But if she sent me that note, she's in for some serious feedback."

A piece of cobalt glass smashed in the kitchen but I resisted the urge to find out which one of my favorite things had been sacrificed to Jakobina's juvenile tantrum.

Nothing more was said of the increased poltergeist activities and disembodied sounds that continued to startle Canary and Punch at odd intervals. Clearly, Jakobina did not relish being ignored. Nor, I suspected, being threatened by Zee. Then the truth struck me. She wasn't simply upset. She was jealous.

Zee went quiet while I cleaned away the dishes. I assumed he was relaxing after an emotional day. But I was mistaken. Zee's even temper had brewed into a monster with teeth. His pent up anger erupted in a shout that startled Felix into a frenzied hiss. I dropped a wet plate that broke on the floor.

"That girl's letter almost ruined my life," he shouted. "If Thatcher hadn't intervened..." he stood and paced the room. "No, it's too much, Aurelia. Getting on my nerves doesn't begin to describe how I feel about the destruction this Jakobina has caused. She may not have killed us outright but she sure as hell sucked the life out of our relationship. She's a shrewd one. But she'd have to be to get you to run away. She must still be a cunning witch to keep you bewitched or enthralled or whatever she did to have held you captive for fifty-years."

Punch tore past me. Canary sat up and growled. "You're angry," I said. "And you have every right to be."

"You think. Sweetie, I'm off the wall, furious."

I grabbed his arm. "But it's over now. Can't it be over?"

He raged on, scaring me. Canary whimpered in a crouch. "OVER! How is it over. How could it *ever* be over. Of all the evil conniving female trickery. I almost hated you after that letter."

He looked up at me, tortured. "I *did* hate you before Thatcher calmed me down. I threw your ring into a dumpster. Thatcher made me go back for it. I dug for hours through indescribable filth to find it. He made me wash it and purify it with one of his weird cleansing ceremonies under a full moon. I had to wear it for months before he let me store it in a box. God… the emotions we humans hide away. And the pointless objects that take their place. Sentimental nothings twice removed, and for what? What are we like. What kind of mindless puppets. Do you know, because it escapes me. We were smart kids, weren't we. I thought we were our generation's savvy clued-in ones."

"It was all my fault. I was the weak link in the whole thing. Be mad at me. Let sleeping ghosts lie." I scrambled for the castle box hoping to distract him. I couldn't have been more wrong. He fingered every object, muttering under his breath, and all the while his seething grew into a rant. "A few useless bits of rubber and paper and buttons," he said. "These are not our greatest dreams. Not the ones I remember."

I countered immediately. "No, of course not," I replied a trifle miffed. "They're sacrifices. Reminders of *my* greatest dreams steeped in love. Memories I wanted to recreate. I was afraid my memories of us would fade with dementia. These few touchstones kept me sane."

I handed him the unsent letter, shaking with unleashed emotion, the world of recent happiness destroyed. Somewhere Jakobina was gloating. The envelope in his hand stopped his tirade. He turned it over and fingered the sealed flap. "It's purple," he said stupidly, stashed it in his pocket, and collapsed onto the sofa murmuring "I'll save it for a rainy day. That cake looks delicious. Did you make it?"

Zee rose immediately he saw my terrified face. He strode across the room nearly tripping over Canary to get to me, his expression as anguished as my own. He pulled me into a bear hug. "Look, whatever happened back then wasn't your fault, and we're getting the hell out of here, okay."

I broke away and dabbed at my eyes with a tissue.

"Come here," he said fuming again. "I'll take care of this bloody mess tomorrow, and in the meantime, dry your eyes. There's a lot to be thankful for. We're together, so, let's make that tea and eat some un-birthday cake. There's a present waiting for you. You should open it before we greet the stars."

Zee's gift had waited patiently for the perfect moment that never arrived. And in the aftermath of Zee's outrage, I was in no mood to open a present and smile graciously at the contents. A flashback of déjà vu reminded me of the betrothed Jakobina, loathe to open her gift of earrings.

Canary barked at the chair when Jakobina moved the package a quarter turn. She materialized to me for effect. I could tell from her body language she was about to hurl it across the room, or worse, into the fire. It was up to me to diffuse the energies of a jealous ghost, an incensed man, and two skittish animals.

Jakobina reached for the box but I lifted it from her hands and sent her a look of pure hatred. "I didn't know it was my un-birthday," I said into her face.

"I guess that makes me the Mad Hatter," Zee said behind me. "Mad, as in angry, being the operative word. Look, I didn't mean to scare you."

"No, it's okay. I'm glad you did. It was necessary. I needed to be shocked out of a complacency I hadn't realized I possessed."

He smiled and looked about the room, no doubt scanning for moving objects. "Possession being the operative word," he said.

The rustle of tissue recalled Punch from her hiding place.

A snowy mountain of tissue caused me to pause. I prodded it. It was soft. Punch helped me get to the centre. I parted the last layer of paper like a curtain. A black face with googly eyes stared up at me. My old Felix toy lay on a bed of crumpled white paper.

I hesitated to touch him. "Felix, is it really you?"

He lay there, black against the white, smiling.

Zee moved behind me and whispered in my ear. "Look at you, all starry-eyed over a cat doll."

"I guess it's Felix's birthday."

"If you believe in reincarnation while a person's still alive, then I guess we're celebrating our re-birth-day."

His reference to reincarnation was unexpected. "I didn't think you would be into such things."

"I had a teacher."

"Thatcher?"

"Yes, Thatcher. He was always a New-Age guy. It was a wonder the school hired him, but then he taught quantum physics, so I suppose they overlooked the weirdness. Nothing's weirder than quantum physics. Anyway, he had this old blue brochure that he swore by."

"The Art of Dreaming?"

Zee nodded. "Have you seen it?"

I tapped the top of the castle box with a teaspoon like a magic wand. "My copy is in there."

Zee snuggled closer, excited, all anger evaporated. "This is so cool. All we need is a good thunderstorm and we can play."

My expression froze his enthusiasm to ice. "Absolutely not. Wishing on that brochure's energy is asking for trouble. Besides, we don't need it. A storm is already brewing. Can't you feel it." I changed the subject, fast so he wouldn't answer. "So, how did you get Felix?"

His demeaner softened. "When I saw the sold sign on your house, I went to see your dad. I wanted something to save for you since I was sure you would come back to me. He was in rough shape but he told me to help myself to your things. I looked for the castle box or a note. He had plans to travel around Europe."

"He was finally free. I'm glad."

"And now, you and I have a second chance. Better late than never, they say."

"Felix is perfect. And now you've given him to me twice. The words thank you don't cover it."

He grinned. "Agreeing to getting out of here, might."

I sent Zee a questioning stare and smoothed Felix's plush fur. "He's in mint condition."

Zee moved closer. "I took good care of him, and by the way, I didn't keep him in a box. He sat on my desk while I studied. In fact, he helped me focus. Those eyes seemed to penetrate my tendency to feel sorry for myself. They reminded me that you were on the run somewhere, alone and troubled. They seemed to say Aurelia must have had a good reason, and now she's out there on her own, way worse off than you."

"My reasons are in that letter in your pocket," I murmured, but he didn't hear me.

We left Punch frolicking in a sea of paper and Canary asleep by the banked fire.

Zee and I took turns with my telescope. It was after midnight when the chilly night sent us inside for cocoa by the dying fire.

Zee checked the Felix clock. "It's late. The B&B closes their doors at eleven, but considering I own the place and have a key, odds are they'll keep the door unlocked for me. It's been a long day and we're both exhausted." He cast his gaze around the living room, a strange definition of a place so recently haunted by a ghost. "We can start making plans in the morning. We need a solid plan. A pact."

"I believe that pacts can sometimes be good," I countered.

I waved goodbye, hugging Felix until Zee's car drove out of sight. Canary barked at the empty drive. A disappearing car horn answered her. She sniffed Felix's toes and whined. "Let's find this chap the perfect place. I know where he belongs. But first, you need a break. She barked a sharp, yes.

"Ah, my twin," Felix exclaimed when we entered the kitchen. "And what a handsome devil he is, too – together we make a double-helix Felix."

"It's too late for wit," I said. "My wits have gone bye-bye."

I cleared a wicker armchair of books and papers and settled Felix against the cushions. "He's going to live right here," I announced to my faithful clock, loud enough for the benefit of the invisible girl who wasn't there. "In plain sight of you. So, please don't let some nasty poltergeist get her protoplasm on him."

Felix's tail hummed like a light sabre. "I doubt Jakobina will be facing Zee anytime soon. He's quite the formidable landlord."

"He's more quick to anger than I remembered."

"He's allowed. He grew up."

Felix's tail stilled. "I hope that time can resume its natural pace, soon," he said. "I'm getting too old for shenanigans. Comeuppances make heavy task masters."

As I climbed the stairs, Felix spoke inside my head. "Believe me child, I'm over the moon that you're happy, but take care. Beyond our beach there be quicksand. Sweet dreams. You will need all your wits about you, tomorrow. We aren't out of the sand traps quite yet. Can you not hear the distant rumbling of a thunderclap?"

Do I dare
Disturb the universe?
In a minute there is time
For decisions and revisions
which a minute will reverse.
— T.S. Eliot

chapter 55
THE NINTH LIFE

Felix 2 fit in, formally accepted by Punch, our family's designated alpha. I found her sleeping on Felix 2's chair curled next to him with an extended paw draped over his legs. One of her claws pinned him to her for protection or ownership, likely both. Cats don't mess around when it comes to staking a claim.

The stramash of the previous night was forgotten. In its place was a day dedicated to rebuilding a new world. Felix the clock nattered as if a bird had landed on the window ledge. "Time for brunch," he purred. "Zee's here."

I checked my hair in the mirror. "Do I look rested?"

Felix snickered. "All things considered, rested might be pushing it," he said. "You look happy."

"Thanks."

"By the way," he continued, "Jakobina put in a short appearance, earlier. She moved a few pieces of your blue glass around but beat it when she saw Felix sitting on the chair. I think he gave her a much deserved shock. You know, it's times like that I wish I had a cuckoo to crow my good tidings."

I pinched my cheeks and smoothed my skirt.

Canary barked at the door a heartbeat before Zee's knock.

"Time is a hard master," Felix said. "I say let the new shenanigans begin and have done with them. None of us are getting any younger."

. . .

Zee was slightly portly in the dignified way of a tall statuesque man. His steely-grey hair was worn longer than usual for a man of his years, tied at the nape of his neck in the manner of an eighteenth-century cavalier. All that was missing was a brocade coat, a lace cravat, and a tricorn hat. Yesterday, his Armani suit had brought him into our century with an aura of success. Today he was the picture of a resplendent beachcomber in khaki cargo pants, sandals, and a black T-shirt. His suitcase in the back seat of the car announced he was moving in.

We walked Canary, dried her with several towels, and drove to The Grail Café for brunch, where Canary, being the only dog, and accompanied by the owner of the island, was welcomed with open arms. I ordered lobster bisque, Zee ordered chicken noodle. Other than that, he was all high-tech to my country mouse. I explained my theory of divination-by-sea-glass, giving examples, and presented my blue specimen as final proof. "I believe this belongs to you," I said.

The shard gave off cobalt sparks in Zee's palm. Neither of us were shocked. Zee held it up to the light. "If this color indicates what you say it does, then I suggest it's a wedding gift. Marry me, Wendy," he said. "Let's get the hell out of here."

The proposal of marriage sat on the table like a mute centerpiece. "Take your time," Zee chuckled checking his watch. "I'm a busy man. I don't have all day."

Canary gave a high-pitched whine from under the table. I reached down and ruffled her ears. "We wouldn't leave without you," I said.

"And Punch," Zee added. "We can all go for a holiday and come back when the place is clear of troublesome guests. I have a house on the mainland. I presume an exorcism is possible?"

"One would think," I mumbled to myself.

After lunch, Zee and I sauntered arm-in-arm through Glastonbury, window shopping, pausing frequently to kiss like teenagers. We made a stop at the bookstore where Zee retrieved a package. Special order, he said. While I checked in at 'The Findings' for my mail, Zee bought a bag of M&M's and a Celtic Claddagh ring that he slipped on my little finger. "For friendship," he said. "No pressure."

Outside, Zee embraced the day with a deep breath. "Do you want to climb the Tor to the standing stone?" he asked. "The view is breathtaking."

"No," I answered abruptly, surprising myself. I shivered, suddenly overcome with nausea. "Another time, perhaps. I'm still catching my breath from last night."

"I was a little out of control," Zee said. "I didn't mean to scare you."

I busied myself tying my shoelaces and spoke to the ground. "It's all good. My head needed a good shake." What I didn't tell him, was that it had been his mentioning the standing stone that had sent a whiplash of fear through me.

I thought Jakobina was gone.

The conversation drifted into an appraisal of the last twenty-four hours. I proffered no immediate compliments, Zee hated those. We shared a knowing glance across a purring cat. "Surf's up," I said cheekily. "I saw your suitcase."

He grinned back like a schoolboy. "I detect a metaphor, darling girl," he said which made me blush. "Is that what you call it?"

I managed to utter "I've missed you," before dissolving into tears. "I hoped you'd find me."

He pulled me close. "You knew I would," he said into my hair.

I whispered into his shirt. "How long can you stay?"

Jakobina slammed an imaginary door so hard behind us we broke apart. Punch retreated to the floor where she woke Canary by kneading her fur into a pillow.

I exaggerated a shrug. "Must be a jealous wee ghost," I said.

Canary proceeded to wash Punch's face in one long lick.

Zee reached into his pocket and placed the Zee Stone in my hand.

"Returned to sender," he said. "If you'll have me, I can stay forever."

I accepted his proposal.

chapter 56
IF DREAMING MAKES IT SO

Back home, in the evening, Zee and I sat side-by-side in front of a grand fire. Canary splayed out like a rug as close to the heat as she could without bursting into flames. Punch curled up between us. My gold claddagh ring flashed blue and gold in the firelight, showing off its traditional design of a crown above a pair of cupped hands holding a heart.

I waited until Zee smiled at me over his midnight cocoa. "It's confession time," I said. "I hear it's good for the soul, and by soul I mean spirit, and by spirit I mean ghost. Are you still with me?"

"Pinch me," he said amused. "I think you'll find I'm not a ghost."

"You know what I mean."

He took a sip of cocoa and licked his lips. "Correct me if I'm wrong," he said. "I'm here to save myself and a damsel in distress. You, as it happens, and just in time as it turns out. Is that the bigger picture?"

I took his hand gently, prepared to die a small death or two for true love. "You can help me exorcize a ghost and annul a legal agreement that doesn't exist on paper."

His smile remained but he squeezed my hand involuntarily. "Back up Wendy. I'm hanging on to the tail of a kite, here."

"I'm sorry to be the bearer of such impossible news. I never thought to believe in ghosts, reincarnation, time-travel, mind-control, and possession, or that I might need a lawyer to exorcise one... or two restless spirits."

"Two?"

My eyes flew into panic.

Zee noticed. "Sorry, I'm all ears. Proceed." He polished the heart in my ring with his fingertip and kissed it like a suitor. "Breathe sweetheart," he said. "The worst is over. We're together, now. You're not alone, whatever happens. The past is buried even if your ghostly guests are not."

I opened cagily with "I've learned, the hard way, what friendship is and isn't."

"If I recall," Zee said, "convoluted was the way you preferred to learn things." He noticed me recoil with my eyes squeezed shut, let go of my hand, and folded his own in his lap, contrite. "Sorry, I'll just listen."

"I know the difference between vulnerable adult and innocent underage child, and who my friends are. But if you've met Catcher you may be well on your way to that realization yourself."

He kissed my hand. "Let's just say, I'm catching up. Catcher is a ghost?"

I hesitated, soaking up the wonderful sensation of being cherished, and began my 'coming clean' speech, gently, reluctantly. "A few days ago I received a shock," I said. "It seems that both Jakobina *and* Catcher are ghosts. Two ghosts who desperately want something from both of us. But it's even more complicated."

Zee cradled his cocoa and spoke softly. "That would explain the double exorcism. Go on."

I planned to outline events slowly but soon my words raced, embarrassed to be aired in front of a man I wanted to stay. "Catcher is, or was, Thatcher. Thatcher was a young man named Mattias who lived in seventeenth-century Holland."

Zee nodded indulgently complacent. I was encouraged and forged on, but speeded up to get the facts over with. I wanted our new life to start with an erased blackboard.

"I may have shared Jakobina's memories in a past life. She told me I was distant family, which I don't believe for a second."

I paused to check Zee's reaction. He seemed to be studying the marshmallow floating in his cocoa. Not good. I needed the reassurance of his smile. "At the very least, I am the manifestation of one of her dreams. For what it's worth, and as far as I can understand, I am a projection of Jakobina's unfinished business. A doppelganger, so to speak, with longstanding identity issues. Not very flattering but there it is. So, now I have an intruder to blame for my idiosyncrasies, past and present. Jakobina and I are related but not actually family."

Zee tilted his head in a question, his eyes never leaving the marshmallow. "And what about me?"

"You are the best of us. I guess this is the time you can ask for your money back."

At last, Zee placed his cocoa on the table and looked at me. There were tears in his eyes. He took both my hands in his and kissed each one in a princely fashion that made me cringe. "I wasn't exempt, you know," he said through knitted brows. "I saw a girl who kept disappearing in front of me to prove something. Maybe that I was nuts, but it wasn't that. She had something to do with you leaving, that much she made clear. She said terrible things I knew weren't true."

My eyes felt kaleidoscopic.

"Thatcher proved to me later, that time was an interchangeable science where dreams were substantial psychological realities with physical consequences. Apart from a lot of unnecessary emotional fallout, he was a good guy in the end. It wasn't easy but I pieced together some of his theories into a sound scientific premise. So, I guess that game I played about subliminal messages in song lyrics wasn't far from the truth. Everything is up for grabs." He cradled my cheek in his hand. "And, Wendy old thing. You are money well spent."

Zee laid his head in my lap and closed his eyes. "This sea air makes a person sleepy," he said. "I feel a cat nap approaching." His breathing evened out into theta waves. Rapid eye movements and a smile on his face informed me he was dreaming.

"No worries," Felix called out from the kitchen. "It's going to be alright, now, IF you follow Doc's advice. Two heads are much better than four."

"If only dreaming made it so," I replied.

Felix hissed. "Has the penny dropped? Catcher is the manifestation of Doc's dreamcatcher gift," he said. "Do you see?"

The next day, Zee presented me with his special order from 'Fisher King's Second-hand Books'. Brown paper peeled back to reveal a thick notebook with blank pages – a writer's dream. On the cover was a gold embossed title: The Memories of Aurelia Marcus Carter – a love story. "I figure we're worth a page or two," he said. "A very merry un-Christmas to you."

That night I checked the sky holding Zee's hand. "I wish I may, I wish I might, have this dream I dream tonight," I said.

chapter 57

LIGHTNING IN A BOTTLE

For two weeks, Zee and I skirted our history – a couple of cagey wolves perfecting the arts of browsing and strolling. Mornings and evenings we strolled the beach with Canary and Punch. When it wasn't drizzling, we browsed the shops in Glastonbury before eating a hearty lunch in the Grail Café, holding hands across a table that overlooked the harbour.

After a happy browse in 'The Findings', Zee produced a small paper bag from his coat pocket. "A message in a bottle," he said triumphantly, "without the bottle." He held it aloft with both hands as if presenting it on an invisible pillow with the words, "It's not made of glass, your majesty, but it spoke to me. I believe it has a message for us. I couldn't resist."

With that, he rapped the package, hard on the table. Colored lights turned the bag into a tiny lantern. Intrigued, I opened it to find a polyhedron-shaped ball the size of a plum that flickered with colored lights when squeezed or otherwise agitated.

We drifted into an hypnotic daydream for two.

"Somewhere in the world movie stars are laughing and chatting," Zee said, staring at it entranced. "Hollywood could never imagine a story as weird as ours."

"I can hear the ice clinking in their glasses," I replied. "They're basking by swimming pools. Wearing their movie-star shades." I flounced imaginary shoulder-length Hollywood hair. "That used to be me in an imagined future that passed me by."

"Passed *us* by," Zee reflected.

Our history came out from behind a dark cloud, prompting me to announce a serious confession. "In all our time apart, I've found no link with any god or super-intelligence other than the apparent 'shadow' of a teacher named Catcher I met on the beach who took me under his wing. Kind of sad."

"Kind of scientific, really. I believe life is mostly a free-dance of hydrogen forming and reforming in myriads of incarnations," Zee announced like a true professor of metaphysics.

I stared at him, impressed. "Spiritual books seem puny and out of context. I'm beginning to understand how everything on Earth is connected. Remember the days when we read to each other from Alan Watts."

I must have looked like a meditating saint with my hands cupped into a mudra holding a planet the size of a baseball. I recalled Alan's philosophy and his artful twists of language: *Earth is the ultimate organism which trees and peoples in verbs.*

I passed Zee the light ball and leaned on his shoulder. "I do remember," he said. "Since trees produce other trees, they're 'treeing' just as humans procreate the species by 'peopling'. Did I get that right?"

I retrieved the ball and squeezed it into life – a wild singularity pulsed methodically through the spectrum. Beside me sat the miracle of Zee, and there I was, close enough to touch, a completely sane human holding a star.

Time ceased to matter. We sat on the porch swing, rocking in the dark as strobing flashes, illuminating us for a few milliseconds or maybe a thousand years.

I imagined the miniature Earth's life sped up, so that, in my hands, it evolved through the risings and fallings of civilizations and ice-ages and meteor impacts. Now and then small puffs of red smoke billowed from atomic bombs and sparks flew out to orbit and return and smash-mashed back into the ball. A few cobalt ones zing-pinged past my ear. The globe felt like a warm egg. It cracked open to reveal a tiny canary, and as its wings grew, it flew, and in its place was a yellow dandelion head that aged white and fluffy with seeds that burst into violet-scented dust.

Zee's voice nudged me awake. "Wendy? Where did you go?" he asked. "You seemed to disappear." He smiled sheepishly and held up his hands in protest. "Metaphorically speaking."

. . .

Zee serenaded me as we washed the dishes. *We are stardust, we are golden, and we've got to get back to the garden...* a gentle reminder of being alive on a whirling rock and lives still promising beyond imagining. *everywhere there were songs and celebrations ....*

And I dreamed I saw...

I stopped him. "It's perfectly logical for a bomber to turn into a butterfly on this island," I said. "So... what *is* that ball you found? Why does it represent us?"

Zee listened to the ball and shook his head. "It's being cagey," he said and tossed it to me. I held it to my ear like a seashell. "Let's recap, shall we. What have we got, here? Give me your first answer."

He grinned like a kid with a secret. "Lightning in a bottle."

"Yes. A captured possibility on an island of impossibilities."

"Aha," he said with dramatic flair, holding it aloft. "Behold. The ghost of a chance."

The business of us began innocently enough as a pep rally for two. Zee's arm was more solid than it had any right to be. We flipped through our yearbook of mugshots that resembled innocent perps in a police line-up. Reminiscing loosened our reserve. Soon we were punch drunk on wine and the sudden release of a strain we'd ignored.

"It was Paranormal High without the recreational drugs," Zee quipped.

I pretended to be a home room teacher. "Please answer present when I call your name."

Zee raised his hand. "May I be excused, Miss? I'm from the future."

"Ziggy Carter?" I called out. *Stifled silence.* I tried again. "Zee Carter, are you here?"

"Definitely present and accounted for," he said.

The reality of his answer sobered me. My shyness returned. The grim reality of our situation replaced lighthearted giddiness. I veered off into an innocent question laced with serious overtones. "Did you know it was me in your office?" I asked. "I mean, *when* did you know it was me? I felt as if I was being watched."

Zee looked away and spoke into the wall of blue glass. "I *was* watching you. I knew it was you. I had a hidden camera installed at Catcher's insistence."

"It was in the frame of the seascape painting, wasn't it," I said. "You didn't trust me."

Zee showed me his face. His expression was contrite. He traced the rim of his half empty wine glass with a finger until it sang. "I could use a refill," he said reaching for an unopened bottle.

His evasiveness unnerved me. "I'm serious. I need to know," I said. "It's important to me."

"Okay okay," he began. "Your signature in your query letter was a big clue. But the clincher was its color. Who else uses a fountain pen with a calligraphic nib? And who mixes red and peacock blue ink together to make purple? Who uses handmade mauve paper the color of amethysts?" Zee raised his empty glass in a toast. "I give you the one and only, Aurelia Marcus."

"I did. I did use mauve paper. And it wasn't contrived. What made me do that? Better yet, *who* made me do that?" and then I remembered how Jakobina had urged me to be creative that day. She'd suggested in exacting words to 'show my true colors' to make the best impression.

Zee continued, blithely unaware of my memory. "And long before all that, your little time bomb arrived in my locker – a time capsule that couldn't be denied. Well, I had to tell someone. I thought I was going nuts. Thatcher was the nearest thing to a counsellor with scientific principles. He calmed me down. I'd recalled our heated discussions about the logistics of time travel in the Stargazy Club based on Einstein's theories. Astrophysics had credibility, and the way Thatcher described it, pseudo-science wasn't the second cousin of woo woo. Over the years sci-fi movies and time travel seemed like pure fantasy but I couldn't shake the newspapers you sent. Published front pages don't lie. But my work claimed my time. I even traveled to England to study castle construction with a vague notion I might run into you camped out at Bodium Castle. I remembered the name."

I sighed, relieved. "And that's where you learned how to shrink Versailles into a pocket sized dream, for me. You designed 'Bodium/Camelot' with a surprise twist of Sistine ceiling."

He accepted my compliment with a shy incline of his head. "Thatcher had specifically mentioned I should visit Tintagel. He was drawn to all things King Arthur, and for a time, he had me hooked, too. Many years after he died, I met your friend, Catcher and he became my mentor."

"I'm surprised Thatcher didn't orchestrate us bumping into each other for shock value or his personal entertainment."

"Thatcher mentioned once, maybe more than once, that timing was everything. And he said something else which I never understood. *Only art is truly immortal,* he said. Right out of the blue and with tears in his eyes."

"I only met Catcher a few months ago," I said. "When did you met him?"

"Two years ago."

I corrected him. "Try fifty-years ago. Our teacher Thatcher had us in his counselling clutches. Thatcher, alias Catcher, and Jakobina, stage-managed us within weeks of each other. Why? The two of us were mentored back in 1965. And when I say mentored, I mean controlled. I don't know about you, but that makes me feel manipulated. We were set up, Zee. That's abuse of a minor. *Twice.* Does that sound too dramatic?"

Zee downed the last of his wine and stared into the glass, swilling the invisible dregs. "I could use something stronger than this."

"I have brandy. Will that do? It's in the kitchen."

He nodded. "Lovely."

I attempted to stand, but Zee grabbed my arm and pulled me back down. "It wasn't a lack of trust, Aurelia. I wasn't hiding from you. I wanted to protect you."

"I understand. You had to be sure I wasn't crazy."

"No. You've got it all wrong. I had to be sure that *Catcher* wasn't."

"He's a tad intense."

"Ten years after I graduated from engineering college, Thatcher died. That would have been around 1979-ish."

I took both Zee's hands in mine. "Sweetie. I don't think he died," I said. "I'm pretty sure he was already dead."

chapter 59
HUMBLE PIE IN THE SKY

Zee made me sit with a cup of tea as he cleaned the kitchen from his elaborate brunch of Eggs Benedict and strawberry parfaits. I waited in the blue alcove savoring the sounds of his presence, lost in a daydream of future happiness.

Felix piped up. "Don't get too lost," he said. "Before you enter the labyrinth pick up the thread at the entrance. It's your lifeline. More importantly, of your dream life."

I'm sure the sea called me after I stared hard into Felix's eyes, daring him to blink first. The beckoning fingers of a salty breeze hooked my nose and I followed. "Hang on tight and don't let go," he called after me. "Hold fast to the way home. That's what lifelines are for. Do you see? The words life and feline combine into an important message… trust me, pussycat, your feline persona represents serious business."

The world ended at the third sand dune. My breath caught in my chest. The beach was in flames. I was betrayed. Outlined against the darkening sky was a moving shape that emitted definitive sounds of anguish. A heart was breaking. I almost turned away but Felix cat-swore from his command post. *"Stay and face the hour of reckoning, skylark. True love is not for sissies."*

Jakobina and Mattias stood as a single entity with four arms and two pairs of legs braided together. Mattias was placating her, trying to shush her with little success. I wanted to run at them, arms akimbo, screaming abuse. "Liars. Murderers. You can't come back here. You're not welcome."

The waves lapped calmly – a cat's tongue licking the shore.

My body dissolved into the spongy sand and sucked me into a cold vortex. I sunk deep into emotional quicksand. The grit of wet sand on my skin informed me I had only dropped to my knees. In the distance, a grey blot that was Canary, lifted her head as if I'd called her. She bounded towards me, tongue lolling, a doggy grin on her face. She reached me, whining hello.

The beach was deserted but I swore there was an outline of shimmering heatwaves where Jakobina and Mattias once stood locked in a furtive embrace. I almost believed I'd been hallucinating but I heard Mattias's voice in my head. *"Aurelia, my dear girl. Forgive us. All will be explained. All wrongs will be made accountable. I promise. Let us in. Please. Save us. Save yourself. Save Zee."*

I grabbed Canary's collar out of habit and buried my nose into her wet fur. The smell revived me. I looked over her head to a sad beach. The surf roared wildly. Emotionally drained, I collapsed, rolled onto my back, and let the cold sand act as a poultice. Spinal shockwaves met the pull of the tides until the planet's rhythms flowed in sync with mine. Canary prodded me. I calmly counted the grains of sand on her wet nose. "Let's go home," I said to Canary, the beach, and the couple who were no longer there.

Canary and I slipped into the deserted kitchen. I gave Felix a cursory glance and retched my fears into the sink. I held my head under the kitchen tap, twisted my hair in a tea towel, and tore it off after I caught a glimpse of myself in the hall mirror, looking for all the world like a senior version of Jakobina. I dried Canary's feet with the 'turban', too damp and miserable to wonder at Zee's absence. "There's a note," Felix boomed. "He's gone fishing."

Zee's note was taped to the fridge. It read: *gone to town for oysters and pearls. Back soon, I love you. Z*

As I climbed the stairs the disturbing lines of a childhood poem, curtesy of my mother, shuddered through my head in Felix's creepy low-pitched mystery voice. *'Yesterday, upon the stair, I met a man who wasn't there.'*

Punch was waiting on my bed. She and Canary curled either side of me like bookends and I slept between them without incident. It was only upon waking from the approach of Zee's car that the nightmare of confronting Jakobina resumed. I loathed her. Mattias disgusted me.

My faith in Jakobina had been entirely compromised… twice in as many days. Our pact was shattered beyond repair. I would have to adopt a more aggressive approach to declare my absolute decision to die naturally, the old fashioned way, without her mumbo jumbo scheme. I pasted a smile on my face for Zee. There was no need to remind him of my troubles.

I needn't have bothered. I descended the stairs, past the man who wasn't there, intending to run smiling into Zee's arms but he held me at arms length and studied my face. "What's wrong," he said. "Something's happened. Tell me."

Mattias materialized slowly in the blue alcove when I was alone. "Hey," he said casually, using the curt monosyllabic speech of a modern teenager. It was almost endearing at first. Strangely, I believed in him, due in large part to the prolonged purring of Felix's approval when he entered the kitchen. Catcher had moved on, whereabouts unknown. As Mattias, his moods stabilized into compassion and the pearls returned to his eyes.

"I'm in no mood to play chess," I said. "Not with you or your self-serving whacko girlfriend."

Mattias stood his ground. "She's my wife."

I shrugged, unimpressed. "And speaking of stalemates, you can tell your beloved self-serving whacko *wife* our contract is terminated."

"She's aware."

I bristled at his flip attitude. "Your childhood sweetheart nearly destroyed the love of my life when she sent him a heartless letter in my name. She returned the ring Zee gave me with calculated coldblooded spite. Did you know?"

"I didn't until after it was sent. It was a mistake."

"It was a slap in the face to a sweet seventeen-year-old boy that almost killed his spirit."

"I know. I was there."

"Yeah. Zee mentioned that you saved him."

"I was there to catch him when he fell, that's all."

I sent Mattias a sidelong glance of indifference. "Is that why you called yourself CATCHer?"

His answer reeked of insolence. "Nope."

"Don't be coy it doesn't suit you."

"Dr. Sanderson's theories on dream analysis were breakthrough. His students and followers called him the 'dream catcher' with great affection. I shortened it to Catcher. You called him the 'Sandman'."

"Hickory dickory dock," Felix recited.

Mattias rolled his eyes at Felix. "The staff called him Doc."

"I know about Catcher *and* Thatcher. So, who else have you possessed? "Were you Vermeer, as well?"

He lowered his gaze to his shoes. "Yeah. Sort of. Once or twice."

His sullen teenage act grated on me. I turned into an old shrill. "Did you even ask his permission, young man?"

He straightened like a soldier. "Yes, Ma'am. I borrowed Vermeer's body when I needed it to play a part." He slouched back against the wall. "No big deal."

I thought back to the time-slip when I experienced being painted by Vermeer, and the feelings of lust that clearly remained within me as the after-effects of Jakobina's sexual fantasy. "That day in his studio when I was inside Jakobina, I thought you were a bit smarmy with your *'welcome to immortality'* line – a cool customer. But now I see it was the work of a consummate actor. You."

Mattias flinched. "I seem to remember you borrowing Jakobina's body to play a part on several occasions. I guess it was okay when you did it."

"I was the innocent party."

"You are part of our story. Never innocent. Just stubborn. A pearl girl. Someone you used to be in a previous life perhaps?"

"If you're suggesting I used to be Jakobina, it's not funny. We've been over all that nonsense. It doesn't make sense. She would have told me."

Mattias chucked me under my chin to make sure I saw he was serious. "She did. She wasn't. But lucid dreams rarely lie. There are laws and rules of conduct and subtle truths. You have to see truths for yourself. Jakobina is bound by silence. She wanted to explain. She didn't handle it well."

"It's a little late, don't you think."

"She tried a few times. In her defense, you forget things."

"In *my* defense there were things I *had* to forget. And, by the way, I was assured I suffered from severe memory loss."

"Zee told me you'd always been selective."

"So, who was I then? Jakobina waited too long. Fifty years!"

Mattias's eyes said *can't you do better than that?* His mouth remained closed as he answered "three-hundred, I believe."

"Three-hundred-and-fifty-four to be exact," I countered. "I happen to know Vermeer painted Jakobina's portrait in 1665. I recall her mentioning the year we met was the 300th anniversary of her creative internment. I studied art for a reason. And, considering my circumstances, did you imagine 'The Girl With A Pearl Earring' wouldn't be a keen subject of interest to me?"

Mattias examined his immaculate cuticles with exaggerated concentration. "Time is tricky stuff. Strange things can happen on anniversaries. Jakobina lived to be seventy-two. She died in 1720. The year 2020 will be the 300th anniversary of her physical death."

He looked familiar. He reminded me of... A rush of buried memories recalled the intimate recurring visitations from a ghostly lover in my twenties.

Mattias took the bemused stance of a patient teacher, his arms crossed, legs apart, waiting with a smile on his face, watching me calculate the math of personal ancient history. And then, I knew him.

The shock of recognition unleashed a flood of sorrow, anger, and embarrassment. "It was you," I shouted. "You were my elemental visitor! All those visits. The passion. Was I just another game to you? Some cruel ghostly sport? And you played it... you played *me*, so earnestly."

"Love is never a game, Aurelia. You of all people should know that. Besides, you needed to, pardon the pun, wake up. Sexually, I mean."

"So, you callously borrowed *my* body, too. Why on earth did you make love to me?"

"I didn't. I wouldn't. I didn't have to," Mattias said looking sheepish. "You were sleeping inside Jakobina's memories."

chapter 61
BINGE WHINGING

Jakobina appeared on our doorstep a few mornings later like a waif in a fairy tale, seeking shelter.

"Sorry, whatever you're selling, I'm not buying anything today," I said. "Clear off." Canary responded to the tone of my voice and joined me with a low growl.

Jakobina reached out to pet her. "Hello girl, it's me, you remember me."

Canary did remember. She snapped at Jakobina's transparent fingers.

Jakobina disappeared with the sound of a balloon popping only to rematerialize behind me in the hall. "I wanted to explain how it was," she whinged. "How the famous 'Dutch School' of artists controlled my life. How it was the *essence* of my life." Her bottom lip trembled and her voice faded to a pathetic whisper. "How it *destroyed* my life." She followed me into the kitchen with Canary whining behind her.

"And how it destroyed *mine*," I chimed in. "It'd better be good. You've got five minutes. Felix will be timing you. But I ask you to consider that there's been far too many schools of thought lately, so give me a break. I'm trying to sort the puzzle pieces of my own high school disaster, thanks to you."

"There will be further tragic consequences if you ignore me," Jakobina said.

I stared back unimpressed. "I prefer to call them incentives."

Jakobina removed an earring and dangled it aloft like a carrot. "There's a prize at the end," she said seductively – "you might say it's a special achievement award."

"Thanks," I replied, with a vicious smirk. "But I have all the earrings I want or will ever need, and besides my ears aren't pierced."

She ignored me. "I met a ghost when I was eighteen," she said. "At least I thought I had." She took a seat at the kitchen table. Blue waves of light played through her transparent form. I wasn't used to such a pathetic ghostly ploy and it unnerved me.

"Don't let my appearance bother you. I have a story to tell, and this is the best way to deliver it. If it scares you, all the better. It should. True love is a terrifying experience."

I turned my back on her and plugged in the kettle. "At ease," I said to Canary. She dropped to the floor, and assumed a position of sleepy indifference. Felix kept a watchful eye. Punch slunk into the sanctuary past Jakobina's shoes and kneaded Canary's fur as if she was a bed. I was protected by three guardians. "You *thought* you met a ghost?"

"I did. Because, in most respects, Mattias *was* a ghost, but I didn't believe in them until… well… after I died."

"But?"

Jakobina held up her hand for quiet and pressed on. She exposed an expression of genuine anguish, covered her face momentarily, inhaled deeply, and smoothed her skirt. "There was a terrible explosion in Delft. It was October 12, 1654. I was six. It killed my father and Mattias. Part of me grieved in silence for the love of my life. Mattias and I were meant for each other. And you know, I knew it the moment I saw him, as young children often do."

"Zee wooed me when I was nine," I interrupted. "I didn't know he was 'the one' until I turned ten."

Jakobina's exasperation showed in her knitted brows. "Sorry," I said. "This is your story."

She nodded her thanks. "When Mattias died the greater part of me died too. As I said, I was emotionally, torn in half. Vermeer captured the troubled side of me in his painting, the part of me completely ready to die and join Mattias. Vermeer was an intense artist. He bragged to everyone that he painted souls rather than people, and included hidden details in his portraits. I don't know how he did this. I only know that this was so."

My expression of disbelief made Jakobina pause. She shook her head and continued. "My remaining half-spirit lived on playing the game of marriage. And after a strange and blissful encounter, the me left behind grew old and died in a foreign country. But *she* was already half-dead. What I never knew was how determined lovers can be to stay together. In any case, I remained a fractured spirit. The hopelessly besotted me was trapped in the painting, the other aimless unhinged me reincarnated many years later as your mother, Emily."

Canary sat upright and barked. Instinctively she moved closer and I hooked my fingers under her collar, and took shallow breaths. "I need a minute," I said, voice shaking. I stared up at Felix but his face was a blank white circle. His hands and numbers were gone. His ticking had stopped.

Jakobina gave me ten seconds and started to speak at breakneck speed. "Through no fault of her own, your mother was doomed to be unstable – half out of her mind, reliving my grief and insanity. As Emily's daughter, you inherited the sadness and fears that she and I shared.

Naturally, you expected to follow her into madness. And I was desperate enough to use your fear to entrap you into saving Mattias and me. Please consider that I did *not* create the domino effect of compound suffering, nor did I want to keep grieving in my next life as Emily. Mattias taught me that acts of compensation inherent in the human soul seek and find in order to mourn and remember. And sometimes they purposely forget in the hopes of beginning a new life to find new love, or better yet, find an old one. But this I *have* learned from direct experience, it *is* possible to meet one's mate again at an appointed time chosen by destiny. But one must be extremely patient. One must wait. Sometimes hundreds of years over several dreary lifetimes.

· · ·

I remained seated in stunned silence trying to absorb the bizarre notion that my mother and Jacobina shared the same spirit. Jakobina ignored my skepticism as her best plan of attack. "So, I hope you can now see, Aurelia, that you come by your negativity honestly. The instability. The anger and grief. The devastating loss, helplessness and isolation, including Mattias's headaches. And losing a beloved parent too soon. My father perished in a moment of needless violence."

"Seeing isn't the same as believing," I said. "But please go on. Fill in the gaps. What am I missing?"

"We were the children of artists," Jakobina resumed. "The boys in our community kept the family businesses alive by growing into apprentices and artists in their own right. As I said, my father died in the Thunderclap."

"Thunderclap?"

"That's what we called the explosion. A few of his paintings survived, but my Mattias, his apprentice, had been working with him and was also lost. My grief was unbearable.

And so I grew up as a teenager, surrounded by the world of art and apprentices I barely acknowledged, including my two older brothers and their friends. One of them, Pieters, took an interest in me. He was kind and life threw us together in our small world dedicated to art. Piet was apprenticed to Vermeer, and I was handpicked, as several of us 'artist's daughters' were, to be his models.

To me, Piet was another older brother. To Piet, I was the one he'd chosen to be his wife.

Eventually, I became convinced that the good man who cared so much for me could make me happy. I wanted a child. And so, I found myself married without being asked. It just happened. Like a daydream. I loved Piet as a friend, and I was trying too hard to forget Mattias to pay attention.

And so, my marriage portrait was undertaken as a great compliment from a master to his friend and apprentice. Master Vermeer finished it in 1665. I felt no aftereffects or pre-knowledge of my future locked inside it. Piet and I married. My portrait went on display for a short time. Time enough for a troubled young man to see it. Time enough to change his life and mine. The young man was Mattias. He had not died in the explosion as I'd feared. His head injuries had been severe enough to cause amnesia. He'd been sent away to an asylum where his drawing skills never left him, and such was his talent, the powers that be, granted him a chaperoned pass to Delft to see the art.

He came face-to-face with my portrait, and by his reports, awoke with instant recognition. Not just of me. His entire life replayed but he was left with terrible headaches and a bizarre ability to know things most of us can't possibly know. Ironically, with the agonies of memory loss came the ability to see the future. It wasn't long after that, he discovered he could time travel in his sleep… or what passed for sleep. His body shut down and he mentally disappeared.

My destiny changed as destinies do, from a plan preconceived beyond our understanding. That these things happen is a mystery. And when you find yourself deep inside one, you have no option but to go with it to see where it will end, hoping against hope, that it ends in a blissful reunion. I assure you, that promise overrides compassion. I am ashamed to admit that a reunion with Mattias was often all I saw. I never hesitated to use you, and in doing so, I implicated Zee.

I am telling you this because, inadvertently, both of you are part of this plan. And there is nothing I can do to change it. Or rather, there was, but I was selfish. I didn't… I *couldn't* wait to meet Mattias at the appointed time and so I rather commandeered you, and here we are."

"I am here, too," a disembodied voice said.

Mattias entered the room through the door in the conventional fashion of the living, and moved over to Jakobina to stand behind her. His hand resting lightly on her shoulder spoke volumes of ownership and bonding. *'She is mine,'* it said. Jakobina reached up and linked fingers. *'I am his,'* her gesture replied.

Jakobina leaned back into Mattias' chest and closed her eyes. Not in bliss but in pain. Mattias disengaged his hand to hug her tightly. He spoke, resting his chin on the top of her bared head. The blue silk turban had been abandoned for quite some time to reveal the color of hair that romantics dubbed titian. "We can lie and plead but unless you agree, our second chance is lost until another time," Mattias said. "And it was possible for me to know when. In our case it meant hundreds of years. The gods alone know who writes these rules. The mythology of children's stories are rife with them. Three wishes. Incantations. Spilling salt, stepping on cracks, full moons, walking backwards, crossing fingers, breaking a mirror. Senseless things on the surface, but life-changing… *death-changing* conditions if left to fester."

They presented a reasonable argument with all their absurdity. I had no such belief in a supreme master who answered to one's bidding on some days, ignored them the next, and shattered their lives with such numbing disregard. "God alone, indeed," I said. "Let's leave God out of this, shall we. Or at least reduce his name to a small 'g' as in the genies of mythology… there are dozens of gods, each with the power to dabble with human lives. If you ask me they have a lot to answer for."

Mattias faced me. "Look, we may not have handled this well. And ironically, under the latest circumstances, we cannot go back again. New life begins tomorrow. Reincarnation is a tomorrow word. A future word. A future world."

I was far from forgiving. "All this time slipping, then? The sandcastles, the lessons, the posturing. The lies?"

"They were meant to serve a purpose," Mattias said. "We bent a few rules. We were a pair of immature children, but we were… we *are*, old souls. My lessons were real. I was a teacher and a healer in my final years. I had a bit of a following."

Jakobina squeezed her eyes in pain. Mattias kissed her hair. "There will be a time for us," he whispered tenderly. His eyes glazed over into a time only he could see. "One day, soon or far. Never forget that this is a truth I have seen that can only be delayed but never changed." He sounded like a soothsayer.

Jakobina came to life, so to speak, to address me. "Now that you have Zee, I expect you won't be inclined to leave him at our originally appointed date for my benefit."

"Nor mine," Mattias added."

I drew my legs underneath me and made myself comfortable with pillows. In a natural muscle memory in homage to my mother, I took a small cushion and hugged it like a teddy bear. "Since you're privy to the rules of reincarnation. Tell me, what may one expect, realistically?"

"You're asking me 'what dreams may come'," Mattias said.

Shakespeare was a poet," I replied being cagey. "Do poets ever hit the mark with their outrageous inspirations?" I knew the answer was an unequivocal yes, but I had to air it.

"Every --- single --- time," Mattias said. "When I wandered in the fog that erased my past, it was the poets and the memoirs of a Roman emperor who showed me the path home. Why did I venture out that particular day? That is, why was I given a day pass from hospice hell the one and only day Vermeer's portrait of Jakobina was on display for me to see? Fortuitous doesn't cover such a wild card. I'd been given a reprieve. More than that, I'd been given the power to connect with destiny that controls the cards in every player's hand."

Jakobina clenched her stomach as if she were about to be sick. She spoke in a voice steeped in fear. "What rules would *you* break, Aurelia? What rules have you already broken? What would you do for a chance to live *your* life over?"

"More to the point," Mattias interrupted. "What *will* you do now so we can live ours?"

I faced both of them with hatred in my eyes. "You couldn't have told me this before?"

Jakobina answered. "No. It didn't serve our… *my* purpose."

"What are you not telling me? I wasn't born yesterday."

"Of course you were, and I was about to." She cleared her throat and indicated I should sit. "It will take a while if you will listen to the end. I would appreciate that chance."

I shook my head slowly. "There *is* no end. At least, no *happy* ending that I can see."

"There are several. Admittedly, not all good. That is, not all in good time."

I glanced at Felix. His eyes were still gone but his hands were back, pointing to 10 o'clock sharp. "Half an hour, then," I announced. "I have an appointment I'd like to keep. Can you pick up the pace a little."

Jakobina needed no further prompting. "After a time, Mattias's reputation as a healer grew. People sought him out for guidance. But I am getting ahead of our reunion. Mattias found me at a time when I was content to be married to Piet, keeping house as any good Dutch girl was taught. But none of that mattered. Mattias and I fell into each other easily. I became with child from our sins and worried greatly for our son's soul. These things, even based on pure love, are said to be punishments that survive several generations. Maybe this is true."

"It would seem so."

"So many years, wasted. For twelve years, Mattias had forgotten who I was. He'd forgotten his own identity. I'd been torn in half, mourning a loss that would never end. I never thought clearly after that."

"Mattias immigrated to England to honor his old friend, Piet, and went to work in an art gallery in London. He wrote to me, once a year, on the anniversary of our reunion. I have eight letters. Our son, Jan, lived eight years. He and Piet were carried off in the plague of 1675. I was sorry for Piet but I suffered agonies of guilt over Jan's death. Had I caused it by my sin?"

"Don't be stupid," I said. "Plagues have no conscience. Hasn't five-hundred years taught you that superstitions are old wives tales with needless, and in your case, devastating consequences that could have been avoided? Ignorance is lifetimes away from bliss. Still, in a way, comeuppance was served. You deserved your punishment. Sadly, Zee and I had to pay for it."

"Some things never change. Even after hundreds of years, we will meet again."

"Mattias?"

"Yes, of course, Mattias, and Jan and Piet. I have already met them in," she hesitated and chilled me with a stare, "certain *waking* dreams. Mattias taught me how."

"Catcher and Thatcher?"

"And one other." She paused. Pearls of tears formed at the corner of her eyes and spilled down her cheeks. "And Zee."

"My Zee?"

Jakobina stared into my eyes. "He was my friend. Mattias' and mine. He was Piet."

FLASHING BACK

'VIEW OF DELFT' JOHANNES VERMEER C.1660

Out, out, brief candle!
Life's but a walking shadow,
A poor player who struts
And frets his hour upon the stage,
And then is heard no more.
— WILLIAM SHAKESPEARE

chapter 62
A PLAGUE ON MY HOUSE

The wooden shutters of a tiny window blow against the hospital wall. Little Jan stands beside his father's bed across from me, clutching the little cat doll stuffed with straw he'd had as a baby. His face is surprisingly clear of the plague boils. His eyes widen with curiosity. He doesn't cry. He blinks slowly but says nothing.

"Go back to bed my darling," I say. "Mama will be right there." But he stays. His form weakens.

"Don't worry. Papa is going to be well. Now go. You mustn't be out of bed."

I am frantic. "*Please* Jan, I need you to go back to your bed." The other beds in the sick room are visible through him. It's unbearable to see my boy wavering in front of me – a small figure insubstantial as smoke. If only he'd go back to bed, he had a chance. But he smiles at Piet and tucks his little cat toy next to his father. The look that passes between them is plain. They are together in this… this adventure of death, and all I can do is fade into the event as a powerless bystander, unable to follow.

I hear a dog barking frantically and the words 'catch her' distract me from the deathbed. "Catch her." The words echo inside my head.

"Aurelia. It's Mattias. Come on luv. It's time to go home, now. Wake up Aurelia… AURELIA!

I woke with Punch massaging my blanket into a nest. Canary was cowering by the door, ears flattened, whimpering. Mattias was standing over me. For a moment I thought he was Piet and I must be in the recently-abandoned bed, dying. But the familiar pattern of the blue windmill curtains in my bedroom flapped in the open window where an icy wind revived me. Mattias pulled up a chair and rubbed some feeling into my numb hands and feet. The healing warmth of his hands settled me into the recovery of half-sleep. I was restored, conscious enough to ask questions.

Canary was on high alert. She pawed open the door and headed for the stairs.

"Catch her," Mattias called out. "Aurelia needs her."

"What is wrong with Canary?" I asked. "Why are *you* here?"

Jakobina joined us having intercepted Canary, and promptly disappeared. I patted the coverlet for Canary to come. "It's okay girl. Up you get." But she held back, leaning against Mattias's leg.

"Zee didn't want to disturb your rest," Mattias said. "He thinks you're having your regular afternoon nap. He had business matters in Glastonbury and will be back tomorrow. He left a note. But Jakobina is a little upset. She's here but she's hiding."

"Why? Has something happened?"

Mattias stopped rubbing my hands but continued to hold them. His eyes showed compassion. "There's no need to panic. You just disappeared for a while. Physically. Jakobina was showing you one of her memories. She feels responsible."

"I disappeared!" I held out my hands to make sure they were there. "Did… did *you* see me go? … How long is a while?"

He grinned mischievously. "I believe a girl in a painting alerted me. Not to worry. It was only a few minutes."

I pulled the blankets from my legs. My feet were there. I flexed my toes. They still obeyed my brain. My bunions were chronic. "Can you see me… right now… *all* of me?"

Mattias answered quickly, obviously a humorous ploy. "Aurelia," he said, "philosophically speaking, you're *always* transparent." He left the chair, plunked his weight on the bed, and Canary leapt up. She sniffed my feet and tentatively licked a toe. I was delighted that it tickled.

Even so, Mattias's *transparent* remark was rude. "I didn't take you for being a cruel person. I trusted you. That's just mean-spirited."

"Funny you should say *spirited*," he said, "We need to have a talk." He pulled a pillow from the armchair and settled down on my bed, presumably to fill me in on a few unsavory details with Canary resting her head in his lap.

I waited, somewhat hypnotized. "Okay, you may as well spill all the beans."

"I won't leave any out," he said, but he revised it to "well, maybe a few. All in good time though. No worries. I promise to give you every last bean."

It turned out to be a riot act, delivered kindly but directly as he asserted "new information is best sown under the stars." As soon as it was dark I followed him outside.

Everything that happens,
happens as it should,
and if you observe carefully,
you will find this to be so.
— MARCUS AURELIUS

chapter 63
ELEPHANT ON THE BEACH

"I prefer to give my pithier lectures outside," Mattias said. His words reminded me of painting *plein air* which was always a hassle playing tag with the wind and a primed canvas that wanted to be a sail. We walked the length of the beach, arm-in-arm, to the far boulders. Canary trotted ahead of us carrying her favorite throwing stick for most of the way but she dropped it to give our resident heron a piece of her mind. "So much for a bird sanctuary," Mattias said.

There was a pregnant pause before I asked the 'elephant on the beach' question we both knew was the reason for our stroll. "Couldn't Jakobina have just told me? What am I not seeing? What did you not handle well? Why did I have to witness those deaths?"

Mattias let go of my arm to throw Canary's stick. "Because sometimes the shortest way home is the longest way around, he said, patting my cheek."

He's overly patronizing. "You're still my old mentor in wolf's clothing, and still, all you can give me is bumper stickers."

He squeezed my fingers. "No need to thank me, Your Majesty. Condensed wisdom is easier to remember. Going backward—is often the best way to advance."

"I live in a castle. And now that I know my stalker was you, and considering you visit me every day, I think I'm fairly safe. I have Canary and you to protect me."

Mattias carried on seamlessly with a snappy rejoinder "Remember, a castle can be an intimidating, impenetrable fortress, but it can turn into a prison when surrounded by foe."

"I still have free will – some agency over my current situation, don't I?"

He sent me a sympathetic look. "One would think so," he said. "I saved the best rule for last, my queen." He picked up the spiral interior of a broken shell and handed it to me, knowing I found them more beautiful than the perfectly intact ones. We had previously discussed their structure as an example of inner strength – enough to withstand the ocean's constant battering and remain smooth as a porcelain sculpture. "Willpower is more about surrender than willing it so."

"You're exasperating. It's like being back at school... only..."

He's a chameleon. A raised Spock eyebrow exclaimed silently: *only*?

"You know something I don't?"

Canary bounded towards us. "Ah, the boomerang returns," Mattias said.

This time, Canary dropped her stick at my feet. She's an equal opportunity gamer. I obliged and wiped the sand from my hand before offering it to Mattias, who clasped it and gave it a playful shake. Our eyes connected with electricity. Mine are puzzled. His are, as always, mischievous when he's about to rattle my world.

"I'd be a sorry mentor if I didn't, now wouldn't I?"

"So it's back to school is it, Professor?"

"Your wish is my ..."

"Command?"

"Is my pleasure. You are *such* a cynic." He burst into song: *'School days school days, dear old golden rule days.'* He stopped to face me with a serious look in his eye. "Sorry."

"Uh oh, here it comes," I said, hoping to diffuse the tension.

I needn't have bothered, his sudden smile made everything okay again. "Keep this in mind... I was *not* your stalker. Catcher was never your stalker. Stay awake. Mull it over."

"Then who was?"

"I shall send you a dream." He rubbed his hands together enthusiastically. "Gosh, I'm starving. I'm picturing Mimosas, soft poached Eggs Benedict with back bacon, spinach, and avocado, Earl

Grey tea, and toast with imported lemon marmalade. Did I leave anything out?"

"An apple for the teacher."

He looked up and to the right, listening. "Zee is home earlier than expected. He's waiting for us," he announced with one of his devastating winks. He danced me around causing Canary to bark madly. "Hold up Aurelia, you've got something in your eye," he said, peering into my face. "I do believe it's an apple. What a clever to thank me."

We froze eye-to-eye for an age. Me baffled with Canary leaping at us, sand flying. Mattias's mouth twitched into a cheeky smile. He was sending me the dream. I closed my eyes to see the image he was transmitting. A realization sideswiped me in a painful clout. "Jakobina was my stalker wasn't she. It was HER all along!"

"Took you long enough," Mattias said. "I accept your belated apologies."

"353 years give or take."

"You're being too hard on her," he said. "I make it 53."

While I made the Mimosas, Zee lounged in a bath, and Mattias read the spines of my books. His fingertips trailed idly over them – a handsome boy running a stick along a picket fence.

"Looking for something in particular?" I asked.

He selected a tall white book. "This one," he said. It was 'The Visionary' my last school yearbook for 1965. He shielded the lower part of his face with it so only his eyes showed and peered at me. "I have some things to confess. You may want to sit down."

chapter 64
NEITHER HERE NOR THERE

Jakobina, deep in the art of eavesdropping, puttered at the sink pretending to wash dishes. Mattias paced the length of the kitchen with a grim expression marring his sweet face. "I've called you many times," he began. "I've pushed and hypnotized you and Zee. I've lied to save my soul and the soul of my beloved."

I gazed at him unfazed. "That probably sounds quite harmless to you."

His laugh was hollow. "In a way, I've lied to save *your* soul and Zee's."

"How thoughtful. You're a real prince. But if you wouldn't mind, I'd really like you to stop pacing. You're making me dizzy."

"Hear my confession, woman. I am contrite. My lies have entangled us all. It doesn't matter that I did so with good intentions or that I now have a plan to put things right."

Against my better judgement, I believed him, but I didn't intend to tell him. I hedged for answers to impossible questions. "How do I know this isn't another one of those times?"

"You don't," he replied. "But if there was ever a time to suspend your judgement, this is it. Pretend I'm your friend. The truth is awkward. Playing with karma is dangerous … future lives are at stake."

"Whose? You're scaring me. Just have out with it and we'll take it from there. You *were* my friend, so, in time, I expect I'll forgive you. Go on, then. I'm listening."

"About your fear of invisibility. It came about because of a dream.

A natural dream shared between you and Jakobina. It was the perfect opportunity to make you feel crazy."

"What dream? When?" The dishwater ceased to slosh loudly as Jakobina perked up. She straightened and dried her hands on her dress. "You were seventeen, beset with anxiety headaches," she said. "And vulnerable. Prime for agreeing to a ludicrous suicide pact."

Mattias's smile of gratitude silenced her. "A month after my death, Jakobina saw the ghost of an old lady in Tintagel Castle. It was a future projection of you, dream-walking in 2018 – a twin dream that bridged her time and yours. You woke dreaming of Tintagel Castle and the ghost of a veiled woman in black. You'd seen Jakobina in widow's weeds. Naturally you didn't recognize her. She was barely thirty-years-old, fading away from grief."

"So," I said. "Invisibility was *Jakobina's* memory. *She* had faded. I *wasn't* becoming invisible?"

Mattias took a deep breath and momentarily closed his eyes. "You were never invisible, but when you're a recluse there's no-one around to *not* see you. Jakobina meant well. And your teenage mind was wide open to suggestions in 1965. She only had to plant the thought. You experienced her helplessness as your own."

I was too stunned to feel anger. "Apparently I'm *still* helpless."

"There's more. The days you time-traveled to the cafeteria and Avalon…" he paused. Jakobina smiled, encouraging him to continue.

I waited, staring unblinking to unnerve him. He was getting no help from me.

"The days you time-traveled to the cafeteria and Avalon were *fabrications* to distort the truth of what might have happened."

To show his loyalty to me, Felix let out a blood curdling yowl. "Shameful. Call a distortion of the truth what it really is… a barefaced lie."

Jakobina faced him and flipped him off. I taught her that. Well, *showed* her, more like, in one of my bad moods. I'd trusted her. She'd seen me through everything, twice: my increasingly erratic behavior, my quick to anger moments when good manners drained away, the growing meltdowns of social graces followed by penances of shame, and my silent reflections of guilt and loss. Regret was a big deal but the embarrassment, now, of being shown to be an old fool even in my youth, was worse. Separated from Zee for fifty years, I'd fallen foul of the need to be touched and cherished, only to be seduced by the shade of a dying patient in twilight sleep.

Disarming a ghost was easier than I thought. Mattias actually blushed and I discovered the remarkable truth that a ghost can be unsettled.

"Dreamers who pass in the night are neither here nor there," Mattias said. "Forgive us."

I finally addressed Jakobina. "I'm confused. I was there in Vermeer's studio when you responded to Piet's attentions. There was no mistaking your feelings of passion."

Jakobina held up an index finger. "No no no," she interrupted. "Absolutely not. I married Piet, but I didn't love him as a wife. I couldn't. I'd given my heart to another when I was five-years-old. Piet was a friend who took pity on me. Grieving for years had left me a sad desolate creature. Piet was patient and kind, another big brother. We became close. I rather went along with our marriage to spare his feelings. I loved him as a friend."

"I was part of you that day. I know Piet aroused your passion because I had to endure it."

"You *did* experience my altered state that day, but I was daydreaming about Mattias and what should have been. It was easier to give Vermeer the lustful expression he wanted by indulging my fantasies. At one point I left my body to be with the spirit of Mattias, and that's when you entered it. Unfortunate timing, I guess."

I responded, justifiably angry. "No way. I don't buy that. It had to be more than that. I couldn't have misunderstood such intense longing. I walked around in a heightened state of bliss for days. I was in love. I could never have been so moved unless my emotions were real."

Jakobina went quiet. After a long time she heaved a sigh, and faced me. "Yes. Your emotions *were* real. You *were* in love with Zee, the Piet in your future, and Piet was in love with you, the future love of his life. I didn't tell you the truth that day because I didn't fully understand it myself. I was even jealous of you for a while. I didn't tell you later because it wouldn't have made sense until you knew that Zee had once been Piet. That he was Piet's incarnation. I'm so sorry."

A sob burst from my chest from the full realization of the love I'd thrown away. "I didn't know. I couldn't have known. What have I done." And then, to Jakobina with deep hatred. "WHAT DID YOU MAKE ME DO!"

She crumpled in tears. "Love blinded me," she whimpered. "It was my fault. Mattias and I had a pact and we were so close. And now there's this mess and a new set of comeuppances that he and I will have to endure."

"So this is what it feels like to be gutted," I said weakly.

Jakobina's mission to enlighten continued as if anything still mattered. She overcame her remorse and became quite chatty. "The saying that a worthy student eventually surpasses their teacher, is true. Doc shared a psychological phenomena with Mattias when they were linked."

"Whatever."

"A powerful visitation known as the ghostly lover, inherent in women's most fervent dreams, is the foreshadow or the past-life memory of a soul mate. The four of us are part of a group soul who incarnate together in order to attain perfection. What do you think about that?"

I squinted at her with disbelief. "You're seriously asking me to think straight after your little history lesson."

"I am. It's what we do. It's what we have to do," she said. "What we've always done."

I pondered the absurdity of her statement and addressed her previous confession. "Wait! You were only *five*?"

"And you needn't scoff. Sensitive children know things. You should know that. You were one of them."

"How do I know that I'm here right now? Maybe all this chit chat is a dream."

"Here and there are relative terms. Wherever you are, that's where you'll be."

My reserve disappeared in a meltdown of cursing. "Again, bumper stickers," I screamed. "What is with you two. I was hijacked into a sexual lather that tore my guts out and all you can give me is glib poetry without a goddam trace of remorse. Unfortunate timing is a slick understatement. Everything about you reeks of bad bloody timing!"

Jakobina ignored me. She calmly seated herself cross-legged on the floor like a true storyteller and spoke with her eyes closed for effect. Her voice was haunting. Like it or not, I felt compelled to listen, a little hypnotized and feverishly curious.

Jakobina lowered her voice to a mysterious timbre. "In 1675, after my husband and son died, I went to London. I was 27, guilt-ridden and sad. Mattias was 32 and in poor health. Mattias and I were handfasted in the tradition of the old ways, and moved to Cornwall to live in the shadow of Tintagel Castle. We were relatively happy for a time. Living together was a blessing we thought never to have. Mattias's headaches increased with the visions that began after he regained his memories in 1666. He knew the future. He gave me hope and a date in time when we would meet again in another life. It was the year…"

"Oh, let me guess. 2020. The year of perfect hindsight. Ironic."

She nodded. "I couldn't endure waiting. And by happenstance, Mattias arrived too early by entering the host body of a kindred spirit who was about to cross over sooner than expected. The man was a professor who studied dreams and psychic phenomenon."

"Doc. Yes, I know him."

"Mattias was drawn into Doc's comatose state to exchange like-minded theories and they became close friends."

"Colleagues," Mattias added.

Jakobina patted Mattias's hand and smiled. "Doc agreed to Mattias borrowing his body from time-to-time. Doc was a willing participant in our predicament and we couldn't lose the connection. He agreed to hang on a few more months so Mattias could be your mentor."

"As Catcher," Mattias interjected.

"Surely, if anything, *that* was against some kind of rule," I remarked.

Mattias turned away from me and addressed the room. "Consent is a powerful rulebreaker. But personalities have conflicting motives. Sometimes Catcher won out and tried to steer you towards independence because Doc was firmly on your side. Something we didn't always see eye-to-eye when I was Thatcher. After Doc heard your story and the history of our meddling, he refused to abandon you or Zee. I see now, he was right. For a time we were at odds and you suffered. It must have been confusing."

Jakobina chose the moment to resume her point of view. "Mattias worked with me to hasten our new lives under a hastily revised plan. And since we are of singular purpose to keep you and your original consent intact, it could seem as if we were against you. I'm not as soft as Mattias."

"Imagine my shock," I retorted with ice in my voice. "It would *seem* that the art of *'seeming'* covers a multitude of sins. Handy for you. Devastating for me and Zee."

Jakobina paid no attention to my sarcasm and pushed ahead. "You and I met several times in dreams. As Mattias explained, I saw you as an old woman wandering a castle, arm-in-arm with your lover. You saw me – an old woman wandering the same battlements, mourning the love I'd lost twice."

I glanced from Jacobina to Mattias and back again. "And my school chums in wheelchairs?"

Mattias stepped up and looked into my eyes, no doubt to spare Jakobina my wrath. "Ah, that," he said raising his eyebrows. He cleared his throat. "Artists have a special dispensation to alter the truth. Poetic license covers a multitude of privileges. You can blame me. I invaded your privacy and created the walking shadows of your high school friends from your memories. I twined them with the definitive image of seniors as elderly citizens. It was a useful dodge to pique your interest."

"And the hospice?"

"Avalon is real. It was Doc's last stand combined with your worst thoughts about your mother's care home, which was, by the way, not as dysfunctional and cold as you remembered."

"You played me."

"I did. I have no excuses. Death is a game that Jakobina and I are still playing to win."

"Then, what's life."

Mattias turned serious grey eyes upon me like a searchlight. His expression was as wistful and fearful as Jakobina's portrait. "Earth is a school. I like to think of it as reform school for the unwashed masses, but it's much more than that, as I will soon prove to you."

Jakobina had a final word of comfort to give. "If it's any consolation," she said brightly, "that encounter in Vermeer's studio was orchestrated to be strange, and due to your ardent desire, my portrait achieved a rare quality that strikes a note of truth with everyone who seeks to truly see it." She sobered and chewed her lip. "But there's much more to it than that. When you're ready."

She withered slightly and vanished before my eyes.

"Love isn't blind," I called after her, "It's cruel."

Once out of nature I shall never take
My bodily form from any natural thing,
But such a form as Grecian goldsmiths make
Of hammered gold and gold enamelling
To keep a drowsy Emperor awake;
Or set upon a golden bough to sing
To lords and ladies of Byzantium
Of what is past, or passing, or to come.
— WILLIAM BUTLER YEATS
'Sailing to Byzantium'

chapter 65
LOVE FOR SALE

It's 1675

Jakobina knows the way. She pushes me ahead of her and steers me through, literally *through*, the clogged streets of seventeenth-century London. No-one parts for us nor do they shift or notice our presence. We simply proceed forward on a distinct trajectory without significant resistance, regardless of street vendors, horses, and riffraff. At most, the bustling population startles momentarily. Their expressions freeze as our molecules collide. One or two faint. A dog sniffs after us until something more enticing wafts his attention away from us.

We walk on, unchallenged. Horseflesh quivers, and dogs cease barking. We meet all manner of physical obstacles head-on without prolonged engagement. The commotions of daily life resume behind us uninterrupted, muffled to me, but no doubt the clamour of London is as loud and chaotic as before we entered their world, no wiser for the visitation of a couple of time travelers on a mission.

I am in no doubt as to the package Jakobina carries wrapped in white cloth and tied with frayed strips of unbleached linen. It resembles a small square mummy, and in a way, it does represent a once fully-alive human. It contains a stillborn life. Jakobina's half-soul lingers under the thin varnish of ten years. I cling to her sleeve trying to keep up as her pace quickens.

Jakobina points down an alley and runs ahead of me. "The gallery is this way," she says. "Don't dawdle."

I wasn't dawdling, I was ogling. Old London town is a nightmare of debris I can't smell and sights I'd rather not see. It's whitewashed with silence.

The toothless mouth of a flower-seller peddling violets on a corner mimes her sales pitch as she thrusts her wares under the noses of every passerby. I grab a posy just to see if I can with no luck. The physics of us are illogical, but that's how dreams unfold. Dual properties allow us to skim subconsciously weightlessness and bodiless, unscathed after slopping through mud and liquid filth and yet our feet meet the cobbled pavements with the solid impact of shoe leather.

Ladies bury their faces in their nosegay violets to escape the stench of rotting fish as they pick their way through carnage of every stripe.

Jakobina sends me a memory of the day my perfumed scarf saved me from the distressing odor of harmless chicken soup that filled the halls of Emily's asylum.

"What was that for?" I ask.

"I saw it too, but it wasn't me," she says. "Every memory has a secret mission to keep, so they connect by themselves. It will make sense later. That was all you."

As we run, fog descends and my body sheds its years until we are two teenage girls. Jakobina can barely contain her excitement. "He's almost here," she shouts. What she means is, we're almost *there*. We leave the murk and enter a square plaza surrounded by red brick buildings stained with soot. A heavy oak door in one of them reveals a sane interior of academia with marble floors and hallways littered with bandaged sculptures in the process of being unpacked. We proceed past piles of loose straw that drift like tumbleweeds and trip over miles of unraveled bolts of cotton.

Jakobina gives a cry and waves to the person we've come to see. Mattias stands tall and elegant beaming with love at her approach. He swings Jakobina in a giddy circle and when the room stops revolving he announces his news. "I've found us a remote cottage by the sea where no-one will bother us. It's near Travena."

I stand back, caught in the crossfire of their excitement, and catch the package as it falls from Jakobina's arms. When they separate, Mattias acknowledges my presence with a curt nod reminiscent of his recent display of teenage indifference. I hand him the painting. "I have a buyer already," he confides. "I hope Jakobina can part from it without a fuss. It holds her soul, after all."

"Travena?" I enquire, puzzled.

"Travena was the name of Tintagel Village in our time," Jakobina says. She explains once more, to make a point, that Mattias has followers who hound him for scraps of hope. "His gift of prophecy is becoming dangerous which is why we intend to disappear," she says.

Mattias winces and clutches his right eye. Jakobina puts her arms around him. "The headaches are getting stronger, aren't they."

Her words remind me of the day we met in my art history class when she asked me a similar question. I feel a twinge of sympathy pain far more intense than the ones I experienced as a teenager.

Mattias recovers enough to lead us into a bright room with easels, and soon the 'Girl With A Pearl Earring' is staring at us from her new perch.

I am astonished at the pure colors of Jakobina's portrait that shine from its surface, smooth as silk – its craquelure being hundreds of years in the future.

Mattias is excited to have a buyer. Jacobina is excited to be with Mattias, and they discuss their plans before any money exchanges hands. The asking price is ridiculously low, but not for the times. I wish I could purchase a few works with 21st century currency and retire home with a treasure chest of lost art, but interacting would have altered the timeline, and I've already paid the price for doing that. I'm invisible here for a reason. Nothing must change.

Jakobina whispers in my ear. "We're going to leave now," she says linking her arm through mine. "We're going home." A sound like a distant thunderclap rolls under the ceiling and the three of us are transported to a rain-drenched clifftop overlooking the English

Channel where the roots of a grey castle cling tenaciously under the thin topsoil.

Tintagel Castle is slowly melting into the landscape. The edges of the exposed walls have been eroded smooth by rain and wind. On one side, a steep drop reveals rough water churning into foamy scum. Facing inland, the sun pokes its fingers through a low hanging mist and paints the gentle slope of hills, pale green.

Jakobina points to a ribbon of blue smoke curling from a copse of trees. "That's home," she says. "But for now it's important to show you the beach of polished stones and the cove where we built our ceremonial fires."

We're suspended on a tour of her past but there's no time to lose. Back where we recently left, the year 2019 is a ticking bomb.

"Was the weather always this abysmal," I ask.

"The south coast is always windy but it was far from bleak compared to a Delft winter and frozen canals," Mattias replies. "And the summers here were plentiful with small game, fish, and fruit."

"I never noticed the damp," Jakobina says dreamily. "We were cozy in love. Peat fires and fine boots kept us warm and dry. My painting fetched a price that provided luxuries beyond our dreams in Delft. And eventually, my portrait found its way home to Holland. Mercifully, Mattias's followers were left behind with printed instructions. The time here, and it wasn't long enough, was for us alone. Mattias kept me in the dark as to his lifespan. He knew to the hour when he would die, and I never pestered for insight about what would come. For a while there was no past or future here. Mattias taught me to live in the moment."

My empathy reaches Mattias. A look of sadness passes between us. "I'm dying," he says in my head. "Whatever time I have left is for her alone. I can't save her from what will be. She has no idea that grief will reduce her to an empty shell. She deserves a better death than this."

I agree wholeheartedly. "And so do you."

"Time is a hard teacher. Will you help us?"

I pause. "I should consult with Zee."

"By all means prepare him," Jakobina says slyly.

chapter 66
LOVE ON THE ROCKS

Jakobina gives me Cornwall in the spring of 1678. I stand in a shallow pool at the base of a tall cliff. Stray foam effervesces around my feet. It reminds me of champagne. I gaze up the side of a chalk cliff and the ruins of Tintagel Castle silhouetted in stark contrast against the bluest of blue Cornish skies. Jakobina stands alone hunched on the battlements making a small black shape. Her right arm extends out in an arc over the sea. Even from my vantage point far below, I can see she is unstable. I think for a moment she is waving to me.

Two stars that sparkle like diamonds fall from her hand. And then I see who has taken her attention. A mermaid sits across from me on a sunning rock, her arms held out to catch the stars. Her mouth, painted with bright red lipstick, kisses the stars. She calls out. "It is done," and spares me a quick smile before silently slipping into the sea without so much as a ripple. Immediately, she resurfaces to slap the water three times with her turquoise tail before disappearing with her treasure.

Jakobina slumps into a dark shape. She calls Mattias's name in a heart wrenching cry of despair. I look away for privacy's sake and when I look back, her shape is different. She looms larger until I realize there are now two figures in an embrace. They part, and I recognize Mattias who waves to me.

Almost immediately, Mattias materializes beside me. "She didn't know I was there," he says. "She can't. I will always be invisible to her until the rules of reincarnation allow her to see me in your time. I can only hope she senses my presence. I never fully leave her, you know."

He wades out to the sunning rock towards two diamonds that glint in the sun. When he returns he opens his hand to reveal two pear-shaped pearls.

I am stunned. "She threw her earrings into the sea!"

"She had to. She wanted to follow them but I taught her well, and even through her madness, she kept her promise to me."

Jakobina is still holding out her arms to embrace her invisible lover. For a moment I think she's going to hurl herself into the sea. I wonder if perhaps that was how she died and didn't want to tell me.

Mattias corrects me. "She wasted away slowly," he says. "Always revisiting the scene of her sacrifice but never seeing me. I couldn't show myself at that time if our future pact was to hold firm. I suffered with her, always by her side, invisible for years, even after her death. We shared a few meagre days when I was Thatcher. After that, we were estranged until she saw that Catcher was me inside Doc's body.

Mattias and I returned to the island without Jakobina. He leaned close to offer a further disquieting tidbit. "And in case you're forming a romanticized image of Cathy and Heathcliff pining away for true love, know this. The powers that be in Travena Village finally had Jakobina committed to a workhouse, a crude mental institution, in present language, for her own good, fearing she would fall or jump into the sea. She endured the proverbial 'bedlam of hell' for forty-two bleak years and died alone, with me invisible at her bedside. Emily's warm dry hospice with nutritious chicken soup was a holiday camp in comparison."

"More karma," I said. "How cruel."

Mattias gave me a lopsided smile. "Compassionate karma."

"And Avalon?"

"It was staffed by a team of dedicated women after the tradition of King Arthur's hospice. It was named Avalon for a reason."

"Jakobina endured madness twice," I said. "The second time as Emily."

"Actually, it was three times. The mermaid showed you that when she slapped her tail three times. The first wave of mental instability was when Jakobina believed I'd died in the explosion that killed her father. She was never quite right after that."

"I know."

"Jakobina blamed him for my death."

"And I blamed Emily for her breakdown and being weak."

"Your mother inherited Jakobina's depression and mental instability as well as my memory loss, and, in turn, passed her fear of the future to you. I'm afraid you were partially heir to my headaches and visions, Jakobina's issues of abandonment, and her deep mourning for lost love."

"Who's luckier than me."

"You could never have fully committed to Zee under the weight of all that. It was daunting, but you have faced every obstacle with determination until the shadows of our pain have burned away. Being your teacher, if only for a few months, made... *makes* me proud."

"I thought I'd pretty much chickened out."

"Hardly. You made a difficult sacrifice even if you didn't realize it. Full psychic consent to Jakobina's pact set your mother's soul free."

"And I'm still a scapegoat. Surely the sacrifices eventually end. They must."

"Sacrifices made for love recycle into new love but the waiting isn't easy. For a time, Jakobina kept her earrings in a box. The dull rattle of pearls against silk brought her comforting visions of me. Those dreams were the only way I could visit her. In essence, she threw me into the sea with her earrings. She was terribly alone after that. Her remaining years, grieving for me, destroyed what was left of her sanity. She saw me for a few hours when I was Thatcher and waited fifty more years until I was able to visit you as Catcher. But in breaking our connection to the past, she insured our reunion in the future. Her loss of comfort cemented us together. Your sacrifices will do the same for you and Zee.

"But Jakobina always had her earrings with her in her portrait, so they weren't really sacrificed."

He reached into a pocket. "Painted earrings are ghost earrings," he said and showed me Jakobina's pearl earrings. "These are the real thing. She kept the empty swan box for the rest of her days, but never opened it fearing to weaken my energy. She's disciplined, but she's becoming impatient. A little more help from you and we're almost home."

"Define little," I said.

chapter 67
MOTHER'S DAY

The fifteenth-century ruins of Tintagel Castle are silhouetted against the waning moon. "Come with me," Jakobina said. "I want, no I *need*, to show you something important."

"I've seen enough. You win. There's no reason to stay. We can go home now."

"There's a special reason. You need to see this."

Jakobina was more than her usual adamant self. She hollered over the raging wind. "WE HAVE TO GO BACK FOR A MOMENT TO THE DAY WE MET." She returned to my side, extended her arm, and once again, I stumbled out of a darkened theatre hanging onto a girl's sleeve. I am forewarned. "It's now May 21st 1961," Jakobina declared. "Stick close to me. You were thirteen-years-old at that time. We're visiting your mother."

The odor of neglect assailed us on the third floor – the site of Emily's last stand.

I lifted my perfumed scarf to my nose and took a deep breath of sanity, drinking deeply of perfumed silk before entering the depressive realm of the forgotten. Despair trapped in the walls oozed into the airless corridor. The stink of chicken soup wafting towards us from an approaching trolley turned my stomach.

The entrance to the elevator was logjammed with several rogue walkers tangled together like wire coat hangers. When the doors opened I sidled past the crush of lost souls and pressed the button for the ground floor. Jakobina overruled my choice by pressing floor 6. "I have something to show you," she said.

The elevator bounced to a stop almost immediately to pick up a male orderly, reeking of nauseating after shave, pushing a cart of cleaning supplies. I nodded a fake hello, snuggled deeper into my silk sanctuary, and squashed myself into a corner. I pretended I was on my beach, where the salt air is divinely fresh even when embedded with rotting seaweed.

"Stop acting like a spoiled brat," Jakobina exclaimed. "You *need* to see this. And I *need* to show you."

"You've made that abundantly clear."

"Mind over matter, Aurelia. It isn't that hard. Think happy thoughts. A moment of misery can change if you give it a chance."

I sniffed. "And the pot calls the kettle black."

The number six button lit up. A bell indicated we'd arrived. Part one of Jakobina's plan was accomplished. The metal doors rumbled open. Apart from the painful sheen from an expanse of shiny beige linoleum and the biting smell of bleach, the sixth floor was deserted. I'd thought I was done being compliant for the day but I slunk meekly after Jakobina's energy as she towed me to a door numbered 613.

The name of its resident, Alice Solomon, had been handwritten in red magic marker on a card inserted into a holder.

"It's unlocked," Jakobina said. "She won't be back for ages."

We were confronted with an immaculate room of military tidiness. Bottles of scent and makeup were lined up on a dresser in precision rows like ranking soldiers. The bedmaking could have passed the inspection of the most discriminating officer. A pleasing scent of lemon furniture polish allowed me to emerge from my scarf and breath deeply.

Jakobina appeared overly excited. "It's in the wardrobe. Behind the clothes, Narnia style."

"What is?"

"What we've come to see, of course."

I pushed back a bursting row of sweaters and housedresses, more than most women could wear in a lifetime, and discovered the clothes were a false wall that revealed a floor to ceiling display of identical white shoeboxes neatly stacked, each one numbered.

Jakobina tapped the one marked with today's date: May 21st, 1961. "That's the one," she said. "I'll let you do the honors. Pull it out."

It came loose with several other boxes that avalanched, spilling their contents which splayed across the floor in a jumble of ornaments, shoes, toys, and books like the disgorged contents of a sunken ship.

I kicked aside the mess and took May 21st to the bed. I waited, momentarily testing the bedsprings. Jacobina's instructions came rather acidly. "Well, open the damn thing," she ordered.

Clean tissue paper greeted me from under a wad of bubble wrap that revealed a teddy bear. I pounced on its familiar face with no eyes. "Virgil! How the...?"

"Oh, there you are," he said. "A box opens like a door, as I'm sure you've discovered."

I stared up at Jakobina stunned, happy, and surprisingly angry. "What the hell!"

"No need to thank me," she said.

"I'm not."

Jakobina sat beside me and stroked Virgil's fur. "Mrs. Solomon was known for her light fingers but the staff humored her. They indulged her and left chocolates in places where she'd be, and placed bets on how long it would take before she succumbed to the bait. They have all sorts of surveillance cameras here. I guess it was entertainment of a sort for the bored staff. It didn't take much sleuthing on my part. Time is no barrier in the spirit world of time-slipping and I move faster than a resident's legs. Anyway, a used toy is not an item of great value, and the cleaners cherrypicked the seriously good stuff. Mrs. Solomon never looked inside the boxes once they were labelled. The entire closet is pretty much a wall safe."

I found my voice and discovered it was still upset. "My Dad reported Virgil missing and asked the nurses to keep an eye out, excuse the pun. He gave them a picture of a child, me, holding her beloved bear, and stressed it was important. He offered a reward. I even cried to get their sympathy."

"Nurses have other things to do."

"Virgil was here all the time. That day you and I visited Emily, he'd been in a box for four years!"

Jakobina touched her wrist to indicate the time. "Look under the wrapping paper."

I found a bundle of missing bear posters rolled into a tube, held together with an elastic band.

"She was a bit of a fanatic," Jakobina commented. "She collected them all. Every one. It was all part of the intrigue. She liked to file things. It was a game."

"She came by the name Solomon, dishonestly," I snapped, keeping a vice-like grip on Virgil under my left arm. I frantically pulled out the remaining tower of boxes with my right hand, throwing them hard over my shoulder. "Bloody old cow." They landed on the bed and chair and a carpet already spewed with forgotten treasures.

We left the closet door open. Empty boxes and confiscated loot littered the room.

I slammed the door on our crime scene and felt slightly mollified, but turned on Jakobina. I stripped the name tag from the door and tore it into confetti. "If you knew Virgil was here, why didn't you?..." My sentence ended in an anguished *agghh*.

"I thought you'd be pleased."

"He's been here for almost sixty years. My god, Jakobina. I was just a thirteen-year-old kid when he was lost. And it seems, stolen. And you knew!"

"I didn't know *you*, though. Not then. *Technically* we met, four years later when you were seventeen. I wasn't allowed to meet you before that. The rules of reincarnation must be strictly observed. They dictated we had to meet, *consciously*, when we were the same age I was in my portrait. From where we stand, right here right now, it's actually Mother's Day, 1961, so *technically*, Virgil was stolen only a few hours ago. Not everything is about you, Aurelia. Zee needed a chance to save you, and I had to be redeemed."

I marched past the nurses station like the queen of everything, clutching Virgil staring passively into his new future, remarkably calm for his ordeal, and inquired if Mrs. Solomon was around.

The receptionist looked up, distracted from her crossword puzzle. "At this time of day our resident ghost is usually in the garden," she said.

I stopped, mid-high and mighty, to stutter in shock. "Ghost? She hasn't died has she?"

"Oh, no. We call her that because she wanders the halls day and night like a ghost."

"I bet she does."

The nurse grabbed a notepad. "Can I give her a message?"

"Yes. Just tell her, Teddy said goodbye."

We swung by Emily's floor in 1965 when I was seventeen.

I thought better of leaving Virgil again. I needed him more than she ever would.

I bent low, mindful not to touch Emily from habit.

"Dementia is not contagious. It's not transmitted by touch," Jakobina said. "You've already inherited your mom's symptoms. Birth does that."

"I think you mean reincarnation does that." The word 'mom' stuck in my guts, loud and sore. But Jakobina was judging me, and after witnessing her anguish over her son's cat doll I felt a semblance of compassion. "In a backwards way, reincarnation may be considered a disease," I added as my last word on the subject.

But some fragment of sentiment loosened. I cleared my throat and addressed Emily from across the room, one foot headed out the door. "Mom. I have Virgil now, so, no harm done," I said, although there was, and it would never heal. We had both surrendered years ago to opposite ends of reality and locked our doors. A sharp memory surfaced. 'It's strange,' I thought to myself. 'When I was very young, Emily was my best friend.'

Jakobina, eavesdropper extraordinaire, added her own thought. "I had a best friend, too, she mused. Marieke died giving birth to a son. Motherhood and friendship are sacred trusts, you know. So, little Miss Sorry Boots, aren't you going to kiss your mother goodbye?"

I sent Jakobina a mental volley of daggers. If only answers could kill. "I don't kiss strangers," I tell her. "But feel free. You go ahead."

She did.

Emily smiled in her sleep from Jakobina's kiss and squeezed her hand. "You're a good girl, Aurelia," she said. "Never forget that. I love you."

I don't remember running down the corridor like a panicky sleepwalker. All I remember is being inside the elevator madly pushing buttons, screaming to get out.

When the door opened, it was 2019 in my castle kitchen. Jakobina was there with her arms folded like an impatient schoolmarm and Felix was quietly sobbing.

CURRICULUM VITAE

How much more grievous
are the consequences of anger
than the causes of it.
— MARCUS AURELIUS

chapter 68
GOING NOVA

– December 1 –
2019

Zee turned on me before he heard the extent of my ingenious new plan. As soon as the words 'I have to save Jakobina and Mattias' were on the table, he blew up. "After everything, you're going to run away from me again!"

I tried to placate him but anger hears nothing. "No, no. It's not like that," I begged. "Listen. I know about reincarnation now. We can meet again. You can join me in the painting when your time comes. So can the animals."

He sat fuming. "Well, thank you. I'm so glad you've worked out my death for me," he said pulling away when I touched him.

I waited.

When he spoke he seemed in a daze, speaking to himself. He cited the month I ran away. *"You might have given me a heads up. You just disappeared on me. We were going to Sam's New Year's Eve party. I felt worse than a fool. You couldn't have loved me. That hurt. And I was still afraid for you. That hurt too. There was a weather warning for big snow. Your dad greeted me at the door waving a telegram.*

'She's run away,' he said. 'She's old for her age. She'll take care of herself. She always has.'

And so I told him. No, she hasn't. Mr. Marcus, Aurelia may be an old soul but she's only seventeen. She's really screwed up. I've been taking care of her for years. We have to look for her. She can't have gone far."

"I didn't," I said hoping to clear the air. "I was right there in the shadows, listening to every word between you two. I stayed silent because it was better to have you angry with me than feeling sad and unloved. It wasn't true."

Zee continued his conversation replay as if I didn't exist. It turned out he'd heard without listening.

"Your dad was calm. Too calm. Perhaps even a little glib with me, all things considered. 'Don't you get it,' he said to me. 'She HAS gone far. As far away as she can get. She's on her way to England. We have relatives there.' He kept waving that damned telegram. 'She may be on her way there, now. No flights will get out with the storm. They sent this telegram. They expect her. Told me not to worry.'"

He looked at me with terrifying finality.

"I told you I went back later to see your dad again. Not for a souvenir for *me* but a keepsake for *you*. To give you when you came back to me. Felix was perfect. He was ours. I figured we had a second chance. I wanted that chance."

My confession *had* registered.

"And now you tell me you were there! We could have fixed things. I thought you would come back. I never doubted that for a second."

Zee let me touch his arm. "I left after you went inside," I said gently. "It started to snow. I couldn't think straight. A headache showed up and Jakobina had my pills, so I walked to a phone booth before the aura hit, and called a cab. Jakobina was waiting for me in a motel. We held up there for a week before hitting the road in a Greyhound bus to Alberta. She gave me sleeping pills to stop my panic attacks. The nightmare was worse when I woke up on the bus. It was a new year. A new beginning. Yes, the telegram was a lie. Jakobina sent it. At first I was livid, but I came to realize that she might have done both of us a favor. That thought got me through the first year without you. I was alone. You were safe. I welcomed the Alberta winter as a punishment. And then, in the Spring, I moved to England to justify the lie in the telegram. I began a new life in 1967. I *did* go to art school."

The shock in Zee's eyes surprised me. He blew past my

justification spiel. "We could have fixed things. Jesus, Aurelia. I was in agony. How could you do that to me! We could have fixed things."

I back-peddled fast, recalling the emotional turmoil of my last day in 1965. "I was in too much agony myself to think clearly. Jakobina…"

Zee covered his ears. "Stop! Enough about Jakobina. I don't want to hear another word about Jakobina. She's dead. Dead but somehow, never gone. And after everything we've been through, you're prepared to leave *me* again, for *her* – a scheming bitch who isn't really here. An apparition who returns a lost bear, fifty-years after the fact, knowing all along her charge was a lonely child. Yes, CHILD. A teenage child pining for comfort. Seriously, this is too much. YOU are too much. And I'm an idiot. You're still a child, and I don't want a child bride."

"I have a grown up reason, if you listen. It wasn't heartless. I'm going through with the transition for *us*. You and me. Mattias explained a lot of things. Jakobina showed me things. It's a matter of priorities. One move leads to happiness for everyone but it requires timing and we're almost out of time. The rules dictate when."

"Everyone? Does that include me as well as the two entities you begged me to banish only a few days ago. Have you lost your mind."

"There's no need to be mean. A few days ago I didn't know the whole truth."

"And you believe Jakobina and Mattias. The two liars who manipulated us when we were innocent teenagers. You haven't consulted me. Was that part of your new plan? Were you even going to say goodbye this time?"

"I was about to."

"What? Discuss a questionable plan, inform me of your decision, or say goodbye?"

"I felt sure you would agree to my change of heart when you knew the terms."

"You've made your decision. And now, here's mine. I'm leaving. It seems I'm destined to live out my years alone. I thought I knew you. I trusted you. I forgave you. But not this. Not for her. Not again. I have to go. Consider *my* heart changed. I release you from our engagement."

· · ·

Our star imploded with the force of a thousand atomic bombs. Zee's words came back to me, biting like shrapnel. His tone was accusatory. He wagged a finger in my face. "You're only agreeing to that cockamamie pact because you got back a stupid teddy bear. Well, have fun with your toys. Maybe Virgil *and* Felix can join you in that damn painting. I sure as hell won't be."

It seemed implausible, but at the heart of things, apart from slurring Virgil's intelligence, what Zee said was true.

chapter 69
WITH HONORS

I am once more able to confide in Jakobina although we're far from being friends. "I miss Zee," I told her. "He was my best friend before we fell in love."

"I had a best friend, too," Jakobina said. "I told you she died giving birth to a son."

"That's terrible. I'm sorry, but it has nothing to do with me."

Jakobina's reply was muffled. "Terrible things happen for a reason."

I resumed the dictates of a twisted advent calendar in a countdown to my death. I was alone on graduation day. A day of revelations, hardly jubilant. I was sad Zee wasn't present to hear the whole truth as unbroken and cruel as Jakobina and Mattias told it. He would have been appalled but he may have stayed.

Jakobina took the lead. "Zee believed you didn't love him, but it wasn't true. It was an old wound because it was a repeat performance. Betrayal had happened before. He once loved me as a woman but I returned his love as a friend. You both carried a fear of unworthiness forward – a fear rooted in the past. My best friend, Marieke, loved Zee and he was *her* friend. A love triangle with too many sides. Wires crossed. Tangled strings. There were things to work out."

"Were!"

"Marieke married my brother and had a son, but she died in childbirth. Her child's name was Felix. He lived three days. I promised to watch over him, and so I did, even from the afterlife. He was destined to be a doctor. Mattias helped him too. He taught the boy everything he'd come to know about dream therapy. That child was born to complete his mission as Dr. Sanderson. Even now he awaits reincarnation. Aurelia, you were Marieke!"

My knees gave way. I crumpled to the floor. Canary nuzzled my shoulder. Her collar was in my face but this time I didn't grab it. I wanted to travel anywhere that wasn't here.

Jakobina knelt down. "I'm so sorry. I didn't mean to tell you this way. The Sandman, Doc, was your son – a natural time traveler. Marieke's son, *your* son, Felix, is with you still. As your muse."

"You're mistaken. Felix could never have been a live person. He's a clock."

Jakobina raised her eyebrows. "Felix is only the voice of your clock. Its brain and heart. He was a human baby. He lived three days. After his death he had some growing to do. School never ends, Aurelia. One of Felix's previous lives flashed past him and he reincarnated as Doc. Doc was born a natural time-traveler. A clock was a symbolic way of imparting his truest self to you. Felix was once a doctor. A Jungian psychologist."

"Strange as it seemed, I accepted my muse was a clock. It was a creative improvisation. I heard him because I thought I was crazy."

"A clock is an inanimate object. But a devoted muse needs to be heard and commandeers mental space in their artist's imagination. That's what imaginations are for. I lied to you when we met. You were never crazy."

"So that's my family? A dementia victim, a liar named Marieke for a best friend, and a semi-conscious doctor in a hospice. Seriously. You're telling me that a clockwork son is my psychiatrist!"

"As family, we do what we can for each other from wherever we are. I sent the telegram to your father, not to hurt Zee but to help your father on his way. He needed to begin the new year with his own second chance for a new life. You left Zee because you loved him too much to hurt him. Under the circumstances, saying goodbye would have been heartless. And you aren't that. You've never been that."

I felt nauseous and acted accordingly while Jakobina turned away.

She handed me a box of tissues and resumed unaffected. "Marieke and I were inseparable. I told her everything. She accepted that my incomplete soul was trapped in Vermeer's painting. And as my closest friend, she agreed to take my place during one of my rest periods between lives, but she died before she could keep her promise."

"And so," I recounted. "As her next incarnation, I inherited her pact with you. That's why you sought me out."

"I was giving Marieke a second chance to fulfill her promise. And by setting her free you will set your mother free as well."

"And Mattias liberated your father's paintings."

"A time traveler may come and go as long as they never corrupt the timeline. One may not go back to save a life, but they *can* retrieve a work of art after it has been destroyed without altering the timeline. Do you see? A burned painting is a 'dead' painting because it no longer occupies physical space. Its molecules are temporarily removed from influencing their time. But after the population of its time passes naturally into memory, a painting's 'ghost' is freed. It's refreshed. Reborn. Healed. If found, a lost painting, may be safely reintroduced to a future time with no adverse side effects."

"You're telling me that paintings can reincarnate and a clock can become a philosopher?"

"Yes. After Mattias's memories were restored he went back to save his master's work but not himself. He managed to store Fabritius's works against any possible future contamination before he returned to the day of the explosion and accepted his injuries with grace. It was an unselfish act of sacrifice – the act of an honorable artist. By 1678, when Mattias died, it was safe for the collection to resurface, but it was wiser to wait for the perfect time. 2019."

A frozen memory replayed in peripheral vision. Jakobina's right earring swung close to my face and paused long enough to deliver a reflection of my face, distorted in its convex silvery surface. Even in my distress on the day of our meeting, it had reminded me of the optical illusions perfected by Vermeer and other like-minded artists of the 'Dutch School'. They'd recorded miniature details of significant figures, out of direct sight, present in a scene, yet obscure and invisible to anyone oblivious to the finer points of fine art.

I envisioned a spectro-camera zooming in to enlarge Jakobina's portrait earring to its greatest magnification.

"Look closely," Mattias said. "See what's hidden in plain sight." The close-up revealed the ghostly image of a woman sitting in a chair holding a cat, trapped under the skin of the pearl. Both stared out of the earring, captured in the act of observing the girl sitting for her portrait. I leaned in close, stunned to recognize myself with Punch, the day we visited Vermeer's studio. We had been there. But what I found even more extraordinary was that, for a brief moment in time, Vermeer had been staring at me.

"Keep your eyes on Vermeer's 'View of Delft'," Mattias instructed. "It's a continual work-in-progress. Did you think a mind like Vermeer's would conceive anything less than a miracle? Do you think he just dabbed a few anonymous figures in the foreground on a whim with a casual paintbrush? He did not. They are guardians. A true master never paints tronies. Vermeer's compositions were well-rehearsed phantoms, adapted to perfection, to tell a story."

"Guardians for whom?"

"Can you not guess."

"For Jakobina, I suppose."

"No, they're for you."

"A few days ago, Zee suggested life was a display of free-dancing hydrogen. Maybe he was wrong. You're the big deal teacher. Was he mistaken?"

"Let's clear something up. I'm *Jakobina's* guardian, which let me assure you, is an enormously complicated full-time *deal*."

"But if you're such a great teacher, surely the essence of your teaching isn't just wish fulfillment in order to dream oneself free of a few mistakes."

Mattias patted me on the back, pity written in his eyes. "Freedom is a difficult artform to perfect. When was the last time you felt free?"

"I'll let you know when it happens," I replied, perfectly serious.

"Look, if you want me to get all preachy. I can, but you might wish I hadn't."

It was too late to stop him. Mattias rolled up his sleeves, gently pushed me onto a chair, and held me down by my shoulders. He cleared his throat and spoke over my head, metaphorically and literally. "The true purpose of life is the relentless pursuit of creative continuity as in procreativity of the species. A galaxy is art. A tiger is art. A molecule is art."

"Well, obviously, art is art," I countered. "So surely, loving is an art."

"Sorry, no," Mattias reflected. "Art is the absolute *chiaroscuro* of atonement (literally, bringing truth into the light) balanced with the *pentimento* of deeper truths (alterations in a finished painting, evidenced by traces of previous work). Love, on the other hand, is a by-product of art. It's the fragile tension between non-resistance and fighting for survival."

I reacted with an explosive "Wow! Emperor Aurelius wasn't kidding."

Mattias grinned and made a bow. "I can state empirically, that Emperor Aurelius had absolutely no sense of humor."

Mattias did everything but wave his hand over me in a spell. "I charge you with listening to a masterpiece carefully for life signs," he said in a truly magical tone. "A barking dog, the wind, muffled conversations… everything. It's no different than holding a shell to your ear to hear the ocean."

Here is the deepest secret nobody knows
(here is the root of the root and the bud of the bud
and the sky of the sky of a tree called life; which grows
higher than soul can hope or mind can hide)
and this is the wonder that's keeping the stars apart.
— e. e. c u m m i n g s
i carry your heart(i carry it in my heart)"

chapter 70
PEARL SOLITAIRE

– December 8 –

I opened the door to an enormous bouquet of sweetheart roses that spoke in Zee's voice. "I read your letter," he confessed, from behind the flowers "And I realized an important thing."

I was overcome with a flood of relief. The flowers suggested an apology but I remained nervous. "Which is?"

His face stayed hidden. "You're my girl. And I'm in for whatever happens next." He lowered the bouquet. "If the wedding is still on I'd like to give you this." He thrust the flowers at me, produced a ring box from his pocket, and snapped open the lid with his thumb, revealing a ring set with a single raw pearl. "It's not cultured," he said.

"Flatterer."

"It's a singularity, like you. Culture is not something that represents either of us. And you've lived in solitary confinement far too long. Will you be my wife?"

My poet friend, e.e. cummings, was right when he wrote *I carry your heart in my heart.* Even though he wrote all his poems and signatures in a lower case alphabet, his sentiments always loomed large in capital letters ten feet high. "And so," Zee said. "In a crazy way, I'll show you

Paris in my dreams and we'll visit Bodium Castle in yours. In time, we will be the dream and the dreamers – the shadows on the walls of our castle. Shadow puppets with no strings."

chapter 71
UNDYING LOVE

"Zee can go with you," Mattias says as if I hadn't already formulated and aired my daring plan. "I mean, he can *follow* you into the painting when his time comes, and until then you can be together. Canary and Punch are invited to your private reincarnation party, too."

"Are you suggesting I haunt Zee?"

"I'm saying, you can continue to *live* with Zee. You lived with the ghost of Jakobina for fifty-three years, so what's a few more ethereal years with the man of your dreams. And from inside a painting inside a castle by the sea. Not too shabby if you ask me."

I snickered. "It's a dream come true. And I didn't ask you."

"Life is but a dream, sweetheart."

"Shaboom," I replied. "Ain't *that* the truth."

The sand was difficult to shuffle. In fact, it shuffled itself and swirled around our feet as Mattias and I walked at a purposely brisk pace with thoughts requiring deep silence, hands in pockets.

He stopped to scoop a handful of sand and held it aloft, pretending to blow it into my face when the wind caught it. Instinctively, I closed my eyes as the grains showered over me. "You can't build a castle with magic dust," he said.

Mattias waited. I waited. Finally, he lifted his eyebrows for an answer. "Well?"

An image formed in my mind, fierce and sharp causing a surprise intake of breath. "There was a child," I said. "A boy. I saw him once, here in the real world, walking to school. I followed him."

"Well done," he said "You're doing fine. What else do you remember?"

"I clung to the schoolyard fence, weak-kneed and woozy for hours. Later he came out for recess and sat alone in the playground. A teacher came out and stared over at me. She called to him. I've forgotten his name but as soon as she said it I cried. I couldn't stop and I was grateful that it started to rain and my anguish was disguised. That teacher was you wasn't it? You made it rain."

Mattias cupped my face tenderly. "Listen very carefully," he said, wiping invisible tears from my face. "*You* made it rain. *You* wanted it to rain. That's all it takes when you're in two worlds. Here and now, you can cry all you want without fear of embarrassment."

I brushed his hands away and smeared my face with the back of my sleeve. "You made me cry. Just then, you made me cry. Because I wasn't feeling sad. I was only curious."

"The tears *were* mine. Well done, you," he said, shaking my hand. He kept hold of my hand and pulled me close until my head found his shoulder. I heard terrible sobs that came from me.

When I was done, Mattias tilted my chin to the stars and kissed me as Jakobina's first husband, Piet. We stood in the heart of Vancouver's busy center. I caught him as his knees gave way.

Piet held me at arms length and scanned the scenery around us. He had made it to downtown Vancouver. "How did I get here?" he said. His eyes were wild and I was certain he was going to shake me.

My words formed without thinking. "You're dreaming, my love. Go back to sleep."

Mattias materialized in Piet's place. "Nice work. You're a natural. But I still have much to teach you if you let me." He pinched my dry cheek. "Teatime," he said, taking my arm to steer me home where Zee waved to us from the porch.

"Nice timing," Zee shouted. "The kettle's on."

Canary barked her happiness bark and bounded towards us. I looked up at Mattias with a question forming in my mind.

He answered right away. "No, I'm *not* Canary. Not always. Once for a few seconds when you met in the animal shelter. She's a dog who adores you. Not that I don't, but you understand my meaning. I experienced her once when circumstances demanded it. That's all. And by the way, the boy in the schoolyard was my son, Jan. I tune in and out of lives to check in for my own purposes. I won't bore you with the details now. Maybe later."

I blinked myopically and opened my mouth to speak.

"No need to thank me," Mattias said holding his finger to my lips. "You created this. Never forget that you are a master artist."

Mattias became Thatcher, Thatcher morphed into Catcher who was replaced with Piet, but it was Zee who enfolded me in a bear hug that made Canary run frenzied circles around us for attention.

"Always and forever," Zee whispered into my hair. When I looked into his eyes they were Piet's.

"This is what will happen," Mattias said in my head. "I will only say it once, so please pay attention. "In a few years, after the world has revolved around the sun the prerequisite number of times, you and Zee will meet as strangers in front of a painting in a gallery. I won't say which one, except that it will be a masterpiece of an almost forgotten artist from the 'Dutch School'. There will be a recognition that lasts an instant and a longing that never ends."

Let us go then, you and I,
When the evening
Is spread out against the sky
Let us go and make our visit.
— T.S. ELIOT

chapter 72
THE POWER VESTED

The Winter Solstice
– December 22 –

Our wedding planner is a smart-mouth clock. Felix ticks off a traditional rhyming list with his tail. *Tick*... "Something borrowed. I'd say a certain painting takes care of that nicely."... *tock*... "Something blue. The cobalt shard you found the day Zee found you." ...*tick*... "Something old. Well, not to put too fine a point on it, the bride and groom spring to mind." His tail paused mid- wag. *tock*... "The difficult one is something new. What say you?"

"Tick tock," I said sarcastically. "An overwhelming release of sadness and a feeling of empowerment."

Felix's tail swished in normal speed. "Atonement it is, then… Nice. Very nice."

"We're not writing vows," I said. "And the traditional spiel about death parting us seemed a tad on the nose, so, Mattias has agreed to say something spontaneous. The whole thing should take two minutes."

Our wedding day dawned calm and unseasonably warm. Zee and I wore the wedding gifts we received from Mattias and Jakobina – clothes Mattias retrieved from 1965. We both wore our old blue-jeans and white running shoes. I embellished mine with the pristine T-shirt Zee had given me as a hug. Zee wore a grey sweatshirt under his red high school bomber jacket with the white leather sleeves and

Monmouth High crest. My high school ring was pressed into service as the wedding ring.

That evening, Zee and I stood under a waning moon, backs against the ocean, holding hands. I held a bouquet of white roses. Canary leaned into my legs as my maid of honor. Punch and Jakobina were bridesmaids. Punch endured being held by Jakobina for a few seconds and Jakobina endured holding Punch in her arms. Mattias performed the ceremony after the Sandman gave me away. Mattias quoted Shakespeare "And in that sleep of death," he said, "and by the power vested in me, I now pronounce you man and wife. Til' dreams do you part."

In the bleak mid-winter
Frosty winds may moan,
Earth stood hard as iron,
Water like a stone.
Snow had fallen, snow on snow,
In the bleak mid-winter
A long long time ago.
— CHRISTINA ROSSETTI
1872

chapter 73
N'EARRING TRANSITION

– December 23 –
2019

I rose early to take a last solitary walk on my beach with Canary and Punch. While the animals scampered over the sand, each in pursuit of their favorite seaside pleasures, I smoothed wet sand together, building a castle for Zee to find as a farewell gift, and left a message for him paraphrased from e.e. cummings, written on a scrap of mauve paper. Darling Zee, *"Come to me and brush the mischief from my eyes… And fold thy unimaginable wings, where dwells the breath of all persisting stars."*

A few hours later, in my time-honoured tradition of leaving without saying goodbye, I ran from the cottage and into Zee's car while Canary and Punch slept. "They'll be fine," Mattias assured me. "They're dreaming of mice and rabbits, curtesy of the Sandman."

I clung to a small bouquet of white roses. "Just think of your body as a heap of molecules," Felix called out after me. "And for heaven's sake let go. And hurry home."

· · ·

The airline clerk eyed our sparse carry-on luggage. "Any other bags to check, Sir?"

Zee held up two flight bags and pointed to my handbag. "This is it."

"Returning home, are we?"

Zee glanced at me and sighed when a chuckle would have eased my guilty conscience. "No such luck. We're just a couple of eccentrics, *leaving* home."

"Anything to declare, Sir?"

"Tis the season to be jolly," Zee said with a straight face.

– Christmas Eve –

2019

Inside the Tintagel train station we were met by an old man selling guidebooks and mistletoe. He took one look at us, a bedraggled pair of old folk, to the airline tag on Zee's bag and my trembling roses, and handed Zee a copy. "On the house," he said tipping the cap he wasn't wearing. "There's room at the Castle Inn on Camlann Street for weary travelers on Christmas Eve. Mrs. Biggs keeps a lovely establishment, she does." He took pity on our exhausted faces. "It should snow later tonight," he added cheerfully. "The weatherman says we're in for a white Christmas. He waved a bunch of waxy green leaves with white berries at me. "Can I interest you in some Cornish mistletoe? It's rather magic."

"Thank you but no," I replied. "Too much magic isn't healthy at our age."

He caught my eye and winked. "Well, Happy New Year to you, missus."

I smiled back. "Not yet."

Outside, the Cornish rain had waited to deliver its payload to greet us. Umbrellas were turning inside out by the wind. Zee held the guidebook over our heads and hailed a taxi. We were off to the tender mercies of Mrs. Biggs and her lovely establishment.

The loveliness meant it was warm and dry and an orchestral version of 'Good King Wenceslas' spilled into the street when she opened the door. She gave us the tour. A lounge revealed the source of music in a room golden with firelight. It wasn't long before we were snuggly ensconced with tea and toast and fig jam, alone in the parlour with Arthur, Mrs. Biggs' black and white cat. In the corner stood a spindly Christmas tree sparsely decorated with tinsel and an ancient string of glass candles that bubbled dangerously with some sort of colored liquid – the sort electricity boards everywhere had banned years ago.

The power blinked, threatening imminent immolation but it was cheery next to the downpour threatening to shatter the windows.

"We do live dangerously," Zee said.

"Dangerous is no way to say goodbye," I said. "Let's end on a high note and confess all our secrets. I have it on good authority by an expert that we're a long time dead."

"Ask away."

"I never met your partner Mr. Zygmont. Is he still around?"

"Actually, he was never around," Zee said sheepishly. "I made him up. He was an imaginary partner. Two names looked more professional on a letterhead. It was a play on my stupid name, Sigmund. Carter & Zee sounded fake. Carter & Ziggy was ridiculous, so I promoted Sigmund to Zygmont."

"Wow! Anything else you're hiding?" I asked.

"You'll be duly informed on a need to know basis."

"Let's end on a promise, then."

Zee read from the guide book, warped from the heat. "It says here that the ghost of a woman known as the 'mad woman of Tintagel' haunts the castle ruins. The article says she is believed to have committed suicide in a leap off the battlements." He made a clicking sound with his tongue. "Now, I wonder who *she* could be."

Mrs. Biggs, who was tiny and deaf as a post, looked in on us with a tray containing slices of chocolate log and Jaffa cakes. She must have caught the word haunted because she launched into what she thought was an inspiring tale. "You've seen our ghost, then, have you?" she said handing around small plates.

I smiled sweetly. "Um, no. We were just speculating. This is an old house and England is full of ghosts." I gestured to Arthur stretched in front of the fire. "But we've met Arthur."

She looked puzzled. "Who?"

I raised my voice a little. "Your cat."

"Oh, right. Well, Arthur's not *my* cat. He arrived only minutes before you did," she said. "Poor little mite. I let him in out of the rain. Soaking wet he was, howling fit to wake the dead. He looked like an Arthur, so Arthur he be."

I spoke louder, enunciating my words. "Well, he's nice and dry now."

"Our ghost is usually seen on the stairs," she offered. "Well, not exactly seen, but one can feel his presence."

"Very Christmassy," Zee said accepting a Jaffa cake.

"The diminutive Mrs. Biggs seemed determined to be even more Christmassy. "It should snow later," she said. "And there's a film on the telly in the common room... Dicken's 'Christmas Carol'- the proper one with Alastair Sims." She checked the mantel clock. "It should start in half an hour."

Arthur stirred and sprang to my lap. "Will you keep Arthur," I asked.

"On the back stairs," she said.

"Sorry?"

"That's' where our ghost appears. On the back stairs."

The door closed behind her, and surprisingly, Zee let out a real laugh. "How delightfully inappropriate, a ghost story to take our minds off our seasonal mission of death."

I held up a piece of toast. "I propose a literal toast to absent ghosts of good cheer."

"Yes," Zee said. "Merry Christmas Dasher and Dancer, Catcher, Thatcher, and Doc, Jakobina and Mattias, Rudolph, Blitzen, et al."

– Christmas Day –
2019

As predicted, Christmas Day was white. Hoar frost bore the semblance of snow but not the stamina. By noon an English drizzle had washed it to Byzantium.

Cornwall's Winter coast with its seasonal storms had reduced tourism to a minimum and gifted us the sanctuary we'd come to find.

But the old parish church of Tintagel bustled with Christmas. Candles dispelled the gloom. Damp as we were, standing room only warmed us. The shoulder-to-shoulder congregation steamed us dry while being charmed by a classic nativity play performed by angelic school children.

Surprisingly, we emerged into a bright day, albeit brisk, and trudged off to the beach with a thermos of cocoa and a bare bones picnic. Pebbles crunched underfoot and Cornish gulls shrieked overhead like banshees. We breakfasted on French bread, strong Welsh cheese, and sweet apples, shielding our food from relentless wings and beaks. Canary would have made short work of their gate crashing.

Tintagel Castle loomed like an ominous grey dragon. Its window holes resembled hollow eyes that peered down on us.

Zee and I marched against the weather determined as a couple of soldiers on patrol until it became apparent we were searching for the familiar couple headed toward us unaffected by the wind.

Jakobina, clearly happy as a clam, waved enthusiastically. Not yet free and clear from her painting, she tempted fate by celebrating her approaching season of mortality. Mattias hailed us. "Well met, brave newlyweds," he said and they disappeared.

"Join us for tea later," I shouted into the space they'd vacated. "We're staying at number 18 on Camlann Street."

We plodded on into the teeth of a new storm as an unexpected wave of black clouds pushed in over the cliffs and descended around us in a bubble of eery silence.

The downpour drew us closer, surprisingly warm and dry. "I know what this is," I said. "This is yesterday's rain. I remember it from Jakobina and Mattias's past. We're not really here."

In a windbreak of piled boulders, two hunched figures in hooded cloaks materialized, holding hands over a dying fire built inside a low wall of stones. A halo of blue smoke hovered over the scene as ashes of sacrificial paper blew around them in a storm of their own. Unaware of us, Jakobina and Mattias continued to chant in Dutch, looking and sounding like a pair of Augustine monks until the apparition melted into its time rift.

Zee and I looked at each other with a singular galvanized thought of Mrs. B's sanctuary where a candle-lit dinner for two awaited. We practically flew back to the village to be greeted by a hypnotic recording of Gregorian chant and the delightful aroma of sage and onion.

After Mrs. Biggs' sherry trifle, Zee produced a bottle of champagne from his bag. "Here's to our 'last supper'," he said. "And a different famous work of art that shall remain anonymous."

I clinked my glass to his. "To girls with pearl earrings," I replied. "May they rest in peace."

They were waiting for us in Mrs. Biggs' parlour at midnight, taking their ghostly form in case Mrs. B descended on us with yet another tray of endless mince pies, Scottish shortbread, and Bakewell tarts. Arthur sat between Jakobina and Mattias as transparent as they were. "I presume you've met our cat," Jakobina said.

I showed no surprise. "Arthur reminds me of Punch. I miss her. And I miss Canary."

Jakobina picked up Arthur and kissed his nose. "Punch *was* Arthur. Cats have nine lives you know. And how, may I ask, can a clam be happy?"

"Maybe they pretend they're oysters that grow nice big pearl earrings inside their shells," I suggested. "And isn't it time you stopped reading my mind. I thought you didn't like cats."

Mattias winked at Zee. For an instant, Arthur's fur turned ginger. "Life is simply full of surprises and promises," he said.

Boxing Day delivered a sky full of snowflakes. We trudged the new fallen snow of the churchyard – a sombre Christmas card. "Mattias and Jakobina are buried here," I said gesturing to the teetering gravestones with my roses – literal touchstones of peace.

Zee huddled deeper into the upturned collar of his wool coat. "They had no markers, so they could be anywhere."

"As it should be," I said. "Still, I didn't bring two roses from my bridal bouquet to give to Mrs. Biggs."

Zee eyed the castle's icy cliff. "If only we could fly, Wendy. We both know there's only one place to offer them."

And so, after a steep climb, I tossed two white roses from the battlements of Tintagel Castle that fell like a couple of stars, and fancied I saw a mermaid lift her hand from the water like the lady of the lake wielding Excalibur, who caught them before disappearing under a sea of champagne bubbles.

chapter 74
HELLO GOODBYE

New Year's Eve

On our last morning, Mrs. Biggs lit a roaring fire in the breakfast room against the worst gale, so she said repeatedly, in the history of Tintagel. Arthur was appropriately invisible in plain sight, staring bold as brass out the room's only window. I sat frozen between fire and rain with my heart breaking as the dying year ironically heralded the eve of my new afterlife.

My last civilized cup of tea grew cold as I memorized the china pattern. From this point on, if tea featured in my immediate future, it would no doubt be served in a crude restaurant mug or a Styrofoam cup. Zee took his coffee black just to punish himself. We let the silence do its worst.

Masking our grief was impossible. We avoided direct eye contact by wearing our sunglasses to breakfast. We looked like a couple of hungover celebrities, incognito the morning after a night of excess revelry. But, I'd stared at the ceiling all night as Zee tossed and turned.

Arthur's claws scraped the windowpane trying to catch the lumps of hail hitting the glass. I waved goodbye to him, from the taxi, still at his post in a different window. I imagined he sent a message to Jakobina that we were on our way.

· · ·

Although widows weeds, veiled hat and all, seemed appropriate for the occasion, I was determined not to wear black. I wore a flowery summer dress under the Sophie coat. Zee wore a navy-blue pea jacket and tied a red wool scarf around his neck.

Sunglasses in the rain caused a few second glances at first, but our grim expressions gave us away as likely mourners in a funeral procession. I got the impression of passersby moving aside respectfully and looking away.

"Greetings and partings," Zee mused aloud to the blurry landscape retreating past greasy train windows animated by rivulets of water. "Humans are gluttons for pain and suffering. I hate storms."

I recalled a painful memory in 1965 when I was drowning in a library, sick with the knowledge I was about to leave Zee forever. Then as now, a rainstorm turned my prison into an aquarium. I had the urge to pull the train's emergency cord. I floundered, drowning in fear. I couldn't lose Zee again. How could I have been so stupid a second time. I needed to stop moving.

I broke the silence to center myself. "Jakobina will be waiting for me at the airport," I said and Mattias will be on the island to welcome you home."

Zee, jittery from caffeine, pulled down his sunglasses to give me a harrowed glare through red-rimmed eyes. "Yes, I know. We've gone over this. Mattias will smother me with kindness and lectures on the nuances of ghostdom. I have my orders to make a fuss over Punch with cat treats and take Canary for several walks a day. Heaven forfend a sinister color of sea glass finds me."

The last leg of the journey to Heathrow grew increasingly strained as we drew closer to the airport in a shiny black taxi that felt like a hearse. We sat far apart, linked by fingertips, each lost in our own window of liquid glass. Low flying aircraft buzzed us farewell. We passed road signs distorted from outside our moving aquarium that screamed the word 'TERMINAL' in a countdown of miles. Zee's grip tightened on my fingers at each one. The tremors in his hands sparked my own nerves until I feared I might shake apart into a heap of smoldering molecules.

When we pulled up to the departures area, our mood shifted from fraught to gut wrenching. The word 'terminal' continued to haunt us. Every sign reminded us we were heading towards a crossroad of no return where we would part ways in a manner we could never have imagined a few short months ago.

Human anguish and joy collided inside the congested terminal, already suffocating with emotional turmoil. Helloing and goodbye-ing stood out in fractious pockets of happiness and tears. It seemed safe to remove our sunglasses but it wasn't.

The anguish in my eyes clearly shook Zee. The overwhelming love and sorrow in Zee's eyes was equally devastating, but the peak of my separation anxiety arrived on the tail of a voice from a loudspeaker declaring final boarding for my flight. Zee gallantly tried to ease my torment by singing to me in Beatle-speak. *"You say yes, I say no. You say yes. I say please don't go.* "Well, old girl, I guess this is hello," he said. He grabbed my shoulders hard and pulled me into a rough bear hug. *"I don't know why you say goodbye. I say hello,"* he sang into my hair. "See you next year, kiddo. Have a safe flight."

I was too terrified to cry. We broke apart, eyes closed, forgetting to kiss, and I hurried off in a dither. Somehow, I composed my face and turned back to wave with a brave smile, but Zee was gone.

I was free to fall apart but the tears didn't come. My body was weightless, dry as paper – a walking mummy, dehydrated and joyless, thousands of years dead. I heard my sunglasses clatter to the floor.

There was no Jakobina in the departures lounge or duty free or any of our prearranged meeting places. No black and white cat slinking between luggage and legs. I boarded the plane with the hope that Jakobina had wrestled her guilt to the floor in an eleventh hour change of heart. The desperate line *'you say goodbye and I say hello'* looped inside my head as musical tinnitus. I decided they would be my first words to Zee when I called him from Amsterdam with the good news.

A sharp stab of nostalgia surprised me as the plane taxied on the runway, its nose facing the Netherlands. I used to tease Jakobina by calling her country 'Never Never Land'. Tongue in cheek, Zee and I called each other Peter and Wendy, representing the reversed roles of a flighty lost girl mothered by a down-to-earth boy. "First star on the right and keep on til' morning," I murmured out loud. And now the words 'terminal' and 'mourning' ran across my mind like the electronic screens in Times Square. This moment, if anything, was definitely flighty. Am I to have no peace. Will I play word association all the way to Delft. "Hogwash," I said under my breath.

The old woman next to me leaned over. "What was that?" she said.

"Hogmanay," I replied, staring at a catalog stashed in the seat pocket facing me. "Tomorrow is Hogmanay. That's what the Scots call New Year."

"Ah. You are Scottish?"

I locked my seatbelt with a metallic click. "Not today but I may have been at some juncture," I replied, hoping to stifle the conversation. I gripped both armrests. "Right now I'm just skittish."

The woman placed her left hand over mine. "I am Dutch. I see you're a white knuckle flier. My dear, nothing can go wrong."

I flinched as the engines engaged, and pulled my hand out from under my neighbor's. When the plane rolled forward, I linked both hands over my stomach in a faux mudra. As the force of liftoff pinned me to my chair, I whispered *what dreams may come* as if was making a wish.

The woman beside me shifted in her seat. Her voice changed to one I knew only too well. "Did you think I wouldn't come?" Jakobina said.

"Yes," I replied weakly without turning my head.

She chuckled. "I had the same thought about you." Jakobina patted my hand. "Nothing will go wrong my dear," she said resuming her disguise. "Flying is as safe as castles."

chapter 75
DEATH BY PAINTING

The Mauritius Gallery, Holland
– New Year's Day –
2020

The Mauritius Gallery thronged with tourists. Jakobina and I stood before her portrait for a long time. People jostled past us until the room was deserted but for a group of nuns in white habits with starched aprons, and a small boy with kaleidoscope eyes who seemed fascinated with us. He stared at me with a cheeky smile on his face, holding onto a woman's hand.

The women were obviously from a strict religious order, although one amongst them wore a jaunty lavender cap. They looked familiar. One of them made eye contact. They turned as one, the way a flock of birds moves across the sky, and waved.

I recognized Baby, Grub, Biz, Blue, Hospital Corners, and of course, Britches in her lavender cap. Mouse pointed to her feet shod in soft carpet slippers. Nurse Clipboard carried her symbol of power and crossed off something from one of her inevitable lists with a dramatic flourish. "You're good to go," she called out, waving a strip of mauve paper. "Officially discharged."

Brisk's smile transformed her into an angel of mercy, nodding approval at Clipboard's side. I hardly recognized her without her stern grimace.

They parted as if performing a surreal ballet to reveal Mattias who immediately morphed into a tall frail man who managed to appear distinguished while wearing pajamas and a striped hospital robe. He leaned heavily on a walker, but when he smiled he straightened his back and transformed into a picture of health. A handsome grey fox of a man. The walker evaporated. He grinned broadly.

"Sandman."

"It's time to dream, Wendy," he called out.

Fear overwhelmed me and I broke away from his gaze. "It doesn't hurt," he shouted. "Honest."

"It's 2020," I repeated several times to myself, stupidly, begging the obvious.

Jakobina was radiant, literally glowing beside me. "Yes, it's finally here," she said.

I gawped at the ceiling to avoid my destination. "So, you're savoring your anticipated victory at my expense. I see your cruel streak has survived. I guess some things remain immortal."

"You have no idea. You are a child."

"When do we do this?"

"In a moment," Jakobina whispered, staring straight ahead at her portrait. "Wait a bit longer."

Queasiness crept up my spine. "The moment is at hand," I whined. "So, what are we waiting for? Let's get it over with before I completely lose my nerve. Are you aware of the term 'now or never'. Can you guess which one of those is uppermost in my mind right now? Can you!"

Jakobina silenced me with an abrupt "shush." She looked miffed but it passed as she smiled into her future. "The waiting is almost over," she said blissfully with her eyes closed. She inclined her head, gesturing to my left. "Look."

The small boy had broken away from his mother and was walking towards us. Concern replaced his cheeky smile.

"Jakobina, please stop this charade," I whimpered. "And let me go."

"You're nearly home," she said. "Act your age. Stop whimpering."

A collective cheer erupted from the nurses. Sandman dissolved into the form of a little girl. "Remember me," she shouted. "I will see you soon." And with that, my farewell committee disappeared like fragile soap bubbles.

I felt a slight tug on Sophie's sleeve. The boy had reached me. He stared up at me with an expression of pure love, his wide eyes shining with bright tears. His sassiness returned. "I'm not crying," he said. "Happy birthday."

I forgot about death, and fear left me. He stroked the fur affectionately. "I remember everything," he said, taking my hand. He smiled radiantly. "Fear is your friend," he said. "Embrace it."

Jakobina nudged my elbow to urge me forward. Sophie slithered from my shoulders onto the floor and lay at my feet like a sleeping animal.

I turned to Jakobina. "Now?"

She shook her head, one last time. Emily materialized in her place, her head still shaking. Her eyes glistened as she opened her arms and embraced me. It was my last chance for atonement. "I'm so sorry, Mom," I gushed. "I should have said goodbye." I kissed her cheek. It smelled of Chanel no.5.

Her touch gave me strength. "Be a good girl," she said and returned my kiss.

My voice caught. "I have to go," I said. "My time has run out."

She answered in a child's voice. "I know."

My mother was gone. In her place, the boy stood up to his knees in fur. His dazzling smile was back. "I remember everything," he said. I looked around for his mother but he was alone. "She's gone too," he said impishly.

The boy was clearly delighted with the fur around his feet. He picked it up gently, nuzzled his face into it, and draped Sophie across his arms, holding the coat aloft like an offering. "I will take good care of it," he said solemnly. "Never forget that I love you."

Jakobina, at my side once more, flickered like a lantern and went out.

I ruffled the boy's hair and managed a feeble smile. "Thank you," I said. "Sophie will like that."

He wiggled out from under my hand and gazed up at me. "I

remember absolutely everything," he repeated with confidence. "I remember being your mother."

"Emily?"

"My name is Jacob, now. I'll always love you."

Even though Jakobina was no longer there, her voice surrounded me. "It's time," she whispered.

"It doesn't hurt," Jacob said. "Honest."

The last sound I heard was the ticking of a clock. "Virgil is right," Felix said in my head. "A painting is an open door. A doorway of many returns."

Virgil's last words echoed down a long hallway of Christmas lights. "Follow the path...*path...path* that was lost... *lost...lost*. It's easy... *easy...easy*."

A cold wind pushed at my back. It loosened my hair until it fell around my shoulders like a maiden's. I walked forward into dazzling white light. A door closed softly behind me with a gentle click. The air quickened. It was warm and smelled of linseed oil and sunshine.

And when I have offered up each fragrant night
When all my days shall have before a certain face
Become white perfume
Only, from the ashes then thou wilt rise
And thou wilt come to her and brush the mischief from her eyes
And fold her mouth the new flower with thy unimaginable wings,
Where dwells the breath of all persisting stars.
— e. e. c u m m i n g s
'If I Believe'

chapter 76
GIRL WITHOUT EARRINGS

– JANUARY 8 –
2020

Of course, I found 'her' immediately. Early morning shadows covered the studio's furnishings like a shroud. Dawn's fingers poked at a wall-to-ceiling display of square windows set in even rows that sent feeble light over Vermeer's easel. I remembered everything. I'd spent a lifetime sitting in that chair positioned just so, with its place marked with chalk. I had to remind myself that I was a ghost here, and for a terrifying moment I was utterly homesick for my husband, my castle, my animals, and my time. What I wouldn't give to feel Canary's furry body pressing at my side offering her canine strength to my legs. I wanted it so desperately I heard her barking in the distance.

And then I remembered Virgil's advice about the inevitable presence of open doors.

I looked behind me and sure enough, the studio door was ajar. Immediately I was through it and Canary leapt up joyously, knocking me off balance. I was home.

Zee had his back to me, staring out the bedroom window. Both his hands clutched the windmill curtains in the act of drawing them together. The first Wednesday evening of 2020 was closing down. My 'life' as the ghost of Tintagel Cottage had begun.

"Peter," I called out. "Is this Neverland?" Zee turned and opened his arms, wide as his smile.

"I haven't quite got my sea legs," I announced, swaying as I walked past the bed where Punch curled, twitching in her sleep. I stroked her fur and she chirped in her dream. I was relieved to be as solid and substantial as ever. I was wild for the sea. "How long have I been gone?"

"A very long week," Zee said. "I was getting worried. Mattias warned me that it would take you a while to adjust to an ethereal state. I found your sandcastle. Come over here, crazy girl, so I can brush the mischief from your eyes."

I ran into his arms. "I will if you fold thy unimaginable wings around me and never let go."

Canary danced around us and crashed into my knees. I bent down to ruffle her ears and we rubbed noses, forehead-to-forehead like the day we met in the shelter when she'd lifted her eyes to mine from her dismal corner. I remembered the feeling of meeting an old friend, and sent Mattias a mental note of thanks.

"We shall be a pair of persistent stars," Zee said.

"We are perfect as we are," I said. "No worries."

I peered over Zee's shoulder from inside his embrace at a square of white light on the wall opposite. The print of the 'Girl with a Pearl Earring' glowed in a friendly way – an open invitation I could use or refuse at will, which was deeply comforting. I owned my place and time more than I ever did in life. "Let's go to Glastonbury," I said taking Zee's hand. "Canary needs a walk and I need to face something."

Zee walked me outside under a yellowing canopy of dawn sky giving up its stars. As an invisible passenger in his car, I wondered, had there been anyone else on the island, if they would have seen a smiling man talking to himself.

. . .

We walked the deserted streets of Glastonbury, past The Keep, The Findings, Fisher King's Books, Pen-Dragons, The Quest, and The Grail. I caught the scent of their demise and saw them as they would look in five-hundred-years – a row of small mounds of rubble and earth, making a straight line of lumps and bumps. From a gull's eye view, the serene landscape languished into the sea, wept over by the ever-present cries of seabirds.

Zee touched my arm, and the Glastonbury he knew, returned.

The grassy Tor loomed taller than I remembered. Its lone standing stone silhouetted against the sunny morning drew my attention like a homing beacon. "We can go up there when you're ready," Zee said. "Or not. It's all good."

"No," I said. "I want to see it. It's part of everything. I need to see it, now."

Canary ran in excited circles around us and bounded after her special throwing stick that Zee kept in the car.

Zee and I stood shoulder-to-shoulder on the grassy summit like a bride and groom atop a green wedding cake. I lifted my face to a spritz of salty wind that showered us like wedding rice. We held hands and gazed out over a calm sea that shimmered with iridescent mother of pearl colors.

The standing stone absorbed our attention. Zee laid some wild grasses from the beach at its base. "It's only a grave of bones," I whispered, leaning my forehead against his. "The painting is only a doorway to another room. My true resting place is with you in the castle."

The rain-soaked granite was stained lime with moss fuzz. Zee hugged me from behind and rested his chin on my shoulder. I stared at the fine Roman letters cut into the stone's surface. As I had decreed, there were no limiting dates. There was no name. I was not there. Zee's gentle voice filled my heart as he read the inscription.

There will be time, there will be time
To prepare a face to meet the faces that you meet;

There will be time to murder and create,
And time for all the works and days of hands
That lift and drop a question on your plate.
— T.S. ELIOT

chapter 77
DISAPPEARING ACT

– Valentine's Day –
2020

Breaking news traveled faster and louder than the alarm bells of the Mauritius Gallery. The 'Girl With A Pearl Earring' was missing. Stolen. Gone. An entire country was in shock, bereft, and angry. I was simply angry.

Last Valentine's Day I'd been sitting in Zee's boardroom waiting to be deemed a tenant worthy of Castle Island, or so I thought. A year later, I lived as a reasonably content fugitive inside a painting in order to pacify a family I hadn't known existed other than in my distant memories of winter canals and old masters. Again, 'lived' is a huge misnomer. I *inhabited* Vermeer's 'Girl With A Pearl Earring' masterpiece as a guest of honor without the honor of being chosen by Vermeer. By virtue of happenchance, I'm involved in its theft. But then, I've been a bizarre victim of circumstance almost my whole life.

I can attest wholeheartedly that, in spite of immortality's obvious singular benefit of consciousness, reasonably content is not a destination worth pursuing after a lifetime spent in forced exile. I had left the land of the living as a swan enters the water – without so much as a ripple. And now, I was drowning in an event that threatened to destroy my future with Zee.

. . .

As an understudy for Jakobina, the work's original tenant, I know where the painting is. At least, I know it's safely housed in a cool dark place among other precious objects that I can sense but not see. Happily, for the time being, I'm still able to use the museum quality print in Zee's bedroom as both door and window.

The thieves purport to be friends of mine. They're great ones for making subversive plans. Other than that, Jakobina and Mattias have kept me, literally, in the dark.

I've been swanning about between Delft and Castle Island, discovering in *hindsight*, that teenage *insight* is still a ticking bomb. When I first penned the words about dementia's seamless arrival on the back of a swan, and a ripple-free transition, it had been without thinking things through. It was romantic teenage poetry. But now, as a 'living' ghost, although I can report unequivocally that death arrives much the same way, it's quite possible I could die a second, more permanent death if Jakobina's original portrait is destroyed. It is, after all, the main gateway to immortality.

After I bypassed mortality, I *suffered*, if I may use that word, from *anti*-dementia. I recalled with 2020, every memory of all my past lives. Every secret, every face, every promise… and every betrayal.

But what I witness February 17th is stronger than betrayal. It's sabotage. It's murder. Jakobina and Mattias, no longer ghosts, haven't the ability to see me when I choose to be invisible. I love this power. It's everything. It's nothing. I am literally, no 'where' to be seen, in a good way.

The smell of acrid smoke leads me to the castle's beach where Jakobina and Mattias chant gibberish over a fire. The frame from the 'Girl With A Pearl Earring' lies empty on the sand. And in the heart of the flames, Jakobina's portrait blackens as it burns. The two of them throw herbs over it with accompanying incantations. They're killing me. They're killing Zee's chance to join me. It is an execution, pure and simple. The painting's cool dark sanctuary is no more. I wait an age but nothing happens.

Zee summoned me a week later. His expression, always an open book, read like an apology in the making. He gestured to the sofa where Canary and Punch slept close enough to resemble a single creature.

"I need you to sit," he said, "because, I'm going to deliver an art history lecture and it's a long story, but it has a twist at the end you're sure to appreciate."

I squeezed myself into the space that wasn't filled with fur, and sat to attention. "Art appreciation is my specialty," I said.

Zee rarely dithered the way he did, now. "Actually, it's more of a love story, so relax," he said. Dithering was the first clue he was hedging.

"Breathe easy," he said with a wink. Resorting to humor to disarm me was the second.

"Very funny."

Zee cleared his throat. I pictured him tapping an invisible microphone to check the sound levels. "Once upon a time, when Mattias was still Thatcher," he began. "We became close friends. So close, in fact, he made me executor of his will. So distant, I hadn't known he'd left me a mysterious wooden crate, the size of a refrigerator. As far as I knew it contained his old clothes and books. He had a fair few. Anyway, he gave me a key to a vault and made me swear to guard it with my life. I promised to keep the crate sealed until he sent me a sign from the afterlife."

I stifled a yawn and toyed with Punch's tail. Zee's story was an old one. I tried not to look bored but he'd headed off into Tangent-ville immediately after his once-upon-a-time intro. Any point he was going to make was destined to curve down a long winding road for a while.

We both knew full well, that at the time of Thatcher's *non*-death, Zee was unaware he was a ghost who had been a Dutch painter's apprentice named Mattias in a past life. And now Zee was revealing how his attachment to his alter ego, Thatcher began. Something was up.

Zee reached for a nearby coffee table book, hugged it like an anchor, and droned on. "I was a desperate teenager floundering in a personal crisis searching for answers," he recited.

I feared that my eyes, growing more incredulous and kaleidoscopic by the moment, would distract him even further, so I closed them retreating into limbo, thinking how loveable he was that he'd remembered Thatcher fondly as more of a big brother figure than a teacher with a menacing agenda. Phrases like guidance counsellor, dire need, and personable role model drifted past. I fixed a smile on my face and remembered how excruciating it had been to sit still for Jakobina's portrait that time she'd commandeered me into one of her memories.

As for real time, although I'd grown into the art of biding it, I now enjoyed wandering the streets of Delft, poking into merchandise in the market and eavesdropping on conversations I automatically understood. I wanted to be there now, sunning myself by the River Schie.

I tuned Zee out. His preamble faded into white noise as I retreated into a reverie of the sinister events he seemed intent on romanticizing. There was no doubt that Thatcher, a cool New-Age 'dude', had strategically positioned himself in the wings of Monmouth High to offer his spiritual guidance during Zee's darkest hour. It had been a calculated move to seduce a vulnerable student while spinning himself as a selfless, spiritual life-coach. In retrospect, it had not been unlike shooting a fish in a barrel.

Both our fates had been sealed 'deals' without full knowledge of their consequences. You might even say the decisions we made were akin to taking a powerful hallucinogen with lethal side-effects. Jakobina and Mattias had staged a flawless takeover.

I'd never minced words after the impact of their selfishness hit me in 2019. Zee and I had been hooked, abducted and kippered, not necessarily in that order, in a paranormal hostage situation when we were still wet behind the ears.

I surfaced momentarily to check into real time. Zee still stood waffling at a podium that wasn't there, gesturing like a conductor without a baton. He addressed his audience of me, a sleeping dog, and a ginger cat cleaning her tail, with a smile. "Thatcher's philosophies naturally evolved into the metaphysical side of the seventies," he said, "but by that time, as I told you, I was open to pseudo-science. It was kind of fun."

"You have a decidedly fuzzy definition of fun," I said.

"Anyway," Zee countered folding his arms, "the day after Thatcher died, he sent me a sign in a lucid dream. *Find Aurelia*, he said. *Keep the box sealed until you do. She'll know what to do.* So, here we are."

"Sir," I interrupted, waving my arm like an eager student. "By my calculations, technically speaking, Thatcher was Mattias, and already dead the day you met."

Zee silenced me with a grim look and pressed on. "And *that's* when I knew, Miss Marcus, that I had to find you. I took the crate out of storage. You might say, I built this castle just to house that crate. And then, Catcher arrived and picked up Thatcher's gauntlet."

"By gauntlet are you referring to Mattias's soul?"

He grinned. "I am."

I couldn't resist raising my hand. "So, just to be clear, a crate of Mattias's miscellaneous effects wasn't as foolish as, say, a castle box filled with whimsical high school mementos?"

Zee drummed his fingers on the book. "Mrs. Carter," he said. "You're one tough audience when it comes to telling a story. And I can assure you there was nothing remotely whimsical or foolish in Mattias's crate."

"And you're going to prove that sometime today. Am I right?"

"If you let me finish."

I smiled sweetly. "Please don't stop on my account. I can wait for an eternity."

"I have a secret in the wine cellar," he said. "It *isn't* dark, and according to Thatcher's message, today is the right time to unveil it."

"How exciting," I said, sitting to attention. "I have to say, as dark horses go, you are the darkest. Goodness, a skeleton in the closet. I mean, dungeon." I rose from my chair and roused Canary. "Let's go girl." Canary opened one eye, lifted her head an inch and went back to sleep.

Zee gestured me to sit back down. "It's more like a family crypt *behind* the wine cellar. I built a safe house for storing valuables, not shown on the architectural plans. I'm showing you now because, I've devised a new strategy that involves both of us in the future. But mostly because of last week's headlines."

Ah, the point at last. "The stolen painting. The one that Jakobina and Mattias stole and destroyed? Yes, I know all about that. I saw them burning it on the beach."

Zee narrowed his eyes. "And yet you come and go from a print copy," he said drily. "So maybe we're okay."

"Or maybe it was a betrayal."

Zee drummed his fingers on the Vermeer book. I sensed guilt was about to be unleashed. "Aurelia, after I left you last December, I read your unsent 'Dear John' letter, and reread the letter you sent from the future. The rest, as they say, is history. And last week I finalized some impeccably elegant legal work of my own, even if I do say so myself, that affects our *future* history." He tapped an invisible gavel. "I propose we put an end to secrets between us."

I stood quickly. Canary startled and shook her head. "Agreed. Bring them on."

Zee led me gently from my fixation on the crime scene. "Right then, follow me. Let's keep it real. Please walk behind me and not through me."

An entire wall of wine shifted easily. The trick was a lever under the bottom shelf. It unhinged a thick door that swung wide. Damp caused the wood frame to creak. Canary whined through her nose and cowered. Punch beetled off after a mouse.

I giggled to lighten the mood. "It sounds like the door of a haunted house," I commented. "How cool is that."

"If you think that's cool," Zee said "Take a look at this." He flipped the light switch.

CATCHING UP...

chapter 78
WAKEUP CALL

After a cool whoosh of climate-controlled air, the sight of a miniature art gallery, superbly curated, was spectacular. Hindsight had never been more 2020.

My first revelation was that ghosts are no more in possession, pardon the pun, of the absolute truth than a kid in high school.

The second, vindicated Jakobina and Mattias as criminals. The stolen original of 'Girl With A Pearl Earring' graced the room, center stage, bathed in subdued lighting. There had been no murder. I had witnessed them burning a mock canvas facsimile of the 'Girl With A Pearl Earring' in effigy as a ritual cleansing.

The entire contents of Mattias's crate were artfully displayed in flattering light. It had contained a dozen or so paintings, several portfolios of loose sketches, and two leather-bound notebooks, all professionally archived.

I drifted over to them, forgetting to use my legs, and inspected them the way a levitating queen might review her troops.

Mattias waited behind me, stating the obvious. "Thatcher entrusted his collection of Fabritius's lost paintings to me," he said.

"Hmmn," I mused. "So I see."

"Provenance is vital to verifying their authenticity."

"It is," I agreed. "Always."

Zee chuckled. "I have to say that our timing is a bitch. We inherit Fabritius's lost works when we're too old or deceased to benefit from them."

"Ironic."

"Quite. The point I'm making is that Fabritius's works were Jakobina's by right as her father's. Theoretically… *metaphysically*, they passed to Emily and on to you. And after we were married, to me. By ethereal rights, these paintings belonged to you until your death."

I gasped. "And I left no will."

"Rather irrelevant given we were married by a ghost and have no valid marriage certificate," he said. "A metaphysical bloodline would hardly hold up in court. The physical line of succession goes to me because I can cite Thatcher's legal will, and, thanks to Mattias's creative flair, stunning watertight provenance. But I have no heir, which brings me to my crazy plan. A confession, actually. With Mattias's genius, I've written a will leaving everything to a future me. My heir will be… me."

I grinned my approval. "I married a con man. Whose luckier than me."

Zee stood beside me, gazing at the 'Girl With A Pearl Earring'. I swooped into it, winked at him and returned to his side.

He took my hand and kissed it. "Nice touch, Wendy. "You know," he went on casually, Mattias is a remarkably creative historian and an unprecedented forger. His list of talents are truly impressive. He charted a brilliant genealogy from his bogus family tree. And being a farsighted mystic who conveniently operates outside the restrictions of time, he has assured me I will be born a healthy boy in the year 2023 who will reach his age of majority in 2044. You and I will be married by then… properly."

"Brilliant," I said. "We're going to be daring young things."

We continued our conversation staring ahead as if including the portrait. "It makes a nice change from being daring *old* things," Zee said.

"Precisely what are we going to do with this lot until then?"

Zee shifted his weight and nudged me with his shoulder. "I rather assumed that *you* were going to tell *me*."

He knocked me off balance intentionally, both physical and mental. I immediately consulted my lectures from Jakobina and Mattias on the nature of living art.

"Here's what I know," I said. "Lost paintings can remain underground for centuries, so we can leave Jakobina's portrait alone for the time being. Our future selves will discover it and reap the reward, if there is one. As for these soon to be 'newly-discovered' works, we obviously can't sell them if the collection is to pass on intact to the future you, and bankroll a lifetime of wealth and travel for the future *us*."

"It's a given the art will increase in value by 2044," Zee said. "Our task is one of maintenance. We will assume the roles of ghostly curators and security guards. As owner of this island I can shut it down and register it as an off-limit bird sanctuary if I so choose. I've already given notice to the residents of Glastonbury. I don't like wasting time."

"Too right," I said. "Time has a history of marching on, waiting for no man."

Zee busied himself straightening a lopsided painting that was perfectly straight. Something was up. "Sweetheart," I called out, "Did Mattias tell you other things?"

"Hmmn? Oh, yeah, there *was* more. Our names will be Jacob and Sophie."

He was hiding from me. "Zee, look at me. Did we not just agree to abolish secrets between us?"

He heaved a sigh and turned around, shamefaced. "We did," he said with a challenging stare. "Jacob will ..."

"Did Mattias tell you the date of your death? Is that why you're in such a hurry?"

Zee's face stayed blank, in recital mode. "Jacob will meet his beloved Sophie in an art gallery in front of 'The Goldfinch' by Fabritius. They will elope and marry as teenagers. And on Jacob's twenty-first birthday he will receive a letter from the legal firm of Carter & Zygmont. It will contain a key and a map with directions to an island in the Georgia Strait that doesn't want to be found, and a safe room with a cache of paintings that does."

Mattias's voice filled my head. "Don't push him, Aurelia. A man has an obligation to protect his wife. Sometimes secrets are vital. Yes, he does know the hour of his death, and no, it isn't soon, but he's also privy to some rules of reincarnation that impact his scheme. Zee's looking past his physical death to a future he's building for you. Something infinitely more complex than a castle. I once told Zee that only art was immortal. Truer words were never spoken." His voice trailed off into white sound.

"I wonder why didn't Mattias tell *me* about the paintings?" I said to be chatty.

Zee relaxed his shoulders. "You can blame that on the convoluted laws of reincarnation. Mattias knows the blasted things inside out. He tried to school me but I'm afraid the details put me to sleep. The gist is, living in the proverbial dark had been necessary because we both needed to learn a lot about rebirth."

"You make us sound like mushrooms."

He chuckled. "Magical ones with hallucinogenic side-effects."

I gave my head a shake. Suddenly it wasn't important to know everything Zee knew. "More like fairy toadstools growing in an enchanted ring," I replied. "An homage to a metaphysical circle with closed doors I once knew."

He straightened and faced me with an infectious grin. "The bottom line, is that Mattias charted our metaphysical genealogy, tasked to help each other over several lifetimes. And you and I are *not* the end of that line. Our children will have the legacy they deserve."

I puttered around intent on examining Fabritius' luminous paintings up close. "That's way cooler than a squeaky door hinge," I said over my shoulder. "These are exquisite." I reached for his hand. "Come. Look at this one."

I still dream.

My old mentor, Catcher, had been spot on when he'd declared that ghosts were the quintessential embodiment of lucid dreaming.

We met in a dream, yesterday, or was it tomorrow. He surprised me the moment I closed my eyes. A familiar gentle wind at our backs pushed us forward. We drifted onto the night beach as the sun sizzled into the water and the sky gave up its stars.

He reached for my hand, kissed it in the manner of his old gallant self, and kept hold of it, pressing it against his heart. "Imagine we've come from one of those stars," he said.

"Planet B-613," I countered. "The 'Little Prince' lives on the planet next door."

"We're human dreamcatchers, Aurelia, little princes and princesses who travel on the astral wings of death and imagination. In the future, the human race will realize it no longer requires atoms and molecules."

"Did I dream you or did you dream me?"

"Dearest girl, we've been dreaming each other a long time. Longer than you would believe."

"Then, neither of us are real?"

"Real is a wobbly term."

I slumped onto the sand and fanned my face with the dream booklet that had manifested in my hand. "I feel a little wobbly," I said reproachfully. My beautiful Canary deposited herself beside me with a graceful flop and whined until I fondled her ears. It was quiet enough to hear Felix ticking all the way from the kitchen. His double-time rhythmic *lub dub... lub dub* felt like a heartbeat that echoed *stay still... stay calm ... stay still.* Hot blood pumped in my ears.

Catcher wriggled a place in the sand next to me, close enough that our shoulders touched. His voice tiptoed around me. I'd never seen him so sad and anxious. I felt sorry for him. "It's okay," I said. "Mattias explained about The Sandman pact ages ago. But I knew there'd be a secret dragon or two beyond his confessions, so give me the last bean. Tell me everything."

As is the nature of dreams, Catcher morphed into Mattias. "Everything would take forever," he replied as if contemplating this notion for the first time.

I patted his knee. "Come on. Start with the worst thing. Freak me out. Don't be careful or kind. I think you owe it to me to shock me into reality or wherever this dream is. Weren't you once my humpbacked beasty man in wolf's clothing."

"Nope. That was Catcher."

"Three shamans in one. How lucky were we, Zee and me."

Mattias chewed his lip, frowning briefly but lifted his head to deliver the truth. He gifted me a wan smile and leaned forward. The silence was almost unbearable but he made me wait. "The worst is also the best," he said finally. Several deep breaths followed that may have been sighs. "Time travel is tricky. I've discovered that deserving trips often require a beasty-man or three to pull off. I don't relish telling lies."

Felix's tail beat a gentle rhythm with the tide… *stay calm – stay calm – stay calm.* Jakobina, silent as a cat, materialized behind Mattias and laid her dainty white hand on his shoulder. She moistened her ruby lips with her tongue, slightly open and breathless, as they'd been immortalized in her portrait and blew me a kiss before she disappeared.

Whatever I was expecting, it wasn't Mattias's next words. "There are days I believe I dreamed the earth," he said. "That I built Leonardo's giant horse and you painted the Sistine ceiling."

Felix stopped cold. The texture of Canary's wiry fur under my hand imprinted with extrasensory detail in the form of gentle electric sparks. I was comforted to have a homespun tweed Canary to ground them. I must have cried out because Canary lifted her head and gave a low growl of protection. I pulled her close, like the old days, and hugged her as a child would cling to a teddy bear in a thunderstorm, my eyes squeezed shut. "You're allowed to imagine anything," I said.

"But not everything. That would be greedy."

"It's only child's play."

"What if it isn't. What if I like possessing people too much."

All three of us popped back to the castle's kitchen where moonlight played over the blue glass. Actual thunder cracked the silence. Canary howled as rain pounded the roof and windows. The room became an underwater echo chamber. I looked over at Mattias. He still clutched the blue leaflet. "What if I can't stop."

"You can wakeup. The way you taught me. Your thoughts made this storm," I said. "But you didn't dream Jakobina, and me, and every raindrop that ever fell."

"So, it's true. The student *does* surpass the teacher. Thank you."

"Maybe Vermeer painted all of us. Jakobina's little mouse teeth always reminded me of pearls," I said. "Her ears were like seashells. Vermeer painted her turban the color of a Greek sea and gave her farsighted eyes, but trust is a tricky thing to paint. Hers were never as trusting as Canary's."

Mattias's wicker chair creaked as he assumed the pose of a teacher on a mission. The image of a fairy flitted across my mind which meant he was about to deliver a fairy tale. I hoped I'd be spared another 'once upon a time' but I couldn't prevent the inevitable anymore than Canary could bark the tide into submission. "Once upon a time," he began, "turns into a forever where children have invisible friends and adults wander off into the organized religions of commerce and fear where it's dangerous to want too much."

"Too true," I agreed. "And is that what's bothering you?"

"Saints living inside terracotta statues replace invisible friends and talking bears. Big daddy genies keep us hostage, dependent on wish-craft. We're puppets, subservient to an imaginary puppet master who sits in a mountainous peacock chair. Our restless fingers dial a perpetual catalogue in the sky connected to us by a telephone line made of rosary beads. Busy signals keep us humbled. Muses are seen as fickle ill-timed angels, who drop in to help one day and look away the next. The living see what they want to see. Believe whatever crackpot theories they choose to stop their molecules shaking apart in fear. Life is a delicate balance of comedy and tragedy. The trouble comes when people limit the number of senses available to them."

"You make us sound like Shakespearian idiots *full of sound and fury, signifying nothing*."

"For the most part ghosts with benefits like mine, are still a race of beasty men. In the Shakespearian sense, lunacy is a compliment.

Human minds have not yet accepted the ability to transcend the physical. Why else would one be in possession of a superior childlike innocence that can embrace the vastness of fiction?"

"Mumblety-peg springs to mind."

"Dull humans disregard the joyful connections between realities. They believe they've grown up. Wise humans believe in the liminal – the mystical boundaries that mark the edges of sleep. I call that place Byzantium. Ghosts swan above all that which can make us a danger to the living."

"Well, thanks for the lecture," I said rising to leave. He stayed my arm. "I may be such a danger. If so, what should I do?"

Back on the beach, Mattias continued to grip my arm. He stared into space as if the horizon was a blackboard. "Subliminal stems from the word 'liminal' but allow me to introduce a higher functioning word: para-liminal – above the magical... outside the measurable... beyond the accountable."

I nodded smiling, and sat back down. "Ah...The Nether Netherlands... Delft... Oz."

He rolled his eyes, leaned closer and tweaked my nose. "Dreaming is no less real when deprived of molecules, little girl. Man's natural vocation is MANifesting. Transcend the body. Enter a painting." He winked. "And if nothing else, exit a life fearlessly."

"Neverland, then – a world where growing up is a criminal offence to humanity. Where sleeping beauty sews a shadow to a lost boy with a magic needle and children can fly."

Mattias squeezed my fingers. "There's no need to wither. No need to suffer debilitating memories. Rise above guilt and shame, they have passed. One's wildest dreams hurt no living thing."

I cringed. "Why are you telling me things I already know?"

He let the silence unnerve me.

"Criminal offences to humanity spring to mind," he said. "What gives me the right to interfere with human error?"

An uncomfortable truth formed in my chest. A memory

materialized into a vision of grey slush and rain. I couldn't resist pointing my finger in Mattias's face. "I remember you, now. You were the man in Tintagel station who gave us a brochure. And, last New Year's Day. You were the boy on the street corner!"

Mattias obligingly transformed into the handsome young street vendor. He winked cheekily, took the blue leaflet from my hand, and waved it in my face. "You mean that earnest young man with pearls in his eyes who interfered with your life?"

I laughed out loud. "I called them stars. You *are* a beasty man."

"All the better to hoodwink you by, Red Riding Hood."

"You were helping out a friend in trouble, as I recall."

Mattias rose, dusted off his pantlegs still coated with sand, and walked away, "No need to thank me," he called over his shoulder. But then he must have thought of a better parting shot because he faced me, all the while walking backwards. "It works both ways, Thanks for helping me out of a silly dream, today. Many happy returns, Missus," he said and disappeared.

chapter 79
THE LEAP YEARS

Glastonbury Retreat closed its doors in 2010, and a mist settled over a new 'Isle of Glass' that disappeared from sea charts and maps into a distant memory. Muses still guide their dreaming artists there, to visit for an hour or a splendid minute where only art is immortal.

A print of Vermeer's 'View of Delft' that hangs in the upstairs bedroom of Tintagel Cottage beside my 'pearl doorway', absorbed a grey dog in 2005, a ginger cat in 2007, and a boy named Zee, in 2010. Our family of four swan about seventeenth-century Delft without so much as a ripple.

Muffled laughter is present under the relentless screeching of gulls in the seascape from Zee's boardroom that graces the stairs. The sound of a dog barking and champagne bottles popping may be heard if you press your ear next to the varnish.

From the rooftop of Tintagel Cottage I can see into the future without my telescope. In time, Glastonbury's standing stone topples and topsoil lovingly covers it with a blanket of moss. The gulls swoop and dive over it, serenading its demise with eternal bird chatter.

After 500 years, the doors of Tintagel Cottage crumble. One by one, the glass windows of our castle succumb to the wind. Rain melts the walls into a giant grey sugar cube absorbed into the dunes thatched with sea grass. Sand drifts through the kitchen sanctuary. Thick white dust settles on the cobalt glass. The toothpick fence is long gone. The ruins of Tintagel Cottage become a castle inhabited by contented shadows. Underneath its main floor, ghosts traipse up and down a lost stairwell.

Zee had inscribed 'Fatum interruptus' (fate continues to interrupt) on a marble tablet, the month I came home, and placed it under the stairs.

The weight of time crushed the cellar into archaeology accessible only by pickaxes and determination. Underneath, preserved in a pocket of musty air, a subterranean cave holds the earthly remains of my love affair with Zee.

Lying face up on the floor, like an Egyptian sarcophagus, half covered in powdered shards of cobalt glass, is the framed print of 'The Girl With A Pearl Earring'. Scattered around it, lies a wealth of human love every bit as extraordinary as a royal tomb. The mottled lid of an empty castle box, dented, and sealed by rust still shows a fading romantic view of Bodium Castle. Its contents, archived in a clear plastic case, have been spared the worst ravages of time and damp: a worn pink eraser with smeared initials 'A loves Z', a silver shirt button, a high school ring, a faded blue leaflet, the marriage proposal shard, and the Zee Stone.

The 'ghost of a chance' ball, the size and shape of a plum, sits in an alcove, and spontaneously bursts into colors whenever a ghost dog barks frantically at the incoming tide.

A pair of pearl earrings rest in an oyster shell on a bed of ultramarine silk beside their original swan box. A slightly moth-eaten Felix doll and Virgil lean, heads together, in a slowly disintegrating wicker chair. Virgil's refreshed black button eyes shine bright as beads in the dark.

Zee's high school jacket and the Sophie coat hang on a wall like pinned butterflies beside Doc's dreamcatcher. It's canary feather wafts lazily in my wake whenever I brush past it.

A self-published book entitled 'The Memoirs of Aurelia Marcus Carter – a love story' sits on a Plexiglass stand under a bell jar. The photograph of the kiss-sealed-in-time from my castle box adorns the cover.

A rainbow of colored sea-glass spilled from broken jars, carpets the floor like tiny stars of honey amber, frosted white, emerald, olive, jade, the palest aquamarine, ruby, and ultramarine.

Hidden, trapped under the rubble of drywall, lies the ominous heart-shaped shard of garnet glass that Punch found long ago on an ancient beach – the same seaside souvenir I'd given my mother as a child – the 'strawberry' on the postcard Jakobina had sent Emily. It is turning amethyst as it reincarnates to cobalt blue.

A symbolic pair of rose-tinted reading glasses hang like a mobile. Happily, I'd been wrong. It was not *all* that was left of me. I am always here, or walking the shore with Canary and Zee, accompanied by the ever-present gulls wheeling over us, riding the updrafts. Punch escorts us when she hasn't darted off, curious as ever to dig for gold in the sand dunes.

Felix the clock's curvaceous black tail detached in the first 'quake' of collapsing bricks and mortar, and landed on the floor like a question mark. From his lopsided perch on a sagging wall, Felix still scans the timeless scene with alert kaleidoscope eyes, roving under a cracked crystal, and so the hands of time continue to celebrate the dreams of a boy and girl whose determination to succeed overruled the obstacles of sacrifice and mortality.

My claddagh ring sleeps in a nest of fragile bones under the standing stone of Glastonbury.

Jacob Carter gave Sophie my pearl engagement ring.

Zee and I remain old at heart and young in spirit.

We rest easy inside the immortal dreams of young lovers with old souls. New dreams replace the old. A fresh supply of gulls continue to screech Tempus fugit (time flies) over our castle ruins in birdsong. Three things are clear to me. Dreaming is more than a game, wishes unfold the way they should if left unattended rather than the way they were ordered, and ghosts sleep far longer than fairy tale princesses under a curse.

After twenty-five years in exile, the lost 'Girl With A Pearl Earring' was restored to the world in a blaze of headlines. Jakobina's eyes, sealed under a craquelure of varnish, gazed into a new generation of rapt faces. Their eyes connected and time ceased to be as art held its breath.

After the painting was cleaned, the hidden forms of a woman holding a cat were discovered in the mirror-like shine of the pearl earring.

In the meantime, Vermeer and Fabritius rest easy and continue the traditions of the Dutch School as muses teaching the subtle arts of hiding images in plain sight to unsuspecting apprentices traveling in their dreams.

Naturally, the universe remains creatively perverse.

I continue to take Mattias at his word and listen often with my ear against Vermeer's 'View of Delft'. I hear my voice calling Canary, and what's even more miraculous, on different days, Arthur the cat may be seen prowling in various locations, on one of the brick gates, a high parapet, a low fence, or one of a dozen windows.

Sometimes *he's* black and white. Sometimes *she's* ginger.

EPILOGUE

To die, to sleep...
To sleep...
Perchance to dream.
Ay, there's the rub,
For in that sleep of death
What dreams may come.

— WILLIAM SHAKESPEARE

Fairy tales can come true.
It can happen to you,
if you're young at heart.

MOTHER OF PEARL

In my recurring dream of life, the tail of the Felix clock acts like a hypnotist's pendulum. "You're getting sleepy," he purrs. And I find myself in part of the castle I've never been. The walls are shiny mother of pearl, warm to the touch. I am six-years-old.

A silvery nautilus shell sits atop a collection of pale sea-glass arranged on a plate on my mother's desk. It gets bigger as I scamper towards it or perhaps I'm getting smaller. I make my way over slick aquamarine boulders to its entrance, big as a cave. It's flesh-pink walls glow seductively and smell of candlewax. The sea is my true home.

My mother found me again, walking her beach of dreams. She picked me up while I was sleeping, put me in her pocket, and lay my house in a silvery patch of moonbeam, high on a window sill, where she can see me. At low tide I creep out and dance for her on the palm of her hand. She tells me stories and peers inside my empty shell to wonder at my fine bed and tiny armchair, and my miniature books all lined up safe into the creamy folds of porcelain wall niches.

As her darling one, I drink from her own teacup filled with honeyed wine. Afterwards, I sit on the edge of her desk and watch her write, her great quivering wings folded close and still. I yawn and stretch to bid her good morning as the sun rises, slide down a spiral staircase, descending into a cool white space where I curl up alone to escape the harsh sunlight.

Her cat, Arthur, sees me go, and in his curiosity, knocks my shell crashing to the floor. Things fall from my shelves, and Arthur's great paws spin us about. His golden cat-eyes wait at the entrance. His purr reverberates deep echoes inside my room, and now my house rolls under my mother's bed, and I am not sure what is to become of me. I pick up the spill of books and pillows, set the place to rights, and pull my knees into a fetal position, huddling nose to tail like a sleeping cat. The giant feline storm hisses and howls outside and finally passes.

Under my mother's bed there are star clusters and tumbleweed dust-planets, and the far off rumbling of thunder when they collide. I'm homesick for the sea, lost again.

When we were both seventeen, whether I liked it or not, a girl named Jakobina was my nemesis. She told me the stars never lied and watched me day and night before she grew old enough to be my granddaughter.

"What book would you like me to read you tonight?" I ask Jakobina, knowing her answer.

"The one about the prince who returned to a star," she answers.

Antoine de Saint-Exupéry's 'The Little Prince' had been my favorite all through my dreamy starstruck childhood. Jakobina had been enthralled by the story but horrified at the lack of skill in the illustrations no matter how many times I explained that intentionally bad drawing was the premise behind the whole book.

Jakobina sits in the kitchen sanctuary amongst the blue glass, watching me scrub a blackened pot. She absentmindedly strokes a cat named Arthur, all the while keeping her eye on Felix. She's warmed to both black and white cats and made her peace with Canary who likes to lay her shaggy head on Jakobina's feet to soak up her energy.

"Grandmother," she says. "Death is sweet."

I flick soap suds at her which fails to impress Punch, sitting on her knee. "You used to call me Grootmoeder."

Jakobina detaches Arthur's claws from her leg, bravely kissing his nose. "And my best friend before that," she says.

Felix's tail points to the floor and freezes. The silence twitches Canary's ears. She alerts us with a single bark.

"It's morning," Jakobina says. "Do you want to check the beach for sandcastles?"

She doesn't hear my reply. I am already there.

Row row row your boat
Gently down the stream
Merrily merrily merrily merrily
Life is but a dream.

ACKNOWLEDGEMENTS

Writing for prolonged periods of time in a vacuum may seem like a relaxing pastime, but writing a full-length novel is a lonely business, and setting aside the joys of writing for a moment, its important to remember that Indie Publishing *is* a serious business. Producing and marketing requires a teamwork of experts and there are people to thank: editors, formatters, graphic designers, media consultants, beta readers, and family to name a few.

This novel required fresh eyes to flag the flaws written in plain sight. Critiquing a fellow author without pulling any punches is not a fun task, nor is it light reading. I am indebted to several beta readers.

THANK YOU Jim Bottomly and Deborah Lambert, indie authors from the Sooke Writers Collective, for bravely taking on my first chapters. Your insight inspired several rewrites.

THANK YOU beta readers Cathy Whyte and Jamie Proudlove.

THANK YOU Arthur the cat for being you.

THANK YOU Charity Chimni for interior and technical graphic design.

THANK YOU Tia Didmon, who continues to talk me through the perils of marketing.

THANK YOU Sarah and David, my adult children who have long accepted the creative quirks of living with an artist mother for what seems like several lifetimes.

THANK YOU Marcus Aurelius whose philosophy has kept writers at their keyboards and note paper, writing towards success through constant setbacks of feast and famine.

And THANK YOU generous readers, who stay with my stories for 300-plus pages.

The Crux Of History Behind 'Disapp'earring Twice'

A core of historical fact always lies pinned like a butterfly at the heart of my stories.

On October 12, 1654, ten years before Johannes Vermeer painted his 'Girl With A Pearl Earring', a freak explosion of gunpowder, known as the 'Delft Thunderclap', devastated the Dutch city of Delft. It killed Carel Fabritius, a promising artist (best known for his painting of 'The Goldfinch') and his apprentice, Mattias Spoors. It destroyed an unknown number of Fabritius' luminous masterpieces and left a fair portion of the city in ruins.

Art history was altered forever, but the nature of fine art decrees that the best paintings pave the way for others to be created. Fabritius, a student of Rembrandt, was likely an inspiration to Vermeer, and so an unbroken chain of creativity binds masters and apprentices.

My story premise connecting Vermeer and Fabritius is pure fiction. But mysteries appear when art disappears from the world. They motivate my quests to bring them home. The epitaph 'now lost' in the art history texts doesn't necessarily mean destroyed. And since great art is truly immortal, it's possible to imagine sentient paintings waiting patiently in an attic trunk or an antique shop to deliver their stories of betrayal and survival that would make Marcus Aurelius proud.

The Emperor, Marcus Aurelius, c.78 B.C. was a prolific philosopher warrior who declared that success can only be reached by accepting, wholeheartedly, every obstacle that comes your way.

That said, obscurity remains an indie authors greatest obstacle. Reviews lead to word-of-mouth promotion that buzzes the vital X-factor for visible success. On behalf of indie authors everywhere, we thank you for taking the time to leave a review.

'Girl With a Pearl Earring' Johannes Vermeer – 1664/65

'The Goldfinch' Carel Fabritius - 1654

apparition has haunted the estate for generations. But rescue only opens a time portal that reveals terrible secrets.

https://smarturl.it/vktwinter

'TIME FALLS LIKE SNOW' – a Y/A time-slip adventure *book two of 'The Bede Series'*. Bede Hall, a sentient building with a timely past, harbors further disturbing phenomenon. The secrets of Bede Hall continue with the sixteen-year-old twins working in league with a team of ghosts and 'twice-borns' who have been monitoring the time portal's secrets for hundreds of years. It falls to Bede Hall's time corridors, the Great Sphinx of Egypt, the rules of twindom, the magic power of nine, and a team of teenagers with several otherworldly allies to save earth from an alien curse. The 'Twinters' have six years to try in a landscape where history is positively ancestral.

https://smarturl.it/vktimefalls

WORKS-IN-PROGRESS

a landscape where history is positively ancestral

THE BEDE SERIES

a time-slip ghost story for children of all ages:

BEDE HALL IS ALIVE, BUT ALL IS NOT WELL

A disgruntled stately home convinces a pair of telepathic twins to save it from being sold to unscrupulous developers in order to fulfill an ancient prophecy, rescue its resident ghost, and save the planet. History, mystery, and magic.

'TWINTER – the first portal' *book one ... completed e-book and print*

'TIME FALLS LIKE SNOW' *book two ... completed e-book and print*

'TOMORROW AGAIN' *book three ... **in progress***

The conclusion of the twins' trials, separated by thousands of miles and years in ancient Egypt.

'SNOW BEHIND THE DOOR' ***in progress***

The prequel to the Bede trilogy. The tale of the child ghost named Snow

Fate is more mysterious than a smile

THE LISABETTA SERIES

a fanciful biography of Leonardo da Vinci's historical half-sister, Lisabetta Buti

THE 'MONA LISA' MAY BE PRICELESS… NOW SHE MUST BECOME A WOMAN WORTH SAVING

In order to reclaim her true identity, the embittered spirit of the 'Mona Lisa', trapped in her portrait for 500 years, must join forces with an autistic boy and his troubled mother.

'LISABETTA – a stolen glance' *book one … completed e-book and print*

https://smarturl.it/vklisabetta

'LISABETTA – a stolen smile' *book two in final editing*

'LISABETTA – a stolen sister' *book three in final editing*

'LISABETTA – a true face… veritas icona' *book four in final editing*

Veronica Knox writes multi-layered stories under the name V KNOX that reconcile historical facts with imaginative fiction: eclectic historical fantasies, art history delivered in ghost stories, paranormal romances, and a magical realism Y/A time-slip 'Bede trilogy' for ages 14-20 in which a disgruntled stately home nestled beside Hadrian's wall (in the north of England) has a mind of its own in a mystical landscape that shelters a pair of teenagers, resident ghosts, mythical elementals, and sentient animals.

She explores the creative inner worlds of autistic savants and master artists, and in one case, the unknown child in the Titanic cemetery. By tapping metaphysical resources such as the discrepancies between reality and lucid dreams, Veronica fishes the depths of the subconscious, the afterlife, reincarnation, the anomalies of parallel lives and dimensions, and the classic psyche of 'the ghostly lover'.

Studying for a university Fine Arts degree inspired an imaginative take on art history that led to other untapped avenues for stories. She discovered inanimate objects are rarely bereft of life and portraits have juicy secrets to tell – snapshots of what was and more importantly, who left their ethereal 'I was here' imprint on the world.

What-if two children aboard the Titanic were meant to marry, and a pair of baby shoes from an exhibit in a museum could reunite them? What if the 'Mona Lisa' was Leonardo da Vinci's kid sister?

Veronica resides on Vancouver Island channeling ethereal echoes from objects in museums and the stifled voices of the Italian Renaissance – the artists as well as their anonymous subjects and companions. She grants them second chances to air their grievances, tell their stories, and together they set the dreariest history books on fire.

V KNOX WEBSITE & CURIOUS ART HISTORY BLOG
https://veronicaknox.com/

V KNOX SIGN UP NEWSLETTER FORM
https://landing.mailerlite.com/webforms/landing/f7e8a1

V KNOX AMAZON
https://www.amazon.com/V-Knox/e/B0094K0Q7Y

V KNOX FACEBOOK
https://www.facebook.com/V-Knox-Author-307047433438123/

V KNOX LINKEDIN
https://www.linkedin.com/in/veronica-knox-233bb51b/